Worship Me

Craig Stewart

HellBound Books Publishing LLC

A HellBound Books LLC
Publication

Printed in the United States of America

Craig Stewart

Worship Me

A HellBound Books Publishing LLC Book
Houston TX

Worship Me

Dedication

Dedicated to my sisters, Erin, the reason this story exists, and Blaire, the first person to believe in it. Without you two, my pages would be blank.

Worship Me

Acknowledgments

It's been a long time getting here, and I didn't do it alone, so here are a few people I need to fall on my knees and ~~worship~~ thank.

For offering to suffer through an unpolished manuscript, I'm forever thankful to Mark Stewart, Christine Stewart, Tim Blackburn, Cameron King, Jacob Sheen, Brandon Forsyth and Kirk Dickinson. You all helped bring this beast to life.

For taking a chance on me, I would also like to thank the amazing team at HellBound Books, in particular Jim Longmore for the invaluable guidance, editor Brandy Yassa for chiseling away at my words until they looked pretty, and Luke Spooner for creating such an evocative cover.

And finally, a very special thanks to my Nathan, you know, for that stuff you do.

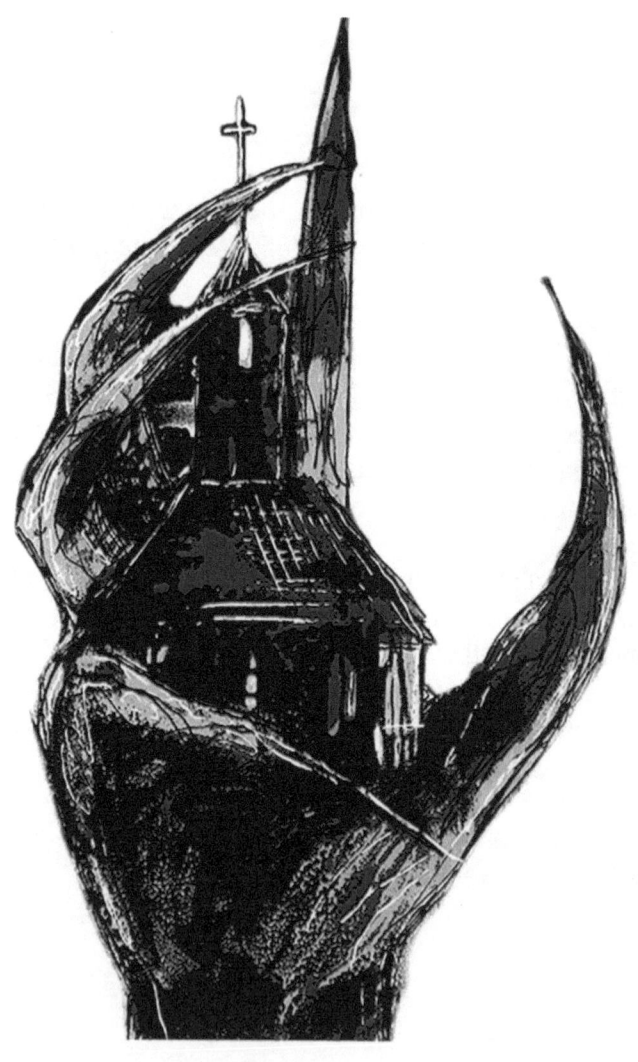

CHAPTER 1

The Burward Forest was unusually cold, even for an early October morning. The clouds hung lower than normal, held aloft by skeletal treetops. Only the most tenacious leaves still held to their branches. Some would consider this a sight of inspiration, these few heroic flags still flapping, but the brutal truth was, they could not hold forever.

Years of neglect had taken its toll on the forest. The old trotting paths were overgrown and the trees had been left to push their way through the wood fencing, which was on the brink of being entirely swallowed, save for a few stubborn posts.

At the edge of the woods, a crude structure had been erected out of mismatched planks of rotting wood. Most of the material was stolen from neighboring barns, made evident by the peeling red paint speckled randomly throughout the structure's exterior. It reached almost as high as the trees that helped support it. Unmeasured angles gave it an awkward stance; the roof leaned heavily to one side as if its spine had twisted. It resembled an upturned coffin, peering out over the Davidson's field, left desolate after the harvest.

Despite the huge opening at the front of the structure, it allowed no light. There were impenetrable shadows embedded within that resisted the prying day; the kind of absolute darkness found in the ocean's depths. It held onto the night, and perhaps, was even the origin of it.

Kneeling at the base of the structure was a man with his eyes turned up to meet the highest point of the temple, his hands stretched out in unabashed praise. A terrible tremor had taken hold of his body; he was no older than thirty, yet looked hardened by a life of heavy labour.

His complete nakedness, save for light layers of dirt coating his unwashed body, revealed the intricate scars that patterned his skin. They spread from the base of his neck, covering every inch of him like tally marks. They traced down his back and across his shoulders, wrapped around his arms and chest, cutting into the crevices of his armpits before continuing down his torso. Even the sensitive flesh of his groin was not spared the meticulous and mysterious documentation. The only blank canvas left was his face, but that was mostly hidden by a wild beard.

The oddest thing of all was his expression of bliss. A gleeful smile stretched out across his face in joyous defiance against the gloom. It was pure adulation that poured out of him: not sorrow, not terror. Kneeling in front of the imposing structure, he could offer only love and worship – his whole body tingled with it.

He fixated on the dark opening like a dead thing glimpsing Heaven for the first time. Thoughts drifted through the light blue of his eyes, and although his pupils remained pinned in place, his irises toiled and drifted just as the clouds above. In the oblivion gaping before him, he found completeness and order. He seemed to feast on it, as if it was something he hungered for.

The man with spectral eyes was waiting for his master. Then, from deep within the Burward Forest, something stirred.

CHAPTER 2

The cat's little paw had just finished twitching by the time Clara scrambled out of her minivan. Her eyes were reluctant to look, but she felt obligated to suffer the damage she had caused. It was far worse than she had allowed herself to imagine.

The animal had burst. Its body reduced to an unrecognizable splash of flesh and fur. She did manage to identify a piece that looked like its head perched near her left signal light. It was grimacing like a gargoyle.

"Oh, dang this day," she mourned, crossing her arms.

She was already late, and now she had this on her conscience. Every Sunday morning, Clara rose to the task of prepping St. Paul's United Church for the day's worship. She had been doing this ever since she returned from teacher's college ten years ago. In all that time, never once was the service held up because of her. Until, she feared, this dang day.

It was not entirely her fault. The family of feral cats had been playing recklessly near the edge of Highway 7. The tragedy was inevitable. Clara was just thankful it was the mother she hit, and not one of the kittens. If it were a baby she had to scrub off her bumper, she might have just turned around and driven back home. Any day that starts with killing a kitten is a day not worth starting.

She rummaged through her van for something to clean with, but all she found was a collapsed box of tissues. She decided they would have to do.

As she brushed off the bones and soaked up the blood, a few cars tore past her down the highway at a speed Clara found more than a little excessive. At one point, the wind from a car almost tipped her over. Briefly, she pictured what she might look like splashed across a hood. Very briefly.

The highway, which had only recently been paved, could lead you to one of two places: either you were heading to church, or you were escaping--far away. Judging by how the cars tore up pavement, Clara assumed they were not searching for God. Everyone was in a rush to find a way out; no one was in a rush to find the Lord.

Clara neatly piled what remained of the cat by the side of the highway and offered it a moment of silence.

Once she was satisfied due respect had been paid, Clara jumped back into her minivan. The church was waiting and she had taken far too much time.

As she shifted the gear from park to drive, she noticed the half-eaten chocolate chip muffin sitting in the cup holder. To call it a muffin was a bit of a stretch. After all, it was more closely related to a cupcake than an actual muffin; it would be, at best, a third cousin, twice removed. It was the same muffin she was taking a bite out of, the exact moment the cat chose to cross the road. She knew as soon as she bought it that morning that she was going to regret it, and she was right.

Before driving off, she tossed it into the field where she imagined the kittens might be congregating. They were going to need it more than she did, she reasoned.

As she roared into the dirt parking lot of the church, she took note of the time. Twenty minutes later than usual. She had to move fast.

She yanked at her seatbelt, but somewhere along the way the strap had burrowed itself under her left breast. This was a constant annoyance for her and her generous bust. Gradually, the strap was wiggled loose and she was finally free.

She hastily climbed the stone steps of St. Paul's United Church. As always, the heavy dark wood of the front door greeted her with a satisfying creak. She had precious little time to appreciate it, though. Her fellow church members could be arriving any minute and there was much to be done.

CHAPTER 3

His fingers clawed at the dry leaves. He crushed them in his fists and let the pain dig deep.

The man with spectral eyes had been forced to his hands and knees by the wound freshly opened down the length of his back. It followed his spine all the way from his shoulders to his buttocks. Despite its depth, there was little blood.

The thin gash had been perfectly placed. It completed his tapestry, as if each of his scars had been leading to this masterstroke.

His breath was slow to return to him, but once he could inhale without his entire torso stinging, he took in as much air as he could. And the air took him in as well, surrounding him, swallowing his entire body.

The hungry breeze chased through the trees and rose with him as he got to his feet. He let the cooling touch of the air wrap around him and ease the burning of his wound. The wind brought life back to the woods, but it wasn't the life it once knew. Leaves rustled and branches swayed, but not because of the hustle and bustle of animals – that life was long gone. A presence had invaded and snuffed it out. Now, there was only the wind shaking the remnants of what life had been.

The man took a step forward and peered through the maze of twisting bark. He looked out from the heart of the woods, and saw all the way to its fringe where the forest ended and the field began. Then, he looked beyond even that.

He saw a little country church by the side of a highway and a little woman getting it ready.

Revelation bloomed in his eyes and filled his thoughts as if the woods themselves whispered to him. His path had been revealed, and he was obliged to follow.

CHAPTER 4

Clara's stained loafers chased across the floorboards as she attempted to get the modest house of God in order.

Known as the mess hall, the first room she entered from outside acted as the main room of the church. From this space, one could enter any of the other rooms, including the sanctuary, the basement, and even the small stage, which inadequately hosted the Christmas concert every year. The smell of the space was a stirring combination of sweet mould and dust, but a homely familiarity with the odour kept it from offending.

She dropped her bags by the old piano, which had been left to rot in the corner of the mess hall since it was about as useful as a wagon with no wheels.

She then laid down tablecloths for the morning snacks and started the coffee maker.

Once in the sanctuary, Clara hurried passed rows of empty pews on her way to the front pulpit. Fresh red carpet ran the length of both the aisles leading to the centre of the room where they met in an explosion of intense crimson. The carpet did not stop there; it led up the steps that elevated the pulpit to the highest point in the room and even reached behind, into the minister's office.

Clara climbed halfway up the steps where a large hand-carved table presented a Bible of biblical proportions. The book would have put the most generously-sized atlas to shame. *Would you expect anything less for a map of the human soul?* she thought.

The sheer weightiness of the text gave Clara comfort. When she pulled back its thick, hard cover, Clara had to fight the urge to grunt. Surely, within its heft, there was something of worth.

She searched through the pages until she found the day's requested readings from the Book of Job. A thin, red ribbon held the page and Clara went about her other tasks.

She laid out the collection plates, readied a glass of water for the minister, and lit the many candles in their holders about the room. After a final check to make sure each pew had its appropriate hymnbook, Clara, astonished she finished in time, stood back to observe her work.

Any minute now, the congregation would start arriving. There was just one thing left for her to do.

She fished through her purse for her pack of smokes. She had been nursing it for a week. Only two left. She removed a semi-bent cigarette, lit it using one of the less ceremonial candles, then exited the building.

Clara was excellent at keeping secrets. Through a life of being invisible, one masters the ease of unnoticeable acts. Her addiction to the smooth smoke, which even then caressed her lungs in the most seductive way, was certainly one of her favourite indulgences.

When her mother scolded her years ago for recklessly abusing her body with known carcinogens, Clara promised she would stop. Now, it played a dual role in her life. On the juvenile side, she was telling her mom to fuck off with every puff; on the darker side, she was entertaining a minor death wish. She could always console herself that the decision to smoke belonged solely to her. She owned it, regardless of its impurity. So what if it hastened her own demise; was that so dreadful? She often rationalized: why should the things that make her happy not bring her closer to Heaven? Maybe God made addiction for a reason.

The smoke crawled up through the morning light as Clara took care in blowing it far enough away to keep the smell from clinging to her clothes. She tapped the ashes onto the parking lot and used the loose dirt to hide them.

Worried that the early birds could start arriving, she decided to finish the cigarette around the back of the building.

That's when she noticed the breeze. Usually it came across the field from the South, but this morning it was coming from the West.

The wind sent shivers through the dried corn stocks missed during the harvest, giving the dead something to chatter about. Most were bluntly hacked off near the base, with a few discarded pieces left scattered like golden confetti across the expanse.

Clara found it depressing, so she turned from the field and focused on the church.

The building was a loner like her. Here it sat with the Davidson's cornfield bordering it on three sides, utterly isolated. As the wear and tear of the passing seasons wore on, it had no one to commiserate with about its failing ceiling or rusting hinges. It had to bear its hardships alone. Then again--and with this revelation, Clara broke into a smile--being alone was all it knew, and all it had ever known. That was its nature. Maybe by this point, the taste of companionship would be too sweet to bear anyway.

She took in two more quick puffs. The cigarette was now half of what it was. She knew she was running the risk of being found out, but Clara was determined to enjoy the smoke to its fullest.

As she savoured the taste, her vision fixed on the sizable stained-glass window that stretched from floor to ceiling on the north side of the church. Its simple depiction of worldly ascension into Heaven was something troubling to Clara. Seeing the Kingdom on high, with its trumpeting angels portrayed so literally, it made the whole thing seem silly to her, like a snippet from a fairytale picture book.

Clara had a more nuanced view: if Heaven really was paradise, then surely earthly limitations, such as flesh and clothing, would have no place there. Clara's eyes closed as she imagined escaping her physical body into an exquisitely inexplicable wonderland. Floating there, wherever it may be, she knew she'd be warm, and feel boundless, and connected, and most importantly, she'd feel like she belonged. When her eyes opened again, however, the image of hungry people clambering up, tumbling like a flood toward a palace of clouds overflowing with gorgeous, winged humanoids was still standing there, twelve feet tall.

It was at this point she thought of Angela Morris and the disappearance of her husband, Rick. There was not a day that passed when she did not think of Angela at some point. Even if it was just a flicker of regret that they had not talked that day, Angela would come up.

The two women had been friends for a long time. They first met in Sunday school when Angela asked Clara to help her pick out crayons so she could colour her drawing of Jesus on a donkey. With their combined artistic savvy, they managed to depict a sickly mule sporting yellowish-green hair instead of the traditional brown, but that's beside the point.

The two of them depended on one another and their trust grew naturally, until they were comfortable confiding every secret they had, transitioning from friends to sisters in a matter of months. As the two matured into young adults, so did their secrets, but no matter how personal, never once did they hold back from each other. Angela learned all about Clara's suffocating mother, and of her lonely lunchtimes at school when the other girls refused to eat with her, claiming her fatness would rub off on them, until the teacher forced them to, which was even lonelier. And Clara learned of Angela's absent father, who spent more time staring down the bottom of a bottle than he did with his own daughter, and the time she almost risked him finding out she visited an abortion clinic, for which he would have cracked his precious bottle over her precious head. Luckily for Angela, it was a false alarm, and even luckier he never found out. They were each other's most trusted confidante, and, Clara imagined, probably the reason she hadn't sent herself to Heaven yet, though this one secret she did keep to herself. She thanked God for having bound them together. That was until Angela met Rick.

It all began when Angela caught a rogue football at one of The Bulldog's big games. Rick was a linebacker and it was his botched pass that had sent the ball flying in the first place. She caught it, as well as Rick's attention. After that, the two never left each other's side. He became all she talked about.

Clara often found herself on the phone reminding Angela that her relationship with the high school sports star was not a race, but the two young lovers' impatient infatuation couldn't be slowed. Angela was eager to leave her old life behind. They were married and had a child within three years. Angela was barely settled into her twenties.

For Clara, this meant Angela had moved on. Her best friend had a family, and, unfortunately, Clara was not part of it. Distance grew, and the echo in the gulf between them reminded her too much of her lonely lunches, so Clara followed in her nagging mother's footsteps and escaped to teacher's college. While there, she discovered a passion that she never dreamed could exist in her. Phone calls between the two friends became few and far between, and the ones that did arise were plagued by awkward silences.

Then, three months ago, Clara received a call that changed all that. It was Angela. She needed help, and there was only one friend who came to mind, the one she had almost fully discarded into her past – her trusted Clara. And so Angela confided in her one more time. Her husband, Rick, had vanished. One unremarkable night, he drove off in his car and never returned. The vehicle was found abandoned in the church's parking lot the morning after he went missing. The driver's door was open, as if he had expected to return, but never did.

Soon after that, Clara's treasured phone calls once again became a nightly routine.

Angela tried to keep the personal details of Rick's last night away from ravenous gossipers – even Clara was not privy to the exact events. But everyone knew from the reports that there were no signs of a struggle, no dubious footprints to track or bread crumbs to follow, only conjecture. With no real leads, the case remained open and Angela was left a semi-widow. Regrettably, her silence on the subject only fueled more rumours with catchy headlines: "Kidnapping on Highway 7", "Spurned Housewife Buries Husband Deep Under Cornfield", "Aliens Answered His Prayers"; all of them absurd and none of them sympathetic. Of course, Clara didn't believe a word of any of it.

Since then, Clara devoted much of her time to Angela's well being. Her selfless endeavours included cooking meals, emotional cheerleading and looking after Angela's son, Alex, when Angela was still regularly dealing with the police. Her generosity was boundless, and Clara could not have been more thankful for this gift of inclusion.

The sound of tires pawing through dirt returned Clara to the here-and-now of the parking lot. The first congregation member had arrived.

Caught up in her daydreaming, she had neglected her cigarette, which continued to smolder away in her hand. She buried it alive in the field without finishing it, prepared her smiling façade for the first arrivals, and took her position at the entrance to the church.

"Good morning," came the first greeting of the day. The honour went to the feeble Flora Thompson as she struggled up the steps.

"Ahoy there, Flora," Clara hollered back. She took Flora by the arm and steadied her. "Matthew didn't bring you today?"

"Oh yes, he did. He drove these tired old bones all the way out here yet again. Precious boy. He's just getting my chair out of the car."

"Looks like it's going to be a lovely day."

"What?"

"Looks like a lovely day."

"Yes, the Lord's offered us a treat this morning, hasn't He?"

"He certainly has."

CHAPTER 5

A car that looked like it had survived some kind of bomb testing chugged into the crowded parking lot. It headed straight past the church and squeezed into a spot between an equally worn-down pickup truck and an immaculately kept van. As the car finally came to a halt, the sound of Annie Lennox belting, *Love is A Stranger* seeped out over the quieted engine.

Angela kicked open her stubborn door and stepped out sporting a pair of sunglasses. Her conservative and gloomy attire was only a veil and a black handbag short of being appropriate for a funeral. After a satisfying inhale, she slammed the door closed.

"She still running?" a disembodied voice called out from behind the van.

Angela searched for the voice's owner. Eventually, Gary Brown emerged from behind his vehicle wearing a grey suit that didn't quite sit right on him. He smiled tenderly and nodded to her.

"You kidding?" she replied with vigor. "This baby's been running longer than I have. I can't imagine her stopping anytime soon."

"Is that so?" Gary playfully teased back with the subtlest sprinkling of real concern.

Alex jumped out of Angela's back seat like a dog after a rabbit and darted straight for the church, his red hair springy and wild.

"Whoa, buddy! Not so fast. Come on back here first." Her command was firm.

"Why?" Alex rebutted, testing his mother's sternness. She immediately proved he had yet to reach its limits.

"Never you mind why, just come on over here 'cause I asked you, mister."

Alex stood his ground, but she could see he was starting to budge. She pretended to pick up an old two-way radio and mimed turning it on. She spoke into it like a gruff soldier, complete with her best impression of radio-static noises.

Gary observed this behaviour from a distance, delight spread across his face.

"Come in echo one," she began. "This is echo two, are you there? Over."

Alex tried to appear unimpressed, but his right hand started to form a grip around his invisible radio.

"Echo one, can you hear me? What are your coordinates? Over," she continued.

"This is echo one, I'm standing right in front of you." Alex had resisted for as long as he could.

"This is echo two, is your message over? Cause you didn't say over. Over."

"Stop being difficult. Over."

"I need you to return to base before heading into the church, that's an order. Over."

"What for? Over."

"That's top secret information, soldier. Over and out."

The walkie-talkies disintegrated back into the air from where they had come, and Alex moped over to his mother. However, when he was just out of her reach, he was halted by a realization.

"You promise not to wipe my face?" he asked innocently.

"I'm not going to wipe your face."

"You promise?"

"I promise."

He took another step toward her and was betrayed in a flash. With inhuman speed, Angela had wetted her palm with her spit and lathered it all over his face.

"Mom! Stop!" His agony was palpable, yet she showed no mercy. She ran her damp fingers through the clumps of his hair to lend some order to the chaos.

"You want your hair a mess?" She took a second to straighten his Sunday clothes then announced, "Okay, now go ahead."

He scampered off toward the church. A few other children arrived at the same time and Alex enthusiastically greeted them. Together, they disappeared out of Angela's sight.

"You're doing just fine, you know that?" Gary offered some encouragement. Although Angela was faintly annoyed that he felt she needed encouragement, it came from a kind place and she accepted it anyway.

"Thanks, Gary."

"You ever need anything, you can give us a call. Only, I will warn that Tina is downright desperate for some, you know, female talk. So, if you get her on the line, she's liable to draw blood with her yammering. Last conversation, I timed her. Three hours. She talked for three hours."

"Thanks for the warning," she replied between laughs.

"And if your old ride there starts falling apart on you, you just bring it on into the shop. I'll take a look at it, free of charge. Alright?"

"Oh, Gary, you really don't have to do that."

"Lending a hand never hurt anybody."

"Unless they don't get it back." Angela chuckled at her own joke, worried that if she didn't, neither would Gary.

"Well, I'll see you in there." He delivered a sympathetic smile and departed toward the church.

"Yep!" Angela took note of the purse Gary carried under his arm as he headed inside. It was a distinctly feminine bag in a soft pastel blue, presumably his wife's. Angela hated it.

She turned to the side mirror of her car and quickly examined her reflection. Angela was not often concerned with her appearance. In fact, she often disregarded it completely. However, there were certain days when she knew she would be scrutinized, or rather, dissected by bladed eyeballs. Once the people in the church heard what she had to say, she knew this was to be one of those days. Though faith brought the congregation together, Angela knew it was gossip that kept them satiated. And they were starved.

A stale gust of wind playfully twirled dirt around her feet. Angela stopped to admire the fluid motions of the dance. It was not that long ago when she would have ignored such a treasure.

She looked to see where the wind originated from, as if expecting to find God huffing and puffing. What she saw was an empty field cowering under the ever-watchful Burward forest, with its lifeless trees crowded together like the tombstones of an ill-planned cemetery.

A decaying well--long abandoned--near the edge of the parking lot, managed to trap some wind and send the doomed gusts howling into its depths. The deathly whistle that resulted gave Angela shivers that overwhelmed the delight she had felt moments earlier.

The beauty had been soured.

She plucked a loose eyelash from her face and headed toward the building, into the den of ravenous lambs.

CHAPTER 6

The mess hall stirred with its usual social fervor. People roamed about the large room with Styrofoam cups of coffee and perky smiles to match.

Most did not deviate from the safety of their family units - each cohesive clan moved as if they shared a single mind. One clan would greet the other and begin an exhaustive update about the week's events. Such events included the weather, the price of gas, or how they mourned the passing of summer and could not wait for its annual resurrection next year. Once this falderal was concluded, they would detach and move onto the next family. This ritual was the same every Sunday and everyone knew their role backwards and forwards.

This cycle could only be broken by the wild cards – the ones who didn't have wives and husbands and children. Solitary people were unpredictable and therefore unsafe. No one knew of the secret life of the loner. The forbidden topic of what one does when they are alone was an affront to the wholesome family. What interesting weekly tidbit could the loner recount? Their struggle to find purpose in their lives or perhaps the number of times they indulged in some dastardly masturbation? Neither of these topics concerned the happily self-sufficient, self-oriented families milling through the space.

Being acutely aware of this, Clara had retreated into the basement to prepare for Sunday school.

Her mother, Dorothy, on the other hand, situated herself as the main attraction by the entrance of the sanctuary armed with bulletins. She watched over the undulating crowd of God-fearing socialites accompanied by the intimidatingly tall Emily Rosenthal, who was yet again wearing an impressively unfashionable dress. Although most of Emily's wardrobe seemed to have been stolen from dead widows, there was something to be said for their charmingly homemade look. No one was fooled, however; it was clear, hidden under her stuffy garments, was the body of a woman who could crush most men--something Emily seemed determined to hide.

Dorothy beamed her infectious smile into the room, while Emily simply looked as though she was standing guard.

"Did you notice the changes?" Dorothy spontaneously inquired.

"To what?" Emily's voice was shockingly sweet and at complete odds with the body that brought it forth.

"To the spacing." Dorothy lifted one of bulletins she had prepared for the day's service. "You know Flora Thompson? At the end of last Sunday's service, she told me she was finding it hard to see the hymn numbers."

Emily's blank stare was unrelenting, but it took more than that to stop Dorothy.

"She said they were too small, 'cause of the spacing. The problem was how they were spaced, so if you look at the bulletins, you'll see I changed the spacing." She took a second to muster her conclusion. "And there's more spacing now. So, you shouldn't run into that problem anymore."

"That's just great. I'm sure Mrs. Thompson will be thankful."

"I just hope the spacing is adequate. Once you change the spacing, you know, even one little bit, then that's it! The whole thing is thrown out of balance."

The two women nodded to each other as if this was a problem they were well-accustomed to.

Emily returned her gaze to the room, marginally warmed from her interaction with Dorothy. Her eyes settled on her husband, Michael. He stood across the room from her and gave a nod in response. Michael was a mountain of a man to match Emily's own considerable form. He looked like the kind of lumberjack that could carry a tree over his shoulder after chopping it down with his bare hands. He had recently taken to only shaving once every three days, so hair generously sprinkled his face. Emily hated that, but had reserved her annoyance to herself as she did most things.

The front door to the church swung open and the wood let out a terrible groan. Heads turned to greet Angela as she spilled into the room, ushered in by the fleeting sunlight creeping in behind her. There was an audible change in the crowd. Conversations quieted and attention shifted; the star had arrived.

As the door slowly closed itself, Angela straightened the wrinkles from her pants, filled her lungs with a breath of determination, and headed toward the coffee table.

"Okay," Emily said to Dorothy, "there's Angela, finally. I saw Alex running around here a bit ago. She really should keep a better watch over him, or she'll lose him, too."

"That poor girl," Dorothy lamented with almost comical emphasis.

"Yes." Emily was obviously annoyed at Dorothy's unbridled sympathy.

"How long has it been now? Two months?"

"Three. Rick went missing in August."

"Oh, that poor thing. Can you imagine not knowing? I think that would be torture. Awful. And now she has to raise Alex all alone." Dorothy's voice faltered as painful memories trickled back. "When I lost Albert, God was all I had to turn to. Of course, Clara was nowhere near as young as Alex, but still."

"Yes, Dorothy, it's terrible. But I have faith everything will work out. As long as she keeps the Holy Spirit in her heart, God will give her the strength to carry on."

"That's right," Dorothy tenderly added, "and she's shown tremendous strength already. I'm sure she'll be able to endure."

They watched as Angela fumbled her way through the cream and sugar, adding liberal amounts of both to her coffee.

"She looks to be doing just fine, doesn't she?" Emily remarked.

"Looks can deceive, poor thing."

"Rick's name is still in the call for prayer, right?" Emily asked, turning her body fully to face Dorothy.

"Of course."

Dorothy's stout little frame stood with confidence until doubt got the better of her. She opened one of the bulletins and hastily flipped through it.

"Oh shit, it's not." Her abrupt profanity sent shockwaves through Emily's entire body. Still, few people could swallow their indignation like Emily could.

"Sorry, Emily," Dorothy apologized. "Pardon me. I should see Don about Rick's missing name. We can't have that go overlooked. Are you okay here?"

"I'll be fine."

Dorothy smiled and patted Emily on the shoulder, despite barely being able to reach it. She then embarked on her journey to find Don in the sanctuary, leaving Emily with the task of bestowing every member with a bulletin.

Angela leaned against the coffee table. The sea of shifting bodies mingling before her was daunting, so the sturdy wooden support provided much needed anchorage.

After taking another drink of coffee, she made a promise to herself; just one more sip and she would venture out onto the rough waters. This promise had also been made five sips ago, but this time she meant it.

"Angela!" A saving grace emerged in the form of Clara, bounding across the room toward her.

"Clara!" Angela tried to match her friend's enthusiasm, but as usual, it was futile.

Clara wrapped both her arms around Angela, almost knocking her coffee onto the ground and Angela off her feet. The pressure built up in Angela's head from the force of Clara's bear hug. Eventually, she was released.

"Angela," she spoke seriously now. "How are you doing?"

"You know, I told you I can't keep answering that question everyday."

"I know, I know, sorry."

"How are *you* doing?"

"My mom's doing well; she was worried about the spacing of the new bulletin or something. You know how she is, fretting about everything, as is the usual. All the kids are settled in downstairs, so, things are good!"

"I haven't seen your mom yet."

"I'm sure you will."

"I have something serious to ask you." Angela's voice lowered as if she were about to slip Clara a secret folder of government documents. "Clara, I need you to discreetly look over my shoulder and tell me if I'm still caught in Emily Rosenthal's gaze of eternal damnation."

Clara's head quickly turned, but Angela brought it back just in time.

"Discreetly!" Angela warned, locking eyes with Clara until she was satisfied they had an understanding.

This time, Clara's head barely moved, but her eyes shifted conspicuously in Emily's direction.

"Yeah, she's still staring."

"I knew it. It feels like a dagger in my back."

"Hey!" Clara announced with gusto.

"Hi?" Angela replied, bewildered, then continued, "we were talking already, right? I'm confused."

"No, that wasn't *Hey* as in *Hi*, that was *Hey* as in I just remembered something fun." From Clara's pocket, she pulled out an old piece of paper, yellowed with age. "My mom asked me to help clean out her basement and I came across this."

She unfolded the precious paper and held it for Angela to see.

What opened up in front of her was a welcome time capsule; a reminder of her life before it got messy. Clara presented an illustration of a tree that Angela had authored twenty years ago, yet the memory of the tree's creation was still surprisingly accessible. On each branch of the tree, instead of leaves, were assortments of seemingly random objects including foods, faces, a soccer ball, a butterfly, a glowing sun, and most noticeably, a cross placed at the peak.

"You remember?" asked Clara. "From when we were in Sunday school. My mom told us to do this assignment. We were given the tree and we had to draw all the things that were important to us."

"Yes, wow. I actually do remember. You found this in her basement?"

"You wouldn't believe the things I found down there."

"I think this one is supposed to be you." Angela pointed to one of the simplistic faces.

"You think?"

"Of course. What? You don't think you're important enough to make my tree? And look, I put a cross at the top. I was such a suck-up. Do you have yours?"

"Mine's garbage."

"That's a little harsh, Clara, don't you think? It's a child's crayon drawing of a tree of love. It's not supposed to be… Mozart?"

"He did music."

"Damn." Angela almost stomped her foot.

"I know it's not supposed to be Van Gogh, but what I meant was mine's literally garbage. I think it was thrown out or something. But, this is going to be today's craft for the kids. So, you can hang yours next to Alex's."

Angela was unprepared for the sudden tenderness. Her words formed slowly and hid behind a thin humorous veneer.

"Clara, you're either so sweet and sentimental that I just love you, or you're lazy and recycling your mom's old ideas. I can't decide which."

Like a crocodile lying in wait for the kill, a hand shot forth from the stillness behind Angela and grabbed her arm. She instinctively turned around, ready with a ferocious swat. Her social refinements, however, saved her from that embarrassment. Instead, she greeted the intruder with feigned, but convincing warmness.

"Sorry to interrupt," Tina Brown apologized. "I just wanted to say hi."

Gary's wife, Tina, lived on the bright side of things; you could tell she was a permanent resident there by the inexplicable glow that she carried with her wherever she went. Sadly, her positivity was rarely an attribute, as she lacked the depth of any real understanding. Tina once brought a batch of freshly baked cookies to a middle-aged man named Rex Walter because he found out his cancer was terminal. They were delivered with a smile. Three weeks later, he was dead. But on the bright side, her cookies were, indeed, still fresh.

"Hi, Tina. I actually just ran into Gary outside. You got your purse, I see." Angela made note, yet again, of Tina's excessively gaudy, but feminine, handbag.

"Yes, what would I do without him?"

Angela almost winced at the comment. Had Tina forgotten her recent loss, or was she just trying to see how much blood would come out if she wiggled the knife?

"Oh, goodness! Sorry, Angela," Tina found herself apologizing again in record time. "That's not what I meant to say. Of course, I didn't mean anything by it. Just one of those silly phrases."

"It's okay. I get it." Angela mused over the likelihood of Tina's honesty.

It was then she noticed Chris, Tina's son, hidden behind his mother. Although he was barely sixteen, he had transcended the awkward teen stage and appeared amiably put together. A sharp haircut coupled with well-fit jeans and a scandalously low v-neck suggested he was looking to impress. Given his surroundings, the question became, who?

"Oh, hi, …" Angela instigated the greeting before she had realized Chris' name had escaped her.

"Chris." Tina rescued her.

"Right, Chris. I knew that, sorry. Sorry, Chris."

"No worries." He offered a meager shrug, appearing distracted from the entire exchange. Something, or someone else, was on his mind.

"I just wanted you to know," Tina interjected, "that we're still praying. Gary and I pray every night for

Rick's return and for Alex to get his father back. If you ever need anything…"

"I'll give you a call, thank you."

"You just hang in there. You haven't heard anything lately have you?"

"About?"

"Well, about Rick. Have you heard anything?"

Tina had made a fatal mistake. Her sloppy questions left a foulness in the air between them, and Angela knew she was just fishing for something really meaty to take back to the horde. Their hunger was becoming insatiable.

"No. Not a thing."

"So, they don't know anything about why his car was here. They haven't put that together yet?"

"If they have, they haven't told me."

"I see. Well, you just hang in there. I know something's going to happen soon. I feel it."

"You feel it, too?" Angela's deadpan voice betrayed her irritation a little more than she had intended.

Tina finally felt the obligation to acknowledge Clara who had been standing next to Angela for the entire exchange. A pitiful grin was all Clara got before Tina and Chris headed into the sanctuary. Clara felt spoiled even by that.

Angela was drained by the experience. Tina, that parasite, probably stole tiny bits of energy with every word she uttered.

"I should really get back down there and make sure those kids haven't eaten all the play-dough," Clara said, half-turned already.

"Okay, get to it."

"You going to be all right?" she asked Angela with refreshing honesty.

"That question is too close to *how are you doing?*"

"Fair enough."

"I'll see you after the service, though. At the picnic lunch, right?"

"Yeah, I'm the tomato cutter. See you then."

The two parted ways.

Angela joined the herd, slowly shuffling into the sanctuary. Still standing guard at the door was the ever-stoic Emily. A bulletin was handed out to each passerby with not a single utterance until she got to Angela.

The bulletin was offered, but when Angela tried to take it, Emily's grip tightened.

"God tests," Emily coldly announced.

Whether this was supposed to be a comfort or a warning, Angela could not decipher. It was delivered with superb ambiguity. Something darker troubled Angela, however. Regardless of what Emily meant, the saying itself spurred memories – it was familiar. Like trying to remember the tune of a beloved song you have sung a million times, Angela racked her brain. Suddenly, it came to her.

"Rick used to say that," said Angela.

Emily's stare collapsed and her eyes went searching, lost in secret thought. Angela watched with astonishment as Emily struggled to piece together a rebuttal, which surely by now was scattered to the wind.

Although the intensity of Emily's distress was puzzling to Angela, instead of pressing the matter, she decided to yank the bulletin from Emily's hand and carry on.

CHAPTER 7

Creaking pews announced every uncomfortable shift as the congregation waited in silence for the service to begin.

Emily was last to enter the sanctuary and did so only after she was positive no one was without a bulletin. She made her way up the aisle and squeezed down a pew, inconveniencing a dozen members in order to claim her seat next to Michael.

On the other side of the room, Angela was sandwiched between two families. The ones closest to the window on her left, though she didn't know their names, she knew they were more than just occasional churchgoers. She judged this mostly by the seriousness with which they sat. To her right, there was Flora and Matthew Thompson. Flora was always the first into the sanctuary as her eighty-year-old bones could no longer handle the trials of the mess hall meet-and-greet. Her grandson, Matthew, who was no older than seventeen, accompanied his grandmother to church whenever his parents could not. He looked just like a miniature adult in a grown-ups' suit.

Angela scanned the room, but after having awkwardly caught too many secret glances, she decided it was safer just to stare ahead and wait for the minister to begin.

A bald gentleman by the name of Sandy finally lifted the silence with some droning first notes on the electric organ. The tune was simple and slow, designed either to induce spiritual calmness or death by boredom. Gradually, a more youthful piano accompaniment chimed in to keep the music alive. Bruce, who was at least twenty years Sandy's junior, and with a full head of lengthy dark hair, played the more lively keys. After a few faulty missteps, the two men eventually found a complimentary cohesiveness and achieved a tone of tranquility.

At the back of the sanctuary, Don Hooper entered wearing his minister's robe and a long piece of embroidered fabric swathed around his shoulders. In unison, the congregation stood up to watch him parade past. His greying hair was slicked back tight to his head emphasizing not only his receding hairline, but also the sharpness of his skull, like Marlon Brando in *The Godfather*. Bushy eyebrows helped to shroud his eyes in mystery, as if they were constantly hidden behind sunglasses. These quasi-sinister features, however, were put to shame by the generosity of his smile.

As if it had been painstakingly rehearsed, the music ended just as Don reached the pulpit. After laying down his personal Bible, which was overflowing with scraps of paper and post-its, he soaked in the faces of the gathering before him.

"You may be seated," he gently commanded while lowering his own hands, as if he were conducting the room. Amazingly, everyone sat in perfect harmony.

The Brown family was seated in the front row, like eager groupies, with Tina and Gary's attention fixed on Don, anxious to absorb whatever Godly insight they could. Chris, on the other hand, was less interested in what he considered the ramblings of a fifty-year-old virgin. Without arousing the suspicion of his parents, Chris afforded himself a quick glance to the other side of the room. He knew exactly who he was looking for and his vision cut through the crowd to catch a glimpse, even if just a fleeting one, of Matthew. He enjoyed the sight of Matthew's messy blond hair, his eyes that seemed to be only seconds away from sleep, and the kind, gentle curves of his face. Memories of having tasted the salty sensations of his flesh when they were supposed to be studying in his bedroom, took their intoxicating toll on Chris, who became worried about the inappropriate reactions his body might start having. Although Matthew took no notice of Chris' voyeurism, Chris had decided his appetite was nonetheless satiated for now. He turned back around and dreamed of the approaching church picnic where Matthew and he could do more than just ogle each other.

"Thank you, Bruce," Don began. "Thank you, Sandy. Once again, we should really be paying you."

"Oh, God's love is enough," Sandy quipped, heartily.

"But a buck wouldn't hurt?" Don's response elicited a polite degree of laughter from the congregation. He waited for the amusement to die down before he continued.

"And thank you, Sandy, for that perfect segue into today's topic: God's love. Now, I do want to be upfront about this. Today's sermon will be a little different than what we're used to. A little darker, maybe. Because, let's face it, these are dark times, aren't they?" His authoritative gaze fixated on Angela. "But I'm getting ahead of myself. I have forgotten about the announcements. Does anyone have anything they'd care to announce?"

From the back of the church, an eager hand sprang forth, waving insistently like a caffeinated Jack-in-the-box.

"Susan Greenfield," Don pointed to the flapping appendage. "You have something you'd like to say?"

Like an ascending sun, Susan arose from the placid crowd with infectious enthusiasm. She was a vivacious young woman and obviously a devourer of every pulp beauty magazine on the shelf. She was immaculately constructed. The tint of her skin, the flow of her hair, the tightness of her blouse, nothing was left to the unpredictability of nature. It was a trait she had obviously learned from her equally fashion-conscious mother, sitting next to her. More recently, however, in an almost desperate attempt to prove she was not just a pretty face, Susan had taken to charity.

"Hello, everyone," she began. "I wanted to remind you that we need your cookies! The fundraiser to fight empty tummies all over the world is happening next weekend and we're short on baked goods. All the money goes to drilling new water wells in Africa. So please, bake, bake, bake! And lets get some water for some Africans. Thank you."

From the moment she stood up, Matthew's eyes were enslaved. He was uncontrollably drawn to her. Although his hormonal urges were titillated by almost anything these days, he was undoubtedly intrigued by her presentation. So much so, in fact, that when she concluded and sat back down, as if he had relinquished all control over himself, he applauded. This died out rather quickly, once the silence of the rest of the room became evident to him. But Chris took notice, and puzzled over Matthew's public fawning.

Dorothy, who was sitting just a few seats down from Susan, offered her support in the form of a thumbs-up.

"Great, anyone else?" Don asked, and Gary stood up. "Gary Brown, everyone."

"Thank you, Don. I thought you all should know that the ceiling above our heads is falling apart, but fear not, I'm on the job and we'll be doing repair work before the first snow. I'm donating my time, and I'm hoping a few others will, too, if you feel so inclined. Thanks." He sat back down next to Tina, who gripped his hand as if to say she was proud.

"Thank you, Gary. Is that it?"

The room was silent for a moment, lasting anywhere from a minute to a week, at least from Angela's perspective. She had been sitting in her pew waiting anxiously to make her big announcement. As the stillness plodded on, a tingling spread through her arms and belly. Her legs felt weak and she became convinced that if she stood up, she would most certainly fall flat on her face. However, she had to act. She would not get another chance to tell everyone in one fell swoop. Opportunities like this were momentary, and this moment was just about over. So, she had no choice. To help support the weakness of her legs, she reached out and gripped the pew in front of her. With one powerful heave, she managed to get to her feet. At the same time, however, Emily also stood. Considering Emily's superior stature, Angela's momentum was dwarfed. Without acknowledging Angela, Emily committed to her announcement.

"Michael and I are in charge of the Christmas concert this year," Emily began. "Rehearsals are not optional. If your child wants to be in it, they must be present every Wednesday at six-thirty. We also need help with costumes. If you want to lend a hand, just let us know. We'd appreciate it." Emily concluded by shooting a couple more daggers Angela's way before taking her seat.

"Looking forward to it. Angela Morris? You have an announcement as well?" Don shifted the attention to the only person still standing in the room besides himself.

Angela looked around at the forty-six anticipating faces beaming up at her.

"Hello. Hi, everyone. I thought I may as well say this to all of you at once. First, I just wanted to say thank you all so much for your compassion and your thoughts." She had made it through the hardest part--the truth that followed was easier to stomach. "Since Rick went missing, Alex and I have been... This has been a hard time for us, and your help hasn't gone unnoticed. But, we're leaving. We'll be moving at the end of the month. We're looking for a new life. We can't just keep waiting for our old one to come back. So, yeah, we're leaving."

The congregation stared like she had just announced there was piss in the communion wine. Angela's pulse pounded a drum solo in her ear. She and Alex were going to move --that was not a lie-- but they were only moving to a small apartment building in town, still within driving distance of the church. This detail Angela decided not to reveal.

"So, again," Angela gracefully finished, "thank you all so much. Really. Thank you."

Once Angela returned to the safety of her seat, she knew she had set the congregation's minds aflame. The Browns, the Rosenthals, the Thompsons, she assumed they were all, at that very moment, constructing elaborate storylines where she orchestrated Rick's disappearance and was now making a hasty escape. Why else would she be so keen on leaving? She fought the urge to stand up again and tell everyone it was just a bad joke. It was tempting, so tempting. But when the murmurs in the congregation grew and the agitation became palpable, she was glad to be rid of the church.

She would not take it back for all the blessings in Heaven.

"Well," Don announced. "I'm sorry to hear that. You and Alex will be deeply missed. But, if you're sure that's the journey God wants for you, then you must follow. Mustn't you?"

Angela nodded vigorously, but only agreed in part.

If this is the journey God wanted for me, then maybe He should have skipped the fucking detours. She smiled as this passed through her head.

Don read it as something else.

CHAPTER 8

The basement of the church was an unwelcoming place, so Clara had done her best to introduce some verve into its cold, tomb-like emptiness. When she first inherited it, it was merely one large room with brick walls and a harsh concrete floor. A small kitchen was attached, but, as it was used mostly for preparing large amounts of food quickly, its industrial feel also lacked warmth.

Originally, the purpose of the basement was as a storage space--a reasonable excuse for its bleak appearance. There were two sets of stairs leading into its depths. The first set led down from the mess hall, the second connected the basement directly to the field outside, but were crumbling, as they hadn't been used for years. A haphazardly-painted door blocked the entrance to the outdoor stairs from the children, who, in turn, had taken to peeling the flaking paint from its wood planks and daring each other to eat it.

Accustomed to working with what she had, Clara brought in portable dividers, which stood the height of the basement, effectively sectioning off the space into different rooms. Each divider was then decorated with colourful drawings and inspirational sayings to keep the maze of makeshift walls an entertaining journey. The contrast of garish primary colours against the dark grey of the stone was quirky to say the least, but better than nothing.

In one of Clara's rooms, the children had gathered around a table, busily committing their tree illustrations to paper. As they worked, Clara circled them like a protective hen. She stopped next to Emily's son, Stanley Rosenthal, who was the oldest child in attendance at an impressive ten years of age. His appearance, much like his mother, was traditional, sharp and crisp.

"What are you drawing, Stan?" Clara asked.

"That's my mom," he pointed to each subject as they came up. "And that's my dad, and that's my dog."

"What's that?" Clara pointed to one of the more indecipherable scribbles on the messy page.

"Pizza!" he replied with simple joy.

"Oh, I like pizza, too. Nice work." It was important for Clara to always be encouraging, even if she considered putting pizza at equal importance as your own parents a sign of severe emotional detachment.

Stanley's doll of a little sister, Samantha Rosenthal, was next to catch Clara's eye. She was four years younger than her big brother, so her attempt at a tree resulted in something closer to bizarre geometric abstraction than anything recognizable in nature. The sight of it made Clara dizzy. However, Samantha had still done better than Bruce's son Dylan, who had gotten as far as sticking the crayon up his nose.

Clara made her way around the table, her shoes tapping like a metronome. The assignment had awakened something unique in each child, despite a few common themes like parents and pets, there were fascinating and often subtle differences to be seen. One child drew clothes because she said she had seen people who couldn't afford any. Another drew stars because he said at night they watched him sleep. Eventually, Clara arrived at Alex.

"Can I see?"

Alex nodded and Clara carefully picked up his paper. Most of the branches were filled with typical bubbly depictions of happy things; however, Alex had included a figure in black crayon that stood next to the tree and as tall as its highest branch. The force with which Alex had coloured the giant, bruised the paper, muddying the image, like something not quite in focus and only half-remembered.

"Who's this, standing next to the tree?" Clara was disturbed by the darkness of the drawing and couldn't take her eyes off it.

"God," Alex replied abruptly.

Although Clara could relate to the formlessness with which Alex had portrayed the Almighty, its undeniable malevolence was troubling. *God was not a looming, dreadful thing*, Clara thought. *He was pure, heavenly, the Father of us all.*

"Where's His big, white robe and beard?" Clara attempted to lighten the mood.

"He doesn't have one."

"What makes you say that?"

Alex just shrugged. Clara was entirely unsatisfied by this response, or lack thereof, so she pressed further. She returned the paper in front of him.

"Can you tell me who else is in your picture, Alex?"

"That's my mom. That's my dad."

"You can't draw your dad!" Stanley blurted out from across the table.

"Yes I can!" Alex hollered back.

"That's very rude, Stanley," Clara reprimanded and stood to her full height to add to her authority.

"Miss Muller," Stanley whined. "You said it had to be important stuff in your life. Alex's dad is gone."

"Shut up, Stanley!" Alex yelled.

"Hey! Enough!" Clara shouted. "Stanley, back to your paper. Never you mind Alex's."

Stanley lowered his head until it was mere inches away from the table.

"Clara…" Alex whispered.

Her livid stare ripped into Stanley for a good five seconds before she could acknowledge Alex again.

"Yes, what is it?"

"My dad's coming back." This whisper was even fainter than the last.

"I hope so, Alex." Her heart broke when a part of her demanded she tell him the truth. "But, we can't really know that, can we?"

She thought, in the heat of the moment, her phrasing was delicate enough. She refrained from flat-out telling him his father was more than likely dead, gone forever. There's a difference between truth-handling and lying, she reasoned.

While watching Alex apply the finishing touches to his God, Clara thought of the conviction with which he had spoken. He did not ask if his dad was coming back, or wish for him to come back, he *knew*. Alex seemed as sure of it as he was of the table in front of him, or the paper in his hands. What had he seen or heard that convinced him so completely?

#

From deep in the Burward forest, the man with spectral eyes stumbled forth. His bare feet were raw from the cruel twigs and stones that assaulted his every step. Like jagged teeth imbedded in a cavernous mouth, this eclectic assortment of sharp points seemed determined to chew up his feet and spit them out. Nicks and scratches bled his ankles enough to leave a thin trail of red behind him, should he choose to retrace his steps. However, his steady stride showed he had an unwavering fortitude and turning back seemed unlikely.

Some of the harsher stones penetrated the same wound more than once, splitting the skin deep enough to scrape out pinkish flesh from the balls of his feet and between his toes. Despite the excruciating pain, the man endured, and marched on toward the edge of the woods.

CHAPTER 9

The congregation's attentiveness had not waned, even though the past twenty minutes was mostly eaten up by dry, scriptural readings. On the contrary, as if by divine influence, there was a rising sense of zeal in awaiting the sermon; then, the wait was over. Don took his position again at the pulpit in the centre of the sanctuary and opened his Bible to the exhaustive notes he had prepared alone in his manse during the course of the previous week.

Angela, unlike the majority of Don's audience, leaned against her pew with her arms crossed. Whatever spirituality had survived in her, she was certain Don's approach, which was obviously geared to appeal to her predicament, would offer little comfort.

Her mind detached from Don as he fumbled through his notes, and switched focus onto the peaceful tapestry that hung on the wall just behind him. It was a symbol of serenity and worship. Dorothy had more than once informed Angela of the tapestry's history, as she had played an integral part in its creation. Thirty years ago, Dorothy, along with three other women, two of whom were still alive, designed the image to the taste of their own spirituality, sewed the fabric with their own diligent fingers, and mounted the fruits of their labour so all could bask in its sanctity. It showed two hands gently unfolding as if recently in prayer. A dove emerged from the hands with a small olive branch in its mouth. Its flight looked calm, gliding effortlessly against the blue backdrop, soaring up to the heavens, rendered in the soft pastel colours of a baby's room.

Angela tried to relate to it, but had never experienced that kind of peace through prayer. She did have faith in a God-like presence operating in the universe, she just didn't believe It listened every time someone clasped their hands together. A Being like that could not possibly care about the goings-on of a country church with dwindling attendance by the side of a highway, not with everything spinning through the cosmos. Yet, here she was on this little planet, in this little church, another Sunday, another sermon. The only way she could bear the ramblings to come was with the knowledge that Don was only human, and therefore could not talk forever.

"We all know pain," he began ominously, "some of us more than others. It's easy, when we feel pain, to get angry. It's natural to wonder why; to ask what did I do to deserve this? Am I being punished? Is that why I lost my job? Is that why I got sick right before the big game? Because God wants to punish me? But let's go even bigger. What about world hunger? What about the millions of people who are destitute? What about cancer? What about murder? What does God think of all this pain? These are tough questions. Really, really tough questions. Now, we've heard a lot from the Book of Job this morning. If you didn't quite follow it, or if you were dozing off, I'll sum it up for you. Job suffers. He suffers tremendous loss. He loses his family, his health, his money. He loses everything he had. Why? Was he a sinner who deserved punishment? No. He was an upstanding guy. He did nothing to deserve that kind of suffering. The hard truth is, pain exists because God allows it. Yet, there is hope. Though the immediate horror of the day may seem bleak, unthinkable, or even unforgivable, and although we may find ourselves at times on our knees asking why; why is this happening to me? To them? To us? And, although despair seems the correct response to this evil that is surely insurmountable, God asks us to trust in Him. Trust that He has not abandoned us."

Panic started to build in Angela. He could not talk forever, right? Right??

#

Across the cracked soil of the Davidson's field, as the congregation listened to the trials of Job, and the children below them drew trees that bloomed with love, the traveling man emerged from the woods, draped in a dirty cloth that cloaked him from head to bloody toe, like Death itself. The parched earth eagerly sponged up the blood from his feet as he made his way towards St. Paul's United Church.

From afar, his limping, hunched form could have been mistaken for a sickly vagrant, but a closer inspection would have revealed hidden strength in his gait, with the dark cloak whipping up puffs of dust behind him. He was driven. By what, was impossible to say, but it pulled him closer to the humble house of worship.

And closer.

#

Don had taken a break to moisten his throat with the water Clara had set out for him. Being a consummate showman, the sip was brief and well-timed.

"He never abandons us. Just as you would never abandon your children, He is with us, always. But that does not mean He will protect us. It's not just hard for us to understand God's scale--it's impossible. How do you measure the infinite? Is it by the teaspoon? And likewise, how do you measure God's plan, which is of equal grandeur? We cannot hope to fathom the reason for pain, but God assures us that He has a darn good one. We send our children to school in order to learn. While they're there, they are exposed to all sorts of pain. Suppose they even get into a fight. The other kid lands a lucky punch and all of a sudden, we're faced with a bloody nose. As parents, we didn't want that to happen, but the truth is we allowed it, just as God allows it. But at the end of the day, when all is said and done, God will be there to wipe away our tears, to sooth our aching nose, to reassure us that we did the right thing by not punching that kid right back. And it helps us to grow, to understand, and to be closer to God. Trust in God. Trust in Him." Don's eyes closed to allow the weight of his last statement to sink in before moving on.

Angela was, as she had predicted, unmoved by the remarks. Though she gave him points for trying, she had problems with the lack of cohesion in his story. Angela's relationship to Alex was nothing like God's relationship to her because, unlike her, God birthed the entirety of the world, not just one child. God, as ultimate Creator, was therefore still on the hook for the remarkably unpopular invention of suffering. At least the sermon got her thinking, even if they were blasphemous thoughts, she told herself.

She looked around the room for someone to share her resentment with, but found Dorothy, instead, with an expression of thankful enlightenment. It was clear she had received some kind of strength from Don's scriptural interpretation. This only fed Angela's annoyance and beckoned the self-directed question: if it worked for Dorothy, then why not her? What part of her was broken?

"I'd like you now," Don stated, "to turn in your hymnbooks, to page one hundred eighty-five, to one of my all-time, favourite hymns. I think the sense of worship it evokes is appropriate. Please join me in singing *Part of the Family*."

The sound of hymnbooks cracking open splintered the room. Tina, whose voice was unsurpassed, stood to lead the congregation in song.

She cleared her throat like a gruff man but hit the first note like a refined flute.

#

The man from the woods stumbled into the parking lot. His hands, which had been bloodied along with his feet, smeared glistening red as he braced himself on the vehicles for support.

His breathing was strained, as if the fabric that cloaked him had tightened and now attempted to snuff out his life before he made it any further. Even in light of all these hardships, he pressed forward.

The heaving gasps choking from his body reached a crescendo as the wet tissue of his feet slapped against the stone of the stairs leading up to the front door.

#

The congregation erupted in a powerful rendition of the cherished hymn. Low male voices rounded out the harmony, while a few sparse sopranos reached for the heavens.

Angela mouthed the words, but did not sing. She occasionally enjoyed belting pop tunes when all alone in her car, but not with these songs or with these people.

The second verse had already begun when the front door in the mess hall cracked open and distracted some of the lesser singers near the back.

A familiar moaning wind, like the one that had danced for Angela earlier that morning, caught her attention again and brushed against the curtains of the three large windows that connected the back of the sanctuary to the mess hall.

The front door slammed shut, echoing like a gunshot, effectively silencing the rest of the singing congregation and startling even Don. There was a pause then, a kind of shock and unease similar to when something breaks the surface of the water, then disappears again just beneath. Everyone waited in excruciating silence for the intruder to make another sound. Soon, all they could hear was the tightness of his breaths as they struggled in and out of his throat.

Tina, who had not moved from the front of the room, stared blankly at the three windows lining the back wall. They stared back at her, with the drapes pulled across them, suspiciously still.

Then, the footsteps began. Their wetness was evident to everyone in the room, which only fed curiosity. The sound was accompanied by something dragging, suggesting they were either hurt, or pulling something heavy. Whatever the case, they were undeniably headed toward the sanctuary.

The sound of the approaching trespasser sent a wave of frantic looks through the congregation. Every step was louder than the last and they seemed to convey a relentlessness about them, a determined drive despite the obvious labour of the journey. Once the footsteps reached the sanctuary's entrance, everyone's gaze abandoned the rest of the room. No more solace could be found in the faces of their loved ones, they had to know for themselves who was at the door. Abruptly, the sounds stopped and the room was again cursed with silence.

"Whoever you are, you're welcome to join us," Don announced from the safety of his pulpit.

The door did not answer.

One of the larger candelabras toppled over as if it was pushed. Its elaborate metal frame crashed against the ground sending spurts of hot wax across the floor.

A few screams escaped some of the more easily startled mouths, but everyone's eyes were enticed to look. One of the candles had come loose and rolled across the carpet toward the door. Its flame flickered sporadically as it rolled past the pews. Dorothy stepped out from the gawking crowd and caught the rogue candle. When she lifted it, a tremendous rush of wind burst forth, claiming its little light.

Dorothy looked in the direction the wind had come from, and it was then she saw the sanctuary door was open. Standing in the doorway was the man from the forest, the man with spectral eyes.

His electric stare was fixed on Dorothy first, who, intimidated by his intensity, retreated back into the crowd.

The dirty fabric that encased him was bunched around his head like a hood and kept most of his face hidden, yet allowed his eyes to peer through.

With his torn foot, he made his first step into the sanctuary. A new stream of sunlight revealed a few more of his features. His beard was greasy and appeared partly singed, his lips were dry and cracked, like brittle paper.

No one made any attempt to help him; they were too afraid to step out of their role as audience.

"Bruce," Don said quietly, "get some water."

Bruce jumped up from his piano and hurried into the minister's office behind the pulpit.

Don stepped down onto level ground with the man and raised his hands welcomingly.

"Friend, you look tired. If you need rest, please..." Don was silenced as the man pulled down his makeshift hood, revealing a surprisingly young, although filthy, face.

Angela's scrutiny focused on the man's eyes. Her powers of imagination were out of practice, but she tried to envision him clean-shaven.

"I think he needs help," Tina spoke up with the certainty of a nine-year-old.

Like a beam of warm sunlight clearing the morning fog, the man's blue eyes cut through the room. He was searching, or perhaps, hunting for something or someone. And like most predators, his vision also had a seductive power, confirmed by quiet gasps and a few bashful, bowed faces from the congregation. When his sight scanned over Emily, she instinctively grabbed Michael's hand; it was as though the man was not looking, but rather touching every part of her. It was threatening, and, although she'd never admit it, also exhilarating.

"Do you have a name?" Don asked, while maintaining his distance.

The man didn't even acknowledge Don's question, let alone his presence.

An eruption of clarity broke out inside of Angela like the sudden failure of a dam. She stood. "Rick!" she shouted.

The man turned to face her and, in that moment, Angela knew she was right. This brutalized stranger standing before her was her long-lost husband, the father of her child. The realization sent her mouth trembling.

"Angela..." Rick replied with a rasp borne of dry dirt and exhaustion. His expression showed signs of uncertainty, as if she were the one caked in mud.

"Holy shit!" Chris let slip out.

Suddenly, Angela's cheeks were covered in wet droplets. To her, the change was instant. There was no bridge between the two states: her cheeks were dry, her cheeks were wet. Rick was gone, Rick was back. Her hand clasped to her mouth to stop it from trying to form words she knew weren't there.

The congregation waited in shock for them to reunite with an amorous embrace, but Rick just stood there. Then, Angela pushed herself past Matthew and Flora into the freedom of the aisle. However, instead of joining with Rick, she charged out of the sanctuary.

Her actions left the room stunned. No one spoke.

Bruce returned from the back office with a glass of water and handed it off like a baton to Don.

Don approached Rick with the refreshing crystal glass. Rick's roaming eyes found the sparkle of the water irresistible, like there wasn't water anywhere else in the world.

As Don edged closer, he noticed Rick's bloody feet soaking into the carpet. Luckily, he thought, they had chosen red.

He offered the glass and Rick accepted.

"Rick, here, drink," Don said, as Rick poured the water down his throat. His gulps were deep and his thirst too impatient to keep from spilling. Streams of water cascaded down the tufts of his beard, but he didn't seem to notice.

"Our prayers are answered," Emily said to herself. "You returned him to us." She smiled sweetly and reached for her husband's arm. Her hands groped the girth of Michael's bicep almost obscenely and she began to nod in agreement with her own statement. God had heard them on this blessed day.

"Come, let's get you cleaned up." Don put his arm around Rick and gently led him toward the modest minister's office at the back of the sanctuary.

Rick's limp made the journey a long one, but people watched patiently for the entire duration until the two men were out of sight.

CHAPTER 10

Once news of Rick's miraculous return finally reached Clara in the basement, she embarked on a mission to find her friend no one had seen since the sanctuary. Guided by her uncanny internal beacon, Clara's hunt proved short and uneventful. When she passed by the kitchen, she heard weeping in the dark. Clara, who loved blindly trusting her instincts, immediately flipped the light on.

The room suddenly appeared and in the back corner, sandwiched between the puke-yellow walls, was Angela. She was sitting on the ground with her knees up to her chin. Her stare was aimed at the floor, but reached far past the confines of the room.

"Here you are," Clara said affectionately. "My mom just told me." She walked over with caution, as if scared she might frighten her away. "Angela, sweetie, what are you doing down here? Don't you want to be with Rick?"

Angela didn't acknowledge her, but something about what Clara had said reawakened the tears looming behind her eyes, and a second wave of weeping washed through. It was the kind of outburst that could be either joy or sorrow, indivisible.

"What's wrong? This is good, right? Rick's back! He's back!" she consoled her friend, though she was not exactly sure for what. Truth be told, Clara had mixed feelings about the news herself. She had grown accustomed to the intimacy in her life that came with Angela and Alex, and she was going to miss it.

"I don't know why I still come here. Old habits, I guess." Angela finally spoke. Despite her tears, her voice came out clear and strong. She lifted her head and used her sleeve to dry her face.

"Angela, what's wrong?"

Before Angela answered, she considered whether or not her secret should remain her own. It was a tempting offer, to keep what she had inside hidden, but this was Clara she was talking to, *her* Clara, so out it came.

"I'll never be free," she began bluntly, with a seriousness Clara didn't recognize. "Rick and I, we weren't like how everyone thinks. It all seemed so great when it began. People always said we were a perfect couple. Well… except for you, Clara. I think people were only seeing what they wanted to see.

"I can't tell you when everything went to hell, but…it did. That's exactly where it went. A week before he went missing, we fought. We fought a lot. Only this time, he bruised two of my ribs with his boot, split my lip and… I didn't leave the house for five days. I had a black eye the size of an orange. He threw me, like I was trash. He just picked me up and threw me. And I was ashamed. He had been getting worse and worse, and I was terrified for myself and for Alex. Clara, Rick going missing was the best thing that ever happened to me. When you were all asking God for him to return, I was praying he would stay lost. I matched every prayer. We were almost free. Just one more day and we'd be free. So, you think this is a good thing? You think God brought him back to me? This is a curse."

"Angela, I…" Clara's inability to form any sentence of value infuriated her. She wanted to say the thing, the one thing that would relieve some of Angela's grief, even momentarily. But she was powerless.

"What should I do now?" Angela's frustration boiled through the sorrow. "Shall I go greet my husband with open arms? Welcome him back like everyone else? That's what they want to see, that's what everyone expects. But I can't. I won't let him back in. He can't come back to us, not now. Not ever again."

"No. No, Angela," Clara grabbed both of her arms. "You've known me a long time and you know my stance on profanity. But if he did that to you, then fuck that piece of shit. You hear me? Miracle or no, he's not coming near you or Alex again."

She froze there, holding Angela's arms in support. Angela was thankful to get a taste of strength, and Clara was relieved, if only modestly, that no one's life was as perfect as it seemed.

Clara helped Angela to her feet. She watched her like a proud parent observing a child's first step.

"Clara, how will we keep him away?"

"We'll think of something." Her optimism was invigorating, but, Angela worried, a bit naïve. But then again, what did naivety matter when desperation came knocking?

In the dirty confines of that excuse for a kitchen, the two women discussed, mapped and plotted things to come.

CHAPTER 11

The cramped minister's office, which was eaten up mostly by an oversized desk, now had to make room for both Don and Bruce. They waited, staring at the closed bathroom door at the other end of the slender room.

"How long has he been in there?" Don demanded. He hated keeping people waiting and knew the entire congregation was holding their breath to hear more about the miracle.

"About ten minutes," came Bruce's timid reply.

Don paced the length of the room. He could get in only four strides before he ran out of space and had to turn back around. Bruce, who, like most of the congregation, was never allowed in the office, took the opportunity to peek behind the curtain. He observed with reverence the strictness of the décor: the clean, sturdy desk with polished gloss, the organized antique cabinet filled with old robes, the perfectly-spaced portraits of the ministers of yesteryear that adorned the walls--it was all exactly as he had envisioned.

Teasing sounds seeped out from the gap under the bathroom door, suggesting it may open soon, but the promises proved hollow. *A man needs time to clean up*, Don had thought, but there were so many nagging questions building pressure in the front of his skull. It was all terribly exciting; he had never been a witness to an actual miracle, let alone be the key instrument through which God's grace had worked. His whole life was a struggle with faith; not only his own, but the faith of those around him. What would the doubters have to say now that his belief had been so undeniably legitimized? And the key to that ultimate triumph was just behind the bathroom door, probably applying shampoo. This maddening tedium of waiting for Rick's simple grooming to conclude was too much to bear. Don had to do something, anything.

"Okay, well there's no sense in both of us standing around in this room. You wait for him to come out. When he does, give him some fresh clothes, whatever he was wearing before smells awful, just awful. I have to get back to the congregation. They're waiting." Don gave the instructions like a true commander.

"Should we call the hospital or something?"

"We'll drive him there ourselves after he cleans up. No sense in calling an ambulance all the way out here. It's not an emergency."

"What if it is? Maybe he's sick. We don't know where he's been."

"We can drive into town faster than they can drive out here and back again. In fact, we can do it in exactly half the time. Right?"

"Yeah." Bruce's eyes hid in his shoes.

"Right. Okay then! Let us know as soon as he's out, yes?"

"Yes."

"Thank you, Bruce."

Don exited the room with a regal gait. Bruce remained leaning against the desk and allowed his eyes to once again search through the space.

The golden tint of the window glass created the illusion of a restful setting sun, suggesting to Bruce that it was later than it was. That's when he noticed there were no clocks in the room. Although it was really only a minor inconvenience, there was also something eerie about this fact. He couldn't remember ever seeing a watch on Don's wrist, so, when Don was in his office, how did he know what time it was?

Just then, the sound of water stopped. Bruce began thinking again of the miracle behind the door. What was he doing now, or, more interestingly, what had he been doing for the past three months?

Inside the seclusion of the meticulously tiled bathroom, hot water had sent billowing pockets of steam to crowd the air. A dampness clung to everything and peeled at the floral wallpaper trim that traced around the ceiling.

The clouds themselves parted for Rick as he stepped forward toward the mirror. The steam settled as if obeying a silent order, giving him an unobstructed view of his own body.

His skin had been washed clean and he stared at himself, admiring for the first time the scars that adorned his flesh. The three deepest and longest marks started at the center of his neck, almost originating from his Adam's apple. The middle one bisected his torso perfectly. It cut between his pectorals, down his abdomen where it had ravaged his belly button. It continued to trace a thick line through his flourishing pubic hair and down the shaft of his penis until it practically split the head. As the scar was a mere suggestion of the brutality itself, one could only imagine it as a failed evisceration. The other two most prominent scars stemmed from the same point as the bisecting one, but persisted on each side at an angle that sliced through his considerable chest and nipples. Those cuts continued down the sides of his body until reaching his feet. The rest of the tally marks grew like a spider's web from these three anchor points.

With his steady index finger, he traced some of his subtler markings. While he was in the woods, there were no mirrors, no large bodies of water to catch his reflection, so to see the fruits of his misery presented thusly, was almost titillating.

Once he was finished with his thorough exploration, he opened up the mirror cabinet in front of him. Inside, he found an old-fashioned straight razor.

As he opened it, the rusted metal joints ground together like bones when the cartilage has worn away. The blade, protected inside the ornate handle, gleamed its sharpness without a single rusted blemish, as though it was used once, then forgotten.

Rick grabbed handfuls of his beard and started cutting. He tossed the disowned clumps of hair into the sink, letting some tumble onto the floor.

What he wanted was a clean face to match his body. More than that, he wanted to emerge to the congregation as physically transformed as he was spiritually. The devastation, the rebirth, the ascension, all of these things that consumed him in the Burward forest he needed to show them – he was commanded to.

The cutting continued and just outside the door, Bruce waited.

CHAPTER 12

Although every congregation member had leapt up from their seats, squawking like a flock of agitated birds, it was Emily Rosenthal who solitarily displayed a sense of serenity. She withstood the contagious excitement and focused on the ever-imposing stained-glass window proudly proclaiming Heaven on high.

With her head upturned toward the tranquil angels populating the top of the window, she was overcome with a feeling of boundless wonder. This was the Heaven she was promised all her life; the one that gave her the strength to carry on through the horrors of the day. God, who had been suspiciously silent when her mother passed two years ago, had, at long last, given her the sign she begged for. She knew it was not proper to ask Him for proof – that's what faith was for – but after bearing witness to the slow deterioration of her mother's health and the agony that spread like a virus through her family because of it, she was desperate. But God was good, merciful; she had no more doubts of that. Her mother had not just suffered, then disappeared forever; she had escaped, just as the window depicted, and had reached Saint Peter's welcoming gates. One day, Emily would make the same journey, only her prize would not be the angelic trumpets or the glorious temple of rolling clouds. All those astonishments would be secondary to feeling her mother's embrace, and seeing her smile once again. Thinking of her mother awakened a familiar ache within her bones, a kind of pain so deep it had become part of her; but this time she had reason to rejoice, for it was only an hour ago that Emily Rosenthal had witnessed proof that by God's grace, her eternal ache would one day be soothed.

Michael had come up behind her and rested his bulky hands on her shoulders. The dead weight of them would have been enough to tip many people over, but Emily had strengthened over the years to support their load.

"Looks like it could use a cleaning." Michael pointed out this dull observation with a flat tone, as he did with all his dull observations.

"Yes, Michael, I suppose it could," she replied, though her thoughts were still elsewhere.

Dorothy had returned to the sanctuary and pushed her way to the front of the room, eager to play an important part in the coming events. Though she attached herself to every social club, church gathering, and charity group she could find, she still longed to be needed. It was like a drug to her and the chance to play a crucial part in Rick's return was too great a fix to pass up. This was the most important event in the history of the church... this was life and death!

When Don emerged from the office, Dorothy was the first to notice.

"Don!" she exclaimed.

"Mrs. Muller," Don graciously acknowledged her presence. "How are things out here?"

"Chaos. Forget about here, what about in there?" she tossed back.

"Don, is it true, is it Rick?!" Emily yelled from across the room. Her zeal gathered the congregation together and everyone halted to hear Don's response.

"I believe it is, yes."

"Praise God!" Emily celebrated.

The room absorbed her enthusiasm and soon everyone was proclaiming similar exclamations, some even raised their hands to the sky. Tina and Gary stepped forth toward the pulpit where Don had situated himself.

"Did he say anything? What happened to him?" Tina asked with her well-manicured concern.

"Is he alright?" Gary followed up more honestly.

"He's fine, now. He's just in no state to answer these questions, yet. It's evident he's been through some hard times, but he's back. That's the important thing. What he needs is space and rest. And I believe, some food." Don's eyes locked with Dorothy and she burst into action.

"Of course! Let's hop to it ladies! The picnic is upon us." She physically gathered people and ushered them out of the room. "You two as well!" she demanded of Matthew and Chris who both seemed disinterested, standing rather unobtrusively to the side.

Dorothy, having been fueled by her proliferating to-do list, charged full steam ahead. This picnic was to be the best the congregation had seen. To call it a mere picnic would be a disservice; after all, you do not serve a picnic to a starving man who was lost in the wilderness. To him you serve a feast with enough food to fill his belly ten times over.

"Thank you, Dorothy," Don said, before it was too late.

"My pleasure, Don," she replied, just before she and her small marching band tromped out the door.

"Does this all seem a little, like, surreal?" Matthew asked Chris as the two of them followed suit behind the other troops.

"It's fucked. What was he surviving on for three months? Berries?" Chris whispered back.

"No, I mean, why are we having a picnic?" Matthew pressed.

"What?"

"If I had been lost, I wouldn't give a shit about a church picnic. Where's the guy's wife? Where's their kid? Why aren't they with him?"

"She's probably getting ready for her steamy reunion with her hot husband. Did you see those eyes?"

"Is your mind capable of a thought without sex?"

"Not while you're around."

"For fuck's sake..." Matthew shook his head, but could not refute the blushing of his face.

The two boys rounded off the end of the picnic line. After they had departed, the remaining congregation in the sanctuary was almost exactly halved.

Michael walked over to Gary and slapped him hard on the back with his meaty palm.

"Well, Gary, what do you say? They're gonna need some muscle getting those tables out there."

"Sure," he said with a grin. "Let's be useful."

"That's the spirit!" Don encouraged from his pulpit. The room was filled with people wanting to help, and although Don was not completely convinced Rick would be in the mood to eat anything, the task brought people together and gave them some much-needed focus. He could not help but succumb to pride as his flock showed the compassion he had been preaching for years.

The room gradually emptied as people busied themselves with tasks until Flora Thompson was the only one left. She sat, abandoned – and perhaps a little forgotten – by the youthful doers flying around her.

Don stepped down from the pulpit and took a seat in the pew in front of her.

"Hi, Flora."

"It's very exciting isn't it?" Her aged voice quivered.

"It is. It's not every Sunday the Lord bestows us such a miracle."

"Life is a miracle."

"That's true."

"I'm glad Matthew brought me today. I'm glad I got to see with my own eyes. He's going to be a fine gentlemen, Matthew, don't you think?"

"As long as he keeps up with his Bible studies."

"Oh, I'll see to that."

"I'm sure you will. Would you like to accompany me to the mess hall? I was going to make sure preparations were going smoothly."

"No. I'm just fine here. I have some things I'd like to say to the Boss first, if you don't mind."

"Oh, by all means." He took his leave.

Flora adjusted her heavily-patterned dress, thick with colourful, entwined flowers, and rested her clasped hands on the pew in front of her. Twenty years ago, when she reached the ripe old age of seventy, she had forgone the burden of fashion and committed to wearing the same dress every Sunday. Her resolve was thwarted only a few times when the gloom of funerals had demanded less jubilant attire. She had recently decided this dress, with all its lively silliness, would be the dress she'd be buried in.

"Dear God," she began. "I want to thank You for Your blessings. For the love You've shown in reuniting the Morris family. May Your kindness continue to shine on them as they try to rebuild their lives in Your glory. Also, regarding my grandson, Matthew. Please, give him the strength to overcome whatever has come upon him. He's distant these days, You may have noticed.

Whatever he's gotten himself into, please help him to climb back out of it. In Heaven's name, I pray. Amen."

Her eyes opened with refreshed energy. She sat alone on the empty pew, in the empty room, with a full heart.

CHAPTER 13

The basement remained blissfully ignorant of the commotion upstairs. The children had completed their drawings and were now playing the clean-up game, which was very similar to regular clean-up and was really a game in name only. Susan, who had been left in charge of the children in Clara's absence, had used this cheeky tactic to clean many houses during her rounds as a babysitter. Though some children were clever enough to see through Susan's deception, they still tidied and dusted with the rest, for no child's will was stronger than Susan's charm.

Through the fabricated hallway, Clara emerged with an almost visible cloud following her.

"You okay?" Susan asked instinctively.

"I'm fine." Clara's performance lacked conviction.

Susan leaned closer and whispered, "I haven't told Alex about anything yet. I thought Angela should."

"That's probably for the best."

"Did you find her?"

"Yes, I did. She's okay, just a little overwhelmed."

"Of course, totally. I'm sure she's just losing it right now. I mean, I can't even imagine." When Susan shook her head, Clara could not help but be distracted by flawless yellow strands of hair sent dancing about her face.

"Thanks for watching the kids. You can head back upstairs now."

"Really, you don't need me for anything?"

"No, that's great. Thanks for helping out."

"No problemo, Clara! If anything changes, just let me know; the kids are adorable."

"Will do, for sure. Thanks again." After the teen vanished out of sight, Clara's attention turned back to the children.

"Alex," she called lightly. "Your mother would like to speak to you."

With that, she led Alex away from the other children and out of the maze of portable dividers. She brought him to the farthest end of the basement where the space narrowed. Angela was waiting for them there next to a pile of old decorations and a rusted, gas generator.

At first, Alex was afraid to approach his mom because she was standing in a spot right next to a terrifying plastic Santa head that was badly deteriorating. One of its eyes had been punched out and that hollow cavity leered at him, following him wherever he stood, like how a cat watches its prey.

"Come here." Angela kneeled down and put her hands out to welcome him closer. He closed his eyes, blocking sinister-Santa from his vision, and joined his mother.

While they embraced, Alex mumbled into her shoulder.

"Dad's back," he said, barely audible.

"Who told you?" Angela pulled back from the tenderness. She looked up at Clara, who only offered a shrug.

"Yes, Alex," she said, returning to her son. "Dad is back. But he won't be living with us. We're going to stay at aunt Clara's for a while. Doesn't that sound like fun?"

"Miss Muller?" Alex questioned hesitantly.

"'Miss Muller'? What's with that, Alex? We're talking about Clara. She's been real nice to us, hasn't she? And you like her, right?"

"We aren't staying with dad?"

"No, no we're not."

"Why?"

It was a simple question, yet it managed to undo Angela.

Because your father is even worse than my father. He's a monster, Alex. He wants to hurt us, even though he loves us, because he loves us. And if we stay with him, we'll die. This played in Angela's head in real time, as if it were a prepared speech, read in a slow, matter of fact voice.

There was only one way out of this, Angela was sure of it. While everyone was distracted by Rick's return, she and Alex were going to make their escape. They would drive home, but only long enough to collect a few things. Then they were going to Clara's house, where she had offered up a spare room for Alex, and a couch in the basement for Angela (though Clara had plans to force Angela to take the bed in her room, instead, while she herself suffered the sharp springs of the couch). They would stay with her for as long as it took to sort through the messy, legal jargon of divorce. Rick would be allowed to visit as little as possible, or not at all, if Angela had her way. Clara also offered to help out with Alex while Angela searched for a job. Then, once Angela could support both herself and Alex, the two of them would move, together, into whatever promising new life awaited them. It all seemed so simple. Simple until Alex asked 'why?', and Angela realized there would be questions, questions she couldn't answer. Not yet, anyway.

"'Cause we need time away from each other right now, that's why. He needs time and so do we. So, we're not staying with him. It's just going to be the two of us, okay?"

"Can I see dad?"

"Yes, just not right at this moment."

"Does he want to see me?"

"Yes, he does, your father loves you." Those words hurt more than his punches ever could. "Alex, we both love you very, very much. We just aren't going to be around him. Do you understand?"

"Yes."

"Yes?" Angela asked, shocked by Alex's curtness. "Good. Okay, we can talk about this more later, alright? We're just getting ready to leave now."

"We can't run," Alex said with the same unnerving certainty. "Not from him, we can't."

Two waves came upon Angela. She rode the first, gliding on the serene connection she felt with her son, who had just pinpointed the exact fear she was trying to hide from him. It was a sense of togetherness she had rarely experienced and one that filled her with tingling light like a jar of fireflies. Darkness was banished, as long as their love and understanding of one another held true. The second wave, however, crested far above the first, engulfed its predecessor and then came crashing down. There was dread to be found in what Alex had said. He was warning her of the dangers swimming deep down below. And what would Rick do if he ever found them? Maybe there was more to fear than Angela knew.

The weight of dark, flooding thoughts drowned her and she sunk deeper and deeper into their bottomless depth, discovering new horrors as she went. Her throat closed somewhat and her breath was cut shorter. Soon all she could think was, *He's going to take my baby. He's going to hurt him. He's going to take him, and hurt him, and make him disappear.* She didn't care if she drowned, but she could not drag Alex down with her. Rick would know that. Rick would use that.

From behind Angela, Santa's demonic face suddenly twisted toward Alex, leaning in, as if for a taste. Alex shifted away from the not-so-jolly, old Saint Nick. The head now stared directly at him, wearing a deformed grin, like the rotting, red smile of a clown. Alex became lost in the secret depths of its missing eye; he swore there was some life there, and it wanted him.

And there *was* life, though not the life Alex feared. All the old decorations started shifting, but not because they were hungry for child flesh; Michael was spotted pulling the old table free from behind the pile, and Santa's head had merely been knocked over.

With a mighty heave, he yanked at the twelve-foot piece of furniture and maneuvered it with surprising ease.

Angela stood and pulled Alex to her, watching Michael closely to discern how much he might have heard.

"Sorry, I didn't see you," he apologized quickly.

"That's okay." Angela kicked Santa's head back into the heap of misfit decorations. "What are you doing?"

"Just moving the table for the picnic."

"Oh, I see."

"You excited to have your father back, little man?" Michael loomed over Alex like an ogre.

Alex, still shaken up by the possessed head, could not assemble a reply.

"I said, you excited?" he forcefully asked again.

"We're not staying with him," Alex replied honestly.

"What's that?"

"He's excited," Angela interjected. "We both are. We'll join everyone in a moment." She wrapped her arms around her son.

Michael and Angela exchanged a smile and he seemed satisfied she was sincere.

He returned to his giant table and lugged it toward the stairs. Angela was not sure what to make of Michael. The man seemed a simple one, but there was a pushiness in his pleasantries that suggested something was being restrained. What it was he restrained from, Angela could only guess, but she had a suspicion it was not something good.

Clara stepped closer to the two of them, but not so close as to impose, just enough to reassure them of her support.

Angela bent down and kissed Alex on the forehead. She rubbed his arms as a way to give comfort, but who actually received more comfort from this action was up for debate.

CHAPTER 14

Bruce, having lost all sense of time waiting in the minister's office, situated himself at the huge desk next to a towering stack of old bulletins dating back two decades ago. He had made it as far down as the early nineties and found humour in the steady decline of clipart integrity. On the cover of the current day's bulletin was an inspiring snapshot of a flower blooming. The vibrant yellow that beamed out from the centre of the oxeye daisy was a classic symbol of nature – and therefore God – at its height of esthetic perfection, like a sunset breaking through wisps of clouds, or the crisp snowfall of a fresh winter day. On the cover dated early September nineteen ninety-two, however, was the unsuccessfully photocopied line drawing of a flock of sheep being herded by a malformed shepherd. As St. Paul's United Church was not, to Bruce's knowledge, providing sanctuary for Quasimodo, he assumed the distorted figure was due to the ineptitude of the copier. The fleeting amusement this offered only urged him to grab the next bulletin that much sooner. So, he did.

This bulletin was not like the rest. While the other dates harkened back to anonymous times and faceless Sunday services, this one certainly brought back memories, and it certainly had a face. It was dated the week before his wife's miscarriage. He remembered it clearly, the way she had excitedly informed all the church members about how the baby was kicking and must be eager to get out. By the end of the service, she practically had a line of people waiting to feel her belly as if it were some holy shrine. They had left the baby's sex as a surprise for the day of its birth, but they were prepared for either. For a boy, they liked the name Ethan, and if they were blessed with a girl, they chose Bruce's grandmother's name, Eleanor, or Ellie for short. After the miscarriage, they did try again a few years later and that's when they had Dylan. During those dark times, Bruce's devotion to the church never faltered. No service was ever without his piano playing. His wife on the other hand could not bring herself to face God after how vehemently she had cursed him. As it turned out, their daughter would have been named Ellie.

He sat, frozen in the tragedy of another time, with the bulletin hanging from his hands, unaware that the bathroom door had finally opened.

Rick filled the doorway. How long he had been staring at Bruce was impossible to gage; but it was clear he was content watching. His soft breath gave no hint of his presence. He was as stoic as the portraits hanging on the wall. The blue clouds that swirled within his eyes were hypnotic in their patterns, like a building storm, and it was all focused on Bruce.

It was not until Bruce escaped his memories and reached for the next bulletin that he even noticed Rick. The sudden vision of the other man sent him back a few feet, while his hand scattered the pile of neatly folded papers across the floor.

Once Bruce had regained some semblance of composure, he pushed his way out from the desk to properly greet him. That's when he noticed the man standing before him was naked.

Though fresh towels were readily available and could have easily been wrapped around for modesty, Rick stood as uninhibited as a freshly birthed baby.

Despite Bruce's attempts to look elsewhere, or anywhere, he could not convince his eyes to abandon the flesh on display in front of him. Firstly, his keen sight focused on the other man's cock – as men's sight often does. There it was, a substantial tube of scarred masculinity nestled in a bed of dark fur. Looking past the obvious slash that scored down Rick's member, Bruce's mind automatically started to compare length and girth, and found himself marginally intimidated. When the phallic shock wore off, Bruce's eyes roamed the rest of his body and gathered as much information as they could. Something about Rick's unabashedly wide stance reminded Bruce of the good old days in the high school change room. Bruce was always a skinny guy, and his physique was never a source of pride, like it seemed to be for most of the other kids in the class. Their muscles had been well formed and bunched into tight knots right where you want them. They had the bodies of sexual, feral beasts, whereas Bruce was endowed with ribs you could have played like a xylophone. While his body suggested death and sickness, the other boys exuded only vitality and virility. Rick would have unquestionably belonged to the later category. His well-formed structure was built from endless physical exertion, which was the only good Rick had ever found to offer the world.

There was no arousal on the part of Bruce for all his ogling, only envy; yet he examined with precision the rising and falling of Rick's chest and how it set into motion a visible ripple effect as his bulk swelled and then relaxed, each cog in perfect support of the other. Bruce had become hopelessly lost in the intricate configuration of the specimen before him.

Upon a more studious inspection, however, he came to realize some of what had appeared as musculature, was in fact deep scar tissue. The reality dawned on Bruce that above Rick's imposing build was a layer of skin that had been methodically carved, but by whom? Bruce could barely slow his mind down enough to form a half-decent response to the question. Was Rick kidnapped by a group of sadists? Could an animal be to blame? Maybe he had done it to himself? The third option was the one Bruce considered most disgusting.

Before he could expect any answers, Bruce knew one problem above all needed to be solved first. Rick had to stop being so naked. Finally, the long awaited first words entered the equation.

"Rick, um, there are some clothes here for you," he said nervously, and pointed to the dresser behind him. "There's lots of stuff in there, lots of things for you to put on. You could put them on right now, if you wanted."

Rick's eyes followed Bruce's finger and searched out the bottom drawers of the dresser. He stepped free of the doorway with a slow, sturdy stride. Bruce understood, then, that he was unfortunately stationed between the dresser and Rick, so every step toward the dresser was also a step toward him. The closer Rick's swinging nakedness came, the more discomfort Bruce felt.

However, when Rick brushed past, Bruce surprised himself by how little effort he had put into getting out of his way. His brief contact with Rick's engraved body was unsettlingly exhilarating. He had allowed his right hand the indulgence of Rick's hip and when their skin met, Bruce felt electrified. This foreign sensation, especially with a member of the same sex, was a reality he had now to toil with.

Rick ignored the bottom drawers, turned and reached into the open cabinet where a dark blue minister's robe hung lifelessly.

Bruce, having become more and more consumed by his teased sexuality, tried to fight the impulse to gawk at Rick's backside, but to no avail. While Rick was turned, Bruce regarded this new skin with the same tenacity as he did the front and was alarmed to see the scar pattern was all encompassing. It was genuine curiosity that brought his eyes down to witness Rick's buttocks, but curiosity was not what kept them there. He saw how the cuts scraped up the thigh, along the muscle and continued until they disappeared into the implicit darkness cushioned between his cheeks. How deep the grooves penetrated was a charged question and one that brought a familiar stiffness between Bruce's legs.

His unwelcome hardness distressed him. His cravings were overwhelming, and Bruce was at a loss to explain where they had come from. In his entire thirty-seven years of life, he had never been enticed by a naked man. Yet, there he was, engrossed by Rick's scored body, wishing he had worn looser fitting pants. Maybe, he comforted himself, it had something to do with the pattern of the scars themselves. They were perhaps primal etchings that conveyed a kind of irresistible eroticism. The truth was, he had talked to Rick many times before without so much as an inkling of attraction, let alone the intense lust that currently boiled his blood. One thing was for certain, he would be in dire need of love making tonight with his wife, both to relieve his restless libido, and reassure himself of his traditional orientation. On top of all this puzzlement was the grotesquery of abuse infused all over Rick's body. Although sadism and masochism repulsed Bruce, to his horror, in that moment he felt inexplicably aroused by it.

Rick delicately lifted the dark robe from its hanger and laid the fabric down on the desk. He took care in straightening out the sleeves and whisked away any wrinkles.

"You can't wear that," Bruce warned, without a drop of conviction. "That used to be the minister's robe before Don changed it. Remember?"

"What would you have me wear then?" His voice was as cold and striking as his stare.

"I think there's some overalls in the drawer. And there's a sweater with a windmill on it." The sentence had come out rushed and Bruce swallowed deeply after its hasty execution.

"That seems hardly fitting."

"I'm sure it would fit fine. I doubt Angela cares much what you wear. She's probably just dying to see you."

"I didn't return for Angela." Rick stopped fixing the robe and turned his body to face Bruce.

"No? What'd you come back for?"

"I returned to lead."

"Lead? Who?"

"Lead you. Lead you all. Back to where you all began. Back to where you belong." Rick, although forceful, seemed to treat this sentiment with gentility. He took a sudden step toward Bruce, who jumped back against the wall and froze like a startled puppy.

There was nowhere for Bruce to go, but he pushed against the wall anyway and hoped he would just fall through it. Steadily, the predator continued his approach.

Rick did not stop until his groin was pressed tightly against Bruce's. Though the fabric of Bruce's pants was thick, it could not diffuse the heat emanating from the two of them, and so, they shared in each other's hospitable warmth. Bruce squirmed, but again, did not fight as much as he thought he would or should.

"Rick, Um... You're still really quite naked," his voice squeaked out.

"I'm going to lead you. But you have to help me first." Rick's hand reached up and caressed the side of Bruce's face to calm the panicked pup. Bruce twitched at the touch.

In an unexplainable way, this was exactly what Bruce wanted; to tenderly entwine himself with the disfigured male form that now dominated him. Yet he knew this appetite was not natural to him, nor did he think it existed in him before this moment. It was something planted within him, something invasive he had no guard against. Despite having realized this, he allowed Rick's hand to continue its sensuous journey down to the base of his neck. Once it rested there against his skin, a calmness and complacency washed over him. As if Rick recognized the passive state Bruce had achieved, he leaned in; their lips hovered dangerously close. Bruce's body shivered under Rick's influence and a wave of prickling excitement danced over his skin.

"You want to help me, don't you? You want to help me lead them back." In response, Bruce barely nodded. "Good. We'll lead them back, then. We'll lead them back to the beast."

Rick's once soothing touch mutated into a violent grip. Bruce struggled against it, but Rick possessed strength far beyond his physical self.

His thumb found its way to the softness of Bruce's throat and pressed into it, effectively trapping whatever screams might have escaped. Bruce's terror had been robbed of its outlet, so his panic spun around inside his stomach and sent his entire body flailing. As he frantically tried to push himself free, he was appalled to discover his erection had not lost any of its rigidity, especially when sent to spasm against Rick's own flaccid member.

The antique razor suddenly snapped into action in Rick's other hand. The blade glinted sharply in the light as he brought it down to meet the top of Bruce's head. The tip of the razor cut into his scalp with ease, like the first puncture into the peel of an orange. As soon as the skin broke, the blood bubbled forth and slid down his face in thin streams between his eyes.

Bruce had become more resigned to his fate once the warm liquid coated his face completely. He wanted to live, but it seemed he had little choice in the matter.

The immediate sensations of his death were ample distraction from the terror of oblivion he might soon face, or the longing for the loved ones he would never see again. Considering the pain, his composure was admirable. His panicked thrashings had stopped. He raised his hands out in front of him as if cradling something small and delicate.

"No, Bruce," Rick warned, with his mouth twisting into a smirk. "Ellie won't be there. Not where you're going."

Bruce's hands trembled at the words and folded in on themselves like wilting flowers.

The blade was dragged through his forehead toward his chin. It slipped effortlessly into his left socket and popped the eye cradled within before slicing down his cheek.

As his blood escaped him, Bruce managed one more thought of comfort. At least, if he was to be drained of every last drop, surely then, his erection would finally cease.

CHAPTER 15

Clara watched the smoke from her lungs trickle up against the brick wall of the church until it vanished into the air.

What was to be born from the ashes of Angela's marriage? Clara could not say, but she nonetheless allowed herself the consolation that things might return to the way they were, the way they should be. If Angela and Alex were to move in with her, maybe she could become a permanent part of their lives. What a treat it would be to have enough hungry mouths in the morning to justify a fresh batch of pancakes. It had been so long since she cooked a meal, a real meal with the gravitas to feed more than one. She considered this longing an unrealistic one, but the mere possibility invigorated her.

She had positioned herself in a discreet nook by the side of the church that faced west into the field. The Burward Forest was within her sights and seemed to duck low to avoid the rays of the sun. She too was hidden from the sun's touch. She tossed the remaining butt of her cigarette far into the field, as if banishing it forever.

If the theme of the day was the end of things, then maybe she, like Angela, should also bid a final farewell to her vices. After all, smoking with a child in the house would be negligent, at best. Could that minute tuft of burnt paper she casually chucked away have really been her last drag? With her newfound motivation, it looked promising.

Just around the corner from where she hid her shame, the back of the church hemorrhaged congregation members who buzzed about with tubs of pre-made sandwiches, sliced fruits, chopped vegetables, jugs of ice tea, paper cups, paper plates, plastic utensils and two large tables – which were the only items carried by men.

Clara remained out of view, listening to the hullabaloo generated by the crowd. None of them knew, except for Clara, that their excitement was born of a deceitful, rotten womb. The festivities were an insult to the truth of the matter: Rick was an abusive degenerate and his return should have been condemned instead of celebrated.

She had left Angela and Alex inside the church where the two of them could collect their belongings. Once they were ready to leave, the three of them planned to escape together, before the drudgery of the picnic could begin.

Once Clara felt confident that the smell of cigarettes had vacated her sweater, she edged out from concealment to get a better view on how the picnic was shaping up. She watched as her mother, Dorothy, led Emily Rosenthal, Tina Brown, Susan Greenfield and a handful of other women into the sprawling landscape of the field. She steered them to a precise spot, which had unique features only discernible by her. Once situated, the rest of the worker ants gathered and the picnic started to take shape.

Clara and her mother were congenial, but not close. They respected each other, but when it came to honesty, their relationship never seemed worth it. Like when

Dorothy, who at the time was feeling acutely vulnerable, had asked Clara if she thought her father, Albert, was in Heaven, and if they would ever see him again. In Clara's mind, their relationship wasn't worth a candid response, as that would inevitably spur an exhaustive debate about each other's beliefs. So, she chose the easy answer and told her mother that she believed they would all be together again one day. This was not a complete lie; Clara did have faith in an afterlife. She just was not convinced by the prevailing version of Heaven that she would one day be floating on a cloud with daddy. That scenario seemed just too clean to be true.

However, despite their disparity, Clara had a sudden urge to seek her mother's guidance. Perhaps it was the fact that, from Clara's angle, Dorothy appeared to be literally planted in the soil of the field like a crop – grounded and wise – as she ordered around the other members. And it had recently dawned on Clara that the escape plan they had proposed could be construed as kidnapping. Before she ran off into the sunset with her two amigos, she needed an outside opinion on Angela's slippery situation, even if the one she sought out proved useless, at least she tried, and at least it would give her mother a chance to berate her one more time before she gets hauled off to prison.

With these burdens nibbling behind her eyes, Clara turned back to the church and glanced up at the stained-glass window once again. The directness of the midday sun had robbed the window of its radiance, and therefore, its life. With no light passing through its tinted shards, the whole thing appeared rather dreary, as if it no longer had faith in Heaven. The angels had dead eyes, muted by shadow, and the paradise of clouds was reduced to a muddy hodgepodge of fragmented shapes, dribbled irregularly around the top of the composition.

The dimness of the glass had transformed the window into the surface of a placid swamp. It was on account of all that stillness that Clara was able to catch, out of the corner of her eye, the subtle movement of someone inside. It was impossible to tell who they were, only that they moved fast. The dark form stirred like a wave through the different shapes and shades before vanishing back into obscurity. Although she barely caught sight of them, she was sure they had headed deeper into the sanctuary, and were therefore still in the room. In fact, they could be just on the other side of the glass, peering right back at her; there was no way for her to know.

Clara backed away and out of view of the glass. Once a few steps were between her and the veiled window, she stopped. It felt like a spider had crawled down her spine and cocooned her stomach. The shadow in the church could have been Don grabbing his Bible, or Sandy checking the organ, or even Matthew helping Flora out to the picnic, but something worrisome had hatched within her that told her it was not.

Maybe Rick was well enough now to search out Angela and his son. What if he found them, what would Angela do? He could be on the hunt for his family right now. He could be hunting for them even as Clara stood there doing nothing. Her distress fed on itself until the spider from her stomach infested the rest of her body, spreading shivers wherever it roamed.

For the sake of Angela and Alex, she had to act fast.

CHAPTER 16

The breeze in the field was incorrigible and meddled with the picnic preparations every chance it got. Its sneaky fingers peeled away the cellophane from the sandwiches, tugged at the tablecloth, and, most mortifyingly, lifted skirts and dresses to improper heights. But still the spot was chosen and Dorothy was not about to let a juvenile gust bully them back inside. Instead, she applied tape to the cellophane, anchored the tablecloth, and simply pretended she did not just get an eyeful of Emily's undergarments. Her delegations were succinct and stately - General Patton would have been impressed.

The food could not be haphazardly strewn about; it needed to be arranged, to be presentable. This was Dorothy's vision and she had conceived a logical order for each dish. The first, and most important items were the sandwiches. The choice between tuna salad, ham or turkey would influence every dietary decision that was to follow. Obviously, the salads were next so people could choose an appropriate green to accompany their main dish, followed by some dip options with sliced vegetables and crackers. Lastly, there were the deserts, but that was a given.

For the sweet tooth, Tina had brought her delectable brown sugar squares comprised of an assortment of nuts held together by baked caramel. She used to bring homemade peanut butter cookies that would send your knees shaking, but after Tom Enright's near fatal allergic reaction that almost turned those shakes into violent convulsions, the church unanimously decided to ban peanuts.

With a formidable knife that looked like it could be used to clear away jungle vines, Tina hacked at her squares with a vengeance. Across the table from her, Emily quietly rolled the extra slices of meat and lined them up on a platter.

"Angela must be so happy," Tina commented between jabs that sent hunks of caramel soaring through the air.

"She didn't look happy," Emily replied without looking up from the meat.

"Her husband is back, Emily. She has to at least be relieved after all the worry she's gone through."

"Did you think she looked relieved when she ran out of the room crying?"

"Well, no, but intense emotions can make people do strange things."

"If your husband went missing, God forbid, and then was miraculously returned to you, how would you react? Would you hold him tight the way the Lord intended, or would you run away?"

"I don't know. I suppose… I guess I would…" Tina refused to finish her sentence, so Emily finished it for her.

"You would go to him, tend to him. You would kiss him and not let him out of your sight again."

"I suppose that's right."

Susan had joined everyone outside and walked past the two women with a basket of buns. When she came within earshot, Tina and Emily stopped talking.

"Hi, Mrs. Brown!" The earnestness of Susan's salutation to Tina beamed from her face.

"Oh, hi, honey. You looking for a place to put those?" She motioned to the basket.

"Dorothy Muller told me they belong on this table."

Susan walked over to the first free spot she could see and laid the basket down. Almost immediately, Dorothy descended upon her like a swooping hawk and snatched the basket away.

"No, Susan, dear," Dorothy corrected, "the buns have to go at the beginning. Otherwise, what will people put the condiments on? It's not much good to have a glob of mayonnaise on your plate before you even have the bun. Right?"

"Yes, sorry," Susan reached for the basket again. "I can take them."

"No, it's alright, I'm already holding them, so…" and with that, Dorothy brushed by her and carried the buns back to the beginning of the table. Susan was left to stand uselessly by, as Dorothy busied herself with her micromanagement.

Tina, spontaneously reinvigorated, continued her conversation with Emily.

"Of course Angela's happy. She's happy Rick is alive. She's only showing it in a peculiar way. It's silly to think she's not."

"I don't think it's silly at all."

"Angela is ecstatic right now. Rick's not dead."

"He only looks dead," Susan interrupted. No one laughed, but worse than that, no one even looked at her.

"You want to know what I think?" Emily baited.

"Yes, of course."

"I think Angela brought it on herself."

"What? How can you say that?" Tina asked out of obligation.

"Things happen for a reason. You saw the way she was, so don't pretend you didn't. She's hiding something."

"Hiding what?" Once again, Susan spoke up as the eager, but completely ignored, audience.

"What are you saying, Emily?" Tina inquired, as if Susan had not just asked the same thing.

"Maybe it's Angela's fault Rick went missing in the first place. She can fool us, but she can't fool God."

"You really think so?"

"Oh, Tina. Yes, I think so. And you do too, I know you do."

"I don't think that."

"Yes you do. After Angela charged out of the sanctuary, everyone knew she was running away."

"Well, are you saying she was involved?"

"Maybe. Maybe she even wanted Rick to disappear."

"Why would she want that?" Tina had become addicted and needed more.

"I don't know."

"What if Rick was fooling around with another woman and Angela found out? And then she was so upset, she decided to get rid of him." Tina's love for late afternoon soap operas was beginning to pay off.

"No. That's not it." Emily was quick to dismiss Tina's hypothesis.

"It could be. I hate to say it, but I always thought Angela had an angry side. You can tell in her eyes. I doubt she even has faith anymore."

Dorothy, who had just barely been able to overhear the conversation, finally spoke up. "You sound like three old biddies," she began. "Listen to this gossip! Angela is a sweet girl who didn't deserve any of what she got. You should all be ashamed."

If shame was to be had, Tina and Emily refused it. The two of them turned their eyes from Dorothy and returned to the tasks in front of them.

"I didn't say it," Susan declared, as if anyone cared to hear.

"Well, Dorothy," Emily began, addressing her plate of folded meats, "time will tell where the shame lies."

At that, Dorothy left in a huff, pretending not to have heard Emily's final cold pronouncement. If their minds could not be changed, then they were not worth being around, was Dorothy's reasoning. She knew how Angela's reputation had gone to seed, and although she had offered her support where she could, she felt a slight failure in her powerlessness to change opinions. But enough of those thoughts; she had to figure out where to station the sliced cucumbers.

From across the field, Matthew had started his journey pushing his grandmother and her wheelchair through the dirt so she could join everyone for the picnic. Flora was capable of walking short distances, but across the treacherous terrain of the Davidson's field, she entrusted her excursion to Matthew's capable hands. It took all his strength to push the wheels through the mounds of loose soil. If he stopped where the dirt dipped between the rows, he would have to roll her back and forth just to gain enough momentum to get the wheels turning again.

By the time the two of them reached the table, Matthew's labours were marked by sweat stains under his arms and around his chest. He leaned on Flora's chair to collect his breath.

"You okay here, grandma?" Matthew asked between heaves.

"Yes. Thank you, Matthew," she said and folded her arms politely.

"Hi there, Flora!" Dorothy shouted from the other table.

Flora responded with a smile and a modest nod.

"Do you want something to drink?" he asked his grandmother.

"Oh, no. You run along and get *yourself* something. You're the one who did all the heavy lifting." She patted his hand and looked up at him. "I'm fine here."

Chris snuck up behind Matthew and playfully jabbed him in the side with his index fingers. The surprise poke sent Matthew's tired muscles into spasms. He spun around and was met with Chris' devilish grin.

"Hey!" Chris said, rather suggestively.

"What was that?"

"Me getting your attention. And look, it works!"

"Yeah, and so would a slap to the face."

"I'll keep that in mind. Can I talk to you over here for a second?"

"Why?"

"I think I figured out a way to get Africans some water, but I want to run it by you first before I announce it."

Matthew, despite his efforts to remain stern, broke out into a smile.

"I'll be back, Grandma," he said.

"Hi, Mrs. Thompson," Chris added, as the two of them headed away from the picnic.

They walked toward the Burward forest, but didn't start talking until they were certain no one could hear.

"I can't believe they keep having the picnic out here," Matthew complained. "Do you know how hard it is to push that thing through this stupid field?"

Chris didn't hear him. He was busy calculating the space they had put between them and the rest of the congregation. Once they had reached a safe distance,

Chris kissed Matthew's neck quickly, like the peck of a bird. Matthew pulled away.

"Hey! Fuck off," he grunted, after taking a step back from Chris.

"What's the matter?"

"Just don't."

"Why not? We both liked it last time. It's fun."

"Not here."

"Alright. If we're quick, we could do it in the forest. No one would know."

"Forget it, Chris. It's not happening. Not at church."

"Who cares where we are? What are you worried about? It was just a little kiss. They won't notice. God won't either."

"I'm not so sure."

"Or, maybe you're just worried Susan Greenfield will notice."

"Fuck you."

"You think she's pretty, right? You like her?" Chris asked as a joke, but the seriousness with which Matthew thought about it disturbed him. "Wait, you actually do, don't you? Cause I thought you were, you know."

"I don't know."

"It's just, you seemed into it before, with me. So… What changed? Did you become un-gay or something? Is that a thing?"

"I don't know. I'm just kind of all messed up right now, I guess."

"Me too."

"No, you're not. You just fucking prance around with confidence."

"Okay, well, fuck you for saying I prance. Also, over confidence is my defense for lack of confidence. It's all fake. And do you really think I prance?"

"Forget about the prancing. I'm sorry I said it. I have no clue what I want, Chris. But that's just another joke to you, so why don't we just drop it."

"I can't drop it. To be honest, I seriously thought after that night, we were, like, together. You know? This morning I thought: oh fuck, another Sunday at church. Then I remembered you'd be there and all of a sudden I cared what I was wearing, I cared about what I was going to say. I cared." Chris's tone was one of vulnerability that he rarely revealed. Usually his feelings were safely hidden by a sarcastic snappiness, but he really wanted Matthew to understand.

"I don't know what to say."

"How about: yes Chris, that night meant something to me too."

Matthew stared at him, paralyzed.

Chris, terrified by the silence, took a step toward him and reached for his hand. With unintentional force, Matthew pushed back and sent Chris tumbling into the dirt.

"I don't know!" Matthew yelled. "I can't keep saying it. Just leave me alone!"

Without helping Chris get to his feet, Matthew hurried back to the picnic.

Chris remained lying in the dirt for a solid three minutes. He gazed up at the clouds, which had gathered in strength, and thought back to the night he held so dearly - the way Matthew leaned into him to show him that moronic video, the way they both danced around how good it felt to be so close, the way they timidly explored each other, first through their clothes, then under. It was all so new. He cursed himself for his stupid crush. His feelings for Matthew could not be denied, but he had to figure out a way to better control them, or maybe even forget them if such a thing were possible.

He got to his feet and dusted off the back of his pants and shirt the best he could before returning to the bustle.

Chris was not the only one headed for the picnic. Clara marched across the field to find her mother. She ran into Susan first and asked her if she wouldn't mind looking after the kids again. Susan, who was just thankful to be acknowledged in any way, readily agreed without question.

Next, Clara spotted the 'general'.

"Mom," Clara said, and tapped Dorothy on the shoulder.

"Oh, hi, Clara, honey. You're early. We're not ready for the kids just yet, but almost." She brushed Clara off and started turning stacks of plates on the table so the patterns matched better. Clara did not just tap her mother's shoulder the next time; she grabbed it and spun her around.

"Clara!" her mother protested.

"There's something I have to talk to you about." Clara stared directly into Dorothy's eyes to lock her in place.

"What is it?"

"We can't talk here."

"Well, I can't just go. Like I said, the food just isn't ready yet."

"Mother, please," Clara pleaded.

"Have you seen Don anywhere?" Dorothy managed to escape her daughter's stare and snuck around to the other side of the table. She moved as though she were chasing a hyperactive fly.

Clara was not about to let her go that easily. She rejoined her mother and stood uncomfortably close.

"No, mom, I haven't seen Don. Can you stop fussing and talk to me?"

"Have you been smoking again?" she asked, followed by a few invasive sniffs.

"Mom! Focus! Please." Clara practically shook her.

"What? I'm right here; what do you want to say? You're always like this. So dramatic, Clara."

"Fine. If we have to talk here, then we talk here. It's about Angela and Alex, they…" She was cut off by her mother's frantic waving.

"There he is!" Dorothy interrupted while gesturing to Don who at long last was making an appearance at the picnic. "Finally! I have something I need to ask him."

"Mother! Did you hear me?" Clara shouted. "I said I need to talk to you about Angela." Her raised voice – not to mention the hot topic name – turned several heads in their direction including those of both Emily and Tina. It seemed the only thing that could earn Dorothy's attention was the threat of embarrassment, and so finally, she fully engaged with her daughter.

"What about Angela?" she whispered and pulled Clara aside.

Knowing how delicate the situation was, Clara took time to allow her thoughts to properly mature before she spoke. The last thing she wanted was to spoil this rare opportunity she had fought so hard for. Unfortunately for her, the spoiling was inevitable.

"Dorothy!" Don yelled from a distance. His powerful voice sent shockwaves through the crowd.

"Yes?" she replied obediently, turning her back on Clara.

Don walked right up to her and placed both his hands on her shoulders. It was over and Clara knew it; there was no way she could compete with Don and his golden touch. She was not going to get any advice from her mother, but perhaps that was for the best.

"I need you to come with me." Don's voice was solemn.

"Sure thing, Don. Just give me a second to finish with the food."

He leaned closer and spoke quietly, a futile precaution against the pervasive eavesdropping as the entire congregation had stopped to hear what Don had to say.

"Something's wrong in the church." After he delivered his foreboding message, he pulled away from her to see if she understood its severity. She did.

Don took hold of Dorothy's elbow to lead her back to the church.

Clara watched, dumbfounded, as her mother abandoned her to follow Don. However, her annoyance was short-lived.

Like a bulldozer careening through a supermarket, the wind suddenly raged and ripped through the picnic. The playful breeze they had become accustomed to was dead and gone, eaten up by something altogether more cruel. The force of the gust stirred up the land and flipped tables over like they were made of paper. There was no warning: just fury, just destruction.

Gary ran across the width of the picnic to be at Tina's side, but before he could reach her, the brutish wind shoved him to the ground. He remained pressed to the soil while the awakened torrent rushed above him.

As the force raged on, even gaining in strength, the congregation fled. The terrified herd of faithful followers galloped frantically toward the church, certain of the security it offered.

Matthew grabbed hold of Flora's wheel chair, but the thrashing wind battered them both and made moving her impossible. Flora covered her face to protect herself from the dirt that whirled fiercely around her. Grit and small stones were forced between her fingers into her ears, nose and mouth. As person after person ran past Matthew and his grandmother, it was Chris who finally stopped to help. He grabbed hold of Flora's left arm, Matthew grabbed the other and the two of them carried her against the storm. The wheel chair was left to the mercy of this most unnatural force of nature.

While the mob charged, Clara took a chance and looked behind her. Although she knew what she saw was real, her mind could not make sense of it. Dark billowing clouds, like smoke rising from a volcano, spilled up from the Burward forest and painted the sky with ash. The terrible wind roared out from the cloud's dark heart. It pushed forward like an avalanche ripping its way toward the church.

One of the tablecloths blew high above their heads, carried through the air like a white phantom. It twirled joyously in the sky as a majestic pre-show to the oncoming destruction. Eventually, the tablecloth fell out of favour and dropped back to earth – a fallen angel into the dirt.

The blackened clouds overtook the congregation before they reached the church. Shadows swallowed the sunlight entirely and suddenly night was upon them.

Emily, displaying her great strengths as an athlete, was first to reach the church door. She gripped the handle and used it as an anchor, afraid the wind would carry her away. After a few other members joined her, their combined strength was enough to pry the door open. People pushed and shoved their way inside with little to no regard for one another; all they cared about was a relief from the terror that chased them.

The last members to escape the foul storm were Chris, Matthew and Flora. The three entered together and the door slammed tightly behind them.

CHAPTER 17

Angela and Alex were in the parking lot when the sky turned. She even had the keys in her hand ready to go, but the fierce gusts swept them inside the church like everyone else. Although Angela wanted desperately to drive off and never look back, she could not fight the primal instinct to take shelter; her body told her to hide, so she did. She followed the flock right back into the building she vowed never to enter again, and as soon as the door closed, she knew it was a mistake. All was not right in the house of God.

Once everyone was securely inside, the sunlight that once nested in the windows became sickly. A shroud draped over the entire church. The room dimmed, and it became harder to tell who exactly was standing next to you. The sound, like a roaring stampede, crashed against the walls of the church and shook the old piano sending faint, dissonant notes into the growing dusk of the room.

The floorboards rumbled and felt as though they might fall away. Hysteria took hold. Frightened hands reached from all directions to pull and push at one another. Screams and desperate cries cluttered the air in an unbearable cacophony of human terror. Feet kicked and stomped despite the possibility that the thing in the dark might have been someone's leg, torso, or even head.

To spare her son from the madness, Angela gripped Alex tightly to her and backed herself up against the wall. Alex covered his ears and tucked his head into the crevice of her arm. As the mob raged on, a few voices could be picked out.

"We should head to the basement!" someone yelled.

"What's happening? I can't see!" came another.

"Someone, get the lights!" This one had some sense.

"Please, God, spare your children." Emily's voice was easy to pick out, not just because of its quality, but also the subject matter.

The wind went still. A few tremors lingered while the church shifted back into place, but the roaring had ceased. Shortly after this abrupt silence, the congregation began to settle. In the wake of the onslaught, there were tears, shaking, and a stunned speechlessness.

Light returned to the windows and it seemed whatever had come, had passed. Tina gripped her mouth tightly when she saw she had purged all down Gary's arm. He did not seem to mind, but she was beyond dismayed.

Angela held Alex at a distance so she could get a better look at him.

"Are you okay?"

"Yes," he said, with just a second of hesitation. Unlike most of the adults, his nerves seemed unruffled.

Angela stood and looked through the crowd to find Clara. The two of them locked eyes and, as if led by a tractor beam, Clara squeezed through the horde to meet Angela.

"What happened?" Angela asked, as soon as Clara was free.

"I don't know."

"What was that?"

"All I can say is, one minute I was talking to my mom, and the next, the wind picked up something fierce. I've never felt anything like it, Angela. It was like we were being chased. It was like the wind itself was chasing us."

"Chasing you?"

"And something else. There were clouds above the forest."

"Storms usually come from the west."

"Yes. This wasn't a storm."

"Listen," Don bellowed above the crowd, "is everyone alright? Is anyone hurt?" He waited for a response. None came. "The important thing is to make sure everyone's accounted for."

Shifting eyes started counting the room, but the way everyone was scattered made it impossible.

Chris and Matthew found a chair for Flora to rest on and sat her down. She breathed out heavily as her airways opened up like tired bagpipes. Matthew's eyes shot up to Chris.

"Thank you."

For fear he might spoil the moment, Chris chose simply to nod in return.

"Chris!" Tina screamed from across the room. She and Gary lunged for him, ensnaring him in a crushing hug. Chris was stunned by the affection. Tina poked and prodded every part of him as if she were testing a tire. Once she was sure he was not leaking air or anything else, she pulled Chris back into the mob, away from where he'd rather be. Chris watched as Matthew gradually disappeared behind rows of frightened churchgoers.

Michael forced his way back to the front door. He pressed himself against its sturdy wood frame, took a breath, and swung it open.

He was rewarded with a bath of sunlight. The storm had not just passed them by, it had vanished. The cotton candy clouds that remained in the sky were light and non-threatening. He closed the door. Although the birds had returned to their chirping, Michael recalled how quickly the winds had changed mere moments prior. The abrupt shift back to normalcy meant nothing, and in fact only proved they could not trust the weather. If those demon gusts trickled up from nowhere before, who's to say they would not do it again?

"Don, what was that?" a voice called out from the crowd.

"I don't know what that was. We may have just experienced some kind of freak tornado, or maybe a rogue gust from down south. It will probably be a while before we know for sure." Don's head swiveled around the room. "Clara Muller, are you here?"

"Yes," Clara said, as she turned to face him.

"Clara, there you are. Could you please go check on the children downstairs?"

"Actually, Susan is with them right now."

"Go to the children in the basement and keep them there, please." His tone shifted and Clara was forced to obey.

"Yes, of course."

"And keep all the children down there until I say, understand?"

"Yes."

"*All* the children," Don repeated looking directly at Alex.

"Okay, Don." Clara turned to Angela and the two of them exchanged a worried look. Clara waited for Angela to make a move, as she wasn't about to snatch Alex away from her.

There was no way for Angela to leave with Alex now. The best thing for them to do was to play along and slip away once things had calmed down. If only she had moved faster, she and Alex would be home. Not here, not in this mess, she thought. But, there was no sense in harping on what could have been. How to deal with the current situation, this was Angela's new problem, and one she intended to solve.

So, she smiled and nodded before she let Alex out of her arms and into Clara's.

"Mom?" Alex asked, looking panicked.

Angela leaned down to his level and spoke with her bedtime voice. This gentle vocal tone was normally used to sooth Alex's night terrors and to distract him from the abominations that lurked in the bowels of his closet. She used it now for that very same purpose.

"It's okay, sweetie. Everything's going to be all right. Go with Clara. I'll see you soon." Her eyes shifted away from her son and up to her friend. "I'll come for you both as soon as I can."

Clara smiled and wrapped her arm around Alex's shoulders. They headed toward the basement together.

"Alex…" Angela added just before he descended the stairs. He stopped and looked at her. Angela was supposed to say she loved him, but she found herself overcome with questions. Was she making a mistake? Should she just take Alex and run? What about the mob and their pitchforks? As she second and third guessed herself, only one thing felt certain, and it was staring her right in the face. Alex. He looked at her as if he would wait patiently for her, no matter what, no matter how long. He needed her, as she needed him.

By the time the shock of her child's candid gaze wore off, Clara and Alex were gone. Angela knew he was in good hands, but the sooner they could disappear, the better. She stared at the basement doorway for nearly a minute, until Susan emerged to rejoin the congregation. Then, Angela's attention reverted back to the panic at hand.

Don and Dorothy had separated themselves from the group to continue their frank discussion that was interrupted earlier. Angela maneuvered herself around the fringe of the congregation to hear what was so important that it must be kept secret. She nudged her way along, careful to avoid the conspirator's line of sight. She was close enough now to make out their whispers.

"Rick is missing," Don said, heavy with concern.

"Missing?" questioned Dorothy. "Where could he have gone?"

"Bruce was waiting for him in the office. He was supposed to come get me as soon as Rick was washed and dressed. He never came. Now, both of them are missing."

"Both? Where have you looked?"

"I waited, but they never came. The first place I looked was the sanctuary, and that's when I saw it."

"Saw what?"

Don's voice found a quieter, more reticent volume, and Angela was forced to move even closer to decipher it. The danger became one of proximity. In order to catch what he had to say, she would need to be right at Dorothy's ear.

Unfortunately Emily emerged like one of Clara's wall dividers and cut secret agent Angela off from her target. It was an annoying move, made even more annoying by the fact that it was Emily.

"What do you make of that wild wind, Angela? What do you think it was?" she demanded.

"I don't know. I didn't see it."

"No, you were in the parking lot. That's right. Were you going somewhere?"

"No. I was just about to bring Alex out for the picnic, but I had to grab something from the car first. Good thing we were a little late getting ready."

"Oh, I see. That makes sense." It was clear Emily meant the exact opposite of what she said and it was also clear she wanted Angela to know it.

"Is there anything else you wanted to ask, Emily?" Angela had grown tired of the needling. If Emily was going to be a prick, Angela thought she might as well be honest about it.

"No, I was just wondering where you two were headed, that's all."

"So, you were worried about us, is that it?"

"I wondered where you were, yes."

"In that case, Emily, thanks for your concern," Angela's smile did not flinch as she continued, "but now that you know exactly what we were doing, maybe you can concern yourself with someone else for a change. You might even be able to mind your own fucking business for once." The words just slipped out as natural as breath itself. They tasted sweet. It took a second for Angela to realize she had spoken them aloud, but once she did, she had no regrets. No more hiding, it was time for truth.

"Angela, I don't know where this anger is coming from, or why you feel you need to speak to me that way, but…" Before Emily could continue, Angela cut her off.

"Maybe because you're interrogating me like a Russian mobster."

"That's absurd. I'm just talking."

"Please…you're a plier away from systematically removing each of my fingernails. You've had a thing against me since Rick went missing. I'm sick of your petty vendetta and your nasty little whispers."

"This isn't the place for your temper tantrum," Emily said and pivoted her head around to make sure no one had noticed their argument.

"No shit. I couldn't agree more. Only, I'm not the one who ambushed me, so I don't really have a choice in the matter."

"It wasn't an ambush. Honestly, I don't know why you're being so aggressive right now. All I wanted to know was where you were. God forgive me for showing concern."

"You don't care about me or Alex. I can't imagine what you actually care about."

"I'm glad you're leaving the church. There's a certain respect we show each other here. If I disagree with someone, I'm civil about it. You aren't. You think you're better than us. Well, unlike you, I don't judge people. That's not my job, it's His. And He alone has that right. But if I'm speaking freely, I'll pray tonight that God judges you kindly, though, I doubt it will help."

"What did I do to make you hate me?" Angela stripped the conversation to its bare bones. It was the only question she cared to hear answered. A speedy, honest response from Emily would end the confrontation in its tracks.

Emily did not say anything, only stared back at her accuser. In the silence, Angela knew Emily was holding onto something and whatever it was it was putrefying within her.

"I don't hate you," the response finally came, "but I do blame you."

Angela was shocked. The statement sent her into a spiral. What blame had Emily referred to? Did she mean Rick's disappearance?

A shattering scream ripped through the room and broke apart the tension that had been snowballing between the two women. Every head turned to see what had triggered it.

A middle-aged woman hugged the side of the doorframe leading into the sanctuary. Her face was pointed into the room, locked in a state of repulsion and hysteria – a most distressing mix. Her scream ran its course and then devolved into a series of whimpers.

"Oh, Lord," Don muttered to himself.

The entire congregation approached in unison, not only to help the poor woman, but also to witness for themselves the source of her terror.

CHAPTER 18

Astonishingly, the first person to make it into the sanctuary was Dorothy. She stumbled past the terrified woman – who grabbed frantically at her dress – and gawked upward at the pulpit.

Her eyes immediately sought out her precious tapestry. It was the subdued blue of the fabric that made the new splashes of red so abrasive to the eye.

The scene of peaceful prayer had been defiled by obscene streaks of crimson blood applied with the most audacious of sensibilities. From the bird's mouth came a flow of gore that poured out into the open hands like a teapot. The blood had saturated the fabric and overflowed down to the base of the wall itself. All the dripping gave the tapestry a sad quality. But, the bloody tears did not end there. The podium itself dripped with red as if it were a candle and the blood its wax. Spotty smudges hinted toward a struggle of some kind, perhaps even a slaughter.

As Dorothy took in the ghastly display before her, her mind managed one quick, practical observation: there was no way something could still be walking around after losing that much blood, so, where was the body?

A dozen more congregation members filtered in with stunned silence at first, but after a few moments, there were some fitting gasps and uncomfortable murmurs.

Half an hour earlier, everyone was outside in merriment setting up for their weekly picnic; now, they were standing in the middle of a macabre Sir Francis Bacon painting.

"My God." Dorothy was the first to speak. She crept down the aisle using the pews to keep herself steady. She stopped halfway at some droplets that had splattered on the floor, but was close enough to smell the conflicting mix of sweaty metal and fresh flowers that wrestled in the air.

"What the fuck?" Chris had consolidated everyone's shock into one simple question and announced it with considerable volume.

"Who would do this?" Gary asked.

"We were all outside," added Dorothy.

"Not all of us." This spiteful comment slithered from Emily's viperous lips. Her not-so-subtle accusation was punctuated by a nasty glare.

Angela's eyes did not meet Emily's, nor did she acknowledge the juvenile attack. She had only recently stepped into the sanctuary and was instead taking in the newly painted room. The matters of her escape with Alex, or even of Rick's ill-timed return, were both momentarily muted by whatever viciousness had recently taken place. It was a morbid mystery that begged to be solved, despite the fact that the solution undoubtedly promised more horrors to come.

Almost unanimously, the congregation shared the sensation of having been violated. This was their sacred space where God made sure no sin could thrive, where pain and suffering were unknown, where the vile beasts of the world dared not enter. Yet, here was their church, besmirched and desecrated, reduced to nothing more than a slaughterhouse. And the lambs started screaming.

"People, please!" Don hollered. "This is an absolutely grotesque vandalism, but we won't find out who did this unless they come forth. We can't start accusing each other at random. That's not what we do. I suggest we all head back into the mess hall."

"We need to call the police."

Don responded quickly. "Yes, of course. We will. But we don't need to do it here. Please, into the mess hall."

"Someone should clean it up before it starts to smell." Gary added.

"I'm afraid we need to wait for the police first, Gary."

"Good luck getting the smell out then," Tina said and rested a supportive hand on her husband's shoulder.

"Alright, we can talk about how to handle this situation in the other room. Now, we've all seen what's here to be seen, so let us all take our leave. Please." Exaggerated hand gestures accompanied Don's reasoning.

He began to lead people out of the sanctuary, but was interrupted by a feeble moan that fluttered forth from behind the pulpit.

"Did everyone hear that?" asked Dorothy. She was the closest to the front and therefore the first to hear the waning voice.

No one answered, but everyone froze.

The moan came again, only this time with a pinch more agony. The cries built as if every moment for the sufferer was more tortured than the last. The echo in the room kept the puling alive, soaking into the space.

"I hear it," said Susan.

"No shit," Chris snapped at her.

"I think it's coming from the…" Dorothy did not finish her sentence – there was no need.

Two shivering hands crawled up to the top of the pulpit. The fingers wrapped around its wood trim like the legs of a tarantula clasping at its next meal. The knuckles had been shaved to the bone, exposing the shifting joints as they popped in and out of place while the hands formed their grip. As they twisted in the light, the pale skin glistened in an unflattering mixture of blood and sweat.

The cries escalated to new, unnerving heights, as Bruce pulled himself up into view. His head was marked with two deep gashes that split the sides of his face and claimed both of his eyes. Clotted blood crowded his wounds and peppered his quivering mouth. He let out another excruciating wail and cocked his head in all directions like he was sniffing for a response. When he opened his jaws, his cheeks opened too, displaying the full cruelty of his wounds. His molars peeked through the slits and winked in the light at the onlookers. His eyebrows no longer rose in unison; each half was a delayed reaction to the other, pulling in separate directions. What was left of his eyes oozed from his sockets and pooled into the wounds.

Dorothy did not scream; the sight of Bruce was beyond that. For some of the other members, however, screaming was the only option.

Although Bruce had no eyes, his sight seemed inexplicably fixated on Susan. He stared at her with two hollowed crevices the way a lifeless statue does. She could not bear the vision and hid her face from him. There, into her own hands, she screamed. Her fingers felt her eyes as if to make certain they had not been lost, too.

"Bruce!" Don yelled and scrambled next to Dorothy. "In Christ's name…"

Bruce's hand beckoned for Don to approach. It waved him forward meekly with a slippery, almost seductive gesture.

It was true Don knew intellectually of cruelty, and of murder, and adultery, and torture, and of genocides and holocausts, of tragedies and disasters, of killings and killers, executions and executioners, but this savagery was always of another time, in another place. It was never standing, bleeding in front of him, moaning and putrid. His own words haunted him: *God allowed this.* God allowed the blades to enter Bruce's face, allowed them to take his eyes, allowed them to coat the walls in his blood like a child's finger-painting. God is great. This is what Don believed; this is what he preached from the pulpit. Did he have the rectitude to do it again? This question disturbed him as much as Bruce's slippery grip that now leaked in his hand.

"Don Hooper!" a voice erupted. Don felt the bass from it rattle deep in his body. It was so powerful in fact, that, at first, he believed it to be the voice of God. "Step back," it commanded.

With his hand still wrapped around Bruce's, Don looked back at his congregation to see if they too heard the voice. Their frightened looks told him they had.

From a corner of the room that was dipped in shadow, Rick stood to his full six feet. His dark blue robe hung from his body and draped down to his ankles as if it were tailor made. His feet, though still bare, were no longer bleeding. His imperial posture puffed out his chest and asserted his authority, making it immediately clear who was the lion and who was the mouse.

"Rick… In the name of God what have you done?" Don tried to match the boom of Rick's voice, but failed.

"I've done nothing in the name of your God." Each word growled out of his mouth, as if coming from the throat of a feral beast.

"Bruce," Don said, turning back to his marred friend, "can you hear me? We're going to get you some help. Someone call an ambulance!"

"I forbid you," Rick proclaimed.

"Forbid me? How dare you!"

Rick took a step toward Don and the church, itself, quaked on cue. It was the same sound as before, only this time there was no storm to blame for the cracks and creaks. Each step brought the building new shivers, as if it were sickened by his very presence.

Angela watched, along with the others, in hushed terror as her *husband* closed in on Don. She recognized nothing of Rick. His voice, his gravitas; it was like he had transformed, emerged from a chrysalis with a new sense of inhuman despotism.

"He's marked," Rick continued, " as you all will be. In time you will come to see it as a blessing."

"God damn you!" The persona of calming wisdom Don had embodied for years was dispelled in a matter of seconds as his blistering anger took hold. "You degenerate monster! May the smite of the Lord fall upon you with all His fury for what you have done."

Rick halted his approach.

"Dorothy! Bruce needs bandages. Go call for an ambulance, and bring the police here. Go now!" Don shouted.

Dorothy snapped out of her trance and bolted toward the door.

"Dorothy." The calmness in Rick's voice was unsettling. "You won't leave this room. None of you will leave this room. Come, be seated." He opened his arms welcomingly like a true preacher.

His lips parted and the edges of his mouth reached for his ears. His teeth and eyes reflected unnatural light – a cheery beacon shining through the gore and chaos splattered behind him; one could not help but feel the preciousness of life was being mocked by the display.

Despite his command, no one moved a muscle.

Angela stepped forth, singling herself out from the crowd. As she was the one who had shared a life, a bed, and a child with this man, she felt a responsibility to try to appeal to his compassion. Having personally tasted his cruelty before, Angela knew he had hidden levels of depravity, but she never dreamed him capable of butchery on this scale. Still, if any part of the old Rick remained, she had to find it.

She walked up the aisle to the spot where Dorothy had been. Her voice was soft, like the one she had used to comfort Alex. Just beneath this placidity, however, was a pounding heart and racing breath.

"Rick, it's Angela." Her pleading stare was not returned. "What's wrong? Why are you doing this? Why don't you just let them go? Let us get Bruce some help. He's badly hurt. I know this isn't you. This isn't my Rick."

"You're right. I'm not me." He finally met her gaze; if Bruce's eyes were craters, then Rick's were an abyss. Angela felt utterly alone in them. "Be seated!" he yelled again. The windows buckled from an invisible force.

The congregation filled the back pews first. They sat uncomfortably close to one another in an effort to keep as far away from Rick as possible. There were a few stubborn holdouts including Emily, Chris and Angela, but eventually even they fell into place. Soon, the only two people in the church still standing were Rick and Don – Bruce's hunched position could hardly be considered standing.

Rick looked over his new flock with pride. There were no whispers or slouched postures, only eager listeners prepped to devour his every word. He inhaled satisfyingly as if the attention he received smelled of roses.

He walked up the carpeted steps and joined Bruce at the pulpit. All the life had drained from Bruce's body save for the frail breaths that trickled from his lips. Rick warmly slapped him on the back as if they were old chums from high school. This stirred a few more moans within Bruce – a waste of what limited strength still remained.

Don let go of Bruce's limp hand and took a step back. He scrutinized Rick carefully, like a boxer sizing up his opponent. He could not allow himself to be an audience to such repugnance. Something had to be done, but Don needed to rally his congregation if they wanted to put an end to Rick's charade. To do that, he needed to conquer the fear that held them captive.

"Bruce was a volunteer," Rick began. "He volunteered to help me. And his suffering will not be in vain."

"He's a maniac!" Don pleaded to the room. "He has lost his mind. We can't just sit here and listen! There's a man dying in front of your eyes – woe onto you who dare ignore it! I'm calling the police and putting an end to this madness. This vile lunatic cannot be stomached any further. We can stop him now, together!"

Every member of the congregation agreed with him, but the danger of separating from the herd kept them in their seats.

Don took one look at their cowed faces and knew he had failed. Words were not enough. If no one would join him, then he had no choice but to act solo. Defiantly, he marched down the aisle.

Angela thought of Clara and what she would do in this situation. *Never fear standing alone for what's right*. Many of their conversations had revolved around this topic. It was something Clara felt passionately about, and worked tirelessly to instill it in all her students. Immediately, Angela rose to her feet. She could not sit idly by and be made obedient by violence anymore. She had already let that happen for far too long, and she was not going back.

Chris was inspired to join the revolution; unfortunately his rebellion was short-lived as his parents quickly pulled him back down against the pew and held him there.

Before Don even reached the door, Rick spoke again.

"We're alone now, Don. Your phones won't work. Running won't work. And praying certainly won't work, so please, be seated."

Don stopped and turned slowly to face the church's new minister. His pride was threatened as much as his morality. He resented Rick's authority almost as much as his savagery. So he stood at the back of the sanctuary with his arms crossed.

"It's distracting having you there," Rick said with eerie composure. "If you remain standing, you'll be disrupting my teachings. And if you do that, you die. Do you understand? Do you understand that I will slaughter you and make them watch? That's the choice. Either I spill you before them, or you sit. And then maybe, I'll let Gary live."

The matter-of-fact delivery left no question that Rick meant it. Don may have been willing to risk his own safety, but not that of his friend and follower. He had taken an oath to guide and protect his congregation, so he swallowed his indignation for now and slid into a nearby pew.

Angela considered running for the door, but knew if Rick wanted to catch her, he could. And she had little faith the room of cowards would do a thing to help her.

There was no choice to be made. She sat back down with her teeth and fists clenched.

Rick waited for the room to settle before he continued.

"You want to know where I've been all this time? I met my god. The one true god. Not this... Not these silly stories." Rick picked up the hefty Bible in front of him and nonchalantly tossed it aside. The tome hit hard against the ground with a thud, its pages crinkled and disgraced. "Rick, three months ago, is not the man standing here today. Rick, three months ago, was a fallen servant. It was a gradual decline. His job was a dead end. He lost his faith, and he found a bottle. He started to hurt the people he loved. He was an adulterer, a bad husband, and a bad father. Something had rotted in his heart, though he couldn't admit it. Three months ago, this was the despair he found himself in. He was drunk and driving without a place to go or to come from. He didn't want to die, but he didn't much want to live, either. Searching. He was searching. He parked the car at the first building he came to: this very church. He was angry. He got out of the car, afraid he might start driving again, and instead stumbled through the Davidson's field. It was then, when he could sink no further, when he was alone with his hopelessness, that *it* found him. It had been waiting centuries to reveal itself. It is the Behemoth. The Beast. It took him into the woods and showed him the mysteries of death, the secrets of life and the eternity of flesh."

"What is this?" Don questioned. "What exactly are we listening to? Tina, Gary, are you two just going to sit there and listen to this blasphemy? Michael, you don't have any problem with what he's saying?"

"What do you expect us to do, Don?" Tina retorted. "He has Bruce."

"I understand your unease, but I have come to you prepared. A miracle. I will show you a miracle, something your God has never done. If you have doubts now, I promise you, they will be silenced," Rick announced to the congregation.

Anxious looks spread through the pews.

Chris' eyes shot across the room and locked onto Matthew. The two of them froze in each other's stare, exchanging their panic. This act did not diminish the potency of dread, but it was a comfort to know they were in this nightmare together.

That was until Matthew noticed Chris' expression distort to new levels of horror. It grew from a look of dismay that Matthew could relate to, to something far more serious, like staring into your reflection, only to realize there's someone behind you in the mirror. When Matthew compared Chris' expression with everyone else's, he found they all shared that grim look, but worse, they were all also staring at him.

Intuitively, Matthew looked to the front of the sanctuary and saw that Rick had fixed his eyes on him. The hungry wolf stalked down from the pulpit toward where he was seated. Matthew's mouth dried out and his lungs emptied. But, something was off. As Rick approached, it became evident he was not quite looking at Matthew. He was staring past him. Rick was staring at his grandmother.

Matthew's head snapped to the right, where he found Flora entranced by Rick's hungry gaze. She looked like a doll-eyed groupie.

Matthew stood up and grabbed Flora's hand, but she didn't respond. He squeezed it hard until he felt her bones slip against each other, but still no reaction. She was hopelessly enraptured.

Rick was only a few feet away now, so out of desperation, Matthew grabbed his grandmother by the shoulders and shook her from side to side. Her head tossed about, but her pale eyes did not lose their focus.

"Grandma? Grandma!" he yelled point blank into her face. He tried to get her to her feet, but it was too late, Rick was within arm's reach.

His firm grip easily encompassed Matthew's wrist and tightened like a python. For fear of hearing his bone snap, Matthew let go of his grandmother. Rick chucked him aside and turned his attention to Flora.

Matthew landed first against the seat of the pew then tumbled off onto the ground, gripping his aching wrist. Chris stood and would have run to Matthew's side if the room had not erupted into pandemonium. Screams tore through the crowd as members jumped over seats, scurrying away from Rick as fast they could.

Don stood, but did not run. He was absorbed in the ritual forming before him. Rick had made a frightening assertion, and Don was compelled to see what miracle Rick's god could muster.

Amidst the hysteria, Rick placed both his palms over Flora's wanting eyes. Her mouth went agape at his touch, and even had the trace of a smile. She offered no fight against his hands; on the contrary, she surrendered to him. Her breath began to falter and the strenuous wheezing reinvigorated Matthew's protective instinct.

"Stop! You're hurting her! Stop it!" he screamed. With his left arm and legs, Matthew punched and kicked frantically at the merciless miracle worker. Underneath the draped robe, however, Rick's body was built like a fortress and withstood Matthew's barrage with ease.

Flora started to shake and suddenly, her head snapped back sharply. A communal gasp broke out from the crowd. Rick released her and held his hands high into the air in praise.

Matthew collapsed next to his grandmother and held her tight. He felt no signs of life in her body. She was wilted and still. Then, after a moment had passed, Matthew detected a faint vibration in her throat as breath returned to her. It came timidly at first, but eventually grew into deep gulps. Matthew gently laid her back against the pew. It was then he noticed her eyes.

There was no blood or torn tissue, but her skin dipped unnaturally into the empty sockets where her eyes used to be. It was as if she never had eyes at all. Her sunken eyelids fluttered uselessly in their search for their missing counterparts. As Flora became conscious, her fingers felt their way into empty holes above her cheek and she started to whimper.

"Matthew... Matthew? I can't see! I can't see you!" she cried. Matthew had never seen her in such a state. He remained a statue at her side, unable to comfort and unable to abandon. He let her hands feel his proximity, which they did desperately. He prayed that would be calming enough.

"What have you done?" Don demanded.

"There." Rick gestured to the pulpit.

Bruce's head gradually rose from its slouched position, and to the astonishment of all, his eyes flickered open. Only they were not his eyes, exactly; they were two pale, old eyes that peered out from his face with the roaming gawk of a newborn baby.

The fear Don dared not entertain had come to pass. Rick was not just a murderous madman; he was indeed touched by something beyond explanation. Something that could have endowed him with awesome – albeit destructive – powers. Backed by his faith in a loving God, Don reasoned that the beast Rick spoke of must have been Beelzebub, the Lord of Darkness, Satan. As a soldier of light, Don felt a new empowerment rise within him.

For the rest of the room, after witnessing such a miracle, all doubts had been dispelled. Even Angela's rage was silenced in the wake of the phenomenon. What they were facing now was an affront to everything they believed true. The gift of sight had been taken away and given back in an instant; flesh disassembled, and then reassembled, like toy building blocks. Minds needed time to fully recognize the enormity of it all. If the leap from believing the world is flat, to the understanding that it's actually a spinning globe hurdling through infinite space, is enough to crack a brain, then this would surely shatter a few. But what Rick promised was undeniably true, and by extension, the beast he spoke of may, therefore, also share that truth. This epiphany not only humbled the congregation, it terrified them.

No one took notice when Don advanced on Rick.

"Satan! Devil! You blasphemous, wicked heretic!" Don shouted with unbridled fervor. "You dare bring your insidious influence here! We serve Jesus Christ and it is in His name I command you to leave. You cannot intimidate us, or tempt us with vulgar tricks. Take your filth and retreat from this house of God!"

"This *is* a house of god, just not yours. Not anymore," replied Rick starkly. "You think me evil? You think I serve your Devil? Pitiful creature, so lost, you don't even realize that you are."

The condescension ignited a fury in Don. The minister of St. Paul's United Church, who, since reaching adulthood had never raised a fist in anger, resorted to raising his fists now. Don grabbed the collar of Rick's robe and pulled back to deliver a blow across the pompous intruder's face.

Rick easily caught Don's forearm before the ill-conceived strike was realized. Don's flesh sizzled on contact, as if Rick's hand were hotter than Hell's most cleansing fire. His digits sank into Don's arm like butter and the blood boiled up between his fingers. Don screamed and tried to pull away, but he was caught and had to suffer for his impertinence. Rick squeezed through Don's scorched appendage until he gripped the bone at its centre. Cracks formed under the pressure and sent Don's nerves shrieking. The sensation of smoldering heat against his naked bone was excruciating, but was at least only briefly endured as the arm snapped off and flopped into the puddle of blood steaming at their feet.

With that, Don coughed up his morning porridge. The offending smell of overcooked meat beset his nostrils – it was all the more disturbing that the smell was his own. He clutched his severed arm and was surprised to find the wound had not cauterized despite the heat. It had melted.

Two hands gripped the sides of his head as Rick pulled him closer. The grip, although no longer burning, felt like a vice that threatened to pop his skull any second. Face to face, Rick flaunted his helpless prey before the masses.

"It's time we give praise to whom praise is due. No more thoughts of an illusive, absent God. A God who doesn't hear you when you cry, or care for you when you suffer. From this day, we praise the one who lives by blood and skin. We praise the Behemoth."

Calmly, Rick repositioned his right hand and slid four fingers under Don's wobbling upper lip, pressing them against his gum line.

Don's beseeching eyes blinked away his welling tears, turned in his head and locked onto the first person he saw: Dorothy. Having been his most trusted aide, he was hurt she had remained so silent throughout his struggle. She watched him, in the moment of his death, with the expression of a frightened, lost child. He had been her abiding guide and mentor since he took over as minister of the church, he counseled her through the loss of her husband, told her God would take care of it, whatever *it* was, yet she was still just a child. In this final moment, when *he* needed something, all she had to offer him was one more searing pain, brought forth by the helpless look in her eyes: were all his readings of scripture, all his sermons, and discussions, and assurances, were they all futile? Did anyone even listen? Would he never be blessed – or cursed – with an answer?

The heat building up against the sensitive pink of his mouth warned Don his demise would be imminent, though not quick or painless. His gums were the first to come unglued and separated from his teeth like taffy as Rick eased his scalding touch under the skin of his face. The burning hand slid all the way up to his forehead and around the back of his neck, effortlessly peeling away the tissue and muscle in one fluid motion. The unsheathed mess that remained of Don's head was comprised of a few meaty bits left jiggling on the skull, but the majority of his face was bunched in the fleshy hood hanging down his back.

Hideous, guttural chokes took over Don's body. They built up inside him, carried by the reflexive spasms of his stomach only to be spat out between his chattering teeth. The squeals born of such anguish were the most unbearable part of his slaughter.

Just when his agony seemed too much to behold, Rick stopped. He dropped the body and it slapped like an old blood-soaked dishcloth against the floor with a grand splash of red.

For the patient witnesses to Don's grotesque peeling, playing the role of audience was no longer possible. The congregation members all tried to flee, but for Angela who stared in shock at the unthinkable brutality Rick had unleashed.

"Silence!" Rick roared.

After their recent lesson on the punishment for disobedience, everyone became perfectly still.

"It's too late to run," Rick said, flicking the blood from his hands. "The Behemoth is already here. If you listen to me, then the Beast will be your salvation, the doorway to eternity. If you don't, it will be your undoing."

"Rick, what happened to you?" Angela asked out of disgust rather than curiosity. She hated herself for not taking Alex and running while she could, for Rick had become far more than an abusive husband – he was now an angel of death. If he was really as divinely touched as he professed to be, then Angela had no hope of escaping him. The fear of this led every rational part of her to fight against his miracles. But, how could she explain it away when his bare hands slid through skin like putty and when the floorboards shuddered at the sound of his voice? She had no answers, but she kept trying.

"I ascended. After three months, I gave myself to the Behemoth. Now, I'm spreading its word to you. The true god is angry. It has been watching you with jealous eyes. It stood silently in the woods and endured every insult as you foolishly praised an insignificant carpenter nailed to a cross, unaware of the majesty that waited just over the hill. Well, it's done being silent. Now, it's time to prove your faith." Rick looked down at the floor before continuing. "Downstairs, right now, there is a room of children. You love them, as any parent would. I have shown you miracles, now you must show your devotion. You must forget this love and choose one child to give to the Behemoth."

"What?" protested Dorothy.

"No!" Tina added.

"This is insane."

"What if we don't?" Gary questioned boldly.

"Then you are unworthy," came the answer, "and you will be slaughtered. If you try to leave, you will be slaughtered. If you fight us, you will be slaughtered like the pigs you are. This is your chance for ascension. Be with us, or be damned. You have two nights to make your offering."

The ultimatum was set and the room was weighed down by it. No one spoke, or even looked at each other. Each member was helplessly drowned by their own torrential thoughts.

Angela's mind took an odd detour – a break from the carnage – and noted how the sunlight in the room remained indifferent to the goings-on, spreading an optimistic radiance throughout the sanctuary, despite what else was inside of it. *Fuck you, Mr. Sun,* she thought to herself.

Two palms slammed loudly against one of the pews. Everyone turned at the sudden commotion. Sandy stood and shook his keyboard-stretched finger in Rick's direction.

"I know my God," Sandy declared, "and he's a God of love, not blood. You can't threaten us. You can't keep us here." He spat at Rick's feet and just like that, he stormed out of the room. Rick offered this slight no response; he did not even seem to notice.

The sound of Sandy's footsteps punctuated the stark deadness of the room. It was easy to tell that Sandy was headed for the front door.

After surveying the shell-shocked faces of her fellow churchgoers, Angela took a deep breath and hurried after Sandy. She was not sure if she was going to follow him outside or try to talk him out of it. All she knew was she did not want to spend another second near the stench of blood.

CHAPTER 19

"Sandy, wait!" Angela yelled as she charged into the mess hall. She was too late. The front door was already closing. A brief glimpse of Sandy's work boot was all she caught, and then the room was sealed like a tomb.

She paused there for a second, only three feet into the mess hall, and waited to see if Rick would come chasing after her, but no one came. No one even stirred, so she pressed on.

Her feet carefully tested each floorboard before committing to the step. Her muscles remembered how to be discrete, to change footing, when to hold position and regulate breath. It came naturally. After all, she had many years of practice tiptoeing around terror.

How quickly things can spiral into chaos, she thought. One minute, you can be in love, the next you are married to a man who terrifies you, who answers you with his fists. You can be seconds away from a new life, and then find yourself trapped with the very devil you were running from. Like a car wreck on the way to prom, futures can crash, dreams shatter, and it can all happen in an instant. You compliment your friend's dress, and then there are bloody champagne bottles rolling down the road.

Yet, there was an odd wonderment to be found in all that grimness. Rick had clearly demonstrated there was magic in the world. Some force at work that was beyond Angela, perhaps even beyond God. She found comfort in the way this minimized her.

As quickly as these thoughts came, they were dashed away by the sound of the creaking floor behind her. Someone had stepped into the room and was either doing a bad job of masking their approach, or didn't care if Angela heard them.

She abandoned her stealth and charged toward the door. If she slowed even slightly, Rick would overtake her. And what punishment would come then? Maybe he'd remove her eyes like Flora's, so she could never see their son again.

Angela reached a full run and the footsteps struggled to catch up. She was only a few seconds away from the door when she realized her speed. She gripped the doorknob and tried to stop, but she overestimated the traction between the old wood and the worn rubber soles of her shoes. She slipped right past the door and into the coat rack. The eclectic assemblage of puffy jackets saved her some bruises, but also slowed her recovery time.

She scrambled to her feet, armed with one of the wire hangers and swung. The thin metal hook came within inches of Dorothy's bunched face.

"Dorothy!" wheezed Angela.

"Yes!" she yelped.

"I didn't know who you were."

"Now that you do, honey, you mind putting down the hanger?"

Angela dropped the flimsy metal wire just as Gary and Tina trickle out of the sanctuary after Dorothy.

"What's everyone doing?" Angela asked.

"We wanted to see, too," replied Gary nervously. "Did he make it?"

"I don't know." Angela admitted.

"I can't hear anything bad. Maybe he made it to his car," Dorothy observed optimistically.

"If he did, then there shouldn't be silence. We should be hearing the motor, the wheels." Angela leaned closer to the door, but the thick wood obscured the sounds on the other side. She listened carefully for footsteps or voices--any sign that Sandy was still out there.

"Does he drive a hybrid? Those don't make as much noise," Gary added. His comment earned another worrisome scrunch from Dorothy's face.

"We shouldn't be here," Tina finally spoke up. "You all saw what Rick did. We should be in the sanctuary with the others. He said no one leaves."

"And you're just going to accept it? Just like that?" Angela questioned.

"Just like that? I just saw Don's face taken off. Don's face! So, yes, just like that, I'll accept it."

"You go back then," Angela snapped.

"Sandy was right, Tina," Gary intervened. "We have to try. We can't just stay in here. That's not an option."

Tina shook her head and stepped away from the group.

"You will be slaughtered." She spun around dramatically and darted back to the sanctuary. Gary watched her go, but said nothing. Tina was a stubborn person, he accepted that, and he also accepted that the only person who could change Tina's mind was Tina. But, he had his own convictions to follow. Eventually, time would bring her back, it always did. He brushed his fingers through his thick, hanging mustache and returned his attention to the door.

Both he and Dorothy nervously watched while Angela's hand slid down the carvings of the wood to the metal handle. Angela was surprised to find her strength wane when she tried to grip the doorknob. Her brain and hand entered an argument over who was boss. She commanded her fingers to clench, but they had doubts.

"Beyond this door is just a sunny day. Right?" Angela asked aloud. Neither Gary nor Dorothy knew if it was rhetorical, but Dorothy decided to answer anyway.

"That's right," she said and pulled at her polka dot dress, which had bunched in weird places from her hunching.

The handle squeaked as Angela turned it. Its pained cry resonated through the room like the warning call of a frightened bird. Then, she stopped.

"What's wrong? What is it?" asked the skittish Dorothy.

There was a subtle vibration from the other side of the door. It was weak and came in pulses, suggesting there was some form of intelligence behind it. It developed into an unnerving scratch, like a desperate animal clawing its way in.

Angela let the doorknob fall back into place. She felt safer with a secured door between her and the phantom scraping. She stepped back to add some distance for good measure.

"What's making that noise?" Dorothy pestered.

"I don't know."

"Should we open the door?"

"I don't think so."

At that moment, the frightened bird's squawking returned as the doorknob began to twist.

Angela grabbed the metal handle before it finished revolving. This time, her grip had no pesky trepidation.

All parts of her were in agreement; whatever was outside should remain outside.

"Help me!"

Gary joined Angela and the two of them pushed against the door.

"What are you doing, what if it's Sandy?" Dorothy said with her hands fluttering.

The scratching Angela had felt did not suggest Sandy. It was the noise of a beast. Sandy would not paw at the door like a dog, he would have knocked, he would have kicked, he would have asked for the door to be opened.

Angela braced herself against the wood, but when Gary shifted into a new position for leverage, the handle slipped out of Angela's grip. The door cracked open.

A hand, soaked in dark red, snaked around the edge and into everyone's view. It emerged from the harsh spotlight of the sun and reached into the shadows where Angela, Gary and Dorothy were hiding. It slapped against the door in an attempt to swat them away.

The fingers, despite their bloody drips, were recognizable to Dorothy. They were the ones she had watched play all her favourite hymns for the past fifteen years.

"Move! It's Sandy for Christ's sake!" yelled Dorothy, as she pulled Gary away from the door with unexpected strength, allowing the door to swing open.

There stood Sandy, or at least most of Sandy. He wavered in the doorway with the overpowering daylight bursting all around him in iridescent yellow beams as if he were Mary Magdalene. His bottom jaw was missing, as was most of the muscle from his torso. His organs heaved in and out, pulsating under the confines of his exposed ribcage. It looked as though his flesh had been torn away in one powerful swipe. His head was turned upwards toward the ceiling, but his eyes peered down over what was left of his cheeks at the three of them. One of his hands reached for help, while the other kept his guts from spilling out of his body.

He took one wobbling step inside and collapsed. When he hit the floor, everything came tumbling out. His bowels scattered messily across the wood like a demented game of curling, bumping and sliding over each other. The life in his eyes vanished as his pupils dilated and rolled back into his head. His eyelids did not close but allowed only a limited view of his dead white globes.

During the course of Sandy's sublime entrance, Dorothy's lips had bunched and tightened, holding back both screams and vomit.

Angela hurried to the door and slammed it closed. The bang of the wood echoed in the church like the clang of a jail cell. She knelt down next to Sandy's body and rested her hands on his back. He was still warm.

Gary had turned away as soon as death stumbled in. He did not see Sandy fall, or the aftermath of his spill, he only heard the wetness oozing out – but that was enough. He looked back to the sanctuary and saw that a group of congregation members had gathered at the door, including Tina.

"Angela…" he said, motioning to the growing crowd.

"Christ… don't let them see."

Gary took the order happily as an opportunity to leave. He blocked people's view and herded them back inside the sanctuary.

"Dorothy," Angela said, "get a sheet. We can't let them see this."

There was no response.

"Dorothy! For fuck's sake, get a sheet!"

Dorothy snapped back into the moment. She grabbed a tablecloth and the two of them lowered it over Sandy's remains. Angela had to nudge a few of Sandy's more overreaching innards toward his body so they would all fit.

The grey fabric inadequately hid the contortions of his mangled form, and as the red soaked through in dark patches, Angela thought it looked like a cloud, only one that rained blood.

"Did he have any family here?" Angela eventually asked.

"No. Not at the church at least."

Angela, in a rare moment of childlike neediness, grabbed hold of Dorothy's hand. Dorothy grabbed back. The two found comfort in the warmth of their respective touches. On a basic level, they needed to be reminded that flesh could do more than bleed; it could also be gentle and offer comfort, it could heal and protect, it was not just there to suffer abuse and be shredded. Two hands locked in a tender touch; this was also the natural state of things.

"What are we going to do?" whispered Dorothy.

"Whatever we can."

"And what exactly can we do?"

"I don't know yet, Dorothy. I don't know."

CHAPTER 20

Flora Thompson never asked for much. She had resigned herself years ago to the encroaching decay of her eighty-five year old body. It didn't seem a terrible fate to her, to allow the natural progression of life, as God had designed it, to slow one down. It was true, she had lost the ability to do many things she loved, such as boisterous nights at the Willow Creek Dance Hall or ice fishing the way her father had taught her, but out growing the frivolities of youth was just a part of getting old. The rule was: if she could no longer manage it by herself, then that was the end of it. Even attending the service at St. Paul's United Church, when she could no longer make the trip up Highway 7, was on the chopping block. The preservation of her impressive church attendance was not her idea; it was Matthew's. She would never have burdened her grandson with lugging her weary bones twenty minutes out of town just so she could enjoy the comfort of her religion. But, he had insisted and he was persistent.

As Matthew stood over her eyeless body, which had been laid across the back pew in restless slumber, he condemned his own tenacity. He should not have brought her; he should have just let her be. Now, because of his meddling, she had lost both her eyes and fallen into a feverish coma. Periodically, her limbs would shake and tease Matthew with the promise she might awaken, but thus far, they turned out to be nothing more than the jittering of nerves.

He sat down next to her and propped up her head on his leg. She seemed to breath easier that way. He brushed the thin, grey hair from her face, which was beaded with sweat.

Chris approached from the other end of the pew with a cup of water and a cloth. Matthew remained hunched over Flora's head, his attention transfixed on her breathing. Chris kept a distance between them, keenly aware of their personal space. He waited patiently, but not intrusively, till Matthew was ready to receive him. Finally, he looked up.

"Here," was all Chris said, and offered the water and cloth.

"Thanks," Matthew replied and accepted both.

Neither was certain exactly how to react to the other, though, in Matthew's case, he didn't much care at that exact moment. Chris, on the other hand, knew he hated seeing Matthew in pain and wanted to help.

Matthew soaked the cloth and gently spread the cool liquid across Flora's forehead. It looked as though it eased her.

From the doorway of the sanctuary, Angela and Dorothy stepped in. Each carried with them more grey tablecloths, bunched in their hands like dreary bouquets. Everyone watched as the two of them marched up the aisle and unfolded the sheets over Don's body. They covered his disfigured corpse as ceremonially as possible, not only to relieve everyone of the sight, but also to reintroduce some order into the chaos. Messes needed to be cleaned and the dead honoured for the sake of sanity.

After the sheets were tucked around Don as neatly as possible, Angela noticed someone was missing.

"Gary," she asked with a grave tone, "where's Rick?"

"I don't know."

"He's gone," Tina interjected.

"Gone? What do you mean? Where did he go?"

"He didn't really go anywhere. We were in here, with him. He started pacing and then he was just gone."

"I don't understand. And Bruce, what about Bruce? Where is he?"

"He's gone, too."

"Tina, you're not making sense."

"What part of this makes any sense?" Emily barked, stepping out from the silent crowd and strolling down the aisle toward Angela.

"Somebody had to see where he went."

"Is that so?" Emily prodded.

"Yes. He couldn't have just vanished."

"You're right. Maybe he turned into a moth and flew away, or maybe a snake and slithered out the vents. Honestly, after everything I've seen today, I wouldn't be the least bit shocked. You think Rick is still just a man? Are you really that ignorant?"

"I think something is happening that we don't understand... That *I* don't understand. But whatever it is, it has to be bound by some rules."

Emily stopped right in front of Angela with Don's body dividing the space between them. She was a good half a foot taller than Angela, which added to her intimidation – not that she needed the help.

"You don't understand? Then let me make it simple. We were touched by God today and He's pissed."

"Emily, that kind of talk is not going to help. It's just going to frighten people," added Dorothy, as she got up from Don's body and took a stand next to Angela.

"They should be afraid. Are you going to tell me you're not?"

Dorothy didn't answer. Instead, she averted her eyes to the faceless, human-shaped sheet that was sprawled at her feet. Its dehumanizing anonymity haunted her and sent her into retreat. She took a seat in a nearby pew. Angela, however, stood her ground.

"Tell me, Angela," Emily continued her assault, "where do you think Rick went? Or Bruce? Or explain to me, how did Flora's eyes end up in someone else's head? We all saw it. Tina and I have been racking our brains, but we can't figure it out. Maybe you can. Go ahead, explain it."

"I can't."

"You can't." Emily glanced back at Tina who remained buried in the congregation. The two of them encouraged each other with a satisfied look.

"Um, excuse me…" Susan's polite voice barely garnered the attention it sought. "I just wanted to say, um, is this helping?"

"That's right. We're wasting time. We should be talking about what we're going to do, not arguing," said Gary in an effort to bolster Susan's message.

"Okay," Angela agreed. "So, what do we know?"

"There's something keeping us here, something powerful." Chris decided to join the conversation. If fates were to be discussed, he wanted to be a part of it.

"Not *something*," Emily corrected him.

"Yes, *something*. We don't know what it is," said Angela forcefully.

"We do know, we just don't want to admit it."

"What is it then, Emily? God?"

"Do you know of anything else that can do that?" she said and pointed to Flora's crippled form. "If we don't start accepting what has come upon us, then we really are doomed."

"Fine, then lets say it is God. Where does that leave us? Where do you suggest we start?"

"We're being punished, Angela. Just like Rick said."

Susan flicked her hair and raised her hand. "Can we talk about how we're going to get out of here?" she asked, like she wanted to be excused from the class.

"There is no getting out of here!" Emily screamed. "Were you all not listening? He's not going to let us leave."

"We have to get out of here," Angela responded. "We have to. It wants our children. Or, did you miss that part? It's after our kids. That's what nobody wants to talk about, right? It said we owe it one child and it'll spare us all. If this thing is God, then we really have no choice. We already know the answer, we know how to get out of here. Give it one of the kids. Is that what you're trying to sell us, Emily?"

"No way. No fucking way," Chris whispered to himself.

Emily felt the eyes of the congregation descend upon her.

"We wouldn't be here if it wasn't for you, you whore," Emily hissed. Perhaps it was not the most amicable response, but teeth were bared and Emily wanted to bite first.

"So, there it is," Angela tried to brush it aside, but the sticky accusation could not be shaken off that easily.

"You got knocked up and brought Rick into this church. You opened your filthy legs, and then you opened the door and welcomed him in. It's your fault. I hope you understand that. I hope you realize that everyone here is thinking exactly what I'm saying. I really hope you do. I hope you feel it."

Across the sizable audience that watched the two titans battling it out, Angela searched for a single comforting face. She found none.

"Rick is not the man I knew. Not anymore. He's something else now, you have to believe me."

"That's great, Angela. But it doesn't change where we are, or the fact that you brought him here. We're suffering for your sins."

"That's enough, Emily!" Gary hollered. "Angela is not to blame. I don't think anyone in this room is responsible for what's happening. We're just fish in a barrel here, and we'll be easy shooting unless we can stop all this bullshit and work on how we're actually going to get out of here."

"Gary, we aren't going to solve anything until..." Emily was loud, but Gary was louder.

"If you're not talking about how we get out of here, then you need to shut up. That's the new rule, okay? Just shut up."

"You can't make rules," Emily scoffed.

"Shut up."

"God won't be defied..."

"Shut up!"

"I agree with Gary. Emily should shut up," Dorothy added modestly.

Emily waited for someone to stand with her, but no one came. Begrudgingly, she stepped out of the spotlight and back into the disjointed congregation. She again found her spot in one of the pews next to Michael, who wrapped his arms around her. Her protest continued subtly through a series of expertly timed sighs and grunts.

Only Angela occupied the front of the sanctuary now. She felt obligated to offer some kind of leadership, or at least general direction. Her thoughts, however, remained focused on Emily's spiteful comments. After all the carnage that confronted them, how could Emily still find time for petty name-calling? What disturbed Emily so much about her relationship with Rick? Angela didn't have the first clue. But, she reasoned, there were bigger peaches to flambé than pondering Emily's grudges. The congregation needed a sense of purposefulness to ward off the impinging despair. It was time to propose some menial job work. Angela, who had once been promoted to the prestigious level of shift supervisor at Bob's Fresh Grocer, felt up to the task.

"Okay, so here's what I think we should do. First, we can't leave Don lying out here like this. We'll have to find a place to move both him and Sandy. Second, like Gary said, if we're going to be in here for a bit, which seems likely, we need to clean the pulpit, the carpet, the walls, everything. Lastly, we may not feel it now, but we're all going to get hungry sooner or later. We should figure out what food we have and start dishing it out per family. Does that sound good to everyone?"

Heads nodded, but no one answered. That's about as much enthusiasm as Angela expected.

Susan's meek hand lifted into the air again. Angela was not sure exactly how to deal with her self-declared pupil.

"Uh, yes Susan?" she pointed to her.

"I have something to add to the list."

"Of course, I'm not the boss. I'm just suggesting what to do. We all have to decide together."

"Okay, in that case, don't you think we should check on the children?"

CHAPTER 21

In the musty seclusion of the basement, Clara had been biding not only her time, but that of the children as well. Much like Angela, she had tasked the children with little odds and ends to keep them busy. They gathered the loose construction paper, organized then reorganized the chairs, and made sure each jar of paint had the correct colour-coordinated lid. However, as ten minutes turned into thirty, and thirty into fifty, the effectiveness of these distractions had begun to wane, and even the children could tell something was wrong.

The gravity with which Don had spoken to Clara had made an unshakable impression. Never had she seen Don so severe, not even when John Crates stood up and died of a heart attack in the middle of one of his sermons. His composure was not easily dispelled, but then again, the windstorm they had just run through would be enough to give anyone the jitters. Clara thought of the clouds she had seen, those contorting masses of black oil. She tried to imagine their hypnotic movement, but found it impossible to recreate. It was unlike any other storm she had ever seen. It didn't move with the wind – it had moved with purpose.

While her thoughts continued to till the mystery, her hand had taken to flicking her lighter back and forth.

The nervous reflex gifted the flame a brief life and then snatched it away as quickly as it came.

Clara leaned against one of the moveable walls, adjusting her loosely-fitted jean capris as she sat down against the cold, stone floor with a weary sigh. What she wanted most was to fall into her snuggly sofa with a cold beer and some reruns of *Buffy the Vampire Slayer*. The tale of a powerful heroine besting bad guys seemed irresistible in that moment.

Once she was seated, her incessant flicking of the lighter momentarily halted and the flame remained on. Her lost and longing sight became trapped in its glow.

The meek light reached into the dark with caution. The dark reached back. A dull moan grew in the basement, as if in protest to the flame itself. It sounded like the pipes had been stricken with an infection and their sore throats sung in pain. Whatever spurred the outburst, it was clear the flame was not welcome and Clara snapped her lighter closed. As soon as she did, the moaning stopped. The basement again was silent but for the whispers of the children.

Stanley Rosenthal shot out from around the corner of the wall, sending a jolt of adrenaline through Clara's body. Once Clara regained her composure, and the wall behind her stopped rocking back and forth, she felt ready to acknowledge Stanley's impatience.

"What is it you need Stan?"

"You're smoking."

"No. No I'm not," she said, more than a little annoyed.

"Yes you are."

"Stanley! What did I just say?"

"You shouldn't smoke inside," he pressed. "My mom told me to tell her if you smoked around us."

Before she could respond, Clara had to subdue the urge to curse out Emily and her self-righteousness. Did

Emily really think she was that careless to smoke around the children? She took a breath and got to her feet, armed with a carefully worded response.

"Well, Stanley, you're mother is right. I shouldn't smoke around you. Smoking is bad. So, luckily for both of us, I wasn't smoking."

"Why do you do it if it's bad?"

"Sometimes we don't always do things that make sense. It's a weird adult thing that you needn't worry about." She waited for him to leave, but he didn't.

"We're finished," he said eventually.

"Everything is done? Are all the paints put away?"

"Yes."

"I mean neatly placed where they should be, not just dumped under the table like they usually are."

"We did that."

"Okay, let me see."

Clara placed the lighter into her pocket and let Stanley lead her back into the classroom.

The children looked as though they had been through war. They were tired and disheartened, dressed in sad, sleepy faces. Samantha Rosenthal rested her head on the table and didn't even turn to greet Clara as she entered. Dylan sat in the chair in front of her with an overstated pout and crossed arms. The only one who didn't seem agitated by all the waiting, but should have been, was Alex. He stood in the corner, facing the room with his hands politely clasped behind his back. He seemed neither pleased nor aggravated; he looked more like he was awaiting something.

"Hey gang," Clara said with exhausted cheer. "I know you all want to leave, but I'm sure it won't be much longer."

"I have to pee," said Samantha, who finally raised her sleepy head.

"I know sweetie, but we were asked to wait down here and we told them we would. We just have to be patient."

"But I have to go *now*."

"You sure you can't hold it any longer?"

"No…" She performed a squirming dance of agony in her seat.

Although Clara was accustomed to Samantha's dramatics, she believed she was telling the truth. The only available bathroom – other than the one in Don's office – was located in the mess hall. She was sure she could trust the children alone for the five minutes it would take to rush Samantha upstairs and back again. What could five minutes hurt? On top of that, Clara admitted to herself that it was a welcome excuse for her to find out what was going on.

"Alright, we'll go." She took Samantha by the hand. "The rest of you just hold tight."

"What are we supposed to do?" Stanley blurted out.

"Have all the pencil crayons been sharpened?"

"No." He regretted his question.

"Then you know what to do. We'll be back before you know it."

She led Samantha down the hallway of temporary walls. Perhaps it was due to the time they had spent in the maze, but the hallway felt like it was shrinking. Both of them were privately relieved once they stepped out of the labyrinth and the room at last fully opened to them.

Samantha's dressy pink shoes tapped noisily across the floor, announcing every little step as they approached the base of the stairs. Each innocent click of her heel added to Clara's anxiety; Don said to keep the children downstairs, but when you have to go, you have to go. Still, she considered picking Samantha up just to spare herself the tap, tapping reminders that she was doing something wrong.

The rusty drain in the centre of the room made a sour hiss as they passed by. Clara was familiar with the sound, but Samantha was startled and wrapped her arms around Clara's leg. She buried her head into the back of Clara's thigh, trapping her breath against her skin. The sudden warmth sent a wave of shivers through Clara's leg.

"Hey, it's okay," said Clara, placing her hand on Samantha's head.

"It's snakes!" she screamed into Clara.

"It's not snakes. It's just the drain."

"The snakes are in the drain!"

"Samantha, I promise, there are no snakes. It's just water that's dripped down there. Just like a sink. Everything's fine."

Everything was certainly not fine, Clara thought to herself, but it seemed like that's what Samantha needed to hear. Angela would not have left Alex in the basement without so much as an update unless something was seriously wrong.

Samantha pulled her face off the support leg. A string of clear snot ran from the inner canals of her nose all the way down to Clara's knee. It was a surprisingly sizable discharge.

Clara helped steady Samantha back on her own two feet.

"Alright, Samantha, you ready to get out of here now?"

"No," came the response, obstructed by the excessive wiping of her nose.

"No? Don't you have to go to the bathroom?"

Samantha did not answer verbally, but the shame that hung on her face said it all. Clara looked at Samantha's frilly dress – as if she needed proof – and saw the stains.

Damn that drain! Now what excuse did Clara have to see what was going on up there?

Just then, an airy creak glided down from the top step of the stairs. The second creak came a few seconds later.

"Oh, good," Clara breathed and smiled at Samantha. "It's about time someone came down."

The two of them listened for the third step, but none came. Their eyes waited impatiently at the bottom of the stairs for someone to emerge. Strange, Clara noticed, the lights were not turned on; whoever was descending the stairs was doing it in utter darkness.

"Hello?" Clara spoke up. "Who's there?"

There was no reply. Clara waited for some kind of response, and then, one came. The third step was not a delicate creak; it was a stomp. More than that, it was the wailing of strained wood on the verge of cracking. Another thump followed with enough force for Clara to feel it in her skull. The thunderous steps suggested a weight and power far beyond anyone in the congregation, or anyone, anywhere, for that matter.

Samantha latched herself once again to Clara's leg, though this time, Clara did not even notice.

Two more booming footsteps called out from the shadows. Whatever it was, it was drawing nearer. Clara backed away. It was then she noticed Samantha's weight attached to her leg. The rest of the children had gathered at the threshold of the makeshift hallway.

Although Clara's primal urge for self-preservation had coaxed her heart into a ramped-up frenzy and warmed the muscles in her arms and legs, she fought the instinct to hide herself. First and foremost, she had an obligation to the children. It was safe to assume that whatever was coming down the stairs was not their friend. It would not be calmed by a kindly welcome or be softened by innocent children. There was a menacing tone in its relentless thumping, like an oncoming avalanche that enjoyed the chase.

Clara picked Samantha up and handed her over to her brother, then kneeled down in front of the children and attempted to appear calm.

"I want everyone to hide, alright?" she said quickly.

"What is that banging?" asked Stanley.

"I just need everyone to find the best hiding spot they can and stay there until I call for you. Can you guys do that for me?"

"It's a game?" piped up Dylan, from the back of the group.

"Yes, that's right."

"No, it's not." Alex refuted. He and Clara shared an understanding of the situation, except Alex didn't seem to care much for putting the rest of the group at ease.

The thumping of the beast on the stairs played in tandem with Clara's heartbeat, bringing her back to the moment.

"Everybody ready? Are you thinking of a place to hide?" she asked, but only saw a few nods. "Alright, go!"

The kids scattered into the maze, but Clara didn't follow. She stood and turned to face whatever might be making those terrible noises.

The stomping had reached such an intensity that it took Clara all her strength not to cover her ears. With her promise to protect the children feeding her courage, she edged closer to the stairs in the chance she might steal a glimpse of what was coming. The shadows denied her even a hint. The harsh bangs suggested a mammoth animal, but the way they slid from step to step gave the impression of a peculiar refinement. It could not simply be a wild thing for, like the clouds before, it moved with a human awareness.

The overhead lights in the basement reached as far as the fourth step from the bottom. Whatever it was, it had stopped on the fifth.

Her right hand grabbed her left and held it tight, as if to offer it comfort. Soon, they were both clasped together in front of her and she found herself pleading to God for support, which in her mind was as mysterious and awesome as the thing on the stairs.

"Oh God, please give me strength. For the children." After the words were spoken aloud, there was a measurable change in her fortitude. It was as if her courage had been recharged, though, it could not be said whether that was due to God's influence or her own remarkable resilience.

The quiet is worse than the thunder, she thought, staring into the silent abyss. She envisioned a rabid creature with drool and teeth, jumping from the darkness, its claws aimed for her throat. She almost longed for it; at least then, she would know where she stood. The torment of uncertainty was far more dreadful than whatever it may be, monster, demon, or otherwise.

While she awaited the emergence of the beast, something wet touched the back of her leg. *Samantha? No, she's hiding. This is colder, wetter.* Clara was reminded of the children and their finger-painting, until the hand slithered under the edge of her pants and up her thigh.

She didn't scream, but quickly pulled away and spun around like a twirling dancer poised for her next move.

To Clara's shock, the algid touch belonged to Bruce, though, it was not the Bruce she knew. What was hunched before her bore a resemblance to the familiar piano player, but was marred with scars and painted with sloppy coats of blood. The two gashes that ripped down his face appeared deeper than before, as if they had been freshly reopened. Most startling were his unbefitting grey eyes that seemed to glow when set against all that red. His foggy pupils followed her with an intimidating thirst.

His body remained squatting like a frog near her feet. A smear of blood trailed from him to the opening of the drain, which made it seem, impossibly, that he had crawled out of its five-inch diameter.

As the shock of his disfigured visage started to fade, Clara discovered she felt pity for his sniveling form, despite his repugnance. He didn't move but for a gentle swinging back and forth like a rocking horse. His hands cupped his mouth, catching a minimal flow of bile that dribbled from his swollen lips like a helpless baby. It was all so bizarre that she completely forgot the footsteps on the stairs.

She knew she had to say something, but what could she say to a man in such a state? She wiped the bloody fingerprints off her leg before she managed her first words to him.

"Bruce? What happened?" was the best she had to offer.

His reaction reminded her of the feral rabbit she once accidentally startled in her mother's garden. The rabbit had attempted to hop away from her, but once it learned it was cornered, it had no choice but to lunge with its teeth bared. She cried for two straight hours that afternoon, not only because the bunny had scared her, but also because it so readily acted against its nature – a disturbing insight she never forgot.

Before she could even raise her arms to guard herself, Bruce was on top of her.

His hands felt like slippery tongues as they fumbled against her shoulders. She tried to push him off, but he slammed her hard against the cement.

Jagged fingernails dug into the flesh of her arms and rooted themselves into the fat just beneath the skin. For the first time, Clara screamed.

In response to her outcry, Bruce's lips tightened into a smile and he brought his teeth down around her exposed collarbone. He bit ferociously, like a dog with a chew toy, and yanked back with his jaws as if attempting to pull the bone loose.

As the blood spilled out and the pain dug in, Clara finally released her suppressed survival instinct and roared like a lioness..

She shoved her recently manicured nails into the open wounds on Bruce's face. Once they were deep enough to take hold of a solid flap of forehead, she pulled with all her might. If Bruce had not fallen off her, she surely would have torn his face in two.

He toppled to the soaking ground and scurried into the corner.

Without so much as a wince from the punctures in her arms or the bite on her chest, Clara shot to her feet, letting the blood fall where it may. She heaved and stared down her enemy as if ready to charge. She could not allow the children to be harmed, so she ignored her fear and took the offensive.

Bruce rose to his feet and reached into his pocket. The straight razor that had carved the stripes down his face was now his to wield. With a mime's flourish, he exaggeratedly flipped open the blade and used it to trace the outline of Clara's body in the air.

She took a step to her right, he reacted with a step to his left and the two began to circle each other.

If he was afforded even one decent swipe with that razor, Clara could be for the worms, and how could she protect the children then? Without warning, she darted into the maze.

Once she was out of his sight, she momentarily succumbed to her wounds. Clara applied pressure to the bite and it reacted with an aching scream. After she learned of its depth, she wished she had not; her index finger could almost feel around the entire circumference of her collarbone. Stilted breaths took over.

Bruce approached the entrance to the hallway and Clara narrowly avoided him by ducking into one of the unused spaces she had sectioned off. She was thankful none of the kids had chosen that room as their hiding spot, or she may have led Bruce right to them.

The stalking abomination made no effort to conceal himself as the sound of his wet, slinking stagger left no mystery as to where he was.

With her body pressed against one of the makeshift walls, she listened to Bruce pace back and forth. With each step came a slight stumble. The sound of his movements gradually faded until they disappeared altogether. Again, there was the return of that unbearable silence.

She stopped moving. She stopped breathing. She just waited.

The delicate, unnoticeable sounds of the basement became impossibly heightened. Clara could soon tell where each little breath was coming from. She hoped Bruce did not share her keen hearing.

From her classroom, a pencil rolled off the desk and interrupted the subtle soundscape like the sound of a dissonant drum. It crashed against the floor at an almost deafening volume and it seemed like the room itself gasped.

Before she could act, the wall she leaned on moved. It bobbed against her as someone on the other side brushed passed. She decided to take the chance it was not one of the kids and shoved the wall as hard as she could. The full-bodied resistance on the other side confirmed that it had to be Bruce. So she pushed harder.

With a physical strength she had rarely utilized, she bulldozed her way through the hallway, toppling the walls like dominoes with Bruce pinned on the other side of the large board. She charged with enough force to lift Bruce off his feet and carry him all the way to the kitchen. With a last barbarian heave, she hurled the board along with Bruce through the doorway. Hanging pots battered his head before he cracked his temple against the metal edge of the sink.

He landed, motionless against the floor with the broken wall on top of him.

Clara leaned against the sturdy doorframe in an effort to remain standing after her rampage. She looked over the man she essentially squashed and was surprised, considering his lacerations, that he still had blood to bleed. Yet, there it pooled.

She placed one hand against her throat as she attempted take control of her panting. Feeling the air rush in and out of her trachea was somehow soothing.

She closed the kitchen door and latched it.

"Kids, it's time to go," she spoke from her gut.

There was no response from the other side of the room. No movement whatsoever. Time stretched like she had never experienced.

"Alex!" she screamed, "Samantha! Dylan…"

Eventually, something caught her eye. Her head snapped toward its direction as Stanley timidly made his way out of the decimated hallway. Tears streamed down his face. Behind him with matching distress was Samantha. The other children, including Alex, surfaced in time.

"Oh God, thank you!" Clara exclaimed as her own tears joined the party. However, her thankfulness was short-lived.

The kitchen door came to life behind her. Bruce was back and the metal hook on the latch did little to contain his furious pounding, so Clara braced herself against it. Every hit felt like the door was about to give way and the thumping quickly bruised her back.

The children scattered back into the dark like frightened mice. Clara knew they had to take advantage of Bruce's entrapment while they could. Judging by the sound of cracking wood and failing hinges, their window of opportunity seemed on the verge of closing.

"No, come back!" she pleaded, over Bruce's banging. "Don't hide, run! Stanley, grab Samantha, grab everyone and run upstairs, now!"

No one moved.

"You listen to me, you little fucks! Get your asses upstairs right now, goddamn it, or I'll spank you so hard you'll shit blood!" Clara channeled the memory of her own mother's occasional rage. It worked. She had fought fear with fear and she had won; the kids ran across the basement and started filtering upstairs.

Behind her, the kitchen door cracked halfway down the middle with a tremendous snap and Clara felt the wood start to shift. Through the split came the tip of Bruce's razor. It lodged itself into Clara's upper back, just under her left shoulder blade. She could almost hear the cold metal grate against her bone.

She leaned forward just enough to escape the razor's reach. In response, Bruce's hammering raised to new heights of hysteria. He growled like a rabid dog and clawed like a bear.

Alex followed his classmates, but stopped at the foot of the stairs. He froze on the spot, staring at Clara. Unlike the other children, now all evacuated, Alex was fully aware of what was at stake.

While the others were consumed by their own terror, Alex was concerned with Clara's. *There she is*, he thought to himself, *the hero holding back the monster.*

She looked back at him with her face red and glazed with sweat. Greasy strands of hair stuck to her forehead. Not even the violent pounding jolted them from the hold they had on her face.

"Alex," she said quietly, "you have to run. Get out of here, please. Go to your mom."

Clara was terrified, but if she could at least protect Alex from the maniac behind the door, then she would have the courage to face whatever might come.

"You're doing the right thing," she encouraged. "Now go! You have to go, Alex."

He did what he was told and charged up the stairs.

Clara smiled and closed her eyes as the door began to fold down on her. She pressed her head back against the encroaching wood to strengthen its resistance.

She thought if these were to be her last moments, it was at least fitting she spent them in the service of children. If her life had had a purpose, then that was it. She had devoted her existence to being a teacher and mentor to countless youth. So, to trade her life for the promise of theirs seemed an affable bargain. But the end was not all ease and satisfaction. There were certainly doubts and regrets she carried with her, as well: she never met someone who loved her, just her, more than any other, she never swam with sharks, or made that trip to Easter Island like she promised herself she would. But, what distressed her most, was the pain that no one really knew her. Her ability to keep secrets now seemed more like a detriment. She admitted that even Angela was not made privy to all of her; not the deep, dark stuff. Who had she kept herself secret for? Was she just a mystery chest filled with treasures, cursed by a lifetime of collecting locks and chains? Perhaps God, whoever, wherever and whatever He was, would know her. The notion was comforting and with Bruce gnawing just behind her head, she prayed it was true.

The sound of hurried footsteps coming down the stairs interrupted her doleful reflection.

"Yes!" she hollered. "Help, quick, I'm down here!"

Clara slammed her palms against the doorframe and locked her knees. If she could just keep Bruce back long enough for help to arrive, then maybe she, too, could be spared. Her muscles had started to shake, and fatigue threatened to collapse her entire body. Bruce by comparison, seemed to have only gained in strength.

Finally, her rescuer emerged. It was Alex, returned to defend his own protector. Though his valor was touching, she did wish he had brought someone who could have actually helped.

Alex grabbed one of the plastic chairs that were strewn across the floor and held it in front of him like a shield. He nodded to Clara as if to notify her he was ready. Clara just shook her head. She barely had the breath to speak, but she managed to steal a few words here and there.

"Alex. Go. I told you to go. Don't worry about me. I'll be fi…" Her last sentence was cut short as the door burst into a thousand splinters. Alex held the chair up to protect himself from the barrage of jagged wood daggers hurling through the air.

Clara was knocked face down onto the ground, letting out a grunt as she hit the cement.

The light in the kitchen flickered on and off like a thunderstorm in the ocean – pitch black with brief, terrifying flashes of luminance, always revealing something you did not want to see.

Bruce appeared, and then vanished into darkness, only to appear again in the next flash. Each time, he was slightly closer.

Alex shook at the sight of the monster's hideous smile.

Bruce grabbed hold of Clara's ankle, which ripped another scream from her. She reached desperately for something, anything she could take hold of.

Alex caught one of her hands in his and with all his limited might, started to pull. He pulled so hard, his rubber shoes squeaked as he kicked against the floor. The three were engaged in a twisted game of tug-of-war and Clara was the prize.

With one arm, Bruce yanked Clara into the kitchen like she weighed nothing more than a husk of corn. Alex blinked and suddenly his hands were empty.

Though the shuttering light masked her assault, Clara's agonizing screams painted a clear picture.

Afraid to stand as Clara's final witness, Alex, at long last took her advice and ran.

CHAPTER 22

By the time Alex reached the top of the stairs, the other children had already found themselves safely tucked away in the arms of their parents.

Over half of the congregation had gathered in the mess hall, but had kept a distance between themselves and the stairs leading into the pit of screams. Alex had emerged from that hell, to everyone's surprise, with only a few nicks and bruises.

With the scattered images of Clara's attack still rolling through his vision, Alex stared through the crowd with vacant eyes. His mind could gather only superficial observations. The day was dimmer than before. Everyone's Sunday clothes were dirty now. There were little red droplets all over everything. None of this distressed him, however. They were simply facts.

"Alex!" yelled Angela, as she pushed her way through the crowd.

Once she broke free of the mob, she rushed over to squeeze the stoicism out of her son. He was jolted back into his body when she lifted him off the ground and planted her warm cheek next to his. Her hands moved all over him as if he were made of something precious and at risk of falling apart.

"Are you okay? There was screaming, what happened?"

"Mom…" came his thin voice.

"Yes, buddy, what is it?"

"I couldn't hold on. I wasn't strong enough."

"What are you talking about?"

"Miss Muller. She's still down there."

"Clara's downstairs?"

Slowly, she lowered Alex back down to his feet. *Maybe Alex is mistaken. Maybe Clara came up with the other children and he just missed her. Please, let him be mistaken. Please!* Angela's gaze searched the congregation but she saw nothing to prove her son wrong. Reluctantly, her vision returned to the cavernous opening of the stairs. The screams she had heard, those pained howls, were Clara's. She escorted her son over to Susan, who had maneuvered herself to the front row.

"Take Alex," she said, handing him over.

"Sure. Why?" Susan inquired.

Angela turned away from her without responding. She knew she could not answer the question without forfeiting her composure.

Dorothy stepped out from the crowd.

"Where's Clara?" she asked Angela. After a moment of silence, she asked again, "Angela, where's my daughter?"

"The basement."

"Oh, Christ…" Dorothy's head began to shake. "No, no, I'm asking you about Clara. Where's my Clara?"

"Dorothy, she's still down there."

Dorothy charged over to the stairs. She had heard the screams as well as anybody else, and her imagination had run wild with scenes of unspeakable torture when the wailing reached its peak, but she had not allowed herself to imagine it was her daughter.

Dorothy stood at the entrance and peered down into the abyss. "Clara!" she bellowed hoarsely. "It's your mother. You get up here right this second. Enough fooling, you answer me now, Clara! Answer me! I said get up here! Clara!" She pounded the wood trim of the doorframe.

Angela waited for Dorothy to finish hurling her demands into the dark before she made her approach. Slowly, she placed one hand on Dorothy's shoulder and gently turned her around so they could speak face to face.

"Dorothy, we're going down there. We're going to find her."

"She never listens. I call her and call her. I tell her things, I tell her to stop smoking, I tell her it's okay to take a break every once in a while. But she never listens, not to me. Never to her dumb mom."

"Why don't you wait up here with everybody? I'll go see what's keeping her," Angela suggested delicately.

"No, I'm going. She's my daughter."

"I don't think that's a good idea."

"I don't care what you think. I'm going."

Reluctantly, Angela agreed.

"I'll come with you," Gary spoke up. He pealed himself away from Tina's arm and joined Angela and Dorothy.

"Fine," Angela confirmed. "Then we all go together."

She waited for other volunteers, but after some time it became clear no one else was going to join the rescue team. Everyone just stood there paralyzed, clutching the very children Clara had no doubt suffered, and screamed, and bled to protect. So the three of them turned their backs on the congregation's cowardice and set forth to find their friend, their daughter, their companion.

Angela reached along the wall of the stairs until her fingers bumped into the light switch. She held her breath and flicked it on. The light blinked to life without any trouble at all.

The dusty carpet that flopped down the stairs like a filthy tongue was not the most welcoming of starts, but if this was the path that swallowed Clara, then they were going to follow.

Their descent felt like they were sinking into a bog. The air was thicker in the basement and carried with it the pungent smell of sweat and death.

Angela was first to reach the bottom step, followed by Dorothy, who clung to the wall as if afraid she might suddenly drop away. Gary was not far behind them.

They noticed the floor first. Splintered wood sprayed across the grey stone almost the entire width of the room. Dorothy tromped through the pieces and headed toward the collapsed hallway.

"Clara, baby?" she called, and began to lift boards and shuffle through debris.

"Dorothy, wait for us. We should stay together," Angela said.

"I'll stay with her," Gary assured her.

"If you find anything," Angela added, before he made it too far, "you holler back. You let me know, and you hide her eyes. Understand?"

He nodded.

A silver glint from the floor attracted Angela's attention. She kneeled down and brushed away a few wood pieces to find Clara's lighter – something Clara was rarely without. Whether this was a good or bad omen, Angela did not want to decide, so she shoved it into her pocket before Dorothy could see.

Dorothy's voice had grown quieter the further she ventured, but still she persisted in calling Clara's name. The basement was not large enough to warrant the repetition, yet every five seconds, the widow uttered the name of her missing child, as if it were a chant to conjure her up. The harsh reality was, either Clara was no longer in the basement, or she was unable to answer.

Angela watched Dorothy and Gary edge deeper into the section of the classrooms that remained intact. In her black jeans pocket, she rolled the lighter back and forth and thought: *Clara should stop smoking*. She would be sure to tell her that, once they found her.

She examined the pattern of the wood splinters on the floor and realized they were, for the most part, all spraying from the same direction: away from the kitchen. It was then Angela noticed the door was missing, and the naked doorway, drowning in blackness, had been staring her straight in the face since she arrived. All the clues seemed to lead into its depths and Angela was left with no other option, but to follow them.

Without too much hesitation, she walked to the edge of the darkness and peered inside. A faint heat emanated from somewhere in the kitchen. Again, Angela's hand slid down the wall in search of a light switch. Her deer-like alertness told her there were eyes upon her; or, if not eyes, there was something in the room that had become aware of her, prompting her hand to roam more aggressively; eager to bring light upon whatever it was.

In her haste, her hand slipped onto something wet. Although the liquid was warm, a numbing sensation chilled up her arm and rested in the joint of her shoulder, effectively freezing it.

For fear that her hand would be drenched in red, should she pull it into the light, Angela decided to continue groping for the switch. Her shaky digits carried on and fumbled over soggy wallpaper before they found what they were searching for. They clenched the plastic light switch like it was a buoy in shark-laden waters. She flicked it on.

A spark flickered out from the bulb at first, giving a brief flash of the room. It lasted just long enough to reveal one detail; there was something lying at Angela's feet. After this tease, the light managed to squeeze out a bit more juice and the kitchen was illuminated.

It was Clara lying on the floor. She looked to be sleeping. Then, like a miracle, a twitch of life stirred in Clara's hand. She was hurt, but she was alive. Her head rose from the floor and she looked at Angela with a smile. The two of them glowed at each other. The love they shared had conquered the evil that threatened to tear them apart. Now that they were reunited, the darkness that surrounded them fell back timidly in the brilliant shine of their compassion. Together, they could withstand whatever life had in store for them.

All of this, of course, was a comforting concoction of Angela's traumatized mind. The effects of this intoxicating fantasy lasted a few moments before dissolving into the unrelenting horror on display before her.

Only a part of Clara was actually piled at her feet; though, which part was impossible to say — she had been so utterly disassembled. It was as though her body had been transformed into confetti, slice by slice. Her legs were spread open, but most of the flesh had been carved away and generously spread to all corners of the room. Like hollowing out a pumpkin, Clara's torso was open and the ribs snapped outwards so she could be effectively emptied. Angela stared into the gaping cavity that used to be her chest – the heart, the lungs, the stomach, everything was gone, meticulously diced beyond recognition. The hollowing procedure continued up to Clara's neck, leading to her head, which had been twisted back as if arched in profane ecstasy. Her eyes were open wide and also the only part of her body spared the frenzied slicing of the razor. The expression on her face told Angela that Clara had fully suffered the obliteration of every inch of her body.

Sometimes dreams are wrong, very wrong.

As the reality of each heinous detail dripped into Angela's consciousness, she could feel her stomach lurch in protest. She turned her back and grabbed hold of the doorway, as her vision grew dim around the edges. Her balance disintegrated and suddenly she was in free fall, though she remained standing with her back propped up by the wall. Uncontrollable gasps sent her body quaking, as if someone were jabbing a knife randomly into her stomach.

Dorothy came running with Gary chasing behind her. He would have restrained her, too, if the debris had not caused him to slip, sending him, face first, onto the cement.

"Clara are you in there?" Dorothy asked with heartbreaking innocence. She stumbled into the doorway and feasted on the full view of the remains of her daughter.

"Dorothy, stop! Don't look!" Angela jumped in front of her, but Dorothy was determined to see. She grabbed hold of Angela's shoulder and shoved her aside with enough force to slam her flat against the wall.

Gary got to his feet, but it was too late; Dorothy was already a witness.

"Clara… What are you doing?" she asked the bloody pile. The mass of torn flesh and cracked bone did not answer, nor did the tortured face that at least still resembled her daughter.

Dorothy collapsed to the floor like a building under demolition. Her knees gave way first, followed by each respective hip. The wave of structural failure followed up her spine until she landed on all fours.

The thing in front of her was not her daughter. It was not possible. Her special girl, who she loved, who she cared for beyond all else, who she had periodically taken for granted, was reduced to this ghastly thing – an inhuman sculpture, the unbearable hideousness of bodily life reduced to bodily death.

"No," pleaded Dorothy, her words fighting through festering sorrow. "God please, no. Christ, no!"

CHAPTER 23

By the time the first night crept upon the church, everyone in the congregation was ready for the sweet escape of sleep. Not just the congregation in fact, but the entire building seemed quiet and ready to forget the atrocities committed within its walls. The church rested, still and alone, on the open field, lulled by the chilled air and silently passing twilight.

People felt safer in numbers, so everyone had remained in the sanctuary, which had been scrubbed clean except for the stains on the fabric mural. This was not the only housekeeping duty that had kept the congregation busy; the bodies of their fallen members had been moved to the basement kitchen, food from the picnic had been reorganized and evenly divided among families, and an overall sense of structure had been established. There had developed two main overseers, Angela and Gary, who naturally became the ones people went to. They filtered, debated and made decisions for the good of the group. Dorothy would have also been part of the elite three if Clara's murder had not pushed her into catatonia.

These tidy, comforting chores of cleaning and organizing were all well and good, but the main problem, the problem of escape, remained ignored for the most part.

Cushions and blankets from various rooms in the church lined the pews, covered the floors, and anywhere else that had been taken for a bed. Candles lit the sanctuary soothingly with a warm, gentle illumination.

Angela remained awake and sat on a pew with her knees pressed up toward her chin. She had discovered in grade two that this was her most self-soothing position, one where she felt protected and solid. Next to her slept Alex, wrapped in a thick quilt Angela had found stuffed away in a forgotten cupboard. Before drifting off, Alex had remarked how the candles reminded him of their Christmas services, which every year used little flames to symbolize the star that announced the birth of the baby Jesus. Angela hoped everyone shared that cheery association. Maybe they did, she thought to herself, noting how quickly the room had succumbed to sleep. However, neither the candles nor the quiet helped Angela rest. She did not trust in the peace they peddled.

A trickle of cold, blue moonlight snuck through the top of the stained-glass window and poured down the length of one of the pews like an elegant brush stroke from an invisible, but gifted hand. *But, whose hand?* Angela asked herself, as soon as the light appeared. She sat a mere three rows down from it. Was that play of light supposed to be God's attempt at comfort, or was it a symbol of His powerlessness to intervene in any meaningful way? Was He merely the God of smoke and mirrors, or was it just coincidence that brought this visual delicacy into Angela's view? She half-hoped there was no reason for the light at all – that it was just nature doing something natural – for if, indeed, there was a Mastermind at work, then He had a lot to answer for. First question Angela would demand was: why Clara? Why was she the one meant to suffer?

Furthermore, why was this beast, this Behemoth, allowed to terrorize them? Was it all a sick test of faith? If it was, then the simple morals Angela had pieced together through her short life were more than enough to convince her that the test itself was bullshit, unfair, and could only be concocted by a God of supreme cruelty and malevolence. If she were God, she considered, she probably would have skipped the inventions of pain and death; it seemed obvious that life would be better lived without those things. And she certainly wouldn't have kept so many secrets and allowed her children to blunder through torture after torture with the hope that blind faith would carry them. Was God's morality so deeply undeveloped? These harsh questions eventually led to a suspicion she had been toying with for a while now – they were alone. There was no Heavenly Father or Holy Ghost. No one listened to the private prayers of the devout, or rewarded the righteous for doing good. All they had was each other, as tenuous as that was. However, if Angela conceded that, then Clara really was gone. She did not shimmer off like a roaring star into Heaven to be reunited with her father, whom she loved. Instead, the reality was, she had been gutted for protecting the children, and there was no eternity of peace as a reward for her valor. She was ended. The notion of such injustice boiled up a repellent nihilism, and brought Angela back to God. Her thoughts continued in this vein and circled around each other like a rusted hamster wheel. Even within herself, Angela was trapped.

Or, maybe that thing from the woods really was God. At least that would better explain the current state of things. The beast was a merciless master, an attentive author of each and every agony that plagued them. Despite that, it had one positive characteristic. At least, unlike the depiction of the crucified man Angela now

171

glanced at, the Behemoth was honest about its immorality.

"Hi, Angela," a voice whispered from behind her.

She turned her head and was shocked to see Tina standing there. The makeup Tina wore so thickly, now stained her tired face like the peeling paint of a neglected house. Needless to say, her usual sense of cheer had escaped her, but that was okay, Angela liked her better that way.

"Hello, Tina."

"Am I interrupting? You looked... pensive."

"No, it's fine. What's wrong? Couldn't sleep?"

"I tried," she said, while taking a seat next to Angela – a seat that was not offered. "But, I doubt I'll get a wink of rest tonight. Gary's out like a rock. You'll probably hear him snoring in about ten minutes. I usually find candles so soothing, but not tonight."

"No? Me, neither. But, it's the best we can do with the power gone."

"There used to be an old generator downstairs."

"It's still there, but we didn't want to use up all the gas just yet, if we don't need to."

"That's good thinking. Who knows how long we'll be here."

"We know. He gave us two nights, Tina. Two nights and this was the first we wasted." Angela decided to be blunt.

"Yes," she said dismissively. "And how about you, are you going to get any rest?"

"I'm not worried about me."

"Well, you need to get rest for your son's sake, then. You won't be much use to him exhausted. How is he doing?"

"I don't know. He hasn't spoken since it happened. I tried talking to him, but he just stares."

"Maybe he's in shock. It's been a hard day."

"Hard?" Angela responded with thick sarcasm. "Oh, I don't know about that. There were some good moments, too. Depends on your perspective." Angela restrained the maniacal cackle that was building within her. A hard day? Was that really the best word Tina could have found to describe it? Angela found plenty of others: a shitty, brutal, fucked-up day. A day so awful, most people would kill themselves before having to relive it.

"Sorry, you're right. That was stupid. I'm just at a loss at what to say, of how to handle everything that's happened. That's all." Finally, Tina had revealed some honest emotions. Angela latched onto them.

"I know. I thought I knew what it was to be stuck in a nightmare, but I had no idea until now."

"Gary told me about the basement. He said how you found Clara and I wanted to say that I'm so sorry." She placed her hand on Angela's knee. "Normally, I'd say she's with God, but, I don't know what that means anymore. So, all I can say is I'm sorry."

There was no response given, nor did Tina wait around for one before she got up and walked away. It was clear she had offered her sympathy earnestly. Unlike her normal gossip-driven self, this display of compassion was solely to show her support, not elicit a reaction. It was tender and genuine, and it was for this reason Angela felt compelled to say something.

"Thank you," Angela eventually uttered quietly, unsure if Tina even heard her since she was already halfway across the room.

Once Angela couldn't bear to look at the stream of moonlight anymore, her eyes adjusted to the dark and soon she could see all the way to the pulpit. Someone was standing there, with their back turned looking upward at the fabric mural of bloody worship. It was a few seconds before Angela realized it was Dorothy.

Angela's pew creaked as Chris slid down closer to her. She started to suspect there was not a single person in the room who was actually asleep.

"She hasn't moved in hours," he spoke softly, motioning to Dorothy.

"I'm not surprised. I doubt she'd move even if the room were on fire. She probably wouldn't care much right now."

"Mrs. Morris, can I ask you a question, and can you answer honestly?"

"Chris, you can ask me anything, just so long as you drop the Morris. It's Angela."

"Alright, Angela, but, do you promise to answer the way you really feel? I asked my parents, but my mom keeps feeding me shit."

"I'll do my best."

"Do you think we're going to live through this?" he asked, seriously. There was a stumble in the question, as if he didn't really want to ask it, or rather, didn't really want it answered.

"Yes. We will. We have to."

"We *have* to? What the fuck does that mean?" His voice rose, but was restrained enough not to wake Alex.

"It means I've decided to be hopeful, for the sake of my son. There's only so much loss you can take before something good has to happen."

"And that's really what you think?"

"Sure. Look, Chris, it's all I've got. Take it or leave it. I'll help you anyway I can, but don't depend on me to lift your spirits, not after Clara."

"I'm not asking you to help me feel warm and fuzzy. I doubt you could do that even if you tried. I don't really like to trust people."

"You're kind of an intense kid. How old are you anyway?"

"Sixteen."

"So, if you're not looking for hope, then why did you ask?"

"Everyone seems content to just sit here, but that's like waiting on the Titanic, hoping it will just suddenly start to float again. It won't. We're sinking. I feel it, Matthew feels it, and I think you feel it, too."

"Yeah."

"I think most people haven't really gotten it, yet. I saw Mr. Sawyer checking his phone, every few minutes, for a solid three hours. Three hours! Non-stop checking his stupid phone. We haven't had any contact out here all day, but he thinks, what? Someone is just going to call him up, out of the blue?"

"Maybe its worth it to keep trying."

"Trying, yes, that's worth it. But he's just wasting time. We're alone, and someone needs to go for help."

"Go outside? That's nuts."

"There's no other choice. No one is going to come and save us. We haven't been missing long enough for anyone to come looking, let alone looking for us at this shitty church. We're fucked, unless we do something."

"You didn't see what that thing did to Sandy."

"Good, don't tell me. I don't want to know .-- not if it will change my mind."

"It would," she said, remembering the horror for herself.

"It's the only plan I have."

"Well, it's not a very good one."

"Angela, I'm scared."

"We all are."

"I'm scared of what people might do once they realize nobody's going to call, and time runs out. There are fifty of us in this room. Only three seem to actually acknowledge what's happening. That's scary."

Angela met his eyes with mutual concern. Until then, her worries had focused mostly on Rick and his beast; she had not considered that her fellow congregation members could, in fact, turn on each other. Or, at least, she had not treated the threat seriously. How much pressure does it take to turn people into rabid dogs? Angela feared that before too long, she'd have the answer.

On this ominous note, Chris returned to the corner he left and Angela lay down next to Alex. She cradled him tightly and let her eyes shut the world off.

If she had taken only a moment to glance at the front of the sanctuary before lowering her head, maybe she would have seen that Dorothy was no longer there. But, as fate would have it, no one had noticed her disappearance.

CHAPTER 24

The mess hall was an empty inkwell when Dorothy stepped into it. She found calmness in the black nothingness that surrounded her. Spatial details were stripped away by the night, which freed her from the church, and from the death of her daughter, into an endless canyon she could wander through and hopefully get lost in, never to return.

What did she have to return to anyway? In just a few years her entire family had died. All the little details which once consumed her, the picnic, the bulletins, the carefully mapped geometry of her garden, all of them had vomited her back out, partly digested, onto a severe stone floor. That's all she was now, a discarded, unwanted, useless slab of regurgitation. The only person who could ever have cared for such a wretched thing like her had been butchered less than twelve hours ago – the full reality of which was buried somewhere deep in the pit of her mind, hiding in the dark, or perhaps she was the one hiding from *it*.

The only comfort that remained was that one day, when she was rid of the curse of flesh, her soul would rise up to join her daughter and her husband in the house of their God. This notion did not ease the ache that clasped at her heart – only hearing Clara's voice again could do that – but it did keep her moving forward.

Then, the wind brushed against the outer wall of the church and produced a familiar sound, like someone humming. It was a somber, disjointed tune, but Dorothy found its melancholy soothing. She folded her hands and listened to the hollow drone.

But the hum changed. It became more distinct. Slowly, it shifted into breathy murmuring, until finally, and impossibly, it formed into words. It was so subtle that Dorothy didn't realize what she was hearing until it was too late to deny it.

"Mother…" it called out, with a decaying shudder. Dorothy's breath stopped and the blood drained from her face. The voice was muffled, barely audible, but Dorothy dared to admit it almost sounded like… *No, it couldn't be..*

Her hands unfolded and she spun herself around the room in search of the voice. The shadows that once liberated her now taunted her with their secrets.

She exited the room for a brief moment and returned with the flashlight that had been left out in case someone needed the washroom in the middle of the night.

Without pausing, she clicked on the beam and pointed it into every bit of darkness she could find. The chairs were still stacked, the stage looked untouched, the decrepit piano still looked as sad as ever. Nothing was out of place.

"Mom…" The voice returned, but this time it felt closer. It was no longer some airy exhalation; it had come from a human throat. It had come from Clara.

The light moved to illuminate the doorway leading into the basement. Dorothy held it there, unsure of what she was expecting to see. The door itself was closed and locked.

"Clara?" Dorothy asked, and waited impatiently for something to react. "Clara, baby? Is that you?"

With even steps she walked toward the door.

Dorothy was not a stupid woman. She was aware the mind could play tricks on you, especially when it was under stress. Though, in this case, the cruelty of the prank was something she hoped her mind was incapable of. Regardless, if it was her imagination, the wind, or some creature luring her, she had no choice but to follow. In light of recent miracles, maybe it was possible her daughter was still alive. It was that slim chance that gave her feet the courage to continue.

She reached the door and pressed her ear against it. Mostly she just heard the sound of her own thumping blood, as the aged wood was thick and insulating.

The metal latch was unhooked and pulled from its locked position with a screech. She swung the door open and immediately chased away the mystery of the stairwell with her flashlight.

"Who's down there?" she demanded.

"Mommy..." came the return from deep inside the cave.

She began her descent.

Despite the thorough wrapping job of the bodies, the smell of death was once again fast upon her. She moved warily to give her feet time to find each step.

A breeze met her once she reached the bottom of the stairs. The windows were closed, yet the gust felt as free as the one that tussled with the chopped corn stalks outside. From where it emanated, Dorothy had no explanation. Although the wind gave her a slight chill, it was the mystery of it all that was to blame for the goose bumps on her arms. Still, she rubbed the shivers away and followed her limited ray of light further into the basement, again toward the partly demolished classrooms.

"Are you down here, Clara?" she asked.

She shoved some of the fallen dividers out of her way and cleared a straight path to where the children had been drawing. Compared to the rest of the basement, the classroom appeared more or less intact. The table was tipped over, as the kids had hidden behind it during the attack. A few of their tree drawings had fallen onto the floor.

Her spotlight moved across Clara's workstation, which was comprised of a Bible, a notepad, pens, pencils, construction paper, safety scissors, paint, and glue paste. The tabletop was dusty with wood shavings and crayon fragments. Dorothy knelt down and flipped open the pad of paper. She found pages filled with scribbled ideas for Sunday school lessons, including some that she recognized as her own.

"Mom." This time the voice was so close, Dorothy felt the words on the back of her neck.

She whipped around with her flashlight pointed straight out in front of her. The room was as empty as before.

Dorothy clasped the silver dove necklace around her neck that her husband gave her for their thirtieth wedding anniversary. Since he died, she had been wearing it every day. Her thumb caressed the contours of the pure metal bird, which helped to calm the shaking of her hands.

"Be with me Al. Help me find her," whispered Dorothy to herself. The next part she announced to the room: "Clara! Baby, where are you? Please, if you're here, let me know. Make a sound. Say my name. Call to me, baby, and I'll find you. God will give me strength to find you. Please, just come back to me."

She pleaded desperately into the ether and begged it to react, but nothing seemed impressed by her sorrow. It was not that she felt alone; there was no question in her mind that a presence was all around her, but if no amount of shed tears could persuade it to let Clara return, then she would have to dry her cheeks and take her grief elsewhere. She could barely suffer her own loss, let alone having it mocked.

One step out of the classroom brought her foot in contact with a stray piece of paper. She pointed her flashlight downwards and found a drawing trapped under her right heel.

Before she could get a good look at it, three delicate droplets of blood tapped onto the page.

Dorothy's flashlight searched out who had shed the blood. It didn't take long; the source was standing right in front of her. The glow immediately illuminated the sweet smile of Clara's broken face. Her features were just as torn, just as wet, just as foul as they were when Angela first found her. Only now Clara's pale eyes were turned in attention to Dorothy, who stumbled backwards at the ghastly sight. She wanted Clara back, but not like this.

The flashlight seemed to fall in slow motion. Its glass cracked against the floor and Clara's mangled form was caught in the fractured light like the flicker of a campfire.

Dorothy had landed on her back, half crushing one of the plastic chairs. She looked up at the sickly leer of her dead daughter, but only managed to stand the sight for another five seconds before she covered her own face.

"No! I can't bear it again! Leave me, please!" she begged and kicked her legs to be sure the dead thing had not started approaching.

"It's okay, mom." Clara's voice sounded as if it were drowned in space, like she spoke from the belly of a huge, ancient cathedral. Her lips moved, but the sounds she made did not quite match up. Although her mother refused to look, she continued, "Everything's okay. I'm okay now. I'm with the beast."

Dorothy's fingers trembled apart and her eyes peeked out between the slits. Clara's corpse bent down toward her, the exposed bones shifting and popping.

"Please God, make it go away."

"I can be with you. I can be with you forever." Clara's eyes never changed. They did not blink, or shift focus. They just kept staring like the painted eyes of a puppet.

"Clara, if that's you. Understand, I can't see you like this. I can't do this," Dorothy sobbed, shaking her head in refusal.

"You can. You have to. Join me, mom. I miss you. Don't keep us apart." Clara had no lungs and when she spoke, Dorothy could feel the air from the room being pulled into her empty chest and through her vocal chords.

The thing in front of Dorothy that called her its mother did not seem much like Clara. However, even this monstrous estimation of her daughter was better than nothing. If Dorothy closed her eyes, she could almost have her back to the way she was.

"How? Tell me how to be with you again," asked Dorothy.

"Follow him. Worship him. Join me." Clara's doll-like smile almost appeared tender.

A piece of paper was then placed in Dorothy's lap. Her eyes dared to look and found it was the torn drawing she had stepped on. By the time her eyes shifted back up to Clara, she was gone. The only sign of her ever having been there were the bloody fingerprints she left on the page.

Dorothy made no attempt to get to her feet; instead she poured her energies into steadying her rampaging heart. Clara's visit had left Dorothy dry in the mouth and dizzy. Yet, she pleaded quietly, "Come back. Come back to me. Please."

Alone in the basement, Dorothy sat with what she just experienced. She thought of the Bible and the visions of prophets. She recalled burning bushes, descending angels, important heavenly stars and obscure apocalyptic omens. None of them compared to the encounter she had just had. She was taught that God spoke in mysterious ways, but what she saw was not mysterious. It was as direct as a bullet to the head. Her daughter had reached out from beyond death and gave her the key she needed to join her in eternity. That key was the Behemoth.

Her hands went limp and hit the paper still resting on her thighs. It was a drawing of a tree. Next to it stood an ominous, dark figure. The author's name was written in big black letters at the bottom: Alex.

CHAPTER 25

For Susan, life had, in some seemingly blessed way, never delivered her a fair share of obstacles. While other kids her age were bogged down by unpopularity, strict parents, acne, or just good, old-fashioned social awkwardness, Susan glided through her existence with a charming positivity, led by the irresistible flick of her golden hair.

Her father had a respectable, steady job as a city lawyer, as did her mother until Susan was born. From the moment the Greenfields brought back their first baby girl, Mrs. Greenfield took it upon herself to redesign the world specifically for her child's success. It all stemmed from an old family philosophy: if you don't teach someone how to fail, then they have no choice but to prevail. In Susan's case, this theory proved true. Piano lessons had taught Susan diligence, gold medals at track and field had taught perseverance, honour role programs had taught her to think critically. To top off her bountiful achievements, she boasted a glowing smile and the kind of body that taught young boys to become young men. Though, she had remained pure and untouched, just as her father requested, she certainly had had her share of adoring suitors. Matthew was one of those hungry puppies, and she knew it, but had decided to ignore his innocent drooling to make room for more pressing matters, such as her future. She had joined her local conservative party to help pass out pamphlets to innocent passersby on the street, and volunteered at both the animal shelter and the Salvation Army. If there were things that needed fixing, she had the power to fix them.

On paper, this seemed like the life to live, but the problem with smelling roses all the time was that it left no room for lessons in personal disappointment, or regret, or fear, or even death. Her parents wouldn't allow animals, so the usual first exposure to losing a loved one was robbed from her. Both sets of grandparents were still alive; not only that, but on one side, she still had a coherent great grandmother who lived only thirty minutes away. To Susan, life was as effortless as another bite of cheesecake. At least it was until Rick had delivered his sermon earlier that day.

Don often spoke of the beauty of the human spirit, but she realized now that he was only trying to separate people from the nasty reality of flesh and rot. In her newly-formed opinion, life was like a pathetic, naked slug that oozed about the surface of the planet with one selfish concern – to continue to live. It was too dumb to realize its drive to exist was also the cause of all its pain. So blindly, the slug continued to bump its way along. What had disturbed her the most, however, was her own powerlessness to change this reality in any way. Unlike world hunger, there were no petitions to sign or donations to be made. Perhaps, if she had been exposed to such darkness before, it wouldn't have been able to consume her so utterly.

She attempted to reconcile everything she had seen with the concept of the Christian God she grew up with. Then, she finished taking her shit and flushed the toilet.

It was the discomfort in her bowels that had awoken her from her much-needed sleep in the first place. She had lain awake on the floor for fifteen minutes before the pressure became too much to ignore.

On the cold, white, porcelain throne she sat, lit by a candle she brought with her. She would have used the flashlight if it hadn't mysteriously disappeared.

While she pulled her pants back on, the flame of the candle faltered and threatened to blowout. Her sudden movement could have caused the disturbance in the air, at least she hoped it had. With her pants only half way up her legs, she froze and watched the candle – her precious and solitary light source – as it struggled to regain its prominence. Eventually, it did and she breathed easy, although carefully as to not disrupt the flame again.

In the mirror, Susan found a young, but visibly troubled woman. Dark patches had settled under her eyes and sweat gave her normally immaculate skin a dirty shine. She couldn't remember the last time she had gone this long without washing, or even basic grooming. The polish she had applied to her fingernails remained intact, but all the scrubbing she had done in the sanctuary left stubborn red stains in the grooves of her hands.

She turned the water on and splashed the revitalizing liquid against her face. She then shook herself dry like a dog, hoping to not only do away with the water from her face, but also the thoughts from her head.

Susan returned to the sanctuary where everything was just how she had left it. She cupped her candle to keep the glow away from sleeping eyes.

In the dim light, maneuvering down the aisle without stepping on anyone was a challenging task. Susan quietly thanked her mother for forcing her to take ballet lessons, as it allowed her to use only the top edge of her feet and move lightly between the bodies. In her tired state, she had forgotten where her mother had chosen to sleep and had to search her out.

She resorted to examining footwear in order to locate her. When she came to a pair of scruffy runners that looked impossibly out of date, she stopped. She knew those shoes belonged to Matthew.

She had not had the time yet to tell Matthew how sorry she was about his grandmother. Since Flora lost her eyes, Matthew had been spending every moment and expending every bit of energy he had, taking care of her. When she lost consciousness, Matthew remained awake for as long as he could in the chance she might need something. She began to think that maybe she had misjudged him.

When she looked up to his face, she was amused to discover he had pulled the covers up over his head like a child scared of the boogeyman.

She grabbed the edge of the thin sheet and gently tugged it down to his shoulders. It was a nice face, she thought. She had not really given his features that much attention before. His eyes darted back and forth under his lids and he wore an anxious expression, emphasized by the dancing of his eyebrows. He looked so innocent. She leaned in and kissed his cheek. It was just something in the moment she wanted to do – to offer him comfort, compassion, or maybe even love. For her, the impulse came and went. For whatever reason she did it, it seemed to have eased him.

A branch scraped across the stained-glass window with a grating screech.

She immediately looked up. The colours had been tainted by moonlight, and the silhouette of a large, leafless tree was waving to her from the other side of the glass. It looked gnarled and old, as most trees in the fall do. The shadows cast by its gaunt branches spread out like a web across the window and shivered in the breeze.

The tree reached all the way to the top of the window where a thicker entanglement had formed – a dark patch that attempted to blot out Heaven.

Although the image of its creeping form evoked an old drawing of a witch that had terrorized Susan for most of her childhood, she could not help but be mesmerized by its undulating rhythm. Her hand, which had been shielding the light of her candle, dropped to her side.

As soon as the flame was opened to the room, the shadows stirred.

Two of the branches started to move contrary to the others and what Susan had mistaken for a tree, turned its head toward her. The more it moved, the more Susan could distinguish what was tree from what was beast, though they shared many similar characteristics.

Susan stopped everything in mortal fear it would draw the attention of the creature.

The beast itself stood as tall as the tree, but most of its body remained hidden by the chaotic interweaving of the branches behind it. Yet, it was clear it had a grotesquely slender human-like shape, like an emaciated scarecrow. The fingers of the beast stretched out like thick needles, each one narrowing to a formidable tip. It almost appeared connected to the tree, like the two were one. Susan had never been able to empathize with an ant until she was in the presence of this awesome and terrifying being.

What was presumably the beast's head tilted in Susan's direction. Suddenly, a pleasing hum reverberated in the front of her skull like a struck tuning fork. Her eyes began to lie. She was no longer in the church, she was in the clouds. Something carried her through the billowing mists and glided her down toward what she thought was the earth. But, this was not the earth she knew. The ground was scorched and bubbling.

Writhing on its surface were strange, malformed creatures, reminding her of the premature birth she saw in sex ed.

Her hand stopped working. The candle dropped. It landed on Matthew's sheet and the flame was eager to spread.

As the fire grew, Susan fell back into her body, back into the church. A scream broke free of her throat that would have given any alarm system a run for its money. Everyone in the room jolted awake, including Matthew, who quickly folded his sheet onto itself to smother the flames.

Some congregation members joined in Susan's screaming, despite not being sure why.

With two mammoth steps, the beast's twisted body strode out of view of the window, leaving Susan to be terrorized only by the shadow of a tree shimmying in the breeze. But, her fear did not diminish.

"Susan!" Gary was the first to shake his brain into alertness. "What? What is it?"

Though she tried, Susan couldn't answer. She found it impossible to put into words what she had just seen. At that very moment, there was a creature, a giant as tall as the ceiling, stalking around the empty fields outside. And it had been watching them.

Matthew stood up from his pew and grabbed Susan by the shoulders in an effort to ground her. He tried to shake the hysteria from her body and was shocked at how well it worked. Her screams quieted as her eyes jostled about the room until Matthew offered them something to focus on. She looked into his steady gaze and rested there for a while.

The room was alive with panicked shouts.

Angela had awakened slightly after Gary and quickly surveyed the chaos, but there was no way of knowing whether the threat was real, or just a dream Susan had.

Most of the children were crying, but not Alex. He looked concerned, yet remained calm. Regardless, Angela pulled him tightly to herself.

"What's wrong?" Matthew asked Susan.

"I saw it! I saw it!" she screamed back.

"What?"

"It's outside! It's real!"

With that, everyone shuffled away from the windows and into the centre of the room, creating a dangerous mob of tangled bodies, sprinkled with knee-high children.

Angela didn't join the others. She instead remained seated with Alex, her attention fixed on the window, hoping to catch a glimpse of the beast herself.

"Mom?" Alex spoke up. Whatever fear was not present in his demeanor certainly came through in the quiver of his voice.

"It's okay. It's alright, sweetie. We're safe in here."

"It's coming for us." He hugged her back tightly.

Gary popped his head up from the crowd and waved his hands in an effort to collect people's attention. It took a great deal of flailing to upstage the beast outside, but he eventually managed.

"Everyone! Please," he yelled, "we have to calm down! We don't know what's out there and we're not going to help the situation by screaming till we can't scream anymore. Is everyone alright?"

"We should head to the basement!" bellowed Emily.

"We're not going back down there," Gary replied sternly.

"It seems a hell of a lot safer than up here," she barked back.

"Emily, we're not going back into the basement."

"Before we decide anything," Angela added, "we should ask Susan what she really saw."

Susan, who was now in the arms of her mother, didn't look as though she had much interest in talking. She looked more like she would rather curl up into a small box and disappear.

Gary nodded and turned to Susan. "Angela is right. Susan, I know you're scared. But, can you tell us exactly what you saw?"

Susan muttered something quietly to herself.

"What was that? Can you speak up?"

"The Behemoth." She finally named it, and everyone in the room felt the chill. It was just as Rick said. The beast had come. They were not dealing with some ambiguous Father in the sky, there was a being outside they could touch and be touched by, a being that had demonstrated its power, and its malice.

Tina pulled at Gary's shirt. "What are we going to do?"

"Listen, everyone!" Gary again spoke to the room. "Nothing has changed. Rick told us that thing was out there. We just have to keep our heads. Now, look around at your friends and your families. Look at them. They are what is going to get you through this. I'm scared, just like everyone. But, no matter how dark it gets out there, no matter what happens, we have to remember that we're not alone. None of us are alone in this."

"Where's Dorothy?" Angela interrupted.

"I'm right here," came a calm reply. Heads turned and found Dorothy standing in the doorway to the sanctuary. She looked unimpressed by Gary's words.

Angela stared at her, but Dorothy refused to make eye contact.

"What if we fought this thing?" Chris' young, but determined voice rose up from the crowd. The question was considered by few, but tossed away by most.

"It's huge," Susan replied.

"Maybe we can hurt it somehow," offered Chris.

Emily swatted the notion down. "Don't be stupid, Chris. You've seen what it can do. How are you going to fight it? With a baseball bat, or are you going to throw your shoes at it? You daft boy, it's the beast we're dealing with, not a wild dog you can just scare off."

"Fuck you!" Chris yelled back. "You're the daft one, you stupid, old bitch." Normally, his disrespect would have been more delicately coded.

"Oh, please, Chris, that's enough!" Tina scolded her son.

"No, mom, I'm right. Sitting here is a bad, fucking idea. We already know we can't give this thing what it wants. We need to fight!"

"We can't fight it. Think about what happened to Sandy!" came another disembodied voice.

After another condemning look from his mother, Chris shook his head and shut his mouth. There seemed to be no way to convince them. The mob had developed a thought process of its own, like a steamroller, and you could either move aside or be crushed. Chris looked over at Angela and could tell she was thinking the same thing. As long as there was at least one other person who saw what was happening, like his father had said, he was not alone.

"What are we going to do if it comes back?" posed Matthew.

"What makes you think it has left?" Dorothy asked from the cusp of the room. She stepped inside and slowly walked up the aisle next to the mob. Her dramatic stride was enough to ensure everyone's close attention. This was a trick she had learned from her years watching Don, and knew he would have been proud to see his legacy of theatrics utilized thusly. "It hasn't left, Matthew. It's still here, cause we're still here. It's waiting."

"For what?" he asked.

"What do you think? The Behemoth is waiting for us."

The ominous statement silenced the room.

"We have to trust in God now," Emily said, taken by a sudden surge of religious fever. "He's the only one who has the power to save us. As always, He is our hope. We cannot lose our faith in Him. We have to trust God."

"Which one?" asked Dorothy. She slipped away from the mob before anyone could answer and sat down in one of the pews with her hands clasped and her head down.

As the rest of the mob started to disperse and head back to their respective beds, Emily recited the Lord's Prayer. She spoke it quickly to herself at a manic speed, but they all knew what she was saying. Everyone, even the children, knew the Lord's Prayer by heart. After she was finished, she began again. She recited it from start to finish seven times before Michael escorted her back to where the two of them had been sleeping.

Angela had watched the chanting closely. There was desperation in Emily's devotion that trembled her hands and drew tears from her eyes. There was no question Emily was begging for some divine intervention. Although Angela was fairly certain by this point that Emily was pleading to an absent God, she did wonder if the praying itself would help. If, perhaps, there was something out there that might listen, that might come to their aid. Maybe the thing outside was listening, and could be appealed to, if the right words were said.

However, the possibility was too slim to bring Angela to her knees.

CHAPTER 26

When the morning no one thought would come finally arrived, the tone of the sanctuary had changed. Each respective family had separated themselves from the group. The situation had become so tenuous that no one, not even Gary, had tried to reassemble the congregation.

Tina and Emily brought around two trays of food to every member. On one tray was a stack of bread and the other, a stack of apples, which were originally intended for a charity event that required massive amounts of apple pies. Each member was allowed to take only one serving.

Tina was surprised by everyone's appetite. Personally, she didn't think she would ever be hungry again.

Once the food had been delivered, Tina and Emily, like everyone else, returned to their families to eat in silence. The quiet was unnerving, but the crunching and squishing of jaws proved even more unbearable.

"Maybe someone will come," a naïve young man finally said. The only response he received was more chewing.

Eventually, the sun awakened the jovial chirp of a single red robin. It unabashedly sang of the joys of life as it fluttered in and out of view of the three small windows that lined the sanctuary wall opposite the stained-glass window. It was a pleasant enough treat, though the screech of a crow might have been more mood-appropriate.

Samantha and Dylan were the first children to be impressed by the bird's flourishing dance and huddled into two of the three windows for a better view.

The Rosenthals had temporarily adopted Dylan, who asked about his father, Bruce, with increasing urgency. Emily and Michael, in a testament to their own discomfort with the subject of death, had told Dylan that Bruce had been called away and there was no telling when he might return. They then bombarded his worried child's mind with ample distractions, and encouraged Samantha and Stanley to play with him. He seemed contented enough.

Stanley pushed Samantha out of the way so he could see the bird, despite there being enough windows for all three of them. Without complaint, Samantha repositioned herself at the other free window.

"Stanley, why can't we be outside if the bird can?" asked Samantha in a whisper.

"Don't be stupid," he replied for lack of a better answer.

"Cause the troll outside doesn't like birds, he likes us," Dylan said.

"Troll?" Samantha was skeptical.

"Yeah. It's what everyone was scared of last night."

"What's it like?"

"It's big, and it eats people. And it wants to eat us."

Samantha, who could barely reach the wood trim of the window, started to lose her grip. Her mind was too distracted by the image of a huge, hungry troll, to pay attention to what her hands were doing. She eventually voiced one of her deepest dreads. "I don't want to be eaten."

"Shut up, Dylan!" demanded Stanley. "You're scaring her."

"No, I'm not! It's true!."

"Even if there is a troll, it can't come in here. We're safe."

"How do you know that?" asked Dylan, who secretly needed to alleviate his own fear as much as Samantha did.

"Cause we're in a church, and churches are special, safe places. Everyone knows that. That's why we're here."

"So the troll can't come in?"

"That's right. All we have to do is stay in here."

After some thinking, Samantha asked, "Can trolls fly?"

"I don't think so," replied Dylan.

"Then it's not a troll," she declared smugly.

"How do you know?"

"Cause it took me flying last night while I was sleeping."

The two boys went silent. Dylan fidgeted with his feet and Stanley scratched some paint off the windowsill.

"Me too… I went through clouds and then it swooped me down and showed me lava," Stanley eventually admitted.

"I guess it's not a troll then," Dylan added.

The three of them remained quietly perched on the windows until the robin lost its charm, then they abandoned their posts for other entertainments.

As they charged down the aisle, they almost bumped into Chris, who had taken on the duty of offering everyone a cup of water.

He approached Matthew, who had been kneeling next to his grandmother all morning, feeding her small pieces of bread. Flora looked drained, lying on the back pew, like her body was slowly shutting down. Her empty eye sockets had become deep bruises that streaked dark purple and red across her forehead and cheekbones.

"Hi," Chris greeted them softly.

"Hey." Matthew answered, with no eye contact. He just kept feeding crumbs between Flora's weak lips.

"How's she doing?"

"She's fine."

"Do you guys need some water?"

"Sure."

Chris poured two generous glasses and placed them next to Matthew on the floor.

"I hope you enjoyed your complimentary continental breakfast this morning of apples and bread," Chris joked. " For lunch I think they're planning apple sauce on toast. They believe in recycling here."

"Not really in the mood, Chris."

"Yeah, no one really seems to be."

"Is there anything else you wanted?"

"Yes, there is something else. I wanted to know how you were doing. If you need any help with anything..." Chris could barely finish the sentence before Matthew interrupted.

"Forget it Chris, if I need a shoulder, it won't be yours."

"That's not what I meant. I'm not trying to just... I'm not just trying to get close, if that's what you're thinking. When I say it, I mean it. Matt, I want to help you. I keep trying to do stuff, but making things better is harder than it looks. The total truth, something inside of me just wants to make sure you're okay, that's all."

"Save it. I know what you want. Thanks for the water, but could you please just go now?"

"Sure, I'll leave you alone." As Chris walked away, an alternate scenario flashed in his mind: he and Matthew nursing Flora back to health together. This would finally reveal to Matthew that, what had started as simple hormonal lust between them, had become something of substance, something that mattered, and compelled them to care for one another in the way that people do when they say, 'I love you', and actually mean it. Before he could wallow in how painfully unlikely his daydream was, Angela interrupted with a request.

"Oh, Chris! Do you mind if we grabbed some water?"

"Here," he said, handing over the pitcher and stack of paper cups before continuing down the aisle without so much as a backward glance.

"Um, thanks."

She poured a cup and turned to Alex, who was awake and sitting quietly, with his vision fixated on the front of the church.

"Here, Alex. You should have some water." She offered him a cup and brought it to his lips. He looked at it, but didn't drink. "Alex, you haven't eaten anything, so please, at least have some water."

He looked up at her, but she could tell he was somewhere else. Not *somewhere*, he was in the basement, with Clara.

"Listen, buddy," Angela said, kneeling down to his level. "I know you're upset. We all are. But you have to talk to me, okay? I know you can, you did it last night. Remember? You said he was coming for us. You remember that? But I promise, I won't let him get you, I just need you to say something." Her hands brushed at his hair and rubbed his back.

Alex turned his head toward one of the stained-glass angels that looked down on him from the window.

Angela had one last trick to reach him. Her hand unhooked the invisible radio from her belt and brought the device up to her mouth.

"Come in echo one, this is echo two."

To her dismay, Alex did not offer any reaction. So, she adjusted her dials and repeated the transmission, "Come in echo one, this is echo two. Do you read me?"

His hand twitched.

"Echo two has an urgent message for you, echo one."

He shifted and almost grabbed his radio.

"Echo one, can you hear me?"

"This is echo one," he replied, "but you didn't say over, echo two. Over."

"Sorry, echo one, that won't happen again. Over," she said, through an uncontrollable smile. She wanted to squeeze him, but fought the urge and tried to stay calm.

"What's the message? Over."

"I wanted to know where you have been, echo one. Over."

"I can't be an officer anymore. Over."

"Why do you say that? Over"

"I failed. Over."

"What did you fail? Over."

"The mission."

"No, echo one, you didn't have a mission."

"Yes I did," he said, without the aid of his radio. "I was supposed to help her."

"Alex, no. Don't think that. What happened to Clara wasn't because of you."

"I couldn't save her. I tried, but I couldn't, and it's my fault she's dead."

Angela recognized the pitch Alex's voice always reached right before he started to cry. As soon as she heard the unsettled stutters, she grabbed hold of him. She wanted to wrap her body around his and protect him forever. Though, she knew she could not.

"Oh, sweetie, she would have been so proud of you. And she knew you did all you could. That's all that matters. You tried. She would have been proud. She would have been so proud."

The two of them rocked back and forth together on the pew, perfectly synchronized in their sorrow. He clung to her just as much as she clung to him, and their loss became a little more bearable, just so long as they promised to never let go.

While safe in their embrace, Angela began to think about what Chris had said. As she comforted her child, and felt his fragile body against hers, she started to agree with him. The sun would not be up forever, and who knew what betrayals would come when the Behemoth returned to collect. She had to do whatever she could to keep Alex safe, and that called for action. Exactly what she proposed to do was a mystery even to her, but she knew she had to do something.

Slowly, she ended the hug and pulled Alex away from her so she could see his face. She wiped his cheeks until they were once again dry and placed two warm hands on either side of his neck.

"Alex, I love you and I'll be here for you whenever you need me," she said, and then repeated the pledge. "Whenever you need me. But there are things I have to do now, okay?"

"I'll come with you."

"No, you can't come with me. You have to stay here. You're going to stay with Susan, alright? She'll look after you until I get back. And I *will* be back."

"I don't want you to leave."

"I don't either, but I'll only be gone a little while."

"Promise?"

"Yes, I promise."

CHAPTER 27

In the centre of the mess hall stage, hidden behind its ragged curtains, Angela balanced herself on top of one of the hefty worktables.

One of its loose legs wobbled as she stretched out and reached with her phone high into the air. She waved it back and forth in the hope that Chris was wrong and she might catch a precious signal. But, the bars remained empty. *Fuck*, she thought, shoving the useless phone back into her pocket.

The only other option was to somehow sneak out of the church unnoticed, that is to say, not use the front door. There was a second entrance to the church through the basement, but Angela was not terribly keen on trying her luck there. The more she thought about it, the more she realized how poorly designed the church really was. True, it was an old building, predating most contemporary building codes, but it was as if no one had taken into consideration basic human safety. With only one easily accessible exit, the church was a firetrap waiting to happen.

She could not pin her hope on the assumption that the Behemoth slept. Sleep was a thing for mortals, not gods – except the Bible did say God rested on the seventh day, Sunday. It was a pity today was Monday.

No, judging from what she had witnessed, the Behemoth was always around, always aware.

"Fuck." Her thought came aloud.

Then she noticed the stage floor was being tickled ever so faintly by natural light. If her eyes had not been cast down, she would have missed it.

Angela jumped off the table with a loud thud.

Burlap curtains hung from wiry strings secreted in the wings on either side of the stage. It was clear, judging by the darkness that crept out from under the hem of the burlap, there was no light to hide. There were a few props, mostly Christmas oriented, like Santa's throne, cutout two-dimensional reindeer and garishly wrapped presents, sure, but nothing to produce the glow she saw.

However, there was a thin sheet of fabric that dangled behind her that had no obvious purpose. Angela pulled it down and found a window about the size of a porthole. The sun beamed through as if she had just unearthed a secret, golden treasure.

The modest window looked out on an obscure part of the field, which excited Angela. Even if the Behemoth were always watching, why would it be watching this wholly unremarkable side of the church? Its attention, she imagined, would be better spent on the front door and the sanctuary, leaving her a literal window of opportunity. From the limited view it offered her, Angela could see where the edge of the dirt parking lot faded into tilled soil. Her car was only a short run from there. If she could make it outside, she could be in her car and driving for help in less than twenty seconds, assuming her car was in a cooperative mood.

She pressed her fingers against the dirty glass of the window and examined its edges. Dark blue paint had been poorly applied to its wood trim and clashed with the scheme of the rest of the stage. Most likely, it was painted to match its surroundings at some point, but had been forgotten, and now showed its age.

Angela pushed on the bottom of the glass to see if it would open, but it didn't budge. She was worried about having to smash the window, as that would definitely draw the beast's attention. She pushed harder and the paint started to crack as the panel shifted its position. After a less timid shove, Angela dislodged it from its cradle with a satisfying Velcro sound. When it moved, it became clear the window was hinged in the centre and would only swing into a horizontal position that bisected the opening. Unfortunately, this did not allow enough space for Angela's body to slip through.

A fresh breeze, that carried with it the rejuvenating aromas of fall, rushed around the glass and into Angela's face. Instantly, she found herself walking through a rested forest, charging through dry corn stalks and jumping into a pile of leaves. It was the smell of change, of a better time, one that she had taken for granted. It smelled like freedom.

She stood there in rapture of the sensation. Without too much thought, she snuck her hand out through the opening of the window and paraded it about. Her limb waved joyfully in the air, intoxicated by the rays from the sun and the cooling touch of the wind. It was a good thirty seconds of bliss before she realized what she was doing.

Her hand tensed up. Technically, she was outside, or at least part of her was, but there was no sign of the Behemoth.

She placed her palm against the outer brick of the building and felt around its crevices. All the while she kept a watchful eye for any movement. At the first sign of something stirring, even if it was just a shadow, she was ready to pull her hand back inside.

It became a game – how long could she keep her hand on the other side of the wall? After a minute, Angela came to the conclusion that the Behemoth was either gone, or didn't care so long as she didn't try to escape. It didn't seem to be aware of her, but for all she knew, it could have been lying in wait just under the window. Maybe what she mistook for the fall wind was actually the beast's breath, or maybe it had grown tired of the church and had left to terrorize the Davidson's farmhouse down the road. The only way to find out would have been to make a run for it, but Angela had decided that was a fifty-fifty chance she did not want to take just yet.

She retracted her arm and swung the window firmly back into place. Her shoes squeaked on the floor as she spun around and headed towards the curtains, back into the mess hall.

Impossibly, the breeze came again, only this time, it was far less inviting. It spilled across her skin and through her hair like cold, greasy fingers and brought similar, yet tainted associations. She returned to the memory of jumping into a pile of leaves, only now the leaves were soggy and rotten.

She stopped and checked to make sure the window was closed. It was.

The invisible force returned and snaked around her ankles before rustling into the burlap curtains of the wings.

The fabric drifted out, then slowly swayed back into place in a most enticing manner. It was as if someone had moved it with purpose.

It had risen just enough for the curtains to part and allow Angela to peer between the slit that separated them. She saw nothing of interest, though light was scarce, before the wall of burlap became whole again.

It swayed a second time, only without the aid of the breeze. The slit, for a brief moment, became a gaping hole. She only saw it for a second, but that was more than enough.

From the shadows behind the curtain, Angela was greeted with a bighearted smile – Rick's smile. His teeth were stained black, as were his lips and eyes, robbing him of whatever empathy Angela might have searched for. He was seated on the prop throne used for Santa during the Christmas concerts. Streams of his blood had defiled the chair, resulting in an ugly mixture of dark red and gold. Every scar on his body had been opened, and he wore his skin, in all its utter nakedness, like a shredded wrapping, pulled so tightly to his body that you could see the strain in every wound.

The vision was so much to take in, and the time so brief, that Angela barely noticed he was holding something.

Then the curtain fell back into place.

Angela cursed her inquisitive impulses. As was true so many times in her life, she should have just kept walking.

The curtains rippled like water, but not enough to give Angela another taste of what lay beneath, not that she wanted a second sampling. Still, the curious movements behind the burlap kept her eyes engaged as she stepped cautiously backwards, away from the wings.

Her left foot came down in a puddle of liquid, but her attention was so focused on the curtains, she didn't notice. After one more step, however, she bumped into something solid, like a wall, only warm.

Her eyes shot down. She was standing in a puddle of blood. Instinctively, her hand reached behind her. She touched hard flesh and whipped around to find that she was groping Rick's slashed thigh. In a split second, she pulled back in disgust and vigorously wiped her hand clean of his blood.

He stood, like an actor ready for his bow with his arms open to his adoring audience.

Angela would have screamed if screaming had come naturally to her. When she was frightened, she usually found herself stricken with bewilderment – an equally useless, although quieter alternative to the standard hysteria.

She took in the impressive carnage of his body, which although disturbing, she couldn't help but appreciate how beautifully symmetrical it all was. The peeled wounds had made his skin raw. The dark puddle on the floor grew as impossible amounts of blood continued to pump forth. His ruby liquid escaped in thin, delicate drips from his lighter cuts and rolled down his overtly masculine form as if each droplet enjoyed touching him. Angela couldn't quite explain it, but part of her enjoyed it, too, no matter how much she damned it. The sticky smile on his face seemed to know this about her, which made her feel even more naked than he was.

Then, she looked at what he held in his hands; a frantically beating heart pulsated in the grip of his left, and in his right, a string of gleaming intestines so shiny, they appeared to have been glittered.

He spoke to her, but not with the voice she was used to. It was soft, yet sent her stomach into turmoil, like the threat of distant thunder. As he shook the organs, he asked cordially, "Whose will they be?"

She fought it, but the image of Alex's torn open body cut into her mind. Her hands covered her face in an attempt to blot out the offense, but like a piece of exposed film, there was no removing what had been captured.

Suddenly Rick's arms were around her. He took hold of her by the throat and stomach, and pulled her backwards onto Santa's throne where he sat her down on his lap.

Angela, defying her own nature, motioned to scream.

Before a sound could be uttered, Rick's weighty hand closed over her mouth like a steel clamp. She thrashed against him, but it was like being squeezed by a steel rope. He didn't budge when she tried to push herself off him, and he didn't flinch when she kicked at his shins. Whatever he was about to do, she could not stop him.

His free hand slid from her shoulder and followed the path of her collarbone down to the centre of her chest. Her heart, as if calling for him to stop, thumped faster and louder as his fingers snuck under the edge of her blouse and teased at the beginnings of her breast.

By this time, the wetness from his bloody body had soaked through the back of her clothes and lathered the skin of her legs and buttocks. It was a slippery, but not completely uncomfortable, sensation. The damp fabric became like a second skin and soon it seemed as though it was just her flesh against his. He was hot, almost feverish. She could feel each sinew of his muscled stomach and groin tense as his powerful legs opened to her, inviting her to slip down between them.

To her relief, he was not yet hard. This came as a surprise to her, having shared a bed with him for fifteen years, she knew him to be a desperately sexual animal. Normally, by the time she could get his pants off, he was already full-grown and would come flopping out just behind the zipper as if he was spring-loaded.

His hand encased the entirety of her breast, but allowed her ripened nipple to squeeze out and be roughened between his two fingers.

Angela grabbed at his invasive touch, but the more she tried to pull him away, the more he pleased her, and he knew exactly where and how to touch her body. In the past, she had resisted his advances on several occasions, but this was different. It was as if she had no choice.

Her body began to revolt against every intellectual, spiritual and personal value she had tried painstakingly to uphold. This man, this creature, this demon, had violated her, beaten her, lied to her, threatened her life and the life of her child, but still her body wanted him. It ached for him, as if it would die without his touch, inside and out. Angela hated the sweat of excitement that formed around the base of her neck, the unconscious movement of her tongue and the itching tremble that ignited from deep within her. She hated each and every betrayal her body made. How could he still have such power over her?

His hand released her breast then flowed down her stomach and into her pants. She gasped at the persistence of his digging fingers as if it was her first time. Her body involuntarily started to bend with pleasure under the force of his hands, which now held both pairs of her lips.

Still, he was flaccid. If only as a distraction from her unwanted ecstasy, Angela started a line of questioning; if Rick was not doing this for himself, then why was he doing it?

He violently pulled her head back, so his mouth was right next to her ear.

"Follow me, baby," he breathed. "I am the way." With a tongue as black as oil, he licked the side of her face along her jaw line. She closed her eyes as this slug of a tongue wiggled down her neck.

By the time she opened them again, she could remember how his tongue felt, but could no longer feel it. She took in some much needed air through her mouth and found no hand holding it closed. Gradually, she came to realize the hardness against her body was the seat of the throne and nothing more.

With shameful tears poised at the cusps of her eyelids, she looked for a sign of Rick, but was surrounded only by dusty Christmas ornaments and tattered costumes. Her clothes were dry, and the pools of red were missing. Had she dreamt the entire thing? If she had, what kind of person was she to have such fantasies? Whether Rick was real or not real was beside the point. She had wanted him, and she had moaned for him.

Her own powerlessness to withstand him dredged up every mistake she had made in her youth and every wrong path she had been forced to follow. The flesh is weak, and her weakness had been made blatantly clear.

She thought herself disgusting, and her head dropped into her hands for the weeping to commence.

CHAPTER 28

"Your mom is gonna be tickled when she sees you ate that entire apple all by yourself," said Susan with feigned excitement as Alex passed to her what was left of his meal. "You sure you don't want any more?"

Alex nodded his head. He was kneeling on the floor using the seat of the pew as his table. Susan sat next to him, trying to coax him into having a few more bites of bread.

"It's really good," she tempted, "fresh, delicious and... bready." In the art of persuasion, Susan was a novice. The only person she had convinced of the bread's irresistibility was herself and she started to rip off a few chunks.

"Will my mom be back soon?"

"I'm sure she will, Alex. She said she'd only be gone ten minutes. So, until then, you're stuck with me. But, that's not so bad, right?"

"I guess not."

"You could be stuck with Mrs. Rosenthal." Susan whispered Emily's name quietly enough so no one else in the sanctuary would hear.

Alex subtly looked over in Emily's direction. She was sitting near the pulpit with Michael, looking like a pile of frumpy gloom. The malaise was so thick about her, it was almost foggy. He had to agree, Susan was the better option.

"So, you want to play a game or something?" she asked.

"No."

"Oh. Okay. What do you want to do then?"

"I don't know," he shrugged.

"We don't just want to sit here, do we?" She ate another clump of bread.

"We can. That's all right."

"Won't you get bored?"

"No, I'm not scared."

Susan was taken aback by the response. She thought about its implications before she pointed out, "I didn't say you were scared."

"My mom's going to protect me. But, it's okay if you're scared. Maybe she can protect you, too."

"Um… thanks. But Alex, I didn't say that I was scared, either. Where are you getting this?"

"Last night."

"Last night…" Susan repeated. It was the last thing she wanted to think about and had pushed it far from her mind.

"It saw you," he said, nonchalantly.

"What did you just say?" her mouth remained open with a half eaten piece of bread soaking inside.

"It saw you, through the window."

"No. No, Alex, the window is stained-glass, you can't see through it. What makes you think that?"

"Cause it saw you."

"Stop saying it saw me," her voice began to rise and drew the attention of the people around them. "It didn't see me, it couldn't have!"

"Susan, is everything alright?" asked Tina, who had been eavesdropping even before the shouting.

"What? Yes. Fine. It's fine," she said, obviously frazzled.

"What's wrong?" Tina asked. Her calculated sentimentality told her to place a hand on Susan's shoulder.

"There's nothing wrong, we're fine."

"People who are fine don't usually shake like you are. Something rattled you. What was it?"

Susan didn't want to say, but it seemed the only way to escape from Tina's trap of care.

"He said that last night, the thing outside saw me."

"He? Alex said that?"

"Yes."

"Well, he couldn't possibly know that."

"He sounded sure."

"Alex," Tina said, turning her attention to the innocent boy at the pew. "Did you wake up last night when Susan screamed?"

"Maybe."

"Then how would you know what the beast saw?"

Alex shrugged his shoulders.

"It's not nice to scare people, Alex," Tina scolded.

"I'm not trying to scare people."

"Then, why would you make something like that up? Something that would clearly frighten Susan?"

"I didn't make it up. It told me it liked her bright hair."

Susan almost whimpered. She had the sudden urge to hide herself, and especially her hair from whatever prying eyes might be searching for her.

"Told you? How did it tell you?" Tina asked. Her tone had grown more severe, and appropriately so. If the child could really converse with the beast, then how could he be trusted? He was, after all, the last person to see Clara alive. Maybe her death didn't happen exactly the way he said it did. It was possible the beast had been influencing Alex from the start. Then again, it was also possible he was just a young, stupid kid saying young, stupid things.

"I don't know," he replied, with his signature shrug.

"Does it say things to you, the way I'm saying things now?"

"No, it says stuff in my head."

"What kind of stuff?" Tina took a step toward him in order to intimidate a quick response.

Susan had been watching the interrogation and had pieced together exactly what Tina's questions were implying. She was also aware of the nosey group of onlookers closing in. She reasoned, if Alex were in cahoots with the beast, then would it have allowed him to admit it so freely? She couldn't explain why the beast had spoken to him, if indeed it had at all, but to Susan, Alex was just a scared boy in a bad situation, waiting for his mother.

"Alex," Tina continued, with snowballing intensity, "did the beast tell you anything when you were in the basement? When you were down there with Clara?"

The question clearly upset Alex, who turned and stared into the wood grain back of the pew. He started counting every subtle variation in the grain he could find.

"I don't think he knows anything, Tina." Susan finally came to his aid, but Tina would not be derailed so easily.

"What else did your friend tell you?"

"He doesn't know anything. And to be honest, I think you need to back off," Susan asserted herself.

"I'm just trying to get to the bottom of why he scared you."

"He didn't scare me. Why do people keep saying I'm scared? I'm not scared. I guess I'm just still a little freaked from last night, sure, but Alex had nothing to do with that."

"Really?"

"Yes."

"You're fine?" Tina asked skeptically.

"That's right. I'm fine," she said with enough confidence to ward Tina off.

Once the confrontation had ended, and people returned to their own business, Susan made a point to sit extra close to Alex. She wanted to show that there was nothing to be feared, that he was just another child.

He was just a child, right?

CHAPTER 29

Though Chris was a big supporter of the escape movement, like Angela, he had not yet figured out a realistic plan. So, he stayed busy doing what he could. Food was a great opportunity for him to talk with people he normally wouldn't. This was important to him since he was going to need their support once his master plan formed – a natural-born politician.

With apple slices wobbling back and forth on his silver tray like shivering red moons, he stepped briskly across the empty mess hall, toward the sanctuary door.

Just as he reached it, the door swung open and knocked the tray from his hands. He had been so careful, but had not anticipated a sneak attack.

The apple moons tumbled from their metal sky and skipped across the floor. The perpetrator of their demise reared his bashful head from around the edge of the door. Chris swore whoever it was, he would never forgive them, but, as it turned out to be Matthew, he changed his thinking. They were just apples, for heaven's sake.

"Oh, shit! Sorry, Chris."

"It's okay," he reassured.

The two of them knelt down in unison and started gathering the slices.

"Matt, you don't have to help me. You have enough to worry about."

"It's my fault they fell, isn't it?"

Chris chose not to answer. He purposely picked up the slices that had fallen further away to avoid the chance that their hands might touch, which he would have enjoyed, but knew Matthew would not.

"How are things in there, are people hungry?" Chris asked to banish the silence between them.

"I'm not sure. I haven't been talking much with people."

"Right, yes, of course not."

"But, I noticed Dorothy has been talking."

"Oh, that's good. I was afraid she had totally lost her shit."

"She and Tina have been talking to a bunch of families," Matthew said, locking his eyes on Chris to make sure he understood the gravity of what he meant.

"What have they been saying?"

"I don't know," Matthew answered with concern, "but people are listening."

Chris got the message, loud and clear.

"Look, Matthew, thanks for helping. I can handle the rest of it."

Well over half the slices had been rescued, but were in need of a thorough rinsing.

"I'm really sorry. I didn't realize you were behind the door."

"It's all right. I should have made more noise, worn a bell or something."

"I'm sorry, Chris." Matthew stopped collecting apples. His voice crackled with sincerity, like when someone says they have something important to tell you and they actually do. He repeated, "I'm really sorry."

Chris stopped fussing with the tray and paid attention to the way Matthew's face had succumbed. It was an awkward, but sympathetic contortion of his features. His light eyebrows quivered as if he didn't know what to do with them.

The display was heartbreaking and Chris stared back into Matthew's dampening eyes, knowing full well that his own were not far behind. Matthew was not usually the kind of guy to wear his emotions on his sleeve, let alone plastered across his face, and Chris took pity.

"Hey, it's okay," Chris said tenderly. "It's all right."

"I'm sorry," Matthew cried. "I'm so sorry…"

Before Matthew collapsed under the pressure, Chris grabbed hold of him and pulled him close. He rested Matthew's sobbing head between his neck and shoulder and supported him there, while endless tears began to storm.

Chris gathered his arms around Matthew's back and squeezed tight, as if trying to crush the sorrow out of him. It seemed to work.

To Chris's delight, Matthew returned the embrace. For the first time since the Behemoth arrived, they each felt safe.

Gradually, Matthew collected himself enough to regulate his breath. When he seemed stable, Chris pulled back from their tenderness.

"I didn't know you liked apples so much," Chris said.

A smile emerged on Matthew's worn face; it was a welcome sign of hope, like finding a flower amidst a field of desolation.

"I do. I really do," Matthew responded quickly, then leaned in and pressed his lips against Chris'.

The surprise kiss lasted long enough for Matthew to thoroughly massage Chris' mouth with his own. The intimate exchange was exquisite and boiled Chris' desire to almost unbearable heights. But, it was more than that. Lust and love had become unified within Chris in a powerful way.

As soon as the moment was over, Matthew got up and continued on his path for some water. It was not meant as a crass exit; it was simply the only thing Matthew could think to do.

Chris was left, kneeling on the floor, to soak in the lasting memory of their dearest contact. The thought of Matthew consumed him the way only young love can. He was exhilarated, electrified; his dreams had been made manifest and proved more miraculous than he dared hoped.

One thing became absolutely clear; they had to escape. They had to escape, if only to be together one more time.

CHAPTER 30

Santa's throne had become a curiously fitting home for Angela and her despair. Though the tears had stopped, a debilitating numbness had settled into their place. She knew she needed to return to Alex and come up with a way to get them out of this nightmare, yet she remained planted in the chair, tucked away in the privacy of the stage.

Rick had, in some way, destroyed her. He might as well have gutted her like Clara. In fact, in a way, he had. He had taken something from her. Angela felt sixteen again and wished she could remember how to be strong, how to fight him, but all she could think to do was hide.

The heavy curtains of the stage rustled as someone stepped into her space. She had no fear it was Rick, unless he was now wearing shoes with sizable heels.

The footsteps clicked their way around the wood floor as if searching for something. Angela was sure if she didn't move, they would never find her behind the burlap. The thought was appealing, but those penetrating clicking noises got the better of her.

"For Christ's sake," Angela eventually blurted out, "what?" She got up out of the chair and revealed herself from behind the curtain. To Angela's amazement, it had been Emily stumbling around. She looked distressed, perhaps even more distressed than Angela.

"Emily… What do you want?"

"I was looking for you," she said, as she scanned Angela up and down.

"I'm right here, behind curtain number three."

"I have something I need to tell you."

"What's wrong, is it Alex?" The question raced from her mouth.

"No, he's fine."

"Okay then… what?"

"There's something I want to say to you."

Angela was not in the mood to hear any of Emily's condemnations, so she beat her to it.

"Don't bother," said Angela. "I can guess every word that comes out of your mouth. Every word. I'm a filthy devil's whore, a dirty little slut, a fucking waste. So, thanks for the visit, Emily. It was grand, can't wait to see you again."

"You're not the whore," Emily admitted plainly.

"Sorry, what?"

"I said you're not the whore. You never were."

"Can you say that again? I want to get it on tape."

"Dang it, Angela! I'm trying to say something to you."

"I didn't realize it was story time," Angela teased. It was clear Emily was not amused. "Okay, go ahead. I'm listening."

"The night Rick went missing, he said he was just driving around without a place to go and ended up here. It's not true. He was coming out here to meet me. That's why he drove out to the church that night. So, you're not the whore." Emily could not even look at her confessor.

A toxic mixture stirred within Angela. Rick's infidelity was scarcely a shock, but Emily's righteous judgment that Angela had suffered for the past three months, which now proved wholly hypocritical, was maddening.

"You and Rick? For how long?" she asked.

"A while."

"Years?"

"Years."

"And for all those years, you've poured that shit out on me. Hated me for being with him."

"The story's not done," Emily said, resorting to her old forceful self. "We met at the church most often. It was a good place -- no one would suspect. I can't tell you how it started, it just did. Please believe that I'm sorry, Angela. I really am. But, I couldn't keep lying to myself, my husband, or my God. Enough was enough. So, on the night he disappeared, I decided I just wouldn't show up. I guess, when he realized I wasn't there waiting for him, he got drunk and wandered off. When I found out he went missing, I couldn't say anything. It would have destroyed Michael."

"So, why are you telling me this now?"

"'Cause in the 'End Times', the only thing that matters is being square with God."

"How about being square with just me? Does that matter?" Angela asked earnestly, and waited patiently for a reply.

The two women stood in silence while Emily considered the question.

"Yes, that matters," she finally admitted. "I'm so sorry for the pain I caused you, Angela. You didn't deserve it. I guess I just couldn't face what I had done. Now you know."

"Yes I do."

Emily swallowed deeply and nodded. For the first time in her confession, she managed to meet Angela's eyes. She had not expected a pardon for her crimes, but she had hoped the sinking feeling in her stomach would lesson once her sins had been spoken aloud. They had only become heavier, but that was her cross to bear. As there was nothing left to be said, Emily started back to the sanctuary.

"Emily," Angela added, "thank you for the truth."

After Emily left her alone on the stage, Angela had time to process the revelation. How many lies were told to her and about her? How many telling looks were shared between Rick and Emily that she hadn't noticed? How many times had her husband abandoned her to be with his mistress? The questions solidified one thing; Rick, even before he attacked her, before he was a mad prophet, before he hit her, was already a ruined thing. When they first met, she was just too young to recognize his inherent malice, but in time it had all become crystal clear.

Strangely, it was Emily's confession that pulled Angela from the murk. After how badly she had been wronged, she could not allow herself to be stunned into such an idle state anymore. If she did, it was as though she believed that she deserved every indignity. By remaining hidden, she was agreeing that yes, Rick could do with her as he pleased, yes, Emily could deal her such lies and get away with it, and yes, the Behemoth could hold her captive and threaten the life of her son.

No, she thought. *It was time to push back.*

CHAPTER 31

Before Angela could open the door to the sanctuary, it opened for her. She pulled back to avoid its blind swing, narrowly missing the momentum of the hefty wood.

Chris, who had been the one so eager to shove the door open, came charging out of the room and nearly ran into her.

"Chris!" Angela exclaimed, catching his shoulder just before it dug into her gut. "Whoa, what's the matter?"

"Angela! I was just coming to look for you. Quick, you have to hear this."

He grabbed her by the arm and pulled her into the sanctuary.

Dorothy had situated herself near the pulpit. Gary and Tina stood in front of her while everyone else in the room watched from the pews.

"I know you don't want to talk about it, but we're running out of time," Dorothy said, forcing her voice far past the two people she was addressing.

"I can't. This is insane," Gary responded softly, and shook his head.

"Do you think this sunny afternoon is going to last forever? The sun is falling even as we speak. You know it, I know it. We all know it. And exactly what do you think is going to happen after dark?" she asked him.

"Dorothy's right," Tina added. "Gary, listen to her."

"No. I won't hear another word of this."

Even from across the room, Angela could piece together the morbid topic under discussion. To her, the idea of it remained too repulsive to entertain. Simply put, giving the Behemoth what it wanted was not an option. It was clear that in her brief absence, much had changed.

"Dorothy bounced back strong," Chris said, almost to himself. "She's got them all freaked the fuck out, keeps waving around a clock and reminding people its attached to a big-ass bomb."

"Why is she doing this?" asked Angela.

"I have no idea. Ever since last night, Matthew said she's been talking to everyone. Look at them, she knows they're watching her." Chris gestured to the crowd of onlookers. They were glued to her.

The heated discussion was interrupted by a deafening thud. The ceiling shook and loosened a few older planks of wood. The room fell silent as the rumble echoed. It sent vibrations through the entire structure of the building. Angela could feel the tremors tickle her feet.

Her first thought was to find Alex.

Another tremendous pound sounded as though it may crumble the roof altogether. A few of the loosened planks gave way and tumbled down against the pews.

As the sky started to fall, congregation members scattered like a panicked anthill. Screams added to the dissonant soundscape and seemed to excite the pounding.

"It's on the roof!" Susan yelled.

It was like the Behemoth, which could not have weighed any less than a truck, had taken to dancing atop of the church. Maybe it was a ritual mockery of the lives contained within, or maybe it was just something the beast liked to do. Either way, it had made its presence known.

It leapt from one corner of the sanctuary to the other and took vast strides that cracked the plaster above their heads. The jovial rhythms of its stomping threatened to collapse the church itself.

Then suddenly, it stopped. The screaming members, however, were slow to catch on that the terror had ended – for now.

Alex peaked his head up from Susan's pew and saw his mother in the doorway. He jumped from his spot and ran to her.

"Mommy!" he yelled. He grabbed hold of her and whispered, "You made it go away."

Angela knew this was not true, but if it helped Alex feel safe, she was willing to play along.

Many of the other children were crying and again, each family separated from the group to tend to their offspring.

To her far right, Angela noticed Emily holding her daughter, Samantha. The little girl's face was flush and full of tears. Emily bobbed her up and down as a distraction from the panic.

"I want to go home…" Samantha sniffled.

"I know, honey. I know." Emily kissed Samantha's tiny hand.

"Where did it go?" hollered a middle-aged man who sounded like a child himself.

"What are we going to do, we can't just keep sitting here!" screamed another.

"Quiet!" Dorothy yelled. She took a few steps closer to the pulpit to give herself some height. It worked. People settled and listened. "You want to know what we're going to do? I'll tell you. We're going to stick together. It's the only way."

"Yes," Tina agreed adamantly.

Dorothy continued, "The time has come to accept our situation. Things have changed. We need to recognize that what we are dealing with, we cannot overcome. We won't out last it. We won't out run it. You think it's scary when it bangs on the walls? Tonight, it won't just bang, it will come crashing through with all the force of nature and take us one by one. We have two options: we comply or we die."

"No! Dorothy! What are you saying?" Angela interjected. Her thoughts had barely formed before she said them. Rarely had her gut spoken with such urgency. She jogged up the aisle as the lead candidate for sanity.

"Angela, do you have something to say?" Dorothy patronized.

"Yes. We can find another way out of this."

"Fine, then tell us your miracle plan to evade the wrath of god."

"That thing is not God."

"Then what is it?"

"I don't know."

"Well, I do," said Dorothy, with abiding confidence. "I know what it is. Woe onto you who still deny the Behemoth. He can be kind, he can be just. He has gifts, wondrous gifts, if only we'd give him what he wants."

"Go ahead and remind us what he wants, Dorothy. Tell us. Name it. I want to hear you say it in front of everybody." Angela had fire in her, and she stoked the flames well.

"The Behemoth wants our devotion."

"No, don't hide behind your careful little words. No more sneaking. Let's hear you say exactly what it wants from us, if you can." Angela had not imagined that Dorothy, of all the congregation members, would be the one to take up the monster's mantle. But, if she still trusted her eyes and ears, then she could not deny that this woman, whom she had cared for and received care from, was proposing to sacrifice the life of a blameless child.

Dorothy broke eye contact with Angela and turned away from her crowd. At first, Angela counted this as a victory, until Dorothy returned to the stage, her eyes reddened with raging sorrow.

"How dare you test me. I have lost my only daughter. I know exactly what the Behemoth means to take and still, I'm eager to give it to him. I, now and forever, put my faith into the only god that I can see. The one who made himself known, and can reunite me with my child. I implore you all to join me and put your faith in the Behemoth. We have no choice." Dorothy spoke with passion and rectitude.

"Oh fuck," Chris muttered to himself.

"No, Dorothy," Angela said. "We have a choice."

"Tell that to Clara. Tell that to my daughter."

"I'm sorry about what happened to Clara; I can't imagine the pain losing her has caused you. But, you don't want anyone in this room to suffer the way you have. I know you don't want that."

"You're wrong, Angela, you just don't understand. Giving the Behemoth what he wants will avoid any more suffering, not cause it."

"Think about Clara. Really think about her. Remember who she was and what she stood for. She would be ashamed to hear you say the things you're saying."

"I'll do better than remember her. I'll be with her again, for the Behemoth promised me so."

Angela conceded her attempt to rationalize. It was clear there was something else at work in the sanctuary now. A desperate, delirious wishing had spread like an infection from Dorothy to at least half of the congregation. If Angela was not careful, she feared she might catch it as well.

"You're saying someone else's child should die?" Angela asked blatantly. The moment had come for her to test just how much humanity Dorothy had lost.

"We need to give the Behemoth what he wants." Dorothy's careful words were back and they served her well. "Emily had it right; we were touched by god. It's either one of us, or all of us."

In the audience, Emily seemed to cower from the resurrection of her own remark. She had not yet decided which side of the fence to plant herself on, but the reference to her own words had left a foul taste.

Angela was taken aback that she had to stand alone against Dorothy. Was there no one else who shared her outrage? Gary seemed to have been adamantly against it, but he remained invisible with his arms crossed. Perhaps his wife, Tina, had been busy in his ear. Out of the entire crowd, it was only Chris who Angela could see shared in her disgust.

"We can't let this happen," Chris said, turning to Matthew. "Someone has to try again."

"Try what?" Matthew asked, but Chris had already left his side.

He watched, bewildered, as Chris snuck out of the back of the sanctuary into the mess hall. It was not until Chris was gone that Matthew had time to realize what was happening.

"Chris?" he whispered. "Chris!"

"We can't just wait for god to go away," Dorothy's powerful tirade continued. "In the night that will soon be upon us, he will come for us all."

CHAPTER 32

Chris raced full speed across the mess hall until he was pressed flat against the front door of the church.

To stand audience to such a grotesque debate – like the one he was currently running from – was something he didn't have the stomach for.

It was clear to him that the congregation had been polluted by a truly toxic sentiment – the needs of the many trumping the needs of the few. He always had problems with *The Many*. Who made up this privileged group and why were their lives of paramount importance? What made them such hot shit? He had witnessed the mobs gather their pitchforks before and had come to recognize it as a survival instinct. Eat or be eaten. Chris easily recalled the cruelty he suffered in school by the hands of *The Many* once they found out he belonged to the few. It was one thing for kids to call him a fudge packer or send Photoshopped pictures of him sucking dicks, but now, the frightened masses had their sights set on the murder of a child. In order for The Many to survive, someone always has to suffer, someone has to be sacrificed. *Well*, Chris thought, *fuck that.*

His hands pressed firmly against the grooves of the wood. He breathed in and held the air in his lungs, letting his left hand slide down to the doorknob. The metal, once he reached it, was cold.

He turned the knob and the inner latch of the door gradually slid out of the frame. He closed his eyes and pulled.

The door did not open. It was locked.

He unlocked the door and tried again, this time with success.

The world opened up to him. Sunlight flooded in like a wave against his body, and although he knew he was about to dangle himself like a worm on a hook for the beast, the warmth that freedom offered still calmed him.

Stepping beyond the threshold would be his next challenge, so he was quick about it. Before his doubt had a chance to catch up with him, he took the leap and found himself standing outside the church in the open air.

At first, his eyes struggled to adjust to the spectacular brightness and he shielded them. As he did, the door gently closed behind him, as if respectful of the risk he was taking. When his vision returned to him, he was amazed to see how very normal everything was.

The tall grass that pawed at the sides of the church had continued to grow. Highway 7, which was only a few feet away from where he stood, remained largely abandoned without a traveler in sight. All the cars were still lined up neatly in the parking lot. It was no wonder no one had come knocking on the church door; in view of its banal visage, who would have suspected the chaos hiding inside?

Chris scanned the rolling plains of the field that stretched on for acres. In all that vastness, he found no giant beast on the hunt, no horrible creature charging to destroy him. He found no Behemoth.

He realized he was still holding his breath and finally released it.

With one of his hands placed firmly on the rail of the stone stairs, he made his way down to the ground, but slowly. With each step he would pause and pivot his head all around like a bird.

As he edged further from the door, he regretted not grabbing his father's keys to the van, but it was too late to go back. The van would have brought too much attention to him anyway. He meant for this to be a covert operation, not a rambling car chase.

His feet crunched against the stony dirt of the parking lot. Crouching seemed appropriate, so he ducked down to the height of the bushes. With small shifts of his feet, he brought himself to the corner of the church. He pressed his back against the brick wall, but before he made the turn, he considered how vulnerable he would be once he was out in the open. Around the edge of the church, there was nowhere else to hide. Aside from the few remaining cars and the old well, it would be just him, the church, and a straight view all the way to the Burward forest. If he was going to be spotted, this was where it was going to happen.

In order to keep himself moving, he needed a way to banish the fears he had for his own life and think of the lives of the people who were depending on him. He focused on Matthew, the first person he truly allowed into his heart. He focused on his parents, even though he considered his mom to be borderline psychotic. He focused on Angela and Alex. He focused on Dorothy in all her horror.

And then he stepped out into full view of the field.

To his immediate relief, he again saw no signs of the Behemoth. However, there was no time to stop and gawk, so he swiftly assessed the distance between him and a thick line of bushy fir trees that separated the fields. If he could make it that far, then surely he would be beyond the Behemoth's sight and could then bring back some help, like the entire army.

When he took his first step, his foot fell further than expected and he stumbled to regain his balance. He looked back to spit in the hole that had tripped him, but it was no ordinary hole. He stared into a deep footprint that was about half the size of his body. Three large talons had carved distinct grooves in the dirt and left a bird-like impression. Judging from its shape, Chris wondered if the Behemoth was actually a giant chicken. Even if it were, the sheer size of the imprint did not allow for much levity. A monster chicken was still a monster. It was obvious whatever had left the footprint could split him in half with a mere flick of its big toe.

His mind started flipping through different configurations of what this creature might look like. Each assembly was more hideous, and intimidating than the last. Some had toothy beaks, some had more than two legs like a spider, and some had giant cat eyes that were cutting toward him even as he stood there. Was it really too late to turn back?

He pushed these thoughts out of his head and again concentrated on the people he loved.

After a purging breath, he clenched his fists and sprinted toward the line of trees. Almost like a cartoon, his feet tossed puffs of dirt into the air behind him. The uneven ground didn't help his speed. Still, his vision remained on the branches of the firs, whose tender sway encouraged him like fans at the end of a marathon. Unfortunately, he had overestimated his athleticism, and the trees were not approaching nearly as fast as he would have liked.

He didn't look back. He had a singular focus that required all his energy. There was no time to worry about what might be coming. If he allowed himself to be distracted, one wrong step could plant him, face first, into the ground. He did, however, imagine Matthew stepping out from between the trees. This illusion inspired him and fed the aching muscles in his legs with untapped stamina, banishing the burn.

His breathing had risen into a steady beat. His sharp inhale worked in tandem with his left foot, while his exhale was joined to his right.

Gradually, there came another rhythm. It was slower and deeper than his and echoed like gunshots across the field. It was impossible to pinpoint where it was coming from, but there was no denying it was getting louder. Eventually, he had to assume that what he heard were the leaping footsteps of the beast galloping towards him.

With only twenty more feet between him and the trees, he decided to push on without checking over his shoulder. If he were to look and find the beast was charging, then what good would it do him? Either way, his best bet was to find a place to hide.

The thumping footsteps were so overpowering, it sounded as though the ground behind him was breaking apart and he was barely keeping ahead of the fallout. He recalled the deafening rumble of a building being demolished when he was ten. He fought the urge to curl into a ball and cover his ears, as he did then, and instead concentrated on the finish line.

The beast gained on him quicker than he thought possible. There was no way to outrun it; he simply needed to reach the trees.

When its next foot landed, Chris felt a rush of air on his back. It almost blew him over. Luckily, Chris's own foot had finally reached the edge of the firs, so he ducked down and dove between the branches, disappearing into their protection.

CHAPTER 33

"It's true," Angela announced to the sanctuary. "I don't know what that creature is, I admit it. I can't offer you answers. I don't have hope to give. All I have is the certainty that if we give this thing what it wants, there will be nothing left of us. How will you ever again hug a friend or kiss your spouse, knowing that it came at the cost of a child's life? Sacrifice may seem like the only way we can survive, but it's not how we're going to live. Don't fool yourselves, those are two very different things. We can't just give up on our compassion because we're afraid."

The congregation was hushed by Angela's plea for humanity. Even Dorothy, who remained planted next to her, had absorbed the words. However, whether or not it was enough to sway her, remained to be seen. For the rest of the room, you could almost hear the brains toiling.

With that, Angela dismounted from the spotlight. She had said her piece and wanted to leave the space open for people to decide for themselves.

But before she could make it back to her seat, Dorothy launched another attack.

"Well, Angela. Those were some pretty words, but being pretty is basically all they're good for, isn't it?

None of what you said really helps us get out of this situation, does it?" she asked, with a vicious bite.

"No, it doesn't. That's not what I was trying to say."

"Forget about what you were trying to say, then. Tell us, what can we do?"

"We can try to escape," Angela answered, predicting with accuracy the reaction it would provoke.

The congregation hummed with skeptical murmurs like a muddled game of telephone. The buzz was one Angela had become accustomed to, but she still resented it. Trapped in that thick cloud of yammering, it was obvious not a single worthwhile word was uttered.

Again, Dorothy focused her crowd. "The Behemoth was very clear what will happen if we try to escape. Do you want us to die? Would that make you happy, if it killed us all?"

"I want us to try!" Angela screamed. "For Christ's sake, all I want is for us to try! I want us to decide there are things that are bigger than our own little lives. Things that are worth fighting for, even dying for. Kindness, caring, mercy, love, and compassion. Without it, who gives a fuck? Who gives a fuck if you survive another second in this godless place? Who gives a fuck about injustice? Who gives a fuck about torture and murder? Who gives a fuck if your husband beats you, or rapes you? No one is ever going to care. And if no one cares, then fuck it all. We've pissed it away."

"So, you don't want to use pretty words anymore; you're using ugly ones. Well, Angela, they're just as empty."

"Dorothy, if you go through with this, you had better pray there is no God, because you'll definitely burn in Hell!." Angela turned her back to her opponent, not only to end the bickering, but also to hide her furious tears. She pushed through the crowd to the back of the sanctuary where she could be calm and secluded with Alex.

Just then, Matthew burst into the room from the mess hall and charged up the aisle.

"What is it, Matthew?" Susan asked, and offered him a soothing touch.

"I think Chris is outside."

"What did he say?" Tina demanded, having picked up on the key word – her son's name.

Matthew repeated loudly, "Chris went outside!"

"Oh, God!" Tina screamed, "Why?"

"How far did he go?" Gary hollered.

"I don't know."

Gary immediately started heading for the door, with Tina following closely behind.

"Did he make it?" Angela asked, desperate for hope.

An answer came, but not from Matthew's lips, and without the hope she had yearned for.

The silhouette of Chris' body slammed against the stained-glass window. A cracking sound was heard above the heavy thud of his torso. Presumably, it had come from his head, where a light dusting of blood erupted.

Tina and Gary instantly recognized the face pressed against the coloured glass. Although it was difficult to make out through the ripples of the molded window exactly what was happening, it looked like three massive claws were holding Chris up by his head.

Gary grabbed the arm of the pew in front of him, as his body shut down from the sight.

Adding to the agony, Chris was still alive and his tormented screams reverberated against the window. The subtleties of his cries were muffled by the glass, which at the same time exaggerated his volume, like a blown speaker. He may have been begging for someone to save him, but it was impossible to tell, and even more impossible to obey.

The Behemoth lifted Chris' body up the length of the window for everyone to see. His face scraped along the smooth surface with an unnerving squeak, coaxing the glass to moan. The rest of Chris' body thrashed wildly against the influence of the beast, straining his neck as his feet swung freely back and forth. He kicked, punched and squirmed in all directions like a deer in a bear trap.

"Chris! Someone help him!" Matthew yelled.

The giant claw pulled Chris all the way to Heaven at the top of the window and lined up his face with that of one of the angels, taking great care in matching up their eyes. Chris stared through the blue glass of the angel's pupils over the entire congregation. He was searching for Matthew, but couldn't find him in the sea of bustling bodies. He was desperate to taste their connection one last time – his dying wish, if he were granted the luxury of one.

Unbearable pressure built against Chris' nose and chin as the Behemoth squeezed his face against the glass. His head came crashing through, shattering the barrier.

The face of the angel broke apart in an explosion of golden crystal shards and thick red spurts. Half the glass scattered on the floor, the other half splintered into Chris' exposed face, imbedding itself deep into the flesh of his lips, cheeks and forehead. His nostrils had been peeled open by the cracking blades of the window, but his eyes, although closed forever, managed to evade any major damage.

His throat partly separated from the bottom of his jaw as the weight of his body pressed his head down against the sharp edge of the opening. A stream of blood gurgled from his neck all the way from the high heavens down to the lowly hordes of the faithful.

The beast left Chris hanging there in the window like a rag doll with his carved red face looking out over the stunned masses. As the final drizzles of life trickled from his body, the muscles in his cheeks started to tense and pulled his torn lips into a devastating smile. Despite its appearance, the expression was not one of happiness or contentment; it was merely the unfortunate byproduct of a body shutting down, of life leaving.

The monstrous theatrics of it all were more than a punishment for trying to escape; they were sadistic. Chris had been transformed into a grisly monument to the Behemoth's savagery and it proved, as if there was any doubt before, that it had no limits.

Tina had seen none of the attack, not that she needed to. She judged from Gary's shivering state and the stilted quiet in the room that her son was dead. Her Chris was dead, her sweet angel.

CHAPTER 34

Susan had gathered the children into the far corner of the sanctuary – away from the smiling corpse that hung in the window – and distracted them with old fairytales that she could only half-remember. A few princesses had switched names and every fable had gained a dragon that was inevitably slain. This specific correlation, perhaps, was not due to a faulty recollection like the others, but rather a wishful hope on Susan's part for a valiant knight to appear that could slay their own beast. Either way, it seemed to keep the kids contented.

On the other side of the room, the rest of the congregation had collected the sleeping sheets and attempted to drape them over the stained-glass window. However, the window was built too opulently to be concealed. Instead they compromised and wrapped one sheet around Chris' protruding head. The excess fabric hung down the window, which more or less covered the blood.

There was no way to get the offending body down unless they ventured outside, but not a soul in the room was willing to take that risk, so a delicately placed sheet was the best they could do.

Since Alex had joined the other children for Susan's story time, Angela again wandered into the mess hall alone. Oddly, she found herself returning to the stage, though at first she wasn't exactly sure why.

She passed through the curtains and allowed herself to be enveloped by the solitude they provided. Rather aimlessly, as if she were in a trance, she floated about the space until she came to the empty throne.

Suddenly, every roaming notion of woe that had rolled through her head like a choking fog became solid, giving her something to focus on and take hold of.

Angela grabbed the chair and swung it into centre stage.

When she stared down at the throne, she realized she had returned to the place of her attack not out of forgetfulness, fear or stupidity, but out of defiance. It was a challenge she was setting, a challenge for her dear husband to reappear. Her capacity for fear and sorrow had been tapped; all that was left was her own fury, and she wanted to share it with Rick and the beast, and if there was a bit left over, she might let Dorothy have a taste too.

"Can you hear me?" she inquired of the invisible person sitting in the chair. It was not clear, even to her, if she was speaking to Rick, the Behemoth or God. Distinguishing between them really didn't matter anymore. She had enough contempt to spread around and each was equally deserving.

"I hope you can. I hope you can hear me. Cause I'll wait, you know. I can wait here for as long as it takes for you to show. I'll wait, so I can ask you to your face. Who are you? I think I know already, but I want to be sure. I want to look into your eyes and I want you to tell me who you think you are. And we'll see if we agree. Personally speaking, I think you're a murdering bastard. You're a degenerate, nasty fucking piece of shit. That young boy, Chris? He didn't deserve to die. But, you took him anyway. His parents don't deserve to suffer, but they suffer anyway. None of them deserved it, not Clara, not Sandy, not Bruce, not Don. But they're dead. It should've been me, hanging by my neck, not Chris. But I'm still here. So, where are you? Hiding? Are you being mysterious to teach us a lesson? To assert yourself? Prove your power? Keep us in line? Why do you do it?" The chair remained very still, and very empty.

"Is pain a joke to you? See, I think maybe you're just afraid. You're pathetic and you're afraid. And you're hurting us 'cause you're scared and sad, but you don't want to be. That's it, isn't it? If I'm wrong, please correct me. I'm asking you to appear on this throne and let me know if I'm way off on this. 'Cause honestly, if you make me judge you from what I've seen, then I'll just have to expose you for the miserable, petty, cruel son of a bitch that you are."

Again, the chair was silent.

"Nothing? Nothing to say? Fine. I guess you either can't hear me, or you're everything I said you were; only worse, you're a coward, too. I'm done. I'm not playing your game anymore."

Infuriated by the indifference of the throne, Angela kicked the golden chair over onto its back. It had heard her grievances and ignored them. This offense, though not the greatest she had suffered, still measured as the most personal. Was the pain she endured so insignificant?

She stomped one of the chair's wooden legs right off and broke the left armrest. The cheap paint was scraped away and she snapped the back frame until it twisted in the wrong direction. All of this she did to make the throne more befitting for its degenerate king.

When her mangling of the furniture was complete, she kicked it back into the wings, where she hoped it would remain wounded and forgotten.

Craig Stewart

CHAPTER 35

Angela pulled back the stage curtain and stepped down into the mess hall. A quiet weeping echoed from across the room.

Next to the old piano were two hunched bodies. Their backs bobbed up and down, set into motion by the wake of their sobbing.

As Angela stared, she came to recognize the two mourners as Tina and Gary. Understandably, they had abandoned the room where their child's body hung and wandered into the mess hall for some solace.

For several minutes, she stood and watched them in secret. The heartache they displayed was exactly what Angela was most afraid of. More than her own death, she feared life without her son. There could be no more terrible a thing than losing that which you lived for. She knew this fear well, as Rick had awakened it within her every time he took to the bottle. Yet, to see it so close, so tangible, it was like she never really understood the extent of the devastation until now. It was the rawness in Tina's cries that taught it to her.

There was nothing she could say to them, and she knew it. The only thing in the world that could bring their tears to an end would be to reunite them with Chris, which sadly was beyond Angela's power. Still, something compelled her to offer whatever it was she might have to give. If they needed someone to blame, they could blame her. If they needed someone to hit, they could hit her. Anything they needed, Angela yearned to provide it.

Without knowing exactly what she was going to do, Angela began her approach, but soon discovered they weren't alone. There was a third person with them. She had been hidden from sight behind Gary's quivering shoulders. To Angela's dismay, it was Dorothy.

Whatever she was whispering to them, Angela had to admit it seemed to be working. Their sobs had subsided and despite their misery, they were listening to every word. Angela had to know what those words were. What could Dorothy possibly have told them that would give them peace? She moved even closer.

Angela brought herself to the edge of the piano where she was caught in Dorothy's eye, and what an eye it was! If Dorothy had given an in-depth presentation with extensive visual aids, she still could not have communicated her distain better than she did with that stare. Her muddy brown irises squeezed her pupil tight, as if trying to harpoon Angela by sight alone. It didn't want her to go away. It wanted her to die.

Despite this, Angela continued her approach.

"Tina, Gary," she began, "I'm so sorry." She placed her hand on Gary's back.

To Angela's surprise, Gary pulled away and slid closer to his wife. He didn't turn around. He didn't acknowledge her in any way, except to recoil.

"If you need anything. Anything. Just ask me," she added.

"I think you should just go, Angela," said Dorothy confidently. Neither Tina nor Gary spoke up to defy her, so Angela had to assume they wanted her gone, too.

She respected their wishes.

Angela backed away from the three of them and headed toward the sanctuary. As she departed, however, a dread grew in her heart. She could feel the church getting smaller and feared that when the air ran out, exile would be on more lips than she ever would have imagined.

CHAPTER 36

Matthew felt a fever warmth building in Flora's forehead. He wet a cloth and placed it against the heat. All of his actions were done absent of his mind, which was focused on the memory of Chris' face, before it had been shattered.

He thought of the first time Chris and he had met. Matthew was quiet in high school. He passed through the halls so silently, that no one took notice even to pick on him. He didn't stand out in any regard, good or bad. His schoolwork was fine, the teams he played on were fine, his clothes, his attitude, his walk, everything was carefully designed to be fine and nothing more. He was so utterly unremarkable. Then Chris came. They were mere acquaintances through church and had rarely bumped into each other, until that day.

On Thursdays his father worked late, and Matthew had to wait for the city bus to pick him up.

With his hand full of change, Matthew stared pensively up the street awaiting the bumbling chug of bus number ten. This was the routine, and the routine was fine, until Chris saw him standing there like a lonely puppy. Matthew could not fathom why, but Chris approached him and offered him a ride. As it seemed likely the bus had died and become carrion meat for its passengers, he decided to accept Chris' offer. Little did Matthew know that Chris only had his bike. Without hesitation, Chris hopped onto its skinny red frame and motioned for Matthew to take a seat on the handlebars. Reluctantly, Matthew balanced himself on the precarious metal rim and Chris took off.

Together, the two of them cut through town. Matthew remembered the speed both frightened and exhilarated him. He had thought to ask Chris to slow down, especially after a few sharp turns, but the thrill of it all sealed his lips with a wide smile. So the wheels spun faster and Chris pushed on, unstoppable. He had a contagious energy. He had life. Matthew felt it that day coursing through his own sweaty grip as he tried to keep balanced on the bike. After that, he was lucky enough to experience it a few more times, but never as powerfully as he did when the ride finally ended, and Chris gave him his first kiss.

How impossible it was that Chris would now forever only be a memory. His infinite life had suddenly become so finite, and it left Matthew aching for more. He wanted more smiles, and more kisses. He wanted to ride those handlebars again, and again. Why did he not embrace Chris sooner? Why did he treat it like a dirty secret? Now, his mourning was a secret, too. No one knew how much he suffered, so he suffered in silence.

Flora's lip started to tremble.

"You need some water?" Matthew asked, not expecting a response.

Her lips curled as if trying to form words. She had not spoken since losing her eyes, so Matthew had little hope to hold onto.

Then came her faint voice. "The children..." she wheezed.

Matthew had never heard such a deathly tone, especially from his grandmother. It was like every word took with it a little bit of her life.

"The children fly…" she continued. As she faded, a few more words dissolved into the air, but Matthew couldn't make them out. He thought he heard something about clouds, which reminded him of a dream he had the night before.

"Grandma?" He gently nudged her shoulder.

It was too late. She had sunk back into a distant sleep.

Matthew bowed his head and wished he could join her.

"I'm sorry, Matthew." A soft, feminine voice spoke up.

Matthew looked at Flora. She hadn't moved. He turned around and saw Susan standing politely.

"For what?" he asked in return.

"Chris. I know you two were close."

Matthew froze. She knew. Someone knew.

"I have to get my grandma some water," he said suddenly, and stood up from the pew.

"Do you want me to grab it?"

"No. I can do it."

He turned his back to her and walked towards Don's office.

Susan looked down and saw a full bowl of unused water sitting by the pew.

As Matthew drifted through the room, he kept his attention set on the office door. If he could make it that far, then he would have a refuge in which to hide the tears he knew were coming. He resented the attention they would bring. His pain was not for their entertainment. Chris meant more than that.

He jogged up the steps, passed the pulpit and into Don's office. Although the door was secure, and his eyes felt puffy and red, perfectly prepped for the show to begin, to his surprise, he did not cry. Instead, he felt overwhelming detachment. He had opened himself up and found there to be nothing. What brought on this disconnect when, moments before, he felt ready to scream, was a mystery to him. Maybe, he thought, his mind was shutting down as a way to protect itself from the pain. Then, he decided, if he was not going to cry, he might as well fill a glass with fresh water to take back to Flora. That way, the journey was not a complete waste.

Matthew sauntered through the lightless office toward the glow of the bathroom. At one time, he may have been tempted to snoop around Don's private things, but it all seemed of such little importance now.

He stepped into the fully tiled room and was greeted by cool, even light. A small window teased in the light from outside, which was then tossed to and fro among the white tiles until it enclosed Matthew entirely. Although there was not a shadow to be found, he couldn't shake the feeling that the room had something to hide.

The pipes screeched, as if in pain, as a sudden rush of water forced its way out of the dirty brass tap. Matthew was waiting with his glass on the other end to catch the spurts. The faucet coughed and sputtered unevenly into his glass, as if sickened by its own discharge. Despite the pipe's whining, Matthew waited until the water flowed over the glass' edges before turning the tap off.

It was when the drain in the sink finished its chugging that Matthew took notice of the sound of plastic ruffling behind him. The crinkling sound of the material had a playful quality to it, like a grocery bag teased in the breeze.

When he first stepped into the bathroom, he hadn't given the shower much thought, nor had he worried about the thick plastic curtain that was pulled closed around it. However, his attitude changed as the noises became more prominent. The window kept the breeze out. In his mind, that left him with only two options: he was either hearing things that weren't really there, or there was someone behind the shower curtain. After he heard what sounded like a hand running down the length of the plastic, he feared the latter was true.

In this instance, his feeling of detachment served him well. It allowed him to ignore his terror and spin around to face whatever it was.

Once he made the turn, Matthew stared into the ethereal emptiness of the opaque curtain. The texture of the grey material resembled an unsettled fog and kept most of its secrets well hidden. It wouldn't even allow Matthew to get an idea of the size of the shower, let alone what was inside it. There was only infinite blankness.

Slowly, a focal point began to emerge from the mist. It was only a dark blotch at first, but it grew larger as it moved toward Matthew. Although it was getting closer, it remained shrouded, almost deformed by the curtain.

Matthew didn't budge from the sink. His suppressed fear had caught up with him and had taken hold of each of his limbs. He was terrified to behold the thing that was slinking forth, yet his curiosity forced him to keep looking. He wanted to see, but was also afraid to get what he wanted.

The approaching phantom finally reached the edge of the curtain and pressed itself against the plastic. It had the makings of a face, the face of someone familiar. It was Chris staring back at him.

The lively eyes of the boy Matthew loved had been stolen away, replaced by two drained, white globes. Chris' features appeared intact for the most part, but the dark red gashes that cracked his face were noticeable through the hazy vista. His ghostly qualities extended beyond the way he looked. Chris remained inhumanly still, like he was fixed on something, and when he spoke, the dead air from his lungs took a stony toll on his voice.

"Matthew…" came Chris' frigid whisper.

Before he could reply, Matthew had to wait for his mouth to stop quivering. Although it was a mere shadow of Chris' sweet voice, Matthew still reveled in hearing it again.

"Oh my God. Chris." The cup slipped out of Matthew's hand and shattered across the tiles. "Chris, I thought we lost you. I thought I lost you."

"Not lost. I'm found. For the first time. You can be too," breathed out the apparition.

"I want to be. I want to be with you. It's all I want."

"Join me."

"How? Tell me!" Matthew whimpered desperately. The tears his eyes had prepared for had finally arrived. He shed them in front of Chris as a testament to their love.

"I'm in the woods now, with the beast. Join me." His head cocked to the side and crinkled the plastic.

"What are you saying? What do I have to do?"

Without answering, Chris' vacant face pulled back from the curtain and faded into the mist.

Matthew's eyes searched frantically for him to return, but there was nothing.

He grabbed hold of the shower curtain and whipped it open, almost ripping the sheet right off the pole. The shower itself was empty.

He had lost Chris again.

Matthew restored the curtain to its closed position, hoping with all his might that Chris would come back. He remained there for ten full minutes, waiting.

Eventually, Matthew left the bathroom to return to the congregation, but his mind remained amongst the tiles, with a pining stare fixed on the curtain and its cloudy unknown.

CHAPTER 37

The sun had grown weak and surrendered to the creeping dark that rose in the east. Still, it held its grip on the horizon, staving off a little longer the horrors its plunge might bring.

An orange light spilled out across the field and lent the stalks a fiery glow. The warmth slid across the church itself and traced along its edge giving it a golden trim. However, the splendor was misleading. As elegant as the light was, it was actually the last taste of what the sun had to offer. Its fleeting beauty meant that all would soon be swallowed by the night – the church's final night.

There were no more songs for the birds to sing, no more leaves for the wind to dance with, there was only a quiet waiting left in Davidson's field. The church stood at attention like a condemned man before a firing squad. Perhaps the gun would jam, perhaps it would not; either way, the palms were sweaty, and the witnesses held their breath.

In the shelter of the sanctuary, everyone gathered in restless silence. Though nobody spoke aloud, there was an energy buzzing up and down the pews. Feet tapped and knuckles cracked while congregation members debated within themselves what was to be done once the light had gone. The nightmare of the past two days saturated their thoughts and washed away whatever ethical certainty they once had. Of course, at first they thought they could not sacrifice a member of their fellowship. Then, once they looked at their husband, wife or child and imagined the beast's ruthless talons slashing them, they reconsidered. It was all so insufferably tragic. The thing that permitted them to delve into depravity was the very virtue they held most dear – love. Any sinister action they were considering could only flourish within them because they cared deeply for another. They were killing, not with kindness, but because of it.

Staggeringly, there were very few members who had taken to praying for guidance. Emily was the most obvious one of them. She had forced both her children to join her and so, on their knees, they recited in unison whatever prayers came to mind. Michael, however, had refused and stationed himself away from his family at the rear of the room where he stalked back and forth. Given his hefty build, his footsteps sounded like a distant war drum.

Matthew, who every few seconds glanced at Chris' body still hanging in the window, had perched on the edge of Flora's pew. Flora remained a prisoner of her deep sleep, and Matthew feared she might never be released. Though, considering how things could turn out, he thought, maybe that was a blessing in disguise.

Angela waited a few pews up from Matthew with Alex nuzzled under her arm. Within the next few minutes, the cowardly sun would be hidden, and whatever foul plan the Behemoth had in mind for its unbelievers, would come shrieking out of the night. Most likely, Angela imagined, there would be blood, savagery and darkness. No matter what devils came to collect them, however, Angela would fight back until her own body was just bones and grit. That much at least was owed for the death of Clara and Chris, and for the life of her son.

On a more hopeful note, Angela dreamed that in the chaos of the beast's wrath, she and her son might have a chance to sneak away through the basement. As unlikely as that fantasy seemed, it was the best she had to hold onto.

"Mom?" Alex whispered sleepily. He had been napping against her stomach, and although he was now awake, his eyelids were slow to realize that fact.

"Yes, sweetie?" she inquired, tenderly.

"Do we have any pizza?" he asked, having been dreaming of the melted, cheesy indulgence.

The innocence of his request inspired Angela to do something she thought she would never do again – she smiled. The benefactor of this gift was beautifully unaware of its preciousness, which made it all the more valuable.

"Sorry, I can't get you pizza right now." She gently brushed her fingers through the confusion of his perpetually knotted hair.

"That's okay."

She brought her face down to his and placed a kiss where it always ought to be, just between his hairline and the single freckle on his forehead.

With her son curled around her, Angela examined the room. The light was dimmer now, and the orange rays, which moments before, had been so prominent, were struggling to pierce the windows. The ones that did were so agonized by their journey, they turned red and lost what vivaciousness they had. Soon, not even the faint crimson glow would be left.

The Behemoth was nigh.

From the congregation arose a galvanizing voice, though not one Angela was thankful for, as Dorothy took to the pulpit. She ascended the red stairs like she was the head of a funeral precession, each step careful and confined. By the time she was ready to speak, she had already captured the attention of the entire room.

"Very shortly, the sun will set. When it does, the Behemoth's footsteps will come pounding through the dark. It will search us out. It will find us. It's our choice to be damned or not. I choose grace, as I know in your hearts, you do, too. There's no time left for debate." Dorothy nodded at Michael and commanded, "Grab him now."

Angela replayed the end of Dorothy's speech in her head, attempting to make sense of it. Despite her efforts, she could not diminish the chill she felt from Dorothy's final militant order. Grab him now. Grab him, she said. Suddenly, the weight from Alex's body was gone. Angela looked down to discover he was no longer resting in her lap. He had been snatched away and was now trapped under the thickness of Michael's python arms.

Alex reached for his mother, but it was impossible for him to squirm free of the suffocating bear hug.

Once the shock had abated, Angela shot to her feet and leaped into the aisle after her cub. However, before she could take two steps, she felt hands press down upon her. Restraining her left arm was Tina, which Angela was not terribly surprised by, but on her right arm was Gary, the man who two days ago offered to fix her rusted car for free. She struggled against them, but their binds held true.

"No!" Angela screamed, as Alex was stolen further and further away from her.

"One of us or all of us," said Dorothy from the pulpit. "We choose one."

Angela pulled her arm forward, almost knocking Gary off his feet. He readjusted his stance to better brace himself against her thrashing.

The rest of the room looked upon her suffering with tacit apathy. They did nothing to stop it. Their silence was their consent.

"Not Alex!" Angela yelled. "Please, not my son!"

"Not your son? What about Tina and Gary's son? What about my daughter? The Behemoth wants a child, so it's only fitting that we give it Rick's own flesh and blood." Dorothy stood her ground.

"But he's just a little boy, he's just my little boy. Dorothy, I'm begging you, you have to stop this!" Knowing that Dorothy had turned to stone, Angela redirected her search for sympathy to Gary. She stared at his face until he made the mistake of meeting her eyes.

"Gary," she cried. "This is wrong. You know it's wrong. Please, don't let them take my baby."

"It's done," he replied bleakly. "I'm sorry, Angela. But it's already done."

Angela's eyes frantically searched the room for someone, anyone, who might be able to help her. Her vision roamed across the shame of the congregation and found mostly bowed heads and averted faces. She peered at Susan, who had turned her back to hide herself away from the kidnapping. Matthew's eyes were still fixed on the corpse in the window.

She saw an abundance of tears running down cheeks, which did little good. Her son didn't need premature mourners; he was not dead yet. He needed just one brave member to stand against the god-fearing congregation. Then, Angela locked eyes with Emily.

Out of the entire room, Emily was the only onlooker who engaged with what was happening. She looked uncertain. She could be reached.

"Emily! You have to do something! Please! My son needs you! Think if it was your son, if it was your Stanley. I know you hear me. For God's sake, you have to act!"

"Dorothy," Emily began hesitantly, "maybe it's a mistake."

Angela considered the half-hearted objection to be the nail in her son's coffin. When murder is questioned so meekly, you know where people stand.

"Have no doubt," Dorothy reassured with her typical conviction. "It's the only way."

"This is wrong! You're killing my son, you fucking devils!" Angela kicked her legs up and tried to swing free of Tina and Gary, but again underestimated their grip. However, her struggling did cause Michael to stop. He stood with Alex flailing in his arms at the threshold of the sanctuary and witnessed for himself the fury stirring on Angela's face. There was hesitation buried within him under all that toughened bulk.

Angela hoped Michael's pause would trigger a wave of doubt in the congregation, maybe even inspire someone to come forward.

"Here!" Dorothy pulled out a crinkled piece of paper she had secreted away in her pocket. As if displaying for the jury, she raised the paper high above her head for everyone to see. It was Alex's tree of love drawing. Dorothy's index finger tapped on the image of the foreboding dark figure. "The child drew this. He drew the beast. Don't be fooled. He is not like the others. There is no innocence in him. He was destined to be given to the Behemoth."

"No! Liar!" Angela's voice cracked.

"One of us or all of us. One of us, or all of us. Trust in the Behemoth. Trust in our god." Dorothy lowered the paper and her head as if in prayer.

Michael was on the move again, hauling Alex toward the front door of the church.

Angela bit like a rabid dog into Gary's knuckle. Her teeth cut easily through the skin of his hand and ground against the joint underneath. One tooth eventually squeezed between the bones and he had no choice but to give into the pain, pulling away with a shriek.

One arm free.

She released a robust punch into the centre of Tina's face, sending her tumbling backwards against the solid wood pew.

Another arm free.

Angela charged down the aisle and jumped onto Michael's back. With her legs wrapped around his torso, she wildly pounded at his neck until he dropped Alex. Michael guarded himself against her blows, but the ferocious attack did not stop. After a few more strikes delivered against him, he swung his weight and tossed Angela into the nearest pew. The wood edge of the seat cracked against her back and stole the air from her lungs.

Angela was on the floor gasping when she saw Alex huddled at the back of the sanctuary. Although he was free, he had not run. After what happened to Clara, he swore he would never abandon anyone again, especially his own mother. This time he would act, this time he would save her.

He got to his feet and ran up behind Michael where he unleashed a flurry of poorly placed kicks against the burly man's leg. Michael barely noticed.

With the help of the pew, Angela pulled herself up. The taste of Gary's blood still lingered in her mouth and fed her animalistic rage. A healthy dose of adrenalin kept her bruises at bay, but she struggled getting her dizziness under control. She had taken blows before but never delivered them. As it turned out, she was a natural at it.

With her fists clenched, she rushed Michael a second time, but he was ready for her. Before she could lay another hand on him, he drove his meaty fist straight into her stomach where her guts were compacted into one solid mass.

Angela's legs gave way and she collapsed onto the floor. She attempted to breath, but it was as if she were under a million feet of water. The more she tried to surface, the more it hurt. She half expected her throat to start filling up with blood.

Michael turned his back to her and again picked Alex up. He tossed the boy over his shoulder like a sack of potatoes and marched out of the room.

Helplessly, Angela remained curled in a ball on the floor without enough air in her even to call out. All she could do was quiver.

When the door to the sanctuary swung closed, that was it. Alex was gone.

"There. It's done. That wasn't so hard," said Dorothy.

CHAPTER 38

Michael dumped Alex in the middle of the parking lot.

The chill from the cooling twilight latched onto the boy's body and reduced him to shivers. In his rush, Michael hadn't thought to bring Alex's coat. Truth be told, he hadn't thought much about anything. In order to carry through with the execution, his mind was purely focused on delivering a package. He was not leaving a boy to die; he was putting something outside, where it belonged.

"Mr. Rosenthal," Alex sniveled through his running nose. "I want to go inside."

"Shut up, boy," Michael demanded, refusing to call him by his name.

Alex grabbed onto Michael's leg, if only to borrow some of his warmth. Michael took the child by the shoulders and shoved him away. The push was not enough to hurt Alex, but enough to scare him off.

"Here! The boy is here!" hollered Michael into the fading blue of the field. His guttural voice bounced back to him, which seemed the only response he would get.

A hungry gust searched them out and devoured every bit of heat it could find. There was a darkness growing in the field, gaping and awesome.

"Where's my mom?"

"You won't be seeing her again." He pushed Alex toward the open field – that bemired lake of shadows – and said impatiently, "Go on. Go. And don't you come back. If I hear you at the door, I'll hit you and your mother until you're as black as night. Understand?"

Alex just looked at him. He understood what Michael was saying, but could not comprehend why.

Michael stepped away from him slowly at first to make sure Alex would heed the warning. To Michael's relief, the boy obeyed. He watched as the large man retreated back into the church and locked the door.

Alex was alone now, set adrift into the night.

He stood still for a while with his arms tightly crossed to preserve his heat. He chose not to move out of fear of what might be lurking in the untold depths that stretched out before him. Without his nightlight, the dark still held power. At bedtime, while tucked away under the sheets, he heard the shadow in his closet plot to swallow him hole and the darkness under his bed salivate over the tender morsels of his toes. The field was no different.

A draft from out of the dark slipped through his hair, much like his mother's touch. The calming brush from the wind evoked memories of Angela's embrace. It was addictive, and he wanted more.

He stepped in the direction from which the wind had come. True, this first step also took him closer to the dark, but if hidden in all that pitch was the source of his comfort, then it was worth seeking out.

After two more steps, the wind returned with equal tenderness. It soothed him and begged him forward. The further he walked from the church, the greater his reward.

It was not long before he found himself lost in the night's deceit without any idea where he should turn next. In the impossible emptiness that filled his eyes, he had lost sight of the church, the road, the forest, or any other landmark that might orient him. The only reassurance that he was still even in the field, and not in some yawning abyss, was the dirt crunching under his feet.

He lingered there, right in the heart of nothingness, and awaited the return of the motherly breeze. Now, more than ever, he yearned for that reassuring touch. Alas, the only obliging wind that reached for him had little interest in providing comfort. Instead, it licked at his warmth as if determined to steal away his very life.

"Echo two, this is echo one. Over," he said uneasily into his invisible receiver. "Come in echo two... Please."

A tremendous and petrifying roar echoed from out of the night like the bellowing death cry of a hundred slaughtered goats. It reverberated unnaturally, as if originating from a crooked throat.

Whether it was meant as an answer to his broadcast was impossible for him to tell. All Alex knew was that he didn't want to excite the hunting beast any further.

This was the first time the Behemoth had called for him with its physical voice. It was true he had heard the beast speak before, but those previous fragments had come to him like dreams, not like the growl of some wild thing. The visions started three months ago, two days after his father went missing. Sometimes he received them late at night, sometimes in the middle of Mrs. Lesy's class, but they were always accompanied by a nasty headache. It never used words, only emotions and disjointed images, like how music speaks. It was as if the messages were not meant for him, and his eavesdropping only allowed for splinters of the truth. Little good his prophecies did him now.

He could hear the beast's massive form stomping in the shadows around him, but due to the echo, could not pinpoint exactly where it was coming from.

As the Behemoth approached, the ground he stood on began to shake, and Alex ran. His direction was chosen in haste, but he committed to it with all his might, though he may have very well been heading straight toward the beast itself.

He charged blindly through the field, hoping with every step he might slam into the brick wall of the church, or maybe even into the ready arms of his mother.

Before he reached any destination, two powerful claws pinched the back of his shirt. The field fell away from under him as he was lifted off the ground. Without his feet against the dirt, there was nothing left to remind him of where he was, and he tumbled endlessly through that loathsome abyss.

CHAPTER 39

Gone. He was gone.

To really believe it was impossible, so Angela became tormented by the impossibility. It was more natural for her mind to imagine herself dead than to endure a single day without Alex. She could pretend he was just out of sight somewhere, quietly reading one of his comics, but it would not bring him back into her arms, it would not refill her. What was lost was lost forever and time promised only to fester the wound.

She tried to picture his face, but all she could see was him being dragged out of the sanctuary, his eyes reaching for her, his mouth screaming her name. It haunted her. Inevitably, he was blotted out by the swing of that heavy door.

Then, gone. He was gone.

Angela found herself tumbling down the stairs into the basement. She scarcely had care enough to shield her head from the pummeling steps. Fortunately, when she reached the bottom, her skull had not been cracked nor had her spine been broken, as much as she may have wished they were. The rest of her body, however, suffered plenty. At least the throbbing and burning that ached through every part of her made her mind feel at home.

As she laid flat against the stone floor with her body and soul pulverized, she listened to the movement upstairs. The door to the basement was gently closed and locked tight. Similar, she thought, to the sound of a coffin's hinges.

The conspirators, those demons in the church, had the malice to murder her child, but not mercy enough to end her. Instead, they had only half-finished what they started and sealed her in her tomb still alive. She offered them no gratitude for this. On the contrary, she despised them for it.

The dank, lightless basement contributed to the feeling of being in a grave. With no power feeding the lights, the only illumination came courtesy of the small trough windows, but that was fleeting.

Her doleful attempts to breathe came and went. The gratuitous filling and emptying of her lungs was exhausting. All it did was help to preserve her. But, preserve for what? She no longer had an answer.

Stiffness in her neck sparked a painful spasm and she tilted her head backwards to alleviate the strain. It was then, with her vision flipped upside-down, she saw the peeling door on the other side of the basement.

The door's existence had completely fallen from her memory, but as soon as she saw it, her original plan returned to greet her like a familiar friend. However, it was no longer an escape plan, it was now a rescue operation.

Beyond the door's rotting wood frame was the old stone stairwell, which climbed precariously to yet another door of similar decay that opened up into the field.

If Angela got to her feet and carried herself to the door, maybe it wasn't too late, maybe Alex could be saved. Maybe she would find him, wherever he was, and never let him go again.

As she struggled to a standing position, her battered limbs wobbled as if they might collapse altogether. She stayed close to the wall and shook the dizziness from her head, all the while keeping her eyes concentrated on the flaking white paint of the door.

Everything hurt. Even her stomach was still in knots over the crushing blow delivered by that brute, Michael.

As she staggered across the open floor, she thought of her lost child condemned to wander alone, hounded by an unspeakable monster. His little legs would only last so long. She knew he needed her. The pain in her limbs was suddenly alleviated, chased away by a fresh injection of determination. The hatred she was keeping warm for her fellow congregation members, and even her own grief, had been temporarily postponed. She shed anything that might slow her down and keep her from finding Alex.

The softened door buckled as she leaned against the wood. It was latched at both the top and bottom by two iron bars that secured it into the surrounding stone. With a great heave, she dislodged the rusted metal from its holding place and the door unsettled from its frame. She opened it carefully, wary its hinges might give way.

Sour air spilled out all around her, filling her mouth with the taste of mildew.

Time had reduced the stairs to crumbling rock, and Angela half-expected them to turn to dust when she took her first step. Surprisingly, she discovered it was dependably solid. The rest of the stairs were quickly conquered with a bounding stride.

The second door was latched just like the first, only this time the metal was even more impossibly fused by rust. She had to utilize all her weight in order to free the bolts. Once she did, she kicked open the door without a second thought.

A blackened field that spanned into oblivion opened up to her.

Is my baby alone in all that darkness?

There was no time to stand and gawk. A deep breath filled her with courage and she walked five feet into the field. The safety net of the church was no longer in reach.

She anchored herself in the dirt and paid close attention to her senses. Smell and taste were useless, as was her sight. Her hearing, however, became her most valuable tool.

Leaves rustled and the dirt of the field stirred mysteriously. The few trees that stood along the road rattled their branches together like the applause of skeletons. None of these sounds were going to lead to her son.

Come on, Angela. Where is he? You're his mother. You can do this. Find him! Before the beast! Find him, save him!

A low thumping sound caught her attention. It was evenly paced, like footsteps. She held hope, that above all the other noises, these faint beats might be a boy running scared.

"Alex!" she yelled. She knew if the Behemoth was not already aware of her, it was certainly aware of her now. But, she had to take that chance. She called again, "Alex, I'm here! Run to my voice!"

The thumping stopped.

She forgot to breathe as she waited for the next clue. The clatter from the branches to her left grew rowdy and muddied her soundscape. She worried that even if the footsteps returned, she may not be able to hear them. She plugged her left ear and took a few more steps into the field.

In desperation, Angela prayed.

God, whatever You are, wherever You are, help my son. He's scared. He needs You. Show him the way back to his mother. Do this for me. Do it, or I swear I'll destroy You. If you let him die, I promise You, I'll dig my way out of Hell, and climb up to Heaven, and I'll destroy You, somehow. And then You'll know the fear of being alone in the dark. Just help him. Save him. I pray in Your name, You son of a bitch, I pray!

Then suddenly, the piercing sound of a snapping tree trunk erupted from the din beside her. She turned left and discovered that the thumping had indeed come back, but it was definitely not Alex.

Some prodigious entity was racing toward her at a tremendous speed, knocking through the trees of the Burward forest as it approached. Although she couldn't see it, she could hear its towering form scraping past the highest branches. She recalled how tall those trees were in the light of day and shuddered at the sheer stature of the beast.

Angela could feel the thumping in her knees. The colossal creature must have been free of the woods now, as the trees had silenced. It tore through the plains toward her with the force of a runaway train.

Her primal instinct took over and Angela ran back to the church.

The first door slammed shut with ease, but she had difficulty fastening the locks. She managed to jam her hand under the rusted latch and shoved it into place. In her haste, she didn't feel how deeply the metal of the lock had sunk into her palm.

She sprinted down the steps leaving a trail of blood tracing her descent.

When she reached the bottom door, she stopped. The rumble from the beast's advance had quieted. Maybe since she retreated to the church, it had lost interest in her.

As she stared up at the lifeless door, the hole in her hand started to sting. She examined it. It was the size of her thumbnail, and just about as deep.

The outer door buckled and cracked, then was ripped off its hinges and sent flying into the night; tossed as if it weighed nothing more than a Frisbee. Once the barrier had been broken, darkness poured down the stairs toward her.

Quickly, she closed the only remaining door between them and attempted to barricade it.

She grabbed anything she could find. A flipped table served as the foundation, anchored into place by a heap of chairs. She didn't stop until the door, itself, was completely hidden.

From the other side of her barricade came horrible clawing sounds, as if the beast was digging through stone, burrowing its way toward her.

It's a monster. It's a fucking monster. And my Alex, he was left out there with it. Maybe he hid. Maybe he's hiding still. Maybe…

She backed away from her barricade.

The roar of shattered stone grew as broken rocks pummeled the barrier and shook a couple chairs loose.

Angela couldn't take her eyes off the trembling pile of furniture, which appeared to be seconds away from collapsing. If it gave way, she imagined the Behemoth would come crawling into the basement to collect her, as it had her son. With her attention elsewhere, an overturned chair caught her leg as she stepped backwards and she fell to the floor.

She landed against the cement in a seated position, absorbing most of the hit with her lower back.

After a few more chairs fell free from the barricade, Angela discovered a hole had been chewed through the centre of the door. The old wood around the opening was frayed and splintered like jagged teeth. From inside the door's lopsided mouth peered a large, black eye outlined by a dusting of grey. After only a brief moment, the eye pulled back into obscurity, but remained clearly defined in her mind. It was the size of a basketball, and had stared at her like a cat would; intensely fixed, measuring when to strike. She was sure of one thing, she never wanted to be caught by its sight again.

Angela kicked the chair free from her legs and readied herself to get back on her feet.

Before she got the chance, however, four knife-like talons came twisting toward her. The beast managed to squeeze its hand through the hole and had lunged for its prey like the strike of a snake. Its huge arm easily spanned half the basement, but was just short of reaching her.

A bloodcurdling scream carried Angela's terror into the room as the talons swiped through the empty air in front of her. If they had been just a foot closer, they would have easily removed her head.

The arm itself was thick and powerful from Angela's perspective, but compared to the Behemoth's size, it was a scrawny appendage. Its flesh was difficult to assess, as it appeared rough, like discoloured bark, yet was as malleable as her own skin.

The beast's largest claw, protruding from the tip of its middle finger, pierced her blouse and managed to pull her closer before tearing through the fabric altogether. Its pinky finger slashed at her belly, but could only scrape the surface. It was enough, however, to draw blood.

Angela immediately moved her arms to protect the vulnerable softness of her stomach. This meant her hands and forearms now had to bear the brunt of the beast's attack.

Any part of her the Behemoth could reach was subjected to a cruel game of ticktacktoe, resembling the brutality displayed all over Rick's body, only the patterns of her gashes were far less orderly. The pain set her skin on fire and cried out for her to act.

She had to do something, or in mere moments she would be shredded to death.

Her right arm abandoned its protective post, again leaving the bottom of her stomach open to the assault – a sacrifice she had to make to survive.

Desperately, she forced her raw hand into the tightness of her pocket. Her jeans hugged the wounds on her knuckles and wrist, pulling the skin away from itself as she dug deeper. Eventually, through the pinching agony, she grabbed hold of Clara's lighter.

The Behemoth uncurled its index finger and placed the tip of its claw against the base of Angela's neck. It was sharp enough that even with minimal pressure, it still easily broke her skin. The pulse in her jugular pumped rapidly against the prick of the heavy talon.

She lifted the lighter and held it under the palm of the enormous hand. It took only one flick to bring forth its flame.

In the presence of Clara's reanimated fire, the beast halted its attack. Angela even felt the claw at her throat retract slightly.

It's scared. Is it scared?

To test, she pressed the naked flame against the Behemoth's skin.

A dreadful growl bellowed out from behind the door and the entire arm instantly recoiled, sucking back through the hole from where it came with such force that it almost snapped the door in half.

As suddenly as that, Angela was released.

She kept the flame lit with her eyes on the door, waiting for the Behemoth to return. She found it hard to believe that a flame from a lighter could threaten a creature of such power. Yet, the beast had retreated.

What kind of god is afraid of fire?

It had run away like an animal would.

What kind of god would fear like that, like an animal?

She placed the lighter down in front of her and, in its protective glow, tended to her sores. To her relief, although the gashes ached, none of them were deep enough to claim her life just yet. With the loose material from her shirt, she cleaned up whatever blood had been shed and again thought of her son. Angela tortured herself with the notion that Alex had suffered the same lashings as she, only he had no flame to ward off the beast. Each cut was also his. Every pain was shared equally between them.

She awoke from her dream that Alex had somehow survived in the open field; that delusion had been entirely dispelled.

How could he survive a beast like that? How could anyone?

The new horrible realization was that Alex had not only been killed, but had suffered a vicious, tearing, ripping, screaming death. She feared that the last thing the world offered him was agony.

Angela had caught a vague glimpse of the congregation's monster when it chased through the field after her. While running back to the church, she chanced one look behind her and out of all the features that might have caught her eye, she focused on the crusty organ that swung between its legs. Now that she had a moment to reflect on it, she assumed this meant it was male. Which also meant it was burdened with the needs of procreation. Despite all its dark miracles and bedazzlements, its body was biological. It was a member of a species, not the lord of one.

There was no doubt in her mind the creature that terrorized her was no more a god than she was. In fact, she had done away with a notion of any god at all. There was no centre to this madness, no reason for the brutality. No plan or harmony, no watchful father or caring mother, no glorious purpose or righteousness. There was nothing but her and the other living things with which she shared her accidental life. And they had made the mistake of crossing her.

Alex was gone. Gone? No, not gone. He was murdered, and someone or something was going to pay for it. Blood for blood, scream for scream.

Angela's mouth no longer tasted of bitter sadness, or the sour sting of grief. She tasted retribution, and it was sweet.

CHAPTER 40

The ungodly sounds that rattled up the old vents from the basement had hushed everyone in the sanctuary. Then suddenly, all was quiet. There was not a whisper alive to tarnish the delicate silence that followed.

Each member looked to the other for answers, but there were none to be found.

Eventually Tina asked, "What was that?"

"I think it came from the basement," said Gary, as if that detail offered some sort of comfort.

"Is it gone now?" inquired another member.

"Please, don't fear," reassured Dorothy. "We gave the Behemoth what it wanted, we will be spared." She took her authoritative stance behind the pulpit.

"You keep saying that, Dorothy, but how much longer are we going to have to wait here?" demanded Michael with his fists clenched. Because he was the one who had physically carried out the sacrifice, the strain of it had weighed on him more than most. He began to worry the child was put out to pasture for nothing.

"We'll wait for however long it takes. The Behemoth will give us a sign."

"Maybe that was the sign!" Tina exclaimed.

"Don't be so eager, Tina. When it's ready to set us free, we'll know."

"What can we do in the meantime?" asked another voice.

"We can pray," Dorothy replied effortlessly. "Tina, grab the rest of the Christmas candles from the box by the window. Everyone gets a candle. I'll light mine, and then pass the flame onto the next. The light will unify our prayers to the beast."

Tina did as she was told and passed out the partly melted candles to each member in the room. Normally, they were also given plastic safety cups to prevent the dripping wax from burning their hands, but that precaution was overlooked.

Armed with misshapen candles, the congregation watched Dorothy ignite the first flame. Its dainty glow was a welcome release from the lingering shadows that steeped the room.

Tina was first to receive the light and she passed it on to Gary. It spread like a wave from there until the entire room was set aglow by shimmering stars.

As the flames approached Matthew, he started to feel a sickness in his stomach. His hand that clenched the candle became clammy and a building urge to vomit bubbled up within him. He asked himself, what could the passing flame represent but their guilt? What had they, as a congregation, have to pray about if not forgiveness for the cardinal sins they committed? Matthew had remained silent during Alex's sacrifice, but he was bewitched then. The promise of Chris' resurrection had been dangled in front of his face, and now he didn't know what to believe. Could the Behemoth really reunite him with his love, or had Matthew been duped into sanctioning a child's murder? He couldn't answer, and so he refused the flame.

"It was a mistake," came a quiet voice from out of the crowd.

Matthew perked up when he heard the sentiment spoken aloud. It was as if his thoughts had voiced themselves. He looked around the room eagerly to see who shared his doubts and noticed that Susan was just as anxious to figure out who the speaker was. Both of them were surprised when Emily tossed her candle to the ground in protest.

"This was a horrible mistake! May God forgive us!" Emily screamed before being stricken with uncontrollable sobbing. Her body coiled into itself. Her hands caught her face on the way down to her knees.

"Emily, it was a hard decision. No one denies that. But we made the right choice." Even if Dorothy shared in the remorse for what they had brought upon the boy, she could not show it. For the sake of appeasing the Behemoth, and for the chance to again hear her daughter's voice, she had to be steadfast.

Emily's face rose up from her hands and met Dorothy's eyes.

"I wish things were different, but now it's more important than ever to trust in our god," Dorothy continued.

"Are you even Dorothy?" asked Emily.

"What kind of question is that?"

"'Cause I look at your face and I hear your words, but, I can't recognize you. I don't know who you are. You keep speaking about God, but I've never felt as far away from Him as I do right now."

"That's because you're looking to the wrong one."

"No, Dorothy. It's because we are forsaken."

"You're going to eat those words when the Behemoth returns. I hope it can forgive you."

Before Emily could respond, the door in the mess hall was blown open. The wood crashed against the wall like a gunshot, igniting a ripple of fright in the congregation.

Dorothy slowly stepped down from the pulpit with her candle held tightly to her chest. Some of the wax spilled onto her dress, but she paid no attention to it. She had not expected the beast to use the front door.

Then came a human voice. At first it sounded like nothing more than a ghostly hum, tickling ears and inducing shivers. From those meager beginnings, it eventually grew into a full whistle. The tune of choice was their beloved hymn, *Part of the Family*.

The familiar melody carried Dorothy back through the bloodshed, all the way to the humble beginnings of that mundane Sunday morning. She recalled the sanctuary aglow with fellowship, and Don speaking of the eternal love of their Holy Father. No matter how bad things may turn, he had assured them, it would all work out in the end, for it is God's plan. Well, things had certainly turned bad, he was right about that. Dorothy wondered if Don really believed his own words, specifically while his face was being peeled off. She did have faith that the past two days had been god's plan, just not the god Don had professed.

By the time the voice began the second verse, it had reached the sanctuary door.

A few of the members moved away, fearing what might come through once the song had ended. Even Dorothy halted her approach and waited at a safe distance for the serenade's conclusion.

The doorknob twisted. The slow turn of the handle stole breath from the entire room.

As soon as it cracked open, an inexplicable gust charged forth and in one quick swipe, snuffed out every candle.

The familiar darkness also brought with it a familiar mystery. Everyone knew there was someone in the doorway, but no one could tell who.

"Did you hear?" a voice asked out of the dark.

No one dared answer.

The silhouette stepped into the room. A stray beam of moonlight snuck through the window and caught the side of his face. The blue shimmer cupped around his cheekbone, but disappeared when it met the dark globe of his eye, as if the light was swallowed by it.

Recognition settled in. It was Rick, who had come to greet his congregation, only the man with spectral eyes now shared the vision of the beast, itself.

"Hear what, Rick?" Dorothy finally responded.

His head turned to her with a hawk's precision.

As soon as Dorothy earned his attention, she immediately wanted to give it away. It was like being caught in a hunter's sights and the little fawn inside of her wanted to bolt.

Rick smiled and stepped toward her. His robe was muddy and its edges torn, as if he had been wearing it for years. The fabric, weighed down by clots of dirt, swayed with his body and left a trail of earth as he approached.

Dorothy gathered her faith and managed to turn her fear into excitement. Despite her nervous instincts, she forced herself to believe Rick had come to reward her devotion to the beast; she had to believe it. She had to. They had done as they were asked, what reason would there be to punish further?

There was also another feeling that had been awakened in Dorothy. This one was even less manageable than the prior. Rick's proximity ignited an unwieldy lust that gathered heat between her legs – a sensation she had all but forgotten since the death of her husband. Whether she was titillated by the surviving handsomeness of his face, the hinted bulge of his body under the robe, or something far more sinister, remained a mystery. Regardless of what caused it, there was no denying the tremble she struggled to suppress. She saw the curve of his lips and could not help but imagine how they would feel against her body. She wanted to live, she wanted to see her daughter again, and now, she also wanted him. Dorothy was disturbed how the needs of her body had come to weigh against the needs of her soul.

Rick walked right passed her as if she were nothing and took a prominent stance in front of the pulpit.

Dorothy hid the shame of her thirst and settled in with the rest of the congregation.

"My children, did you hear the boy's screams?" asked Rick with delight. "Did you listen to his cries from way down deep? It was beautiful. You should have been there. You should have heard it. The boy, Alex, was well-chosen. He had such spirit." The zeal with which Rick spoke only salted their collective wound.

"Is the Behemoth pleased?" Dorothy interrupted, unable to bear anymore talk of Alex's fate.

"Oh, yes. Yes. Joyous. Ecstatic. Exquisitely satisfied. It finally has what it always wanted."

"The boy?"

"No, you. Faithful followers. It has you, devoted and loving. You are all now the Behemoth's precious congregation and you have given the beast the awe it deserves."

Michael stepped into the aisle and blurted, "We did it. Can we leave now?"

"Leave? Before seeing your god? Do you not wish to behold it?"

Dorothy was overcome by the idea and dropped to her knees at the offer. She clasped her hands together and begged for a chance to witness such divinity.

"Please, yes! We do!" she exclaimed on behalf of the congregation.

The devotion started with Dorothy, but soon everyone in the room had joined her, groveling on the ground. By this point, most were sincere in their worship, though there were a few pretenders, including Matthew, Susan and the disheartened Emily, who prayed with the others only to preserve their anonymity.

Rick raised his hands to the pleading congregation with a look of sympathy.

"Yes, children. Your ascension shall begin." He turned his head upward to the heavens and announced with booming force, "Behemoth, lord of all that rose from the dust, master of earth and sky, we beseech you. Bless us this night, your faithful, loving children, and let us look upon your splendor that we may praise our true father. We humbly ask this and forever love thee. Our god, the Behemoth, ruler of wood and stone, of blood and bone, and keeper of our eternity. We pray."

CHAPTER 41

With Clara's lighter leading the way, Angela headed into the cluttered storage space near the back of the basement. She found herself standing in the exact spot where she first told Alex his father had returned. The ghost of the moment lingered there. She picked up the plastic Santa head and tossed it across the room. It shattered against the cement.

She ripped through the rest of the junk until she unearthed the old generator. Its red paint was in severe need of some patchwork and the instructions were faded and illegible.

Hidden under some oily rags she found two jugs of gasoline. She shook the first one but there were only a few dribbles left. The second, however, was filled all the way to the cap.

She poured a quarter of the jug into the generator – the rest of the gas she had need for elsewhere.

She primed the engine, adjusted the choke, and then grabbed hold of the pull chord.

She paused. Once the generator was started, there would be no going back. She needed to be sure of her plan. It was not an easy thing to commit to. What she had in mind was not about saving herself, nor was it about saving anyone else for that matter. In fact, it had nothing to do with life at all, but rather, death. Brutality had become the common tongue, and it was Angela's turn to speak. To her, life was a cruel proposition – you give someone the world and then take it away. This vicious practice was all there was. As much as she hated it, as much as she wanted it not to be true, she could not escape it. Just as Alex did not escape it, and just as the congregation upstairs was not going to escape it.

Angela pulled the chord.

The motor squealed to life like a pig. Its screech chased away the settled quiet of the basement, while the exhaust grumbled up a thick pipe that carried the fumes outside. Power spread through the basement, giving Angela the light she needed.

The rattle from the generator suggested it probably didn't have long to live. That was fine. It would all be over soon.

CHAPTER 42

The ceiling lights flashed on and off above the congregation like a battle in Heaven. Emily grabbed hold of her two children and pulled them closer. Eventually, the power stabilized and the room was brought back to normalcy, if that's what it could be called.

Rick squinted. His beastly eyes were accustomed only to the dark.

In the clarity the lights offered, everyone could see the extent of Rick's transformation. His teeth had blackened as much as his eyes. It was as if he was rotting from the inside, only he appeared strengthened by his deterioration, not weakened by it.

"Was that him?" cried Tina.

"No, my children, it was not," Rick answered dismissively. His arms remained outstretched and the fabric of his robe hung down like tattered feathers, displaying an impressive wingspan.

"Matthew, why are the lights on?" whispered Susan.

"The generator," he replied.

Rick's head bowed down as he spoke, "Everyone, be silent and gather close to me. The Behemoth comes now."

The first person to join him was Dorothy, and even she hesitated. Eventually though, she was down on all fours with her hands clamouring about his torn, bare feet.

"What are you all waiting for?" she asked the others, "come and worship our saviour."

The sound of a rustling sheet brought the congregation's attention to the stained-glass window. To everyone's shock, there was only an empty hole where Chris' body once hung. The sheet that had covered him had fallen onto the pews beneath.

Tina immediately spun around to her husband.

"Gary! Where did he…" her sentence was cut short once she realized it was not her husband standing next to her. She stared into the bleeding eyes of her son's shredded face.

It smiled at her, but not in the way he did when he was alive; it was his death grin.

Tina brought her hands close to her chest as if to protect her heart. She screamed when her dead son lurched forward and reached for her face. The corpse didn't move in a human way. Like a marionette, it was only an estimation of true life.

Gary took hold of Tina's arm and dragged her away from the hideous vision, but not before she saw Chris' head, which was barely attached to his neck, begin to roll around his shoulders like a grotesque pendulum. The image of his smiling face, swaying back and forth, made her think of the first toy she ever gave him – a Jack in the box.

The two of them hurried to the front of the church, where Rick was waiting.

Matthew shook his head in frightful wonderment. If what he had seen before in the bathroom was not evidence enough, there was no longer any doubt of the beast's power over death. His breaths grew short and he kept repeating, "My god... My god..."

His astonishment was interrupted by a hand scurrying up his back. The fingers were wet, soaking through his shirt. He turned around and saw Bruce's carved carcass rise up from the pew behind him. The gashes down Bruce's face nearly split through his wide grin.

Matthew abandoned his doubts, as well as his grandmother, and ran toward Rick. The rest of the congregation followed him, scrambling to the front of the sanctuary as Bruce slid over the pews toward them.

All the scared little lambs were now herded around their shepherd, trembling as the dead closed in around them.

A third body appeared in one of the aisles. It dragged itself along with its one good arm, heaving the bloody mass of its mangled form across the red carpet.

Dorothy looked up from Rick's feet, afraid of what she might see, and rightly so. She recognized the twisted abomination as her daughter. The dead thing's pale eyes were fixed on Dorothy, and even had a hint of recognition.

"Clara, my baby girl," Dorothy wept. "It brought you back. It brought you back to me." In the thralls of her wretched hysteria, the edge of Dorothy's mouth even curled into the beginnings of a smile.

"Silence!" Rick demanded. "The Behemoth is near. Children, prepare to behold the maker of your miracles. The air becomes death, and so we let the shadows rush in. It is upon us."

#

The weight of the gasoline pulled on Angela's arm while she made her way steadily up the stairs. The liquid sloshed about the jug, a tactile reminder of what was at hand.

She reached the door to the mess hall, which had been locked. However, it was hinged from her side and so with the blunt end of a piece of wood, she started hammering out the metal pin that secured the door to its frame.

It was a noisy process, but Angela had no worry of being found out. After all, what could they do that they hadn't done already?

The top pin popped out and bounced down the stairs. The door shifted. After the bottom pin came loose, the entire thing dislodged. Angela then kicked her way into the mess hall. The door came crashing down at half speed like a great oak tree. She emerged from the basement and stood over the fallen barrier.

Across the room was the sanctuary. The door was still closed. Nobody had heard. Nobody knew she was coming.

Her gaze moved to the three large fabric windows that joined the two rooms. A few silhouettes floated passed the thin sheets. The congregation was on the move, but not toward her.

Her grip around the handle of the jug constricted and the plastic let out an aching moan.

She marched toward the unsuspecting congregation with the look of punishment promised in her determined eyes.

#

Although the deathly visions had forced everyone to the front of the sanctuary, they had not pressed any further. The bodies of the lost had halted, as if standing guard.

Dorothy hadn't left Rick's feet during the entire migration. She felt safe being so close to him; her head was almost ducked under the shelter of his filthy robe. He was the promise that made it possible to endure it all, even her daughter's agony.

The children were brought to the centre of the mob, protected on all sides by the rest of the congregation. Susan and Matthew were among the youth being safeguarded and had taken it upon themselves to calm the frightened kids. There was something comforting about making the children feel safe; perhaps because if the kids believed it, then they could too.

Everyone else's attention remained with their prophet, silently begging for his guidance.

Eventually, Rick's head once again turned upward to the sky, but this time, with a look of ecstasy. A series of grunts erupted from the depths of his throat with a perverse intensity that would have made anyone blush. His breath became shallow and his body quivered. His feet, which Dorothy still clung to like an anchor, began to pull away from the earth.

There was a detectable charge in the air that pricked at the skin of the congregation and built pressure in their ears. Everyone became as silent as death.

Rick rose a foot off the ground and floated in space as if held there by some cradling hand. A few awe-inspired tears dropped at the sight, and still Dorothy did not let go.

The pews started to shake and banged against the floorboards like a restless audience. The noise was deafening, and filled the sanctuary. It sounded as though the pounding might break through the floor. Their trusted room, their haven that had sheltered them from untold terrors was transforming.

"The Behemoth is here!" Rick proclaimed.

Desperate hands groped at Rick's robe. Anyone who couldn't reach him shoved their way through the crowd for a chance to be closer to god. There was only one singular thought shared between the entire congregation; *the Behemoth is here. The Behemoth is here!*

#

Angela twisted the lid off the jug of gasoline with such haste, the precious fuel spilled out over her hand and dripped to the floor.

She found herself feeling surprisingly sturdy in front of the sanctuary door. She clearly heard the banging coming from the other room, but closed her mind to it. She had no care for what the awful noise was or what made it. No devilish mystery was intriguing enough to dissuade her from completing what she had set out to do.

The jug poured easily. The clear liquid splashed under the door and snaked its way into the sanctuary carpet.

After she was satisfied the gas permeated the only entrance to the room, Angela generously soaked the entire wood frame of the door and carried a trail all the way to the thin curtains. They too were rendered dripping within seconds.

She didn't stop until every last drop of gas was emptied and the fumes dizzied her senses.

Her son was not in Heaven, despite how much she wanted him to be. There was no eternity amongst the clouds for him with his long lost dog. Dead was dead, she was sure of it now, and fairytales, no matter how appealing, could not change that simple truth.

And more, if nothing lies beyond this world, then there would be no final judgment to punish the congregation for what they did. The thought of Dorothy,

Tina, Gary, Michael, Emily and all the others going about their days in blessed ignorance was unbearable and chased away any hesitation or pesky moral concerns she might have had.

So, the duty of jury fell on her. Since Heaven would never come, she took it upon herself to deliver them unto Hell.

Angela pulled Clara's lighter from her pocket and sparked the flame.

CHAPTER 43

The rapture was too engrossing for anyone to notice the gas, or its accompanying odor, which now saturated the carpet running through the aisle.

The congregation was too busy pawing over each other like excited puppies starving for their mother's milk. Escape from their hell seemed, at long last, mere moments away and their sweet freedom was made all the sweeter knowing the price they had paid.

At the cusp of their ascension, many of the members saw fit to give thanks. They were relieved that at least the boy had not died in vain, at least the darkness could be overcome, and at least they still had a god to praise.

In the midst of all this clamouring, the sanctuary was ignited. The first and most obvious to be swallowed by the flame was the door. The ravenous fire devoured the wood in seconds and proceeded to let itself in without waiting for an invitation.

Quickly, it chased up the aisle, reducing the red carpet to a foul, blackened sludge. The fabric of the three rear windows burst into rolling balls of flame in succession, like carefully timed fireworks. The orange blaze tumbled upwards in a grand display, leaving scorch marks against the back wall as it rose. The upsurge dispersed against the roof, birthing several new fiery offspring.

Already, the impenetrable fire had cornered the congregation. All their escape paths were burning and the heat was only getting closer. The roar of the flames competed with the congregation's screams as the fire jumped eagerly from one pew to the next.

"No!" yelled Dorothy in an attempt to frighten the fire away as if it was an animal. It didn't work.

The glow of the devastation settled in Rick's eyes, lending his coldness some much-needed emotion. He knew who was to blame for this inferno and was compelled to whisper her name, "Angela…"

One of the side pews suddenly caught fire.

"Grandma!" screamed Matthew. Stunned by the undeniable majesty of the encroaching bonfire, he had momentarily forgotten about his slumbering grandmother.

With his shirt pulled around his face, he left the children and forced his way through the heat, but it was too late. By the time he reached the pew where he had left her, Flora Thompson had already been eaten away. Crispy flakes from her flowery dress – the one she wished to be buried in – were caught by rising pockets of heat and twirled into the air. Faced by the sight, Matthew's body told him simply to breathe and keep breathing. Unfortunately, there was no more air to take in, only smoke, and Flora's ash.

He coughed uncontrollably, as if his goal was to retch out his lungs. The heat crowded in around him and he fell to his knees, unable to withstand the weight of the tenacious flames. With his forehead against the ground and his fist pressed tightly to his chest, he resigned himself to suffocation. The sounds of panicked cries and scurrying feet faded from his ears. All he could hear and feel was his body attempting to sift out oxygen where none could be found.

Before he was completely overcome, however, an angel intervened. Susan – who was as close to an angel as anyone was going to get – arrived at his side and propped him back up on his feet. She helped him from the thralls of smoke and back to where the air was slightly more breathable, but even at the pulpit, the dangers did not abate.

The fire took to the old wood like a kid in a candy store, hasty to gobble up every morsel.

Gary, along with a handful of assorted congregation members, ran to the stained-glass window in the hopes of smashing their way through it. As they approached, it became obvious the conniving flames had predicted this move and had already crawled all around the window's trim. The glass mural was completely enclosed by a blazing arch and although this made getting near it impossible, Gary noted how it also made the colours radiate brilliantly like winking gemstones. It was a beautiful thing, even in such perilous circumstances. *If only Chris could have seen it*, he thought to himself.

A sizable plank from the roof came loose. It swung down through the air like a flaming baton and landed on Gary Brown's head. He wasn't aware that the sky was falling, nor was he allowed time to ponder his last moments before he was crushed. The weight of the plank collapsed his neck; his spine compacted, then snapped and down he went. The greedy fire was impatient to get a taste of him.

In a flash, his body was engulfed, as was half the room by this point. The sanctuary had become a furnace and its searing heart was growing ever brighter.

Dorothy shielded herself from the harsh light of their impending cremation and looked again to Rick. She grabbed hold of his ankle, wrapping her hands around the top of his foot like a chain.

"My god, save us! Please! Do something!" she pleaded desperately.

Without offering Dorothy so much as a sympathetic glance, Rick kicked her away, sending her skidding across the ground into the front row of pews. Despite this, the other congregation members continued to beg for his help. Rick, untouched by their cries, floated effortlessly into the air and disappeared into the billowing smoke that had gathered on the roof. Even then, a few believed he would return.

Dorothy, bewildered and destroyed, remained sitting against the shattered wood of the bench where she landed and looked around at the hell that had come to pass. She folded her hands in her lap and let the destruction sink in.

It was more than just the church that was being destroyed. Over the past two days, the ugly struggle for life, or rather, for what she wished life to be, had ushered in unthinkable pain. She had lost too much and so she had become a crusader against death itself. She strived to maintain the promise of ever-lasting life, the comfort that nothing really ends, that no one is gone forever. She was determined to earn Heaven at any cost, even at the cruel bargain of one of their own. However, in the madness she witnessed now, as congregation members dashed about the room, choking, and frantically searching for a way to save themselves, she had to admit, it hardly seemed worth it.

Then, someone called for Dorothy. Though filtered through char and carnage, she could still recognize the voice.

Gradually, Dorothy's sweaty face turned to behold Clara climbing up the aisle toward her. She was wearing a dress of fire that had melted most of her dead flesh away, but somehow her eyes had once again survived. Despite the cracking wrinkles singed across the abomination's face, Dorothy could still see her struggling little girl.

"Mommy…" the burnt thing whispered, smoke spilling from its mouth.

"That's right, baby. I'm here. Come to mommy," Dorothy responded tenderly, with a smile. She opened her arms and welcomed her closer.

At the sight of this warm gesture, Clara's corpse sprang into action and scuttled forth like a beetle. Its crispy hands latched onto the pews on either side like the rungs of a ladder and propelled it forward.

Dorothy Muller's burning child pounced on her with a devastating embrace. Once the corpse's arms entrapped her, Dorothy felt the incredible heat of the dead flesh scorch her skin, almost fusing the two together, before the fire even had time to acquaint itself.

The daughter leaned its sweltering head against Dorothy's bosom. It was like a searing frying pan held to her nipple – she was being suckled by the devil's lips, a depravity to which she felt deserving. As Dorothy's nerves exploded from the surging pain, she was compelled to express her torture. She arched her head to the smoky roof where Rick had retreated and released a wail that grew from her gut into the storm above. The sound was like the final, piercing note of a most extraordinary libretto.

Her mouth suddenly became very dry as the flames passed from one body to the next. Fire picked apart her arms before rushing up to her neck only to become engrossed in her hair. Once the first strands caught flame, it was only a few seconds before her entire head was bubbling like an overcooked marshmallow.

The two of them fell backwards together into a bed of coals, releasing a burst of fresh sparks into the room.

For the rest of the congregation who still dreamed of escape, the only hope for survival that had yet to be burned away were the trio of small windows on the east wall. The problem was, only the children were small enough to make use of them.

CHAPTER 44

Through the connecting windows in the mess hall, Angela bore witness to the full extent of her vengeance, but the misery she had unleashed was – in some cases – more than she bargained for.

It wasn't until she heard their screams that Angela remembered the children would also be caught in her fiery fury. Upon the realization, she wished she could have thought more clearly, she wished she could have spared the innocent. Yet, she could not take back the flame, nor could she leap through the inferno to save them. All that was left for her to do was watch as the devastation washed over the church, obliterating wood and flesh alike, indifferent of their struggles and protests, until nothing was left but ash.

Angela became audience to a melodrama of survival, played out on a glowing red stage. Every scene ended the same – in cinders. She witnessed lovers sacrifice themselves in vain, and strangers push one another into the flames. Everyone was driven by the killer instinct to persist. Even in the end, the war between kindness and callousness raged on. It was a mesmerizing montage of human ugliness and human beauty, both made irrelevant by the certainty of utter annihilation.

Some commotion from the far corner of the sanctuary attracted Angela's weary eyes. At first, she hesitated to look, for fear of witnessing more of what she had begot. To her great relief, however, she saw Susan and Matthew using one of the long steel candleholders to hammer out the remaining windows. Angela couldn't hear over the crackle what they were saying to one another, but it was obvious what they were trying to do.

The children had been gathered around them like skittish ducklings. Susan laid down her sweater on top of the broken glass for protection. Then, one by one, Matthew started feeding the kids through the window. Angela counted anxiously as each passed out of the flame's reach until she was certain not one child was left behind. It was a refreshing sight of heroism, one she was thankful to have beheld.

Matthew and Susan then crawled out the window themselves, though they didn't easily slip through like the children. They had to squirm and struggle, but eventually they made it. Angela was less enthusiastic about this. Both Susan and Matthew were present when Alex was condemned, so they, like the remaining congregation members, deserved the fate Angela had prescribed.

So resolute was her castigation that, although it pained her to watch such suffering enacted, in her wounded heart, she felt it was justified.

There were no innocent souls left in the sanctuary now that the children were safe in the fields outside. Being *safe* and *outside* had become two contrary notions, but Angela knew the Behemoth would not come after them, at least not with the fire still burning so brightly. If Susan and Matthew were wise, they would take the children and run. Angela hoped they would be led far away from this place. She hoped they would, in time, forget about the deceit of the church, the cruelty of the congregation, the tyranny of gods, and most importantly, the fire she had used to destroy them all. She hoped they could somehow escape the traps life had so intricately laid out for them. *But, like lambs to the slaughter*, she thought.

As the heat reached new levels, it became more and more difficult to distinguish what were human remains from what was just burnt furniture. It was as if everything had been coated in tar. A few hymnbooks burst into shimmering blizzards and scattered into the smoke.

Angela focused on two bodies near the pulpit where the flames had not yet reached. She recognized them as Emily and Michael Rosenthal. Both were lying face down against the searing carpet. Emily's body slightly overlapped Michael's, like they had fallen together. Because of the way Emily's hand clutched her throat, Angela assumed the smoke had claimed them both. The fire, however, wasted no time once it reached their feet. Their clothing took to the crimson flames as if they, too, had been soaked in gas. Emily's body shriveled rather quickly, whereas Michael's density took longer to penetrate. His mass was a feast for the fire and it seemed to savour lapping him up.

Something awakened from out of the flames. Angela immediately shifted her vision to the right. What she found was a horror as honest as she could bear it to be. A screeching figure, blackened and hairless from the heat, tore through the crumbling pews toward her. Fire stretched out behind the blazing banshee like the fluttering wings of a dying phoenix. Its scream was utterly inhuman, as even its vocal chords had been seared.

The miserable creature was at the window before Angela realized it wasn't some demon from Hell, or a haunting spectre. The squealing thing was actually all that remained of Tina Brown.

This was a woman whom Angela had always hated, even before the madness. Yet to see Tina's writhing form slumped over the frame of the window and her scorched fingers break apart like brittle chalk, was worse than just bitter sweet; it was pure agony. Though Angela undoubtedly wanted Tina dead for the part she played in murdering her son, comfort could not be derived from such a repulsive spectacle, no matter how much she tried.

With the solid wood stand that once held the binder for signing in and out of the church, Angela smashed through the back of Tina's head. The charred flesh ripped away like tissue paper from the force of the blunt attack. What blood remained in Tina's body bubbled out and sizzled against her exposed skull.

The stand rolled out of Angela's hands and thumped against the floor. She waited in silence for Tina's final convulsions to run their course. Once all movement had ceased, Angela took a step back.

There were no pews left in the sanctuary; the walls were now supported solely by a floor of flames. Not even the pulpit had been spared. On the contrary, the fire seemed to burn brighter there than anywhere else in the room. Angela had stripped away the façade of the building and found hell underneath. Soon, she thought, although the fire had remained obedient, that same hell would come spilling into the mess hall to claim her as well. When it did, she asked herself, would she run?

Then, the unmistakably artificial keys of the electric organ began to harmonize. A hypnotic melody, unfittingly banal, rose above the fire's grumble.

The notes piled on one another in a simple musical grid, almost tribal in nature. Angela stalked by the windows to catch a glimpse of who might be playing.

Just as she had guessed, it was Rick who sat at the instrument, surrounded by a climbing blaze. His calmness made his presence all the more surreal.

Angela was almost lost in the music. It bypassed her mind and whispered directly to her soul.

A wall of smoke rose suddenly and obscured her view of Rick. The organ hit a piercing chord. If the instrument could cry, surely that was the sound it would make.

Angela rushed to another window, anxious to get Rick within her sights again. However, when she reached the opening, although the music remained, Rick was gone. Dorothy's smoldering corpse had been placed on the organ, pressing down on the dissonant keys.

There was nowhere left for Rick to hide. The fire had laid claim to every inch of the sanctuary, so where did he go?

She stepped closer to the window, as close as the heat would allow her, and surveyed every corner of the burning room.

When she approached, the smoke stung her throat as it poured forth from just under the ledge of the window. It reached upward only a few feet away from her.

Out of that thick cloud emerged Rick like a phantom materialized, his robe billowing from the updrafts. With an animalistic roar, not unlike the one she had heard from the Behemoth itself, Rick lunged from the burning frame of the window and seized her, pinning her to the ground.

Despite the terrible destruction she had wreaked upon his congregation, he greeted his wife with a perverse smile.

CHAPTER 45

Bits of burning debris had followed Rick into the mess hall and scattered around the two of them like fallen stars.

Angela pushed against Rick's body, but he weighed down on her as if he were filled with stone. She stared up with the inferno she had unleashed now smoldering in her eyes.

Rick stared back, unflinchingly. He straddled her, holding her legs down with his own, then pinned her shoulders to the floor. It made her feel like she was buried alive. Yet, Angela continued to fight him.

"Angela... You've been a naughty girl."

"What makes you say that?"

"You have no idea what you have done." Piercing red pupils formed in the centre of Rick's eyes as if the blood was pooling there.

"I know exactly what I've done."

"The Behemoth will be very angry."

"Fuck you! And fuck that thing!"

He moved his mouth down to hers so she could feel the coldness of his empty breath. It chilled her skin and ate the heat from the fire.

He spoke calmly. "You still resist the beast? Are you so blind? If these past trials could not convince you, then what?" Rick paused as he considered the question, then continued. "I'll show you firsthand what the beast taught me. It taught me so many things, Angela; things only a god would know. It showed me how nothing is truth. Through the will of the beast, everything becomes as you desire it. Even bone, even flesh."

He rested his face against hers and gently fit his jawbone into the groves of her neck, just like he used to.

Her body, which had been primed by heated exertion, was disturbingly quick to lust. Angela felt her famished hunger for Rick reawaken inside her. Within seconds, the mutinous yearning took over her senses. Her mind pulsed with memories of him pumping into her. She recalled, during their few years of enjoyable sex, how the tense musculature of his back felt as it rolled into a variety of lovely configurations with every grinding thrust. Now, trapped against the floor of the church, she quivered at the opportunity to feel those sensuous assemblies again.

As if her face had somehow betrayed her passions, Rick brought his hips down against her own. She became enraptured by the thickness maneuvering on top her. Yet, it was a nocuous partnership, as with the pleasure came a tangible level of disgust and repulsion.

"Whatever I want you to be, you are," he whispered. "If I want you steaming like a dripping virgin on prom night, then your flesh will obey. The Behemoth taught me this. I can make you do anything I want."

"No, Rick. You can make my body want you, but I never will," Angela turned away.

He suddenly withdrew from her.

"What if I don't want you hot? What if I want you to burn?"

Rick grabbed a fistful of her hair and pulled it hard. Angela yelled and beat at his chest. The strands wrapped between his fingers started to fry, as if twisted around a curling iron. The offending odor of burnt hair filled the space, with smoke seeping from his fist.

To restrain her, he took hold of one of her wrists. Instantly, her skin blistered at his touch.

"Do you understand?" he bellowed furiously. "The physical is nothing. You are nothing. I could sink my palm into your stomach like clay, if I so chose. I could snatch out your beating heart and shatter it between my hands like glass."

Angela reached out with her one free arm and grabbed hold of a piece of fiery coal. Despite its smoldering heat, she formed a tight grip all around it. Then, while Rick gloated above his helpless prey, she ground the searing wood deep into his cheek until finally, he released her.

Both of them sprang to their feet. Angela picked up the wood stand and held it like a bat, ready to knock something out of the park. Rick on the other hand appeared weaponless, but Angela knew not to trust that.

"You took away its congregation, do you think it will let you live?" Rick smirked at her.

"Do you think it can stop me?" she spat back.

"The Behemoth could snuff you out in…"

"Then why doesn't it?" she interrupted. "I'm right here! Why doesn't your god come on over and stomp me dead?"

She was not afraid to die. Without Alex, there was no point in reaching dawn, so what was left to be afraid of? Her despair was her liberator. It took away the beast's power, and freed her of the fear that ensnared the church, and kept her captive in Rick's embrace. All she had left was her hate, and all she could do was let it burn.

The fire had been gaining momentum and overflowed into the mess hall. Neither Angela, nor Rick seemed to pay much attention to the flame's expanding feast, even as the room lit up.

"It's scared, you know. Your god is afraid of fire, just like an animal. Like a dog, or a rat. It's no god, Rick, and you're no fucking prophet."

"Careful Angela. You could suffer worse things than dying."

"I'm not afraid. Not anymore. Not ever again." Her hands tightened around the wooden mace.

"Not since Alex," Rick teased.

"Don't you say his name, you son of a bitch!"

"Alex, my little trooper."

"He isn't yours. You gave him away, to that thing. So don't you dare talk about him."

"Or, what will you do? Please, I implore, let me hear the threat. It'll be cute."

"I'll find some way to hurt you."

"Like you did the congregation?"

"Worse."

Rick released a jackal's laugh that bruised Angela's conviction. Even if hurting him did prove impossible, Angela would try to her last breath.

"And what of the hurt you've already caused? The entire congregation lies in ashes because of you. You are more a monster than I am; at least I offered to spare them."

"At an impossible price."

"Still, you gave them no choice at all. For no reason, they're all dead now."

"They killed my son!"

"Who said Alex was dead?"

"What?" Angela froze on the spot, unable to move, unable to do anything but try to process what Rick had just said.

"He's alive, Angela."

Her eyes locked onto Rick's face to measure the truth of his words, and oh, such words they were.

"He's alive?" she repeated. The grip around her club, which at one time seemed strong enough to crack the wood, had begun to loosen.

"He's with the Behemoth, but he's alive." Rick peered into the stormy depths of the inferno before he mused, "You punished them for a crime they didn't commit. Now, tell me, how does that make your vengeance taste?"

It was not a matter of trusting what Rick had said; it was matter of wishing it to be true.

Suddenly, Angela didn't feel like a crusader; she felt like a murderer. Suddenly, she was the destroyer of lives, yet her own life had been returned to her. Suddenly, she had thoughts of tomorrow, beyond the rage of the fire. Suddenly, she had her son again, and was a mother once more. She was no longer fearless. In fact, she was terrified. Angela knew what losing Alex was like, and now that he was back, she feared his loss that much more.

While Angela was stunned, Rick had reached into his pocket and retrieved his straight razor. He unfolded it slowly before her, like the excruciating reveal of an engagement ring.

Angela sized up the blade.

"Take me to him," she managed to demand, despite the fresh threat of Rick's knife.

"No," he said dismissively, taking a step toward her.

"Take me to him." Angela stood her ground and, once again, lifted the wood pole as menacingly as possible.

Despite her false swings, Rick continued to creep forward, with his piercing eyes jabbing into her.

"No, you won't be seeing him again. I won't take you to him. I'm going to split you open, empty you out,

307

and cook you over the burning coals of the church. Maybe I'll make Alex watch, if he still has his eyes."

Before Rick could lunge, the generator in the basement choked out an awful death moan, and the power failed.

As soon as the lights went out, Angela darted into the shadows, out of reach of the fire's glow.

Rick swung the razor frantically, in the hopes it might catch her. His ferocity could be heard in the hum of the blade as it cut through the air.

Angela silently slid herself across the floor, spreading her weight evenly to avoid any creaks from the wood. In the dark, she relied on her hands to search out a place to hide. Though one of her palms was still raw from the chunk of coal, she managed to feel her way into a spot behind a flimsy stack of old chairs.

There she was concealed by shadows, but as the fire blazed on, she worried how long she could stay hidden before the glow reached her.

Adding to the race of her heart, Rick joined her in the darkness, brandishing his blade, which, even in such pitch black, seemed to find fire trembling in its reflection.

He moved methodically about the room and was light on his feet. If Angela didn't keep him in her sights every second, she might lose him and she didn't want to be bumping around blind in the dark with Rick and his razor.

"You just sit tight, little lamb," he taunted. "Sit tight for the slaughter." He flung a table across the room. Once it smashed against the floor, it, too, was quickly consumed by the encroaching flames.

Angela shifted herself closer to the stage, which seemed her best hope if she wanted to stay hidden. She focused on thinning her breath for fear her heaving might give her away.

While Rick ripped through the other side of the room, Angela slid across the floor. Her knee nudged one of the chairs stacked in front of her. A ripple coursed through the pile and the second chair from the top shifted out of place.

Across the room, Rick suddenly stopped.

Angela peered through the stack into the depths of the mess hall. Rick was gone, yet, she could feel him everywhere, in front of her, behind her, right beside her. The dark held him and seemed to come alive.

His voice slithered from out the shadows and asked, "What are you thinking about right now as you wait? Are you thinking about poor Alex? You think maybe, just maybe you can still save him. And maybe you could, if you only knew where he was. But, dear Angela, you can't let yourself become distracted, or you'll end up making mistakes. And you'll spoil the hunt."

Angela ignored the dark and continued crawling toward the stage. Her hands reached into the space in front of her, each time hoping they would meet the wood boards, and nothing more.

She felt a familiar cool breeze tickle the back of her ankle. The tickle grew. Then, a sharp metal edge pressed against the skin of her heel.

Upon recognizing the razor's sadistic stroke, Angela immediately started kicking. Her foot came into contact with someone. In her panic, she shoved the stack of chairs on top of her assailant and ran.

Her knees hit against the elevated floor of the stage first, but adrenaline didn't allow for the bruising to slow her down. She hurled herself into the folds of the curtain, and then turned to meet Rick as he approached.

A loud cracking sound, like the growl of a thunderhead, pulled Angela away from the chase. Something in the mess hall had given way and the fire, as if awakening for the first time, rapidly grew to a blustering intensity. In an instant, streaming flickers of orange light cut down the darkness. The powerful glow spanned the entire stage curtain like an army of spotlights.

Angela stood in front of the glowing sheet with an honest, but ill-timed appreciation for its menacing majesty. She guessed that half the church must have been burning to cause such brilliance.

Its beauty didn't last long, however. Shadows were quick to creep back into view. Rick's silhouette emerged into the light. Angela snapped out of her admiration. He was only a few feet away from the front curtain. The ripples in the fabric morphed his hands, giving them a slithering quality as he reached toward the stage.

Angela raced to the small window hidden on the back wall. She wasted no time trying to unlatch it, and instead smashed it open with a thick ceramic baby from the pile of props.

She glanced through the window into the night's expanse, which had benefited from a sprinkle of moonlight. It was laughably serene. No sign of the Behemoth, just as she had predicted. She then lifted her body up, and started squeezing through, legs first.

Angela was halfway out the window before she noticed Rick's shadow had disappeared from the curtain. If he wanted to gut her so badly, where did he go? What called him away when he was so close?

Without the answers, she pushed herself the rest of the way through.

CHAPTER 46

Angela's feet were welcomed by soft grass. It was the first time in the past two days she had not been standing on something flat and solid. She found it delightful.

Her first instinct was to start sprinting in a straight line, not only to get away from the church, but also to celebrate the fact that she could. The endless open space, free of walls, doors, and people, was an inspiring change of scenery.

A few crumbs of loose dirt sprinkled onto the top of her head. So insignificant was the dusting, that if she hadn't been in such a heightened state of awareness, she never would have noticed. But, as the situation would have it, she looked up to see what had shaken loose, and almost immediately regretted it.

Perched like a spider against the brick wall was Rick. He had been silently crawling down the side of the building just above her. The red pupils of his eyes had been stoked to such intensity that they produced their own luminance, competing with the moon that hung against the brick behind him.

Before she had time to run, Rick took hold of her by the hair and dragged her up the wall at a tremendous speed. Angela was certain the force would scalp her, so she kicked and pounded against the brick. The rough stone tore through her clothes, leaving scrapes down her legs and back. If she was curious what burning alive might have felt like, these fresh wounds gave a decent estimation.

Rick tossed her like a rag doll onto the roof where she landed hard against disintegrating shingles.

Her head throbbed and her body stung, yet what was most distressing were her lungs that refused to fill. Angela grabbed her throat to encourage the air. Strangely, it worked.

The heat ate away at the roof and made it impossible to stay in one spot for more than a few seconds.

Angela struggled to her feet, but as soon as her weight became concentrated, the shingles gave way. Her right foot sank into the oven below. Instantly, her limb felt like a dinner roast. She quickly pulled it out, ripping off more of the roof as she did. The hole she created became a makeshift chimney and a funnel of smoke spiraled up from the opening.

She looked around. The roof was collapsing in patches. It was like she was stuck on a fragile island, slowly being cracked apart by streams of lava – a children's game turned horribly real.

Adding to the good news, Rick gracefully emerged from the side of the church to join her. Although he weighed considerably more than she, the roof had no trouble supporting him.

In a bizarre juxtaposition, he now appeared rather gentlemanly to her. With his grin complimented by the warm glow of the fire below them, the scene could almost be mistaken for romantic.

Angela tried to back away, but every move she made brought more holes and more heat.

"Careful, watch your step," Rick said, almost genuinely. He didn't approach; there was no need to. He knew she was trapped.

"Rick," pleaded Angela. "If there is any part of you still in there, please, if not for me, then for our son. Don't do this."

Rick responded with a gaze of reticence. Angela was not sure how to take it.

In one smooth motion, he stripped off his robe, retrieving the straight razor from it before tossing it over the edge. A mixture of fire and moonlight unabashedly detailed his impressive nakedness.

He presented it for her to explore every inch, like some sadistic fashion show.

"The Behemoth transformed me. Each cut is born of my own progression toward grace, and was documented on my body by its magnificent teeth. We are intimately connected, the Behemoth and I. More connected than I have been with any other living thing." He began fondly outlining his scars using the blade of the razor, enjoying the memory of every excruciating cut. Then, he continued. "It taught me how to fully exist for the first time. Not only that, but how to master existence. That gift showed the most profound love. Can you even understand that, Angela?"

"Is that what you wanted, Rick? You wanted love?"

"This has never been about what I want. That's far too small. It's not even about you and me, or our son. Forget Alex, he is nothing compared to the will of the beast."

"You can't mean that."

"You just don't understand. I tried to show you, reveal all your trivial obsessions, but you refused to see; adamant in your ignorance. You were given the chance to join us. You failed. Now, you die."

"You're wrong, Rick. Whatever amazing thing you think it taught you about life, or how to exist, or whatever the fuck… You're wrong. Your god is just as petty as anything else, which makes you just another asshole. A womanizer. And a shitty father." Angela felt particularly secure in her judgments.

"Well, in that case, as my dad would often say, 'The bitch and the brat never meant much to me.'"

With that, Rick stalked toward her. His militant stride carried no hesitation. He didn't even shy away from the terror in her eyes. Quite the contrary, he basked in it.

Angela watched his determination course through the pulsing muscles of his legs. It was like every part of him, down to his toenails, was elated by the promise of her death. His body wanted to experience her blood all over; it was itching for it. On some primordial level, she experienced this sweeping threat, and knew his desires.

She had but two equally unattractive options: to try to outrun him across the sizzling roof, or stand still and hope he would be quick about it. If not for Alex, Angela might have chosen the latter.

Running on the roof was more like trudging through molasses as the melting shingles swallowed each step she took. It was obvious she could not muster the kind of pace needed to escape Rick, especially since he remained inexplicably supported by the same charred boards that so quickly caved under her. It was then she noticed there was about a two-inch space between the soles of his feet and the roof.

Rick's hungry blade was only a few feet away from tasting deeply of her flesh. Angela needed a new plan fast, but she was trapped in the middle of a burning wasteland suspended two stories in the air. Her options were not just limited, they were nonexistent.

By the time her mind grappled with her precariousness, Rick had already caught up with her.

With one foot stuck between two stubborn shingles, Angela lost her balance and collapsed in front of him. She tried to dig her foot free, but the roof refused to let her go.

Rick loomed above his trapped prey, savouring the sounds of her struggles. He lifted the razor to admire its sleekness. To his delight, the lengths of skin it had already cut had not dulled it. Not one bit.

Angela's decision to either fight or succumb had been stolen from her. She really had no choice. It seemed that life had made escape impossible, almost as if someone had carefully designed each element to ensnare her. When she was still just a kid, she had followed her heart and it led her right into Rick's arms. From there, everything spiraled downwards. Even being a loving mother to Alex, which was, seemingly, the most innocent of her endeavours, had led to the mass murder of an entire church. Tragedy seemed so unavoidable. Angela started to believe she deserved whatever butchery Rick had planned. The war had been lost and she awaited her end.

Rick placed the knife against the side of her temple. She felt the blade shiver. Rick was excited.

Then, in a split second, Angela reconsidered. The notion that her life had been designed required for there to be a designer. And who might fill those shoes? Was it the abusive washed-up jock that stood before her, or perhaps the cowardly giant stumbling about the field? Even better, maybe it was the celestial Father from on high who professed love but looked upon the suffering of His children with indifference. None of them were worthy of the title. The only author up for the job was herself, and she didn't care much for downer endings. She was not going to be bled out atop this collapsing church, just as Alex was not going to be food for the beast.

Angela punched her fists through the roof underneath Rick's feet. She withstood the heat just long enough to grab hold of a substantial bundle of shingles and ripped them free, opening up a gaping hole beneath him.

A tornado of smoke slammed into Rick, and for all his uncanny abilities, he yielded to it as any normal man would. The furious cloud, fueled by the burning corpses of the congregation, attacked his face, and he was forced to shield himself.

He dropped the razor.

Quickly, Angela snatched up the weapon. The next step was to decide where to plunge it. She couldn't reach any of his vital organs from her position, so she considered settling for his knees, or maybe one of his thighs. However, she ended up focusing on the part of his body he prided the most. It seemed an appropriate point of attack, keeping in mind that it was Rick she was attacking.

She drove the metal sliver up between his legs, deep into the hanging flesh of his tender sack. Her cumbersome hand was the only thing that stopped the razor from continuing all the way up his body.

His burst genitalia oozed over her fingers. It looked as though she had tried to push her arm up through the bottom of a squid. She knew she had hit her mark right between his balls as she could feel their meatiness dangling on either sides of her fist.

Every section of his body tensed and shivered, like he had been overloaded and could explode at any moment.

Angela looked to Rick's face, eager to witness the agony she had wreaked upon him. To her great disappointment and revulsion, he looked as though he was enjoying his mutilation. In fact, she recalled he wore a similar expression when they had sex. His cheeks were flushed and veins stressed like lightening up his neck.

She underestimated the tolerance for pain his scars had afforded him. Compared to what the beast had done, her attempted castration was but a pleasurable tickle.

He rocked his hips slightly, swallowing the blade an inch deeper into his scrotum.

"That's the spot, Angela." He smiled at her with bated breath, as if moments away from ecstasy.

Despite the gaudy masochism on display, Angela could tell Rick was bluffing. She knew his intricacies very well. Part of how she had survived their marriage was by becoming a student of his mannerisms. She knew every inflection his voice could take, and although he had attempted to mask it, she heard his secret pain in the dropped vowels of his speech.

She returned his smile like an obedient mate, and then pulled the knife toward herself, splitting the bulk of his groin in half. Every excruciating detail of the blade's journey was broadcast through the nerves of his body as if it was a two-hour epic event. The razor's edge glided through his muscle and severed his urethra near the root of his cock. In a spectacular explosion of red, the blade erupted from the looseness of his skin, snapping through his weighty member like torn elastic.

A healthy, red, waterfall gushed between his thighs. The profuse flow of dark blood seemed eager to drown Angela, but proved only ambitious enough to paint her arms and face.

Rick's piercing scream announced his agony to the world and made the entire ordeal worthwhile. The whimpering that followed was just gravy.

Angela watched, partly in shock, as Rick's trembling body curled into his drooling wound. He was a deflated man, with all of his mass reduced to the vulnerable coiling of a fetus.

When her mind finally caught up with her actions, she tossed the dripping razor into one of the fiery pits surrounding her and rose to her feet. She took advantage of Rick's immobility and pushed hard against his shoulders.

His weightlessness failed him as he tumbled backwards against the roof. The shingles caved under him, and he plummeted into the tumultuous depths of the inferno.

Although she wanted to enjoy her victory, Angela was allowed only a brief moment of satisfaction. The structure of the roof was compromised, and soon, if she didn't move with haste, it could claim her, too.

With balanced steps, she moved as fast as possible to the edge of the church. A quick peek over the wall revealed a guaranteed bone-shattering drop.

She lowered herself, timidly at first, until she found solid footing on the protruding ledge at the top of the stained-glass window. From that point, she lowered herself further, this time holding onto the ledge with her hands. Her body dangled precariously in front of the shimmering window, her face even with heaven. To her morbid amusement, the angels were on fire.

She considered falling from this height. Angela estimated there would be about a fifty percent chance of her snapping an ankle, though she had no experience to base this estimation on.

A countdown started in her head and when she reached zero, it would be time for lift off.

Five, four, three, two…

Before she could finish, there came a tapping at the window. Angela looked down.

Rick's hairless, blistered body was pressed against the glass. Layers of skin had been stripped away, giving him a painful red hue, like the clichéd image of Satan. His swollen eyes caught her and he opened his foaming mouth.

The barrier between them, that nostalgic corner stone of coloured glass and simplistic faith, came crashing down like a magnificent fountain of glistening jewels.

Rick lunged from the sanctuary and wrapped his arms around Angela's legs. His hot flesh stung her ankles. He snarled and clawed his way closer to her vulnerable midriff.

Like a worm on a hook fighting for its life, Angela thrashed wildly against the jaws set on devouring her as Rick continued climbing up her body.

She managed to deliver one knee against the side of his head, which momentarily stunned him. He dropped down her body to the level of her feet. Taking advantage of his loosened grip, Angela pulled one of her legs free and stomped on his face.

The force of her blow condemned both of them to fall.

As soon as Angela's fingers slipped from the ledge, and the nauseous uproar in her stomach announced that everything solid in the world had been lost, she again considered her odds. The fall could shatter her skull, break her femur, knock her out, or perhaps, if she were taken pity on, maybe she would just land on her feet. Whatever the outcome, there was little she could do about it now.

She waited for the ground to make its decision.

CHAPTER 47

The first thing Angela saw when her vision returned, was a wall of flames. The church had reached full glow. For this, Angela was thankful; if not for the punishing heat, she may have remained unconscious until dawn.

She quickly checked herself for any new wounds – something she had become rather proficient at doing – but found no surprises. She got up from her soft bed of grass and scanned her surroundings for Rick.

Since she was still breathing, she assumed the fall had either killed him, or knocked him out. Neither proved true. There was no sign of him anywhere.

While the fire continued to gorge itself, Angela stepped out into the field. The air was cooler there, and her mind freer.

Once her eyes adjusted to the dark, she spotted what she was looking for. Halfway across the field, where even the fire's impressive glow couldn't reach, was a naked man stumbling toward the Burward forest. He took small, plodding steps like a child, with both his hands clasped around his groin.

She wasted no more time deliberating her next move. She charged after him. Her body, that beleaguered collection of cuts and bruises, tore into the night as if fresh for a marathon. Of course, she knew the beast was waiting for her in the shadows. In fact, she was counting on it. Rick would lead her to the Behemoth, and the Behemoth would lead her to Alex. She had to follow, or be damned.

It was easy for her to keep pace with Rick's lumbering steps, though she was careful to maintain a healthy distance.

A thunderclap rumbled behind her. She immediately turned to meet the storm, but instead saw the church crumble into itself. The roof fell first, followed by three of its walls. The sacred bonfire stretched to towering heights, far beyond that of the meager trees that framed it, and far beyond any glory preached about in all its history.

Angela found herself mesmerized by the death of the church. The body of the building snaked up into the sky, wood and stone made lighter than air, tossed into nothing. She even imagined for a moment the streams of smoke were actually the souls of the condemned congregation. Maybe there would come a day, she supposed, that she would mourn them, perhaps even feel remorse for what she had done. But, for now, she just watched them climb.

As the fire's hiss rolled through the field, echoing back on top of itself, Angela turned her attention solely to the Burward forest and the man who was about to stagger into it.

The rest of her journey through the gaping deadness of the field was uneventful, almost welcoming. Though she found herself drowning in night, guided only by the moon's disposition, she, nonetheless, reached the edge of the forest without a single stumble.

The first peculiar detail she noticed was the utter absence of life. There were no paws trampling through leaves, no anxious whistles from high in the branches, no scratching sticks or shuddering bushes. The silence was so absolute, it was deafening.

She had marked in her mind the path Rick had taken. He didn't enter the woods as she had expected, but rather traced along its exterior. She lost him when he lumbered around a protruding point that carved out into the field.

Her hands found what remained of the old fence. The wooden posts were mostly disintegrated, but a rusty wire still ran the length of the perimeter of the forest. She pinched the metal strand and headed toward the protrusion.

To her right was the field, still sparkling in the glow of the church. To her left, however, was a different matter. The woods intimidated her with their cold gaze and thin, scratching arms. The moon brightened the sky, but was not invited into the heart of the forest, where the emaciated trees crowded densely like spinsters with their secrets.

Then came a sound from the woods that seemed entirely out of place. Angela heard footsteps scurrying in the dark. Although the idea was absurd, she couldn't deny it. Somewhere, hidden away, there was a group of little feet running through the woods.

She stopped and turned. The footsteps faded.

"Alex?" she whispered.

A terrible thrashing erupted in response. It sounded like a whirlwind of cracking trees, as if they were being decapitated by a flurry of ferocious swipes. It was the temper tantrum of a titan and Angela had never heard such pure rage. Not only that, but the song of desolation was getting louder.

Angela gripped the wire with both her hands; afraid she might be swept away by the oncoming torrent. She imagined the line of trees exploding from the force of the beast and her being trampled out of existence under its feet as if she were nothing at all.

In her determination to save her son, she had forgotten the enormity of the creature she hunted.

A tree shattered and fell toward her, smashing into the ground mere inches from where she stood.

The sudden shock of it sent her tumbling backwards. She managed to land on her side, and chose to remain very still. She lay in the dirt and waited for whatever had dislodged the tree to make its next move.

Nothing happened.

She began to question if maybe the tree had fallen by itself. Then, she received her answer. The Behemoth released a gruff exhale from its stony throat. The beast was looming just above her. She didn't look up – she did not dare. Any movement, even the rotation of her eye could bring attention to her, so she played dead.

At least, by this point, her body was too tired to tremble.

She heard its giant limbs shifting, like the grinding of stones. It sounded as though it was returning to the forest.

Apparently, she played dead well.

Once she could no longer feel the tremors from its footsteps, she lifted herself up and stared into the tunnel of flattened trees the Behemoth left in its wake. It reminded her of when she was a child and a tornado ate up one of the farms outside of town.

Despite this, Angela had no choice but to follow the path the beast had laid out for her, especially now that her safety wire had been severed.

She stepped bravely into the passageway; resolute in her pledge to follow it where ever it may lead. Be it her death or her son that awaited her, she was marching toward the end.

CHAPTER 48

As she made her way through the corridor of fallen trees, Angela had not noticed the subtle curve of the passageway that led her back to the field. The walls were too gnarled and sporadic to allow her any orientation.

Eventually, she arrived at a small clearing, that had been hidden all this time, behind the dense, protruding arm of the forest. Like in the tunnel, the trees had been demolished, allowing for an open view of the field and, indeed, even the church.

She stepped out from the entangled archway and walked cautiously into the hollowed space. Once she was free of the path, she noticed the immense wood structure to her left. It was as tall as the beast and was held together by uneven nails. Flaking red paint dusted the tower's exterior like it had been dipped in blood.

Angela circled the primitive temple until she arrived at its front, marked by an enormous opening. The structure gaped at her; its maw threatening to devour her. The darkness inside looked so infinite, it was like she suddenly realized she was standing on the edge of a cliff and had to take a step back, for fear she might fall in.

Though the tower would only give enough room for the beast to stand inside it, Angela knew this was its home.

Shuffling dirt announced the approach of someone through the field. Angela immediately ducked into the thicket and positioned herself where no one could see. A twig dug into her back, but it was too late to shift her body now, she had to bear the pain.

Rick came stumbling into the clearing. He crunched through the wood splinters until eventually he collapsed on his knees in front of the temple.

Angela watched with surprising pity, as Rick pawed obscenely at his mangled manhood, whimpering with every gentle stroke. One of his hands stretched upwards, as if reaching for the peak of the structure. A thick sleeve of blood dripped down to his shoulder.

"Dear god," he whispered, "gentle Behemoth, ruler of wood and stone, of blood and bone, and keeper of my eternity, I pray. Your faithful servant has failed you, and I am undeserving of your mercy. But please, help me. Heal me! I beg you, do not forsake me!"

A deep moan like bending wood called out to him from the opening. It sounded sympathetic, but could just as easily have been a yawn.

The beast's arm unfolded from inside the temple and extended across the width of the clearing toward Rick. Its jagged hand glided through the air like drifting milkweed.

Angela was, again, chilled by how silent the beast could be. She had been standing right in front of its home. Why did it not snatch her up? Perhaps it had been sleeping, or perhaps it didn't care to. Either way, she was lucky to still be living.

Rick opened himself up to the beast's caress. Its palm covered his entire chest, while its talons tickled his neck and shoulders. The monster's touch seemed to put

Rick at ease, as if his pain could simply be rubbed away. He closed his eyes and leaned his head back.

"Save your servant." Rick's voice was soft, as if he were speaking to his lover.

The Behemoth's hand slid down to Rick's waist and pressed firmly against his tenderness. He winced with pleasure, as its spindly fingers wrapped around him, pricking at his buttocks. If his cock had been in a more functional state, then a titillated gasp wouldn't have been the only thing to have spilled out of him.

Suddenly, its grip tightened.

The beast's other arm shot forth from the temple and took hold of Rick's upper body.

Before Rick knew what was happening, it began to squeeze him. He could feel his bones buckle under the pressure, like wobbling support beams.

"My god," he wheezed, with what little air he had. "I worship you!"

The beast's grip did not falter. It didn't even hesitate.

Rick screamed and flailed his limbs, as if it would make a difference.

The tiny, toy man was no match for the Behemoth's mighty arms. It twisted both halves of his body in opposite directions. His hips popped first. Then, his stomach contorted as his intestines pulled tight. Bones shattered, snapping through tendons and muscle as they exploded like cherry bombs from the pressure. His front swung around to meet his back, and, finally, his spine cracked free of his pelvis. Once this last hold-out gave way, the squishy flesh that connected his two halves burst like a balloon of blood.

Red waves crashed against the fallen trees. Rick's top half gargled on his own juices before both sections of him were tossed back into the field. With a dead thud, Rick was returned to dirt.

The Behemoth stepped out from its decrepit abode.

For the first time, Angela was treated to the full spectacle of the beast.

It looked old, very old. Like a thing born of stone and earth, yet somehow organic. It had human attributes, like legs and arms, though the proportions were distorted. The beast's craggy torso hugged its ribs and dipped in around its stomach as if it had not eaten for years. Its coarse flesh balanced dark, grey tones as if it predated colour. Oversized eyes loomed from the harsh structure of its skull, that seemed to celebrate the viciousness of nature; every point that could be tipped with a horn, was. An equally fierce spine ran down its back. In the beast's mouth were teeth shaped just like its talons. They hung from scabby gums like hundreds of thin stalactites, each one with a slight curl and dagger tip. It was almost reptilian, but that description, alone, would not have done its horror any justice. It was the thing that had inspired myths of ogres and dragons, and haunted fairytales since before they were put to paper. It was the beast that made us afraid of the night.

Angela took all this in with a single, staggered breath. Her limbs went numb. She could not deny it was an awe-inspiring sight to behold. She understood, now, how Rick had mistaken it for a god. It really was a majestic beast, but she worked hard to keep in mind that in the end, that's all it was, just another beast.

The Behemoth moved smoothly and precisely, as if invisible anchors weighed it down. It rotated away from Angela and leaned toward a large, flat stone that rested against the edge of the woods. Sleeping on the surface of the rock was her son.

Feeling returned to her limbs. Alex was in her sights. Yet, she held back, knowing full well that, if the Behemoth found her now, it would destroy her.

She watched helplessly as the beast reached toward her son, with Rick's blood still dripping from its hand.

The Behemoth smeared the warm red liquid all over the boy's body as if he were a paper towel. Yet, it seemed gentle enough.

However, knowing how quickly the beast's tenderness could become lethal, Angela stirred and started to push her way toward the clearing. She would not sit idle and witness her son meet the same fate as Rick.

In her haste, she misplaced one of her steps and her foot broke through a brittle stick of wood.

Angela's courage dwindled when the Behemoth turned its head in her direction. She froze.

It was impossible to know just how visible she had made herself. There were only a few slender trees between her and the clearing, but maybe that was enough to remain hidden in the dark. Adding to the uncertainty was the strange stillness in the beast's expression. Its stare seemed able to observe everything all at once like an insect. Angela was afraid she had been swallowed, like everything else, into the pits of its eyes. The beast's stoicism was torture. She had no idea what it was thinking, or even if it had thoughts at all. Was it waiting for another noise, or just biding its time before it charged her?

Then, without any warning, the Behemoth took to the forest. It galloped back through the tunnel and within seconds had disappeared altogether. Angela was shocked to see just how quickly it could move.

She waited until the sound of its crushing stride had faded completely before she started toward the clearing again.

Once she stepped out from the cover of the trees, she paused, testing to see if it was a trap. But, the Behemoth didn't return and the woods remained still.

She made her way to Alex as quickly, and as quietly, as possible.

His eyes were closed.

He wasn't moving.

Then, when she was only a few feet away, she saw his chest rise and fall, and rise again. A shock of joy weakened her knees, but she managed to press onward.

Angela fell on the rock next to him, with her hands held just above his body. They hovered there; quivering with dread that, if she tried to touch him, she would discover he wasn't real. How could he be? How could this nightmare end with the two of them reunited? Eventually, even that fear could not hold her back, and she grabbed hold of him. Her hands were treated to the warmth of his skin and the soft fabric of the shirt she had dressed him in. She cradled the back of his head as she pulled him tightly to herself. Tears came, though not the ones she was used to. These rolling beads were not born of sorrow like the rest. They were forged from the disbelief that her love could be so wholly restored.

"Alex... Alex..." She repeated his name until he began to awaken.

His sleepy arms stretched out lazily into the night as if he had just been napping in his own bed. Angela, however, needed to hear his voice.

"Alex, you're okay. Right? You're okay?" she pleaded.

"Mom?"

"Yes!" she exclaimed. He had spoken. Angela couldn't remember hearing anything so simply beautiful. She melted into a full-blown weep.

"Mom, are you okay?"

She cleaned up her sniffles and kissed his forehead before answering.

"Yes, sweetie. I am now." She cradled his face in her hands and examined his features as if afraid they might slip away. Alex remained calm and subdued, even in the presence of Angela's near hysteria.

Once she had had her fill of him, she forced her mind back into the reality of their situation. The beast was still somewhere in the woods, and it was only a matter of time before it returned.

"Come on, we have to go," she said, lifting both of them to their feet.

"Where?"

"Home."

"I can't," he said, regretfully.

"What do you mean? Of course you can." Angela grabbed hold of his arm and jogged toward the field.

Alex pulled free of her.

"No!" he yelled. "I can't go."

"Alex! Please, you have to be quiet. We don't have time. This is serious and not up for discussion. We're going home. That's an order, okay? Over and out."

"No." He stood defiantly against her.

"What's wrong?"

"He needs me."

"Who needs you?"

"The forest man. He asked me to stay with him."

A sick feeling grew in Angela's stomach. What lies had the beast been telling her son?

"You mean the Behemoth?" she scorned. "You can't trust it, Alex. Don't listen to anything it says."

"He's just lonely, mom. He's been here for a really long time and all his friends are gone. He's sad. Like when I was sick. He just doesn't want to be alone, I think."

Could it be that simple? Was the Behemoth just some ancient lonely thing, the last remnant of a secret, mythical species? Angela had to admit, in some strange way, it made sense. How else would a beast like that relate to a group of churchgoers but as their god?

"Whatever it told you," Angela pleaded, "it's not what it says it is. It's just pretending – trying to trick you. But it's dangerous, Alex. It hurt lots of people, even Clara."

"It didn't burn them up, though."

"No… No, it didn't burn them."

"The forest man said *you* did."

Angela was rendered speechless. It was no use lying, Alex knew her too well for that. She shook her head, not in denial of the charge, but in refusal that she was as monstrous as the beast.

"I thought it had taken you," she finally muttered. "So, I did something terrible, something really bad. But, I thought I'd never see you again. I know you can't understand that. Please, just come with me, honey, and we'll run from here. We'll run and leave it all behind us."

"I told you, mom, I can't."

"You have to!" Angela screamed, and lifted him off the ground. There was only so much negotiation she could take at this point, and she was not about to just leave him behind.

With Alex secure in her arms, her aching legs carried them through the field. She pushed herself beyond exhaustion, beyond the complaints of her muscles, or the protest of her wounds. All this she did simply to maintain a slow, but steady, pace.

The trees tore open behind them.

Angela turned and saw the Behemoth stampeding toward her. Its soaring stature grew as it approached, giving Angela a subtle case of vertigo. In no time, it was standing directly above her, gazing down.

Its rough lips peeled back like horizontal curtains to reveal its dagger teeth. The beast's mouth snapped open, and its head descended to swallow her whole.

Soon, all she could see was the reach of glistening bones as its jaws closed in around her. Overwhelmed by the tunnel of teeth, and the odd, strawberry scent of its breath, Angela fell backwards.

Before the beast could enjoy its first sampling however, Alex stood up between the encroaching mouth and his mother. The Behemoth suddenly stopped, sheathing its teeth.

The beast headed back to the seclusion of its temple. It was almost like Alex had power over it.

Angela started to breathe again and managed to sit up.

"See?" Alex asked rhetorically. "Just like I said. I can't go."

Angela's voice had lost its courage, trapping her thoughts in her head. She wanted to tell Alex that leaving him was impossible. She could never let him go. But her mouth wouldn't cooperate.

"Bye, mom. I love you," he said simply, like he was heading for the school bus. He flipped around and followed the beast back to the clearing.

Of all the ways she had lost Alex during the past two days, none had hurt more than this one. She stood up to get a better view as he receded into the forest. He was a stubborn child, Angela knew that, but this was more than defiance. Alex truly believed he belonged here with the abhorrent creature. Angela became convinced there must be a spell laced around the trees, or maybe a hypnotic charm lingering in the air. Something had laid claim to her son, but she was not going to give him up without a fight.

She slowly turned and looked upon the grand fire of the church. Although it had lost some of its gusto, it still had a bounty of fury to spread, and Angela was looking for a bit of fury.

CHAPTER 49

It had been a long time since Alex had a proper father. Rick had started off well enough, but as time stretched, and the baby became a boy who could talk, and ask, and need, it became clear Rick was never really there, even when he *was* there. So when the forest man swept Alex up and brought him to the clearing, and offered him a home, he was more than ready to accept the friendly giant.

In some primal way, Alex just wanted to be kept safe. The world had shown him time and time again just how dangerous it could be, and although he knew Angela loved him, he also knew she could no longer protect him. She had tried valiantly, but she had failed. The forest man, on the other hand, had given him refuge, and could promise safety from all the foulness of the earth. For once, Alex felt truly secure.

In return, the beast was provided with what it desired most – companionship. The boy, it had discovered, was deeply in tune with its own frequency. Unlike the other insects, who could only receive messages, Alex was able to hear, and indeed message back. Throughout the beast's lonesome centuries of existence, it had rarely come across another living thing it could talk to. Rick had been a promising pupil, but was nothing more than a class clown compared to Alex.

And the boy offered insight of his own. He could tell the Behemoth's thoughts were poisoned by isolation. The beast had grown cold and angry. When it found the people of St. Paul's United Church, who had been begging week after week for God to show up, it answered their prayers out of sheer desperation. They offered praise and it accepted.

In the end, the beast had lost its precious congregation, but it had found something infinitely more valuable. There was a time, it could faintly recall, when there were other beasts much like itself, moving through the secret cracks in the world. Alex reminded the Behemoth of this forgotten time, a time without loneliness.

As the beast slept in its elongated temple, a fluid exchange of disjointed thoughts emptied from its head into Alex's. The charge that linked their minds hummed through the air and deepened Alex's understanding of his slumbering companion.

The boy spread himself across his rock using his hands as a pillow. He fixed his sight on the moon and listened as the Behemoth recounted tales of a molten earth, where the storms were fierce, but the inhabitants fiercer. The details of this foreign age were communicated to Alex through the language of emotion, which, although not the most specific language, was perfectly understandable. He was guided through a time before life was solidified, when existence flowed like water from one being to the next. Each body was shared equally between them all, like communal conduits. Some creatures had necks stretching up into the clouds, while others were no bigger than a thumbnail. There were no teeth for biting or claws for scratching. No existing thing was valued any more or less than the next.

The only fear they knew was of fire's hunger. Flames poured over the surface of the earth like rivers, but as long as they kept away from them, life had no pain. That all changed when some of the beings decided to settle into their form, and grew possessive of their physical state. In order to defend against the others, they taught their bodies to become hard, and gave themselves shells and tails armed with lethal clubs. Their bones grew jagged and broke free from the fleshy nubs of their fingertips. Mouths contorted into grinders to reduce their enemies into meat. The weak were crushed and the strong inflated to untenable sizes. Then, the world split and ice suffocated the flames that had been stirring. Few survived, but all were alone. Other eras with other creatures came and went, but none quite so magnificent as what had been lost.

The Behemoth, born from this world of giants, became a voyeur of sorts and Alex was treated to spectacular memories of ferocious dinosaurs, drifting landscapes and even primitive man. With the beast, he plunged into the ocean's depths, then turned skywards and discovered obscure creatures soaring through hills of clouds. All of this the beast considered commonplace, but to Alex, it was like riding on the wings of a god.

Adrenalin from Alex's fantastical journey brought life to his body and warded away any notion of sleep. His newly acquired perspective not only on his life, but on the life of the entire earth, ignited a studious appetite.

He sprang from his rock and tasted the wood splinters on the ground. They were rough against his tongue and left flakes of bark and dirt in the crevices of his teeth – the same dirt that was once the fragile flesh of a bird's eye. He dug his fingers into the bodies of plants, allowing their roots to hug his digits like tickling caterpillars. Everything had been so marvelously transformed. The interweaving of existence had unified him with the moon itself. It was a most brilliant revelation.

With his face pressed against the side of the wood temple, Alex began to hum an old lullaby from his past to thank the beast for its generosity. The slumbering creature seemed pleased by the delicate timbre of his voice.

However, the gentle tune could not last forever. Once it reached its end and the night returned to its silence, a faint rumble could be heard.

Alex lifted his head and checked all around him; the sound was so faint that it could have been coming from anywhere.

He jumped onto his rock – the ancient history of which he now had an intense appreciation for – and scanned the surrounding shadows of the field.

A small, glowing dot had separated from the church's robust fire and was moving across the vastness. It maintained a steady speed, like the approach of a calm and purposeful firefly. As it neared, the rumble became more distinct and Alex recognized it as the growl of a car engine. The flickering dot grew bigger, and soon the boy realized it was not headlights shining in the night; it was a formidable fireball cutting through the earth toward the clearing – a meteor destined for impact.

Angela's car had once again defied the odds of its age. For its tenacity, she was eternally grateful. After she had coaxed the vehicle to life, she opened the hood and stuffed it full of burning planks of wood from the church. She used the cover from her back seat to protect her hands from the heat while she worked. If the beast would not allow Alex to return to her, then it had to be destroyed, and fire was the only way she knew how.

Now, she was barreling through the field at full speed, tearing up dirt as she roared toward her destination with the mouth of her car filled with all the fire it could carry. The flames blew wildly across her windshield. She had become a captain of her very own torpedo, with her crosshairs set on the beast's temple.

Her hands were so tight on the wheel, she could almost feel it bending, though the rising heat might have had something to do with that.

Alex leapt from his rock and ran toward the slumbering giant. He kicked and pounded against the side of the temple.

"Hey! Wake up!" he cried, "You have to get out of there!" His fists were bloody by the time he had given up trying to wake the beast. There was no way of stopping the approaching apocalypse, so he stepped away from the temple and hoped he could at least hold onto the dreams the forest man had gifted him.

Angela had neglected the gearshift and the engine was screaming by the time it met the slope of the clearing.

Mere seconds before impact, the light from the flames invaded the darkness of the temple, revealing the Behemoth curled up into a ball at its base. It was surprisingly compact, almost like a puppy, flopped on top of itself.

Despite this, Angela's foot remained planted on the gas.

The front of the car smashed into the structure. It would have cut the temple down if not for the considerable mass of the Behemoth.

The burning planks shot forth from the hood like golden, projectile vomit over the beast. The old wood of the structure caught fire quickly, and the flames raced to the top. In the blink of an eye, the Behemoth's temple had become a cage of blazing timber.

The beast rose, trembling, into the inferno. There was nowhere to escape; the fire had already taken hold of its limbs. Its skin sizzled and popped unnaturally in the heat, while pockets of steam bubbled forth from its belly and face. It remembered the earth as it once was, that melting hell, filled with rivers of fire and clouds of ash, and so it screamed. It released a strident shriek towards the moon – a lament to echo through the eons. It thrashed in vain, swinging its burning arms from side to side in a beautiful, but desperate dance.

Angela lifted her face from the air bag in time to see the entire temple come crashing down on the beast. The ceiling of flames flattened the creature and sent it hurdling toward her. She managed to jump out just before the burning mass of flesh and wood exploded through the windshield and filled the car.

She crawled across the ground on all fours until she could no longer feel the heat gnawing at her legs. Once she was at a safe distance, she turned to see if the beast was still in flames. Indeed it was, trapped under the rubble of its own burning monolith.

Angela watched until she was certain only its bones were left.

Guided by the light of the fire, she searched the clearing for Alex. She found him laying a good distance from the fallen tower. He was unconscious, but breathing.

She scooped him up, held him firmly against her bosom, and again ventured into the field.

In the east, the dawn was rising.

CHAPTER 50

The sun seemed to freeze on the horizon, as if stunned to find Angela and Alex alive, and walking hand-in-hand down Highway 7. Angela, herself, was in shock that the night had not claimed them both, so she squeezed her son's palm just to be sure. It was true. They had survived, though not unscathed.

The awakened day revealed every battle wound Angela had collected. Her arms were bestrewn with deep gashes from the Behemoth's claws, while colourful bruises and scrapes from the roof of the church marred her legs. A double coat of blood was unevenly lathered over her torso and face. She smelled like smoke and metal.

Although they walked together, Alex had not spoken a word to her. He lumbered alongside Angela like a zombie. His eyes looked straight ahead of him, as if staring at the impossible end of the endless road they traveled.

Once the repetitive sound of feet against pavement became too grating, Alex finally spoke.

"Where are we going?" he asked.

"Home," Angela responded with a deep-seated rasp.

"Home?"

"It's where we live, Alex."

"I don't want to go there."

"Yes you do, sweetie. It's best we keep moving. We're just going to walk and walk and walk, until we reach our door."

"But, I want to see the forest man."

"You can't," she said, shaking off some soot from her shoulder.

"Why?"

"You just can't."

"But why?" he hollered.

"Cause mommy burned him up!" Exhaustion had dismantled her parental filter. She was raw. Alex could have asked her anything and she would have answered with the truth, even if it hurt, even if it was terrible.

"Like everyone in the church?" questioned Alex.

"That's right, just like everyone in the church. I burned them all up."

"Even dad?"

"Yes, especially your dad," she said quickly, then amended, "Well, no, not your dad. He was popped in half by the forest man, just like breaking a loaf of bread."

Alex remained silent as he considered what his mother had just confessed. She was a murderer, as he had come to understand the definition. Then again, it sounded like everyone was. He didn't want to walk down this road anymore. He was tired and confused. He wanted to be swept away by the grace of the forest man. Within the beast's presence, Alex had found an alluring tranquility. All he could think about was being wrapped up in that cozy blanket once more.

He pulled his hand away from Angela.

"What are you doing, Alex?"

"I'm going home."

"Yes, you are, that's exactly where we're headed."

"No, mom. I'm going to *my* home. You go back to yours."

"It's *our* home we're going to, not mine. You're still my son, no matter what lies that beast told you."

"He didn't lie!"

"That's all he did, Alex! That's all anyone did. Everyone lied. Everyone."

"I'm not going with you."

Angela's attention was diverted when she spotted a van approaching from far off, down the road. It was still about a minute away, but she nonetheless started to wave it down. So hectic was her flailing, that her arms were liable to be thrown right off her body.

"Yes! Oh, please see us," Angela yelled excitedly. "Alex! We're getting out of here!"

She secured her arm around Alex and pulled him close. Angela was anxious to get as far away from the church as possible. She was sure as the distance grew between them and the beast, Alex would gradually come back to her. All they had to do was get in that van.

The routine of opening a car door, taking a seat, and buckling up crossed Angela's mind. It seemed so hysterically mundane that she couldn't help but release a brief, if slightly insane, chuckle. Imagine, clicking the seatbelt into place. Click. Safe. Done. She laughed again, this time with full force of her gut.

Her amusement stopped when the van failed to slow down. On the contrary, it had gained in speed. And the vehicle..she had seen it before. The problem became one of placing it to a time and location. Yes, in the church parking lot. Underneath the dirt and ash it had collected, it was Gary's van. But it couldn't be Gary behind the wheel. Rick would have been just as impossible, and she doubted the Behemoth knew how to drive. Who ever it was, they didn't look interested in offering a ride.

The van swerved off the road, onto the shoulder, and aimed its wheels straight toward Angela and Alex, tossing up an angry fog of dust behind it.

Angela had two options in front of her, but not enough time to properly consider either of them. She could jump with Alex into the ditch and hope the van would not follow, or she could push Alex out of the way, and guarantee his survival by sacrificing hers. The choice between life and death had almost become tiresome, and she worried she no longer had the energy for it. Her mind was detached, as if it floated ponderously three feet to her left. So, she let her hands decide for her.

She pressed both her palms against Alex's shoulders and shoved him down the grassy slope. He rolled through the green thickness and settled, gently, in the bottom of the ditch.

Angela had no time for last words, or even a final glance. The snarl of the spinning wheels was already upon her.

She turned to face it.

Suddenly, her mind returned to her. A rapid succession of desperately meaningful images, people and moments from her lifetime, coursed through her head. She wondered if she should have forgiven her father when she had had the chance, what her grandmother would have been like if she had ever met her, and what had become of the boy, Steven Brachmayer, who had taken her virginity in the ninth grade. Some proved more trivial than others, as she found herself wondering what happens to the two lovers in her trashy, pulp novel. She assumed, by the end, they worked things out. This mixed-bag of snapshot memories had no continuity. Each thought shuffled through to the next, as if nothing was connected. Finally, she recalled the great bonfire of the church. She saw the faces of the congregation melted and wrinkled, their eyes replaced by spouts of smoke, their reproachful tongues, cooked and swollen. They had wronged her, but she had also wronged them, and she regretted it. She thought of the disintegration of her beliefs, and her new abiding faith in faithlessness. She thought of her son having to continue on through this godless world without her. She thought of the lessons she never got to teach him. She thought of being remembered. She thought of being forgotten. She thought of Clara. She thought of the determined, yet futile beating of her heart and the ache of her body. Her final thought was of the mysterious patterns of her thoughts – the simple miracle of the act of thinking itself. She focused on how many more she might be able to fit in before the van hit, and what thought might come next.

Nothing came next.

The bumper connected first. It cracked her shins in half and sent a devastating ripple-effect through her joints. Her bones shivered loose from her flesh, as the brunt of the van compacted her torso. Her elbows and knees unlocked from their counterparts, and spun wildly in all directions, as if she were a windup toy. The less-solid parts of her body, such as her stomach, poured out over the windshield, and rained down upon both the van and the ground on which it drove. Angela Morris was spectacularly undone.

The van, with a new, brilliant red paint job, skidded to a stop once Angela's body had been exploded from the face of the Earth. Not much of her remained – at least, nothing recognizable. A few strands of her hair gave away which part of the spill used to be her head. Her face, splashed in blood, was nestled next to the contortions of her spine. Her left eye was open, the other locked shut, like a devilish wink to greet the Reaper.

The collision happened so fast, Alex missed his mother's grand martyrdom. He raised his eyes and saw only red. Everything was red. Although he hadn't witnessed the act itself, he understood what had happened, and what Angela had done. His mother's body, it seemed, was just as malleable as the forest man had said. Life really was made of mere globs of putty and the proof was on display, splashed all across the road.

The van rattled into reverse and backed up next to where Alex lay. The front of the vehicle was badly dented, contributing to the chug of its engine.

Alex stood and brushed off the grass that clung to his shirt.

The side door of the van slid open with a tremendous metal clang. Like a curtain being lifted, Angela's murderers were suddenly revealed.

Looking entirely out of place behind the wheel was Matthew, still wearing the soot of the fire that had claimed his grandmother, as well as his congregation. Manning the sliding door was Susan. She too appeared to have been brazenly seared. They both stared at Alex expectantly.

Alex stared back.

"Come on, Alex, we're taking you home," Susan said warmly, as if she were rescuing him.

"Home?" he asked.

"The Behemoth wants you back."

"He does?"

"Of course he does. He needs you. We need you. We're all in his service now." She smiled and offered him her hand.

Alex hoped it was true. With both his mother and his father gone, there was not much family left, in fact, none that he knew of.

"Alex," Matthew added, "you belong with us. Trust me. We've seen it too. Hop in and we'll go meet the beast together."

"You saw it?"

"Yes. We saw it all. He found us in the field and showed us the world, the real world. How it used to be."

"The world on fire," Alex added quietly.

"You're meant to lead us, Alex. You can hear him like no one else can. Please, come back with us," Susan pleaded. She stretched out her hand to make it a little more enticing.

More than anything, Alex wanted out of this tragedy. He knew his mother would never again be by his side to guide him. He had no delusions about that. So, what choice did he have but to return to his precious giant in the woods?

Alex took the hand that had been offered.

CHAPTER 51

The carcass of the church smoked like an ashtray, balanced on the edge of Davidson's field. A few twisted pillars of brick and scorched wood still reached for the sinking clouds above, but no matter how hard they stretched, they could never hope to recapture what had been lost. The home of fellowship had been utterly devoured. St. Paul's United Church was no more.

A handful of firefighters tromped through the coals, while police cruisers encircled the area. A dozen emergency vehicles had gathered around the steaming pit, which was set aglow by flashes of red and blue lightning.

Once they confirmed that the fire had not only claimed the building, but also its congregation, waves of devastation began rolling in. It hit everyone at different times, but no one was spared the weight of the flood. These singed bones were once their friends, their family members.

The local paper called it Judgment Day. Headlines dramatically declared it the greatest tragedy in the history of the county, which, to that point, was true. Alas, despite the media hubbub, headlines and breaking reports, the ones left behind would never be privy to all the sordid details. However terrible the fire looked – and it did look terrible – no one could have imagined the profound horror that had taken place. The secret agony of the congregation had been buried in ash, reduced to a featureless black smear besmirching the flattened planes.

While the rest of the world was busy sorting through the carnage, the sound of little footsteps echoed through the Burward forest.

The children of the congregation, led by Matthew and Susan, marched merrily toward the Behemoth's clearing in an orderly line, with their feet bouncing along the ground like playful goose steps. All the kids were present and accounted for, including Alex, Stanley, Samantha and Dylan. Each one wore a look of reverence, with their eager heads turned toward what was left of the beast's temple.

Earlier that morning, before the first emergency vehicles arrived, the children visited the remains of the church and had taken certain keepsakes. In their arms, they carried pieces of what was left of their parents. Stanley gripped a dusty bone from Michael's leg, while Samantha lovingly hugged onto Emily's ribcage as she would a teddy bear. Each child brought with them their own ashy bit of memorabilia as an offering to the beast.

However, the bones swinging in Alex's hands were not blackened by soot like the others. Clenched in his left fist was a bloody jaw, while in his right, he held the rest of his mother's skull with his two fingers hooked through the eye sockets. Both items looked freshly peeled.

Twigs cracked under their delicate feet, as the children gathered around the scorched car. The sagging vehicle jutted forth from the pile of wood like an old bombshell. The roof of the car had melted into itself, and the interior had been completely hollowed by the fire.

Burnt wood beams that used to comprise the temple sprayed from the front of the car like a living Rorschach test. The inky swell of the wood had a reaching quality as if it attempted to eclipse the car, and perhaps, the children along with it.

"Well kids," Susan announced to the group. "Did we bring anything for the beast?"

A few of them nodded, and then placed the bones of their parents among the remains of the temple.

Alex cleared a flat space for himself, near the centre of the scorched monument. He gently laid the jawbone down as a base, then fitted the skull into it with a satisfying click. The two pieces snapped together rather nicely.

"I love you, mom." Alex's whisper was so modest, even he could barely hear it.

He took a step back to admire the altar they had raised from the rubble. The bones extended naturally from the twisted coals, but it was the shimmering red of Angela's skull that stood out like a ruby and gave the composition focus.

Susan continued, "We entrust to him the bodies of the ones we have loved, and know that if we remain faithful, they will never truly be lost."

"Praise the Behemoth," added Matthew.

"Will we ever see them again?" asked Stanley, who hadn't taken his eyes off his father's bones.

Before Susan could speak, Alex stepped out from the cluster of children. He stood in front of the burnt temple and drank deep of its smoky air.

"Of course we will," Alex responded. "The Behemoth showed all of us the path. We just have to follow."

"That's right, Alex." Matthew wore a proud smile.

Susan clapped her hands together, and with a bright face asked the children, "We'll never forget what he showed us, will we? No, no we won't. And we praise him for it. He saved us. Now, lets hear it. All together..."

The children recited in unison, "In the name of our god, the Behemoth, ruler of wood and stone, of blood and bone, and keeper of our eternity, we pray."

Despite these words, and an exhaustive search, the new congregation could not find their god. It was no longer stalking the tunnels of the Burward forest, nor was it slumbering in its desecrated temple. The field was empty, and all had grown silent.

As Alex stared into the pitch-black underbelly of the rubble, a few wisps of smoke drifted up through the boards. Whether this fog was just the remnant of forgotten cinders, or the precious breath of their god was impossible to say. So, he took it on faith.

THE END

ABOUT THE AUTHOR

 Craig Stewart is a Canadian author and filmmaker who learned how to count from the rhyme, "One, two, Freddy's coming for you."

He's a creator and connoisseur of everything horror; never afraid to delve into the dark, and then a little further. His written works include short stories, film scripts, articles, and most recently, a novel. He has also written and directed several short horror films that have enjoyed screenings across North America.

Don't be afraid to reach out to him on twitter: @TheCraigStewart

Or visit his website: everythingcraigstewart.com

Craig Stewart

<u>Other HellBound Books</u>
<u>For You To Enjoy</u>

**All available now in paperback and eBook from
Amazon, iBooks, Barnes & Noble, Kobo etc.
For full details, visit our official website**

<u>www.hellboundbookspublishing.com</u>

**Or
Download our App from iTunes / Google Play – or
simply scan the QR Code below**

No Rest For The Wicked

A modern day ghost story with its skeletons buried firmly in the past.

From beyond the grave, a murderous wife seeks to complete her revenge on those who betrayed her in life; a powerless domestic still fears for her immortal soul while trying to scare off anyone who comes too close; and the former plantation master - a sadistic doctor who puts more faith in the teachings of de Sade than the Bible

When Eric and Grace McLaughlin purchase Greenbrier Plantation, their dreams are just as big as those who have tried to tame the place before them. But, the doctor has learned a thing or two over his many years in the afterlife, is putting those new skills to the test, and will go to great lengths in order to gain the upper hand. While Grace digs into the death-filled history of her new home, Eric soon becomes a pawn of the doctor's unsavory desires and rapidly growing power, and is hell-bent on stopping her.

Demons, Devils and Denizens of Hell Vol. 1

A hellish collection of short stories from some of the best in the business - compiled by the award-winning author P. Mattern. Featuring tales from the darkest pits of Hades by Tania Hagan, Lily Luchesi, Jay Michael Wright II, Ken Goldman, Sergio "ente per ente" Palumbo, Emery LeeAnn, Crystal Barnard, James H Longmore, Toneye Eyenot, James Richardson, Lori Fontanez, Marcus Mattern, Lance Tuck, L. Ashby, P. Mattern, Elizabeth Cash, Bryan A. Tann, Elizabeth Zemlicka, Michael Sutton, Thomas S. Gunther, Feind Gottes, and the incomparable Nik Kerry

Blood and Kisses
By
James H Longmore

The definitive short story collecting from James H Longmore - an eclectic mix of dark horror, bizarro and Twilight-Zone style tales of the downright disturbing.

Welcome to the long awaited collection from the writer of horror novels *'Pede* and *Tenebrion*; a forword by Richard Chizmar (co-author of *Gwendy's Button Box* and author of *A Long December*), 18 short stories, 5 flash fiction and even a poem - all skin-crawling, soul-shredding tales of terror, of the darkest things that skulk amongst the night's inky shadows, and of the everyday gone horribly awry.

Discover the alternative implication of technology becoming self-aware, enjoy the acquaintance of a charismatic new pastor who promises his flock a brand new place in which to worship his God, and spend a little time in the company of a nice young man who is inexorably caught up in his home town's terrible secret. Then there is Cupid's revelation that personally he has never experienced love, yet we discover that very emotion alive and not so well amongst the ruins of a post zombie apocalypse world, and we bear witness to a childhood innocence forever destroyed in a war-torn city. There is more, Dear Reader, much, much more; for within these pages we have devils, demons and ghosts, lycanthropes and demi-gods, all rubbing nefarious shoulders with vilest of Hell's offspring who have slithered from the netherworld to doff their caps and wish us all the sweetest of dreams...

The Big Book of Bootleg Horror 2

The second volume in HellBound Books' flagship horror anthology - this one bursting at the seams with even more fantastically dark horror from the cream of the rising stars in today's horror scene!

Featuring: Tracey A. Cross, Elizabeth Zemlicka, Shelby Thomas, Matthew Gillies, Spinster Eskie, Stephen Clements, Ken Goldman, Nathan Robinson, K.M. Campbell, Cody Grady, Sebastian Bendix, Leo X. Robertson, David Owain Hughes, Timothy McGivney, Kane Gordon, Todd Sullivan, Mike Mayak, Edward Ahern, Rose Garnett, Jaap Boekestein, Brandy Delight, Stanley B. Webb, D. Norfolk, and Thomas Gunther.

A HellBound Books LLC Publication

www.hellboundbookspublishing.com

Printed in the United States of America